Mistletoe Treasures

Mischief and Mayhem in Mistletoe
Book 1
Mistrust and Medicine in Mistletoe
Book 2
Misfortune and Mystery in Mistletoe
Book 3
Misadventure and Murder in Mistletoe
Book 4

By

Ronna M. Bacon

Matthew 6:20
"But store up for yourselves treasures in heaven, where neither moth nor rust destroys, and where thieves do not break in or steal;

Luke 12:24

"For where your treasure is, there your heart will be also."

Mistletoe Treasures

Mischief and Mayhem in Mistletoe
Book 1

Jacob Whitson was handed his Grandfather's journal at the gravesite, along with a letter addressed in his Grandfather's hand, directly him back to the town of Mistletoe, specifically to arrive the first weekend of December during the start of the Christmas Festivities. Jacob arrives to find the owner of a antiquities store, Finola Bronagh, under attack and rushes in to help. He soon realizes that Finn, as she is known as, has the key to unlocking the secrets in the journal, secrets someone will go to any length to prevent coming into the open. To honour his Grand's memory, Jacob digs deep, pulling Finn into the adventure, not realizing the danger he puts them.

Mistrust and Medicine in Mistletoe
Book 2

Arriving in Mistletoe to find he is a descendant of one of the town's founding fathers, Levi Blackwell searches for a place to fit in. On the run from an abusive stepfather who will stop at nothing, including murder, to get her share of the town property, Julia Bronagh comes under Blackie's protection. Keeping her safe means putting his own life on the line. Falling in love with her was not what he thought would happen, but God had other plans. Staying barely one step ahead of their pursuers, Blackie and his Jewel come to realize just how much God cares for them and how much they care each other.

Misfortune and Mystery in Mistletoe
Book 3

Abducted as a young child and transported across the country, Leah Bronagh has always felt the missing part of her life. Drawn to Mistletoe on the advice of a friend, she encounters danger before she even arrives in town. Joshua Smithson steps in to help Leah after she seeks refuge in his restaurant, falling in love with her and marrying her in an attempt to help her survive. Deeply in love with one another, the couple are faced with constant harassment and assaults by an unknown assailant. Standing true in God's strength, they meet their assailant and danger head on, resolving a mystery that had plagued Mistletoe for over a year.

Abandoned as a newborn, Eavan Walker has made a life for herself and her beloved Gran, being a photographer. Unknown to her, she snapped a photograph of a murder while still a teenager. She was drawn to Mistletoe on a suggestion and made a home for her studio there, not realizing she was related to one of the town founders. Simon Gardner, detective with the county police force, is drawn into Eavan's life when he tackles her and saves her life. Encounters and adventures lead the two to fall in love and marry, not realizing that someone was after them and only wanted one thing - both of them dead. In discovering who that was solves the mysteries of why Simon's three friends were brought to Mistletoe. Even when faced with life and death, Simon and his beloved Eavan don't waver in their trust in God.

Table of Contents

Mischief and Mayhem
in
Mistletoe

Mistletoe Treasures
Book 1

By

Ronna M. Bacon

Dedicated to my niece, Fiona, who loves Christmas stories and asked if I had written one. This one is for you, Fiona. Luv you lots.

9

Verses

Jeremiah 29:13. You will seek me and find me when you seek me with all your heart.

I Chronicles 16:11. Look to the Lord and his strength; seek his face always.

New King James Version

Table of Contents

He stood over the grave, tears flowing down his face, not wanting to say goodbye to the man who had raised him. He would miss him so much. He would miss the quiet words of wisdom, the sharing and the prayers. He raised his head to stare across the grave, his eyes searching the gloomy sky, thinking it matched his mood.

He turned as he was approached, taking the letter he was handed, not hearing the words spoken to him. He tucked the letter into a pocket, his head bowing once more.

He finally turned, his steps slow and heavy as he walked away. He would come back later, on another day, to say his final goodbyes. It just didn't seem real.

He slid into the vehicle waiting for him, his eyes staying on the grave until it was out of sight before he turned with a sigh, not wanting to face the empty house, the fact that he now was all alone, no one to care what he did or didn't do.

The man under the trees watched at the car moved away before he turned back to the grave. He had been successful, he thought. No one suspected anything. Now to continue with his plan. He would succeed, even if it came down to a matter of murder. It wouldn't be the first time that had been the outcome, nor would it likely be the last. A lot rested on this, he thought.

He moved away to his own car, following the young man until he entered his own home, parking his car across the street and just waiting until the lights in the house went out. Somehow, he had to make sure that his plan went forward. He would find some way to get that young man to do exactly what he wanted. His plans depended on that very fact.

He put his car in gear, driving away, an evil grin of satisfaction filling his face. Now to wait. But he only had some much patience and the men after him were not that patient.

Chapter 1

Sitting on a bench near the centre of the little town of Mistletoe, Jacob Whitson shrugged his jacket collar higher. He had not expected it to be so busy. Nor could he understand his grandfather directing him to this town, village, he wasn't quite sure how to categorize it, or at this particular time of year. Christmas this year wouldn't be the same, not with Grand gone, he thought. It had just been the two of them for the last twelve years or so, since Grams went home. He rose, shoving his hands into his pockets, shivering against the coolness of the air. He squinted at the sky. It looked like snow, he thought, and he still had to find a place to stay. The small hotels or motels, or whatever you called them, were booked, had been for months. The proprietor at the second one had taken a look at him, went to say something, shook his head and then told him to find Finn at the local antique and used bookstore. He thought Finn might be able to help.

Lord, I have no idea why I'm here, other than Grand asked me to come in his letter. I have no idea what the journal is about. I know it's his. I recognize his handwriting. I really don't need a trip down his memory lane. I just want to pack up and move away somewhere I don't have to live with so many memories.

He stood for a moment, head tipped back, as he reached to pull his hat from his head and stick it into his pocket, his eyes on the sign of the store. Finn's Antiquities. This is it, he thought, as he reached for the old-fashioned knob on the old fashioned door, pushing it open to the sound of an old-fashioned bell. He stood, his eyes sliding closed, as he took in the smell of the building, clean but with the scent of history mingling with it. His eyes flew open as he heard a rough voice from somewhere in the back. He walked that way, a frown appearing on his face.

He stood, standing in the shadows just back from the doorway he saw led to the office at the back of the store. A roughly dressed man stood there, hands on a person Jacob couldn't see, angry words spewing from his mouth. He couldn't hear the other person's response, couldn't tell if it was a man or woman that stood there.

Jacob moved forward, knowing he couldn't stand back and let someone be assaulted. The man turned slightly at his footsteps and Jacob caught sight of the person he was threatening. A young woman, his own age, he thought. No, he could not walk away. He had to step in.

"Can I help you, ma'am?" Jacob soft baritone broke through the anger words, causing the man to turn and glare at him.

"Butt out. This is none of your business." The man turned back to the woman. "You're coming with me. No backing out this time. You belong to me."

The young woman stood, eyes blank, not moving as the man tugged at her arm, frozen in place. Jacob drew a deep breath and then caught at the man's arm, pulling him away from the woman.

"She's not going with you, man. Now, back off. If you don't, I'm sure the police would like to hear that you're threatening someone or assaulting them."

The man swung at Jacob, who ducked the blow. He sighed to himself. He had served in the armed forces for eight years and this was nothing compared to what he had faced. He caught the man's hand and wrist and twisted it behind his back, forcing him through the building and out to the street before letting him go. He stood, facing the anger the man threw at him.

"I would suggest you leave and don't come back to bother her." Jacob watched carefully as the man finally walked away before he turned and entered the building, flipping the lock on the door and the sign to closed for now. He stood for a moment, eyeing the young woman where she still stood, unfocused.

He walked forward, gently guiding her to a chair, and then searching for water. He held the glass to her mouth, watching as she finally swallowed, the fear gradually loosening its grip on her.

She finally looked at him, a grateful look fluttering across her face. "Thank you."

Jacob crouched down in front of her. "Are you okay?" He spun slightly so he could stare at the door. "And just who was that?"

She shuddered, bringing his hand to the glass she held, taking it from her and setting it down on the desk.

"Are you sure you're okay?"

She finally nodded, her eyes clearing of the fear that had gripped her. She swallowed hard, knowing she had to explain.

Jacob stood, his hand raised. "Don't explain if you don't want to. I'm a stranger here." He looked back at the store. "I was sent here to talk to Finn."

"I'm Finn. Who sent you?" She stood, walking through to the counter in the store, frowning at the sign on the door, her words causing Jacob to spin and stare at her.

"The man in the small hotel near the downtown. I'm looking for somewhere to stay and all the rooms are taken. He seemed to think you might be able to help." Jacob withdrew his keys from his pockets. "It's okay. I don't need to stay here in town."

"No, that's okay. This has just shaken me. Before I forget, thank you for stepping in. No one else in town would have. He's a bully, used to getting what he wants."

"What did he mean, then, that you belong to him, if you don't mind my asking?" Jacob watched as Finn grimaced, her hand rubbing at her wrist.

"He thinks I'm his, that whatever he says I'll do. He's been told to stay away. I have a restraining order against him, for all the good it does."

"He should stay away, then. Why don't the police get involved?"

—

15

She snorted in a very unladylike manner. "Because the police chief is his father and according to him, Gerry can do and does not do any wrong. It's always the other person's fault. I had to fight to get a restraining order, going to the judge myself. I'm not the first one to seek one against him. He backs off if he finds out a lady he's harassing gets herself a boyfriend or husband."

"Well, then, I'm Jacob Whitson. Happy to meet you and I would be glad to stand in as a substitute friend if you need it."   His deep gray eyes sparkled with mischief as he reached to push back a lock of deep red curls that had dropped over his forehead, taking in the amber eyes and golden hair of the lady standing in front of him.

She shook her head at him. "Really? I might just take you up on that. Seeing as you've locked me up for the day, just let me ring off the cash, stick it in the safe, and I'll take you to my parents' B&B. I know they still have a room there." She paused, looking at him in a strange manner. "Have you ever been here before?"

He shook his head. "No, I haven't. My grandfather died about three months ago and his last request was that I come here during December and search for something he's hidden in a journal. He used to live here when he was a teenager."

"What was his name?"

"Aaron Whitson." He watched her reaction, not expecting it.

"Aaron? Oh, my! He was a friend of my grandfather. Pops used to talk about him a lot, wondering where he was and how he was."

She soon had led him through town to her parents' home, his car following closely behind hers. He stood for a moment at the bottom of the wooden stairs, staring up at the two-story sprawling wood clad house, feeling like he had come home. A sense of danger and adventure coursed through him. Lord, I've come home, I think, but I feel the danger out there. We need your protection, both Finn and I.

Finn pointed to the closet where she had hung her jacket and set her shoes, waiting for him to do the same, before leading him towards the back of the house. He hesitated, knowing he was a guest and knowing she was heading for their personal quarters.

She turned, frowning as he hadn't followed her. "Jacob? Come on. Mom's here in the kitchen." When he still didn't move, she caught his arm, pulling him with her. "You're not a guest, Jacob. You're a friend. Friends are allowed back here." She threw him a grin as she pushed through a door. "Mom?"

"In the kitchen, love. You're home early. No trouble, I hope."

"Yeah, well, that's a story for another day." Finn hugged her mother.

"Not again, Finn. When will he leave you alone?" She didn't look up from where she was working at the counter.

Finn shrugged. "I have no idea. I don't think he ever will, Mom." She looked up at Jacob, over her mother's bent head, and shook her head. "Mom, I brought home someone I think you'll be interested in meeting."

Finn's mother, Mary, looked up from the cookies she was icing at that, seeing for the first time Jacob standing there. Her hands froze for a moment before she dropped the icing bag and came around the counter, wiping her hands on a damp towel as she did so.

"Aaron?"

Jacob shook his head. "Jacob. Aaron was my grandfather."

"You look so much like a photo Timothy Sr. has of the two of them." She reached to hug him, surprising him.

Jacob gave a small smile. "That's what they tell me."

Mary turned to frown at her daughter. "And just how does Jacob fit in to what happened?"

Finn sighed, knowing she'd have to confess. "He walked in on it. John sent him to me to see if we had a room for him."

"Of course we do. He can have Dad's room. It's empty and I know Dad would have liked to have met his friend's grandson. Where's your luggage, Jacob?" She turned back to face him, studying his face.

Jacob stared at her, not quite sure of what had just happened, but feeling that he had been welcomed home. "It's, uh, it's in my car, out front."

"That's fine, then. Finn, get your chocolate out and make you both some. I just have to finish these for the guests' tea and I can join you." Mary bustled away, leaving Jacob staring after her, feeling as if he had been caught in a whirlwind.

Finn laughed. "She's always like that, Jacob. Better get used to it." She pointed at a sitting area off to the side. "Have a seat in there and I'll be right with you. You do drink hot chocolate, don't you?"

He shook his head. "No, actually, I don't. I never have acquired the taste for it."

"What will you have then? Coffee, tea, hot cider, or something cold?"

"Tea sounds good." He grinned. "How many flavours do I get to choose from?"

"About a dozen. If you've no real preference, I like English tea."

"That sounds wonderful. Thank you." He waited, taking the tray from her and watching until she had seated herself. "Now, about today."

She frowned at him, then paused to sip her tea, gathering her thoughts. "What about today?"

"Just what I asked." His eyes watched her intently, so intent she shifted in her chair. "Does he come around a lot?"

She shook her head. "Not really. Although in the last couple of weeks, I've seen him watching me from a distance and walking back and forth in front of the store. Today was the first time he has approached like that in a long time."

"What would have happened had I not been there?"

She shuddered. "I have no idea, Jacob, and I don't even want to think about it."

He nodded, his eyes watchful, his thoughts turning into a prayer for his new friend. He looked up as he heard a commotion from the front of the house.

Finn sighed as she set her cup down on its saucer and rose. "I just knew he'd show up sooner or later."

"Who?" Jacob rose as well, his hand reaching automatically for his phone and turning on the video recorder. It was a habit he had in certain circumstances, and he felt this was one of those. He set his phone down, propped up against his mug, even as a large man stalked through the doors from the front of the house, a belligerent attitude flowing from him.

"What's the meaning of this, Finn? What did you do to Gerry?" The venom and hatred towards Finn spewed from him.

She snorted. "I did nothing to him. He did it to himself."

"Right. Sure he did. He said he was attacked and hurt." The man's eyes never left Finn's face.

Jacob eased up behind her, reaching to envelope her in his arms, crossing his around her just below her own that she had folded across her body. Finn tensed for a moment, then relaxed subtly, enough that she leaned back against Jacob. His arms tightened just enough that she felt the strength of his character in how he held her.

The man shook his head. "I know you, Finn. I know you did something to him. You've always lied about him."

Finn stared at him, her mouth slightly open. "Really? After all the complaints that went in to the department, that were never followed up on? Not just by me, either. The ladies in this town know the character of Gerry. It's his family that doesn't recognize it."

Jacob watched the darkness settle deeper on the man's face and sighed inwardly. What did you just go and do, Finn? Why did you say that? And just who is this man?

Finn shifted her weight closer to Jacob even as he watched the man approach closer. His eyes lifted to the man entering quietly from the front of the house, catching a glimpse of Mary coming in from the dining room, and vague movement of a younger man entering through the back door. His focus returned to Finn and the man standing in front of her.

"All lies, Finn. All lies. You know that."

Finn shook her head. "And you know they're not." She drew in a sharp breath as she watched the man's hands clench into fists. With that, Jacob had released her and swept her behind him.

"I think you should leave now, before you do something you regret." Jacob's words were soft but forceful, drawing the man's attention to himself.

"Stay out of this. This doesn't concern you."

"On the contrary, it does. I will not stand by and watch a lady of any age bullied."

Jacob's words drew the man's focus totally to him. Anger and another emotion Jacob couldn't define crossed his face and then the man's fist was heading for Jacob's face. Jacob felt the force of the blow he didn't have time to duck, the force driving him backwards and down into darkness. His backward motion caught Finn and took her down with him, their bodies hitting the floor in a solid thud. The younger man sprang forward, his stance protective as he stood in front of them.

Timothy Bronagh sprang forward as well, his hand going to the police chief's arm to prevent further blows being lodged on their guest. He wasn't in time to prevent the heavy kick the man launched at Jacob.

"George. Enough of this. You've gone too far this time. When this gets reported to the council, you'll be done."

George spun, almost spitting in Timothy's face in his rage. "It will be my word against yours. I always win."

"Not this time, George. Not this time. You entered a private residence without cause or a warrant. You've assaulted someone without provocation. No, this time you're done. Now leave." Timothy swept his arm towards the door, one eye on the man, the other trying to assess the two on the floor.

"This isn't over, not by a long shot. If he stays in town, he will be arrested for assault on Gerry."

Timothy shook his head in a sorrowful manner. "I don't think so, George. Your time of running the town is over, I think. Not with who you just assaulted."

George Adams scoffed. "He's just a stranger in town. What's the big deal?"

"He's more than just a stranger, George. I understand that's Jacob Whitson, Aaron's grandson."

George's face whitened as his mouth opened and closed, his lips unable to form words. He finally spun, his footsteps heavy and hurried.

Mary rushed forward, dropping to her knees beside the young couple even as Finn struggled to sit up, her brother's hands reaching for her.

"Finn? Are you okay?" Timothy crouched beside them, his eyes on his daughter.

"I am, Dad. Jacob?" Her eyes flew to him, her heart in her throat at the thought of how he had been injured stepping in front of her.

Jacob rolled to his back, his eyes flickering open and closed. "My phone!"

Peter's eyes flew to where the phone sat and he frowned even as he reached for it. "Jacob? Your phone? At a time like this?"

Jacob nodded, regretting it as pain spread through his face and head. "Video."

Peter's eyes brightened as comprehension dawned. "Wonderful! We have proof we can take somewhere."

Finn stared between the two men even as she heard quiet footsteps approaching the door and saw her father rising to greet one of their guests who stood there. "What's so important about his phone?"

"He has a video of what just happened, Finn. We have proof. It's timestamped and everything."

Jacob's eyes slid shut against the pain. "A habit I have." His words were mumbled as he fought to stay conscious.

Timothy stared at his guest, wondering that he had come into their private quarters. Then his face cleared at the man's words.

"I don't want to intrude, but I was in the lounge and heard what was said. I was a medic in the armed forces. May I take a look?" The younger man's eyes drifted past Timothy and lit on Jacob, a sound of recognition pulled from him.

"Whit?" He too dropped down beside Jacob, his hands reaching to assess him.

Jacob pulled himself back from the blackness he was drifting into. "Blackie? What are you doing here?"

"I'm moving to this town. I thought it would be a nice quiet town." Levi Blackwell stared down at his friend, concern on his face even as he grinned. "At least it was until you showed up. And that's something we need to talk about. But first. How's the head?" Long fingers gently probed at Jacob's jaw and head, before Blackie turned his attention to Finn. "Are you all right?"

She nodded. "I just had the breath knocked out of me for a bit. How is Jacob?"

Blackie reached down a hand to pull Jacob to his feet, a hand steadying his friend before he guided him to a chair. "He's fine. He's got a hard head."

Timothy and Mary exchanged glances before Mary spoke. "But you seem to know Jacob. How?"

"We served together, Ma'am. I lost track of him when we both left the service." He studied his friend. "There have been a couple of other friends looking for him. Something has drawn us to this area."

Jacob stared at his friend, eyes narrowed, knowing they would have to talk and that there was something Blackie wasn't saying. "We'll talk." Jacob's attention turned Finn. "Are you okay, Finn?"

She nodded. "Don't ever do that again, Jacob. Don't ever step in front of me like that." She glared at her brother as he snickered.

Jacob stared at her without blinking, until she looked down. "Don't even think I won't, Finn. I won't let any man bully a lady, not if I can help it." He looked around at the five staring at him. "What's his problem, anyway?"

Timothy sighed as he accepted the mug of coffee his wife handed him before he too sat in one of the arm chairs. "He's pretty much run the town for years now. We've had issues with him, but the council is running scared of him and his bullies. Any recruit we get to the force that is decent moves on within a short period of time."

"Toxic." Blackie spoke up.

Timothy's head swung his way as he frowned. "Toxic? That's a good way to describe it. We've gone to the next level of law enforcement but he's always been able to talk his way out of anything. But you, Jacob. You've come here for a reason." Timothy pointed to the younger man. "I have no idea what brought you here, other than God."

Jacob shrugged. "I never knew this town existed, not really. Grand never talked about when he was real young. I was handed his journal and a letter from him at his grave, but I had no intention of coming here, even though he asked me to. His lawyer finally convinced me I needed to, to come find "my roots" as he put it. I haven't read the letter yet and only glanced through the journal, just enough to find the name of this town."

The four Bronaghs exchanged glances before Mary spoke. "Then, you really have no idea of what this town means to you."

Jacob shook his head, a sudden dread filling him. *Lord, what did I go and walk into? I have a feeling I'm in over my head right now. I really really need Your strength and guidance right now.*

Timothy sighed as he stared at his wife, waiting before she gave a reluctant nod. "Then, let me fill you in on what this town means to you. First, Mary, let's dish up our dinner. Blackie, may I call you that?" At his nod, Timothy continued. "Please, join us. A friend of Jacob's is a friend of ours. We need to talk. Then, Jacob has some decisions he'll need to make. One, I hope, is going to the next level of law enforcement with his video."

"Next level? As in the county police?" Blackie suddenly grinned, drawing frowns from those watching him. "Jacob, Simon's on the county force. You'll have someone who'll believe you."

"Simon? Oh, that's wonderful." Jacob set his fork on his plate, the casserole there forgotten for the moment, arms resting on the table as his eyes sought Finn, watching her for a moment, unaware of the interest he was garnering. "Timothy, what was it you had to say?" His attention turned to Timothy.

Timothy sat back, folding his arms across his chest, as he studied the younger man. "Your great great grandfather founded this town, along with my great grandfather. Your roots run deep here, son, deeper than you know. I'm glad you're back. I wish Aaron had come back to stay. He was in and out the last couple of years, here for a couple of hours and then gone. We never had a chance to speak. But I do know this. Your grandfather owned about half the buildings in this town. If he passed his estate on to you, then you now own those buildings. That would be why you were pushed to come here."

Chapter 3

Jacob lay in bed late that night, his eyes on the white of the moonlight as it filtered through the window sheers and reflected in the mirror of the antique dresser on the opposite wall. He shivered, not from the cold, but from the coming difficulties he sensed he faced. He rolled over, pulling the blankets up around his ears, trying to find the sleep that eluded him. He sighed, knowing he wouldn't get much sleep that night. His thoughts turned to the events of earlier, and he frowned. How had the police chief gotten away with so much for so many years?

Then his thought drifted to his grandfather. Grand, was this what you wanted to talk to me about that night? You were gone, graduated to heaven, so quickly that day, I never got to say good bye to you. He wiped at the tears that wet his face. It had been just him and Grand for so many years after his Grams went. He had been a young teenager. Grand hadn't wanted him to join the forces, but hadn't stood in his way, pride in him reflecting every time he saw his Grand after that. They had taken him in after his parents had been killed in a typhoon serving overseas as missionaries.

He rolled over again, restless with his thoughts. He had never imagined his grandfather owned so much property. He had never said, never talked about finances at all with him. He wished he had. Then he would have been better prepared to hear what Timothy had told him. He sighed, his heart turning to prayer. Lord, I have no idea where this is going. I am so over my head in this situation, even more than when I had to arrest a fellow soldier. I never wanted to be an MP but that's what You chose for me. Guide us here, Lord.

He finally drifted off, his thoughts on Finn, a smile on his face. He knew without a shadow of a doubt he wanted to spend time with her. He prayed for his new friends, not knowing just how much those prayers would be needed in the coming days. He felt the sense of doom approaching, but ignored it.

❁ ❁ ❁ ❁ ❁

Finn stirred in the early morning light, her eyes opening to the early winter morning. She squinted at the clock and sighed. There would be no more sleep for her. Today was a big day in their town - annual Christmas festivities starting during the morning. She still had to finish her decorations outside her store.

She pushed back the covers and swung her feet out of the bed, stopping as she saw the bruising on her wrist. Jacob had noticed it the previous night when her sweater sleeve had pulled back and insisted Blackie check it out before he took pictures of it. She tried to get him not to but he just shook his head and continued. Lord, I have no idea who he is or what he's here for, but I sense that You brought him here. Protect him please.

She paused as she pulled the soft jade sweater over her head, a frown appearing. Lord, Jacob's here and I just know he's going to change things in this

―

town. I just know he's going to change things for me. She drew a deep breath, realizing finally that she had let him encircle her with his arms, holding her against him, and she had let him. In fact, she had moved backwards against him, into the strength of his body and character. This was not her. Not since the attack so many years ago when she had been beaten by a high school acquaintance. She hadn't let any male touch her, just her father and brother. She stared at her image in the mirror. Lord, am I finally healing?

She greeted her mother, grabbing her tea to go and her usual bagel, and headed for the street. She usually walked to work if she could. Today, she needed that time alone just to try and figure out her feelings. And somehow, she didn't think the fifteen minute walk would work.

She stood for a moment staring at the town centre, the large pine tree with the lights ready for the lighting ceremony that night. She spun in a circle, studying the other businesses in the square, noting she was the only one not yet ready. She sighed. This year, she hadn't been in the mood to decorate, even though she knew she had to. Some years, she despaired of ever finding the spirit she needed for that time of year and quite often not finding it.

She shoved open her shop door and headed for the office, dropping her purse into the usual drawer and locking it.

She dug around to find the decorations, standing back and staring at them. She put the same ones up year after year, just because it's what her Pops had done with the shop.

She sighed and turned to the front of the store as she heard the bell. It had to be a visitor to town, she thought. Townspeople never came in that early. She stopped, her eyes on Jacob as he laid a journal on the counter, then turned to study the shop, moving quietly and slowly through it before he ended up in front of the door, his eyes meeting hers before a smile lit his face.

"Finn! I didn't see you standing there." He turned back, his arm sweeping around the view of the store. "I like this store. Your mom said it used to be your grandfather's?"

"It was. I grew up in here with him. He taught me what I knew, sent me to study with experts and paid for college courses for me. We shared the same love of the old." She moved towards him. "You're out and about early."

"Habit." He grinned at her. "I got used to being up and about early in the armed forces and can't shake the habit." He followed her back into the office as she shook her head. "Your mom said you had to decorate your shop. Let me help."

She finally nodded, a pensive look on her face. "I've done it on my own for the last few years, since Pops went. It's not the same."

Jacob froze for a moment, realizing how true it was. This would be the first year without any of his own people. "It's true."

———

She turned, catching the momentary look of sadness of his face, before he smiled.

"These boxes are the ones you're working from?" At her nod, he gathered up some and headed for the front of the store. "Where do we start, inside or outside? And do you have to do the same thing every year?"

She started to laugh. "Inside, and no. Why? Do you have fresh ideas?"

He grinned as he nodded and then opening the boxes, starting going through them. "Oh, this is wonderful. I have so many ideas. You shouldn't let me loose, you know."

"All I can say is go for it. I'm glad for some fresh ideas. I don't have the heart to change what Pops always did."

"I don't want to offend anyone, Finn. If it will, I won't go ahead with any of my ideas."

She shook her head even as she laid a hand on his arm, her eyes focused on that movement. He's changing me already, Lord. I'm not sure I'm ready for this but as long as You're not saying no or stopping me, I'll go along with it. "No. It's time I changed things and made it my own. Rather, your own."

Two hours later, Finn stepped back to the edge of the sidewalk to study the decorations outside the store, her face flushed with laughter, Jacob grinning at her unrepentantly. Her parents watched from the other side of the street, smiles on their faces.

"He's good for our Finn, Mary." Timothy sighed inwardly, knowing her happiness might not last.

"He is. I haven't seen her that happy or laughing so hard since before her attack. I pray he stays here."

"That's all we can do, dear. Dad would have liked him."

"That he would have. I wish he could have met him." Mary drew in a deep breath as she saw the officer approaching Finn. "Not now, please."

Timothy's hand tightened on his wife's. "Jacob will look after her. Trust him."

Finn looked up as she heard her name, freezing momentarily as she saw the police uniform, not hearing Jacob call to her or feel him moving behind her, an arm coming around her.

The officer, a friend of Peter's, stood for a moment watching the two, his eyes thoughtful. He had heard from Peter what had happened the night before and had promised he'd watch out for Finn, a lady he considered a sister. His eyes searched Jacob's before he nodded.

"I had a complaint there was too much fun going on here, Finn." He grinned as she shook a finger at him.

"And who complained? Peter?" She leaned back on Jacob, not realizing she was doing that, drawing Tom's eyes to the movement. "Tom, this is Jacob Whitson. You've heard of Aaron? This is his grandson.

Tom reached to shake Jacob's hand. "Welcome to your town, Jacob. Sorry the welcome wasn't so good last night." He looked around. "Watch your backs, you two." He moved past them, his eyes watching the crowds.

Jacob watched him walk away before his own eyes searched the crowds and before he looked down at the lady he still held and who hadn't made any move to step away from him. He liked the feeling of her in his arms.

She tilted her eyes to search his face before she moved out of his arms, her eyes back on the building.

"I like what you've done, Jacob. This is so unique and so true to what we have inside." He had used her grandfather's decorations in a different way and they had been getting compliments from the neighbouring businesses.

"I'm glad." He stepped back towards the curb with her, his eyes assessing what they had done. "Your work in the window helps. I like how you've used objects from the kitchen to make believe you're cooking an old-fashioned dinner."

She laughed, something she had done a lot of that day. Something about Jacob had released the lock on her emotions and her heart and she finally felt free of what had held her back. She felt a sudden shove and screamed, finding herself falling towards the street and the oncoming traffic. There was no way she could avoid being run down.

Jacob, hearing her scream, spun, his hands and arms reaching for her and cradling her to him even as his feet shoved him away from the street. He hit the sidewalk with a heavy thud, protecting Finn as much as he could, rolling towards the building even as the pedestrians scattered around them and ran, a few heading their way to help.

Tom dropped to his knees beside them, even as he reached for his radio. He knew the call would go nowhere, the chief would make sure of that once he knew who was involved. He frowned. There had been something different about the chief as he walked through the building that morning. He wasn't as arrogant in his manner as he usually was and he didn't stop to berate any of the men and women milling around during the shift change.

"Finn? Jacob?" Tom reached to help entangle the two, the man from the neighbouring bakeshop on his knees to help.

"Finn was pushed, Tom." Ed's words were breathless. "If it weren't for this young man, she'd have been under someone's tires."

Jacob pushed back Finn's hair even as they sat up on the sidewalk, his hand resting for a moment on her cheek. "You're okay? You're not hurt? I tried to protect you."

Finn's eyes were wide and frightened before she took a deep breath and then slapped Jacob's shoulder. "You have to stop doing that, Jacob. You'll be killed next time." She shoved to her feet and stormed through her store door, the door banging shut behind her.

Jacob stood, hands shoved into his jacket pockets, as he watched before he felt Tom's hand on his shoulder.

"Give her a moment. She reacts like this when she's scared. She gets mad." Tom looked around. "No one will have seen anything. I can guarantee you that. I'll ask the normal questions and that will be the answer I get."

Jacob nodded, even as he watched the crowd once more hurrying by them, the excitement over. "What's really going on, Tom? She shouldn't be treated like this, not in a town called Mistletoe."

"No, no one should, but the chief has made it clear that she is persona non gratis, because of his son. We've tried to talk to him and usually end up with a report on our file because of it. Those of us who are loyal to our people and town have made a pact to protect the people the chief has taken a dislike to." He paused, searching for the right words. "And you'll be at the top of his list. Peter talked to me last night. Watch your back." He nodded towards the door. "Watch Finn. She's letting you do things no one else can. I saw her back up to you when I approached. She's never done that before. Never let any male other than her family touch her. She's let you. For some reason, the trust is there before she really knows you. Don't break it."

Jacob nodded. "I won't. I think it goes back to our grandfathers being friends. She may feel like she knows me."

Tom stared at him for a moment, then shook his head. "That's not it, Jacob. You have a presence about you, a presence that demands respect. You can intimidate if you have to. I hear tell you did that last night. We need you in this town." He nodded towards Finn's store. "She needs you in her life, Jacob, whether or not she realizes it. And not just to stop what's been going for years, something none of us have been able to stop or even figure out what it is." He slapped Jacob on the shoulder before walking away.

"He's right, you know?" Jacob spun at the voice behind him. Ed stood there. "I've had my shop next to this one for as long as Finn can remember and even longer. She's never reacted to someone like she has to you. I haven't heard her laugh like she was and for her to giggle like she was? No one has heard that since she was a young child. Stick around. I knew your grandpa. You look like him and it appears that you act just like him."

Jacob stared, openmouthed, after him as he walked back into his store even as he heard the bell jingle at Finn's. She stood there, eyes on him.

"Well, get in here already, will you? I have your tea ready for you. Ed sent over some sweets for us. Then I need to check my online orders while you research your journal." She watched with sympathy as he froze beside her at those words. A hand was laid on his arm. "He would want you to read it here in Mistletoe, Jacob. This was his hangout when he was young, this store. It wasn't what it was then, but he and Pops hung around here with my great grandparents."

———

27

He stood, nodding his head, willing the tears back down. He couldn't and swiped angrily at the ones that escaped to roll down his cheeks. He heard a soft sound from Finn before she drew him into the store and hand wrapped around his arm, back to the office where she turned to him and hugged him. He stood for a moment before his arms reached around her and his head rested on hers, accepting the comfort she was giving. He finally released her, not looking at her for a moment. When he did, he saw the tears sparkling in her own eyes. He reached to trace the track of one that had escaped.

"Thank you."

She nodded, then pointed to the chair he had used the day before. "Sit before our tea gets cold."

He watched as she worked away at her computer, rising every once in a while to help a customer. He wandered through the shop, his eyes drawn to the books and journals she had on display. He frowned for a moment as he reached for one.

Finn watched from where she was gift wrapping an old small globe for a tourist, her attention wavering for a moment, before it returned to her customer. She smiled at the man's thanks and watched as he walked away. It would soon be closing time, but then the festivities in the square would begin. This year, she just didn't want to be in a crowd. She didn't feel safe, even though it was her town.

She walked over to where Jacob stood. "What did you find, Jacob?"

"This." He help up the journal. "It's got a cover like Grand's." He carefully opened it, a frown on his face. "This is strange. This is Grams' handwriting. How did it end up here?"

Finn shook her head. "I think I took that in with a bunch of books someone found in a house they were renting. They were told they could clear out the attic and get rid of anything they didn't want." She paused, her eyes shifting to stare into the distance. "I think it was a house your grandfather owned." She placed a hand on his, finding his shaking, and closed her fingers around his. "It might have been your grandfather's house. Mom or Dad will know. But I'm not even sure that's how it got here." She reached for it. "Come to think of it, I don't remember seeing it before."

He nodded, a somber look on his face. "I need to buy this from you, Finn. I need to read through both of these. Maybe it will give me answers as to why Grand wanted me to come here."

He looked up at her as her fingers tightened on his and frowned, a puzzled look on his face, his eyes searching hers. Lord, what is it about this lady that draws me when no other one ever did? Guide me here, please. I don't want to hurt this lady, not at all.

"It's yours, Jacob. I can't charge you for something that belongs to your family." She shook her head as he opened his mouth to protest, a finger laid across his lips. "No. It's yours. It should have always been. I'm not sure why your grandmother didn't have it with her or how it got here. She wasn't from here, not that I know of."

He shook his head. "No, she wasn't. I wonder." He stared down at the journal, a distant look in his eyes. "Grand disappeared for a couple of days after Grams died. Maybe he came back here and left it here." He sighed. "I suddenly feel like I'm caught in a whirlwind or something, that I'm lost on some path where I can't see around the bend." He glanced at the clock. "Your mother's expecting us for dinner before we come back here. Let me help you lock up for the night." He stacked the two journals together with his coat.

Tightening her jade patterned scarf around her neck, Finn dug into her pocket for her gloves. With the sun going down, it was getting chilly. Snowflakes drifted lazily down and she tilted her face to feel them caress her skin. Jacob smiled at the picture she make, not aware of how her parents were watching and then exchanging their own smiles. He reached for her hand, surprising her. She stared at their linked hands before she shrugged and followed as he tugged her towards the downtown.

Jacob led Finn among her fellow townspeople and the visitors, finding just the right spot to watch the activities where they would be sheltered and out of sight.

"Will this do?" Jacob smiled down at Finn as she glanced around.

"Perfect. It's my favourite spot for watching the festivities but I don't often get it." She reached up to drop a kiss on his cheek. "Thank you."

Jacob stood, his eyes on her as she looked around the crowd, waving to friends. He wanted to touch the spot, but didn't. He sighed to himself. He had no intention of living in a small town, but he also had no intention of living in the town he grew up in. He searched the crowd, seeing people who had approached him over the course of the day, talking about his grandfather and his ancestors. He was drawn here but he just didn't know.

Movement to his side caught his eye and he turned, a frown on his face that smoothed out when he saw Blackie standing back from him, watching the crowd. He looked past him as the man standing next to Blackie nodded at him. He grinned suddenly. Simon was there. Now, where was Joshua? A movement to his other side had his head turning that way. Joshua. Joshua nodded before his eyes dropped to Finn and then back up. Jacob's heart stilled as he got the message. Something was up tonight that involved Finn and his friends had picked up for him.

Finn turned at that point, her eyes on his face, a smile on her face. She seemed relaxed, more than he had seen in the couple of days since he met her.

"Thank you, Jacob."

"For what?"

"For being who you are. You're like what Pops always said your grandfather was like."

He hugged her at that, tears prickling at his eyes, tears he willed back down. "Thank you for saying that. He was a wonderful man. Sure, he had his faults, who doesn't? But he stayed true to his course and that was being a man of God."

They turned back to the square, watching as the festivities started, listening to the local band playing the carols and Christmas songs, the cheers as the tree was lighted, the oohs and aahs from the children as they watched the lights flicker to life on the tree.

Jacob finally pushed away from the wall, his hand catching Finn's as they moved through the crowd.

"What happens now?"

She shrugged. "People stay here, mingling meeting old and new friends. A service club serves hot drinks. Another one hands out candy canes to all the kids."

He nodded, his eyes searching for his friends and not seeing them. That didn't worry him, he knew they were with them.

"Jacob?" He looked down as she said his name. "You seem distracted tonight."

He shook his head. "Not really, although you are a distraction, one of the nice ones." He laughed as she blushed. "My friends are here somewhere, and I was hoping to introduce you to both Simon and Joshua."

"Joshua?" She mulled over the name. "Is he a cook by chance?"

Jacob nodded. "He was. I'm not sure what he's up to now. We lost track of one another when we left the armed forces."

"There's a new cafe in town called The House. The owner's name is Josh. Would that be him?"

He nodded. "It would be. I'll need to check it out next week. Knowing Josh, it won't be open on Sundays."

She agreed. "He's been here for about a year, I think. He's been pressured to open on Sundays. The police chief has been one of the ones after him. He has refused."

Jacob sighed. "Is there nothing that man isn't involved in or won't do?"

"Not much." She turned as she heard running footsteps approaching them.

A hand went across her mouth as an arm swung around her, trapping her arms as she was picked up. She heard a sound from Jacob and then was out of his sight, carried through a back alley to a vehicle. Her hands were bound behind her and a gag tightened over her mouth before she was dumped into a trunk. She heard murmured words and then felt the car shift as someone sat in it. She felt the movement as the car moved away. Her heart sank. Who had taken her and why? She had a good idea who was behind it but without proof no one would ever believe her.

She felt desperately around the trunk, trying to find a weapon or something to release her bonds and found nothing. She stared at the lights, and then raising a foot, kicked at one of the lights, finally breaking the plastic. Cold air rushed in and she shivered.

—

Maybe that wasn't such a good idea after all, she thought. I'm going to freeze to death. Lord, help me. She laid her head down, too stressed to cry, too worried about Jacob.

Jacob struggled to sit up, Blackie's arm around his shoulder holding him upright. The blow had caught him in his back, at the site of an old injury that still plagued him. The sudden pain had sent him down to his knees even as Finn's hand was ripped from his.

"Finn?" His breath came in gasps as he tried to control his pain.

Blackie looked around. "She's not here, Whit. Simon and Josh are after her. We weren't close enough to stop it." He looked down at his friend, before reaching down a hand to pull him to his feet. "I'm sorry."

Jacob leaned against the wall behind him. "This was planned, Blackie. For some reason. I think you'll find the police chief and his son are somehow behind it, though why I have no idea."

Blackie looked around, saw an officer approaching them and hand on Jacob's arm, drew him down an alley where he stuffed him into his truck. "I don't think you want to talk to the police in this town."

Jacob shook his head, his breath finally evening out as the pain subsided. "Not really. I know there are good ones, Tom for one, but I can't be sure even about him."

Blackie pulled his phone out. "Josh says they're on the trail of the car." He started to laugh. "Your lady's good, Jacob. Josh said it looked as if there's a light out on the back. Would she have known to kick it out?"

"I have no idea, Blackie. I just met her yesterday. Our grandfathers were friends, but other than that, I don't know of any connection to her." His eyes searched the vehicles ahead of them, not knowing which one was Simon's and not knowing which one held Finn.

Blackie stared at Jacob for a few seconds before his eyes returned to the road ahead of him. He couldn't believe that. Those two have a connection like I've never seen. Lord, protect Jacob's lady, whatever it is she is involved with. Guide us to her tonight.

Josh read the text he had received from Blackie. "They're behind us, somewhere, Simon. Are we following the right car?"

Simon Gardner nodded. "We are. I had my eye on that car earlier. The way it was parked just shouted something was off about it. I don't trust the police in Mistletoe enough to alert them."

Joshua Smithson nodded. "I know there are some good cops there. I've met them. But their hands are basically tied by the chief. We need to get him out of there."

Simon pointed. "There. That's our car. What on earth?" He started to laugh. "She's kicked out a light by the looks of it."

Josh stared at Simon for a moment before he looked back at the car. "Smart lady. She's a good match for Whit." He stared around. "Hey! Didn't we just leave the town?"

Simon nodded, a grim look on his face as he reached for his phone. "We did. We can arrest him now, whoever he is, and charge him in our county. He won't get away with kidnapping in our jurisdiction. My boss has been looking for information and evidence on the chief in Mistletoe for years."

"Blackie said Whit taped what happened last night. You know Whit. He set up a video recording when the chief entered their private residence."

"He did? Wonderful. David will be so glad to hear that. We need to get it from Whit."

"We do." He watched as the car ahead swerved across the road and back. "What is he doing?"

"I have no idea." Simon stared ahead. "I can see the lights from the county force heading our way. We'll trap him between us. There are no roads or lanes he can turn off onto in this stretch." Then his breath caught and he slammed on his brakes. "He really didn't just go and do that, did he?"

"He did." Josh had his seatbelt off and was out of the truck, heading for the car.

The kidnapper had spun his wheel when he realized he was trapped, sending the car trunk first into the trees. The two men running that way winced at the sound of metal crumpling. They slid to a stop, taking a look at the driver before heading for the trunk, their hearts sinking as they saw it crumpled badly.

"Watch him, Josh." Simon ran for his truck, flagging down the patrol officer responding to his call for help. The officer nodded, reaching back in for his radio.

Simon grabbed his tire iron and another pry bar he had dropped into the tool box just by chance. He stared at it for a moment. No, he thought, it was not just by chance. It was God.

He slid to a halt beside Josh, who was frantically trying to open the trunk, handing him the pry bar. Together, the two men worked feverishly to free the twisted metal without success. Simon looked up as he heard the sirens and then the sound of a diesel engine. He stepped back, pulling Josh with him as the firefighters ran their way, dragging the equipment they needed.

Josh looked up as he heard another vehicle stop. "It's Whit. Let me go see him."

Simon nodded as he cast a look that way before watching the crumpled metal give way. He drew closer as the paramedics traded places with the firefighters and worked on Finn.

"Is she alive?" Simon could barely ask the question.

—

"She is, and I don't know how." The paramedic shot a glance around the trunk. "The way it crumpled, that saved her. She was thrown forward against the back seat when the trunk crumpled from the top back."

Simon nodded, then turned to make his way towards Jacob, Blackie, and Josh. He could feel the tension and anguish radiating from Jacob before he reached him

Jacob shot him a look and then turned to watch where the paramedics were working on Finn.

"Jacob." Simon sighed. "Jacob!" His voice raised a bit and Jacob jumped and turned to him.

"She's alive, Whit. Somehow, she's alive. She's unconscious, which is not unexpected. They'll be transporting her soon." He watched the relief flood over Jacob before he shared a look with their two friends. "I have a patrol officer on his way to find her parents and her brother, I think Blackie said?"

"Peter. Please." Jacob walked rapidly away from them towards the ambulance. A few quick words and he was on board, watching Finn's face intently

"Is that really Whit?" Josh's voice was quiet. "And you said Finn?" At Blackie's nod, he continued. "I know Finn from town and from church. I didn't realize Whit knew her as well."

"Not until last night." Blackie filled the two in on what had transpired. "I think he's smitten, whether he realizes it or not."

Josh nodded, a thought crossing his mind. "Did you say he hugged her last night and then was holding her hand tonight?" He grinned suddenly. "She doesn't let any male that close to her, except her brother and father. I think Whit has himself a lady."

The two other men shook their heads. Blackie then spoke. "I'll head in to the hospital. Josh, you with me?"

"No, I'll stay with Simon. I think I have to give a statement or something like that."

Blackie nodded as he walked back to his vehicle, his heart raised in prayer for his friend's lady. He searched the traffic stopped by the accident, his eyes zeroing in on a certain truck. He pulled out his phone and took a photo, making sure he took one of the plate, before he slid behind the wheel and pulled away, being waved through the scene.

❀ ❀ ❀ ❀ ❀

Two hours later, Jacob looked up and then stood as he found Mary standing in front of him, Timothy and Peter flanking her. She reached to hug him, then sat beside him, his hand in both of hers.

"Mary. Timothy. I'm sorry."

—

Timothy shook his head. "Not your fault, Jacob. He would have taken her no matter who she was with. At least you were there and because you were, your friends were and found her so quickly." He leaned back in the chair, his eyes sliding closed. "Thank God you were all there." His eyes opened as he assessed the younger man before he nodded. "Finn has let you into her life in a way she has never let anyone else, not even us. I know you'll be careful with her."

"I will." Jacob looked up as he heard footsteps. "Any word on her condition?"

"She's conscious. They're running some more tests and want to keep her overnight but I'm not sure they'll win that battle."

Jacob nodded. "If she goes home, Blackie can check on her for you." Blackie nodded his agreement from where he stood close to them.

Jacob excused himself, walking towards his three friends. "Simon. Josh. It's so good to see you two again." He reached to hug his friends.

"And you." Josh looked around. "Is there somewhere we can grab a coffee? We need to talk, Jacob, and not in front of her people."

Jacob shot a look backwards and then shrugged. "I have no idea, Josh. Simon?"

"There a little cafe just around the corner. We can go there. Just let me speak to her people and I'll catch up."

Jacob looked at his friends over his coffee cup, seeing the grim looks on their faces and sighed to himself. This was not the way he hoped to reunite with them. Something big was happening and he was in the middle of it. Suddenly he felt like he had been caught up in a tornado and had no way of escaping.

"Simon?" Jacob's eyes fell on him. "You start."

Simon grinned. "I never expected we'd all end up in this area. We all had plans to go different ways. I didn't realize it was a home area for you, Jacob."

"I didn't either, but apparently it is. Mistletoe - who calls a town that?"

"Your great great grandfather apparently." Blackie grinned at him, then sobered. "We need to talk seriously, guys. Something is going on in Mistletoe and it revolves around both Finn and Whit."

"And I have no idea what it is. Finn doesn't either, I can tell you that. She thinks whatever has happened in the last couple of days goes back to an incident when she was a young teenager." A black look crossed his face. "She has told me she was attacked, beaten up, and threatened. She hasn't said who, but from what happened yesterday in her shop that I walked in on, I would said it was the chief's son who was the culprit." He brought the other two friends up to date on what had happened. He figured Blackie had told them what had gone on the night before.

The three other men exchanged glances. Finally, Simon spoke up. "But what brought you here, Whit?"

—

35

"My Grand left a letter and a journal for me, to be handed to me at his grave. I refused to read the letter, had no interest in coming this way. The lawyer finally tracked me down and specifically told me that Grand wanted me to come here, that his will would not be released or read until I had. So, you see? I had no choice." He paused, a thought crossing his mind. "I wonder how much he knew of what was going on here. I found Grams' journal in Finn's shop. She thought it came from a box of old books she had bought. But I wonder. Grand had gone on a trip about three weeks before he passed, when I was away overnight, or so his lawyer said. I wonder if he brought it here and stuck it in Finn's shop. He would have known I'd end up there. He knew my love of old books."

The three men with him stared at him for a moment before Josh spoke.

"You know, about that time an older gentleman came into the cafe, asked for tea and toast. He reminded me of someone and now I know it was you. I wonder if it was your grandfather. I meant to sit and talk with him but by the time it had settled down in there, he was gone."

"It likely was him, Josh. He wouldn't have mentioned it to me. Mistletoe had no meaning for me at that point. Now, I don't know. Timothy tells me I own half the town buildings because Grand did."

"Can your lawyer tell you if the police chief lives in one of your buildings?" Blackie was thinking ahead, knowing Jacob's troubles were just starting.

Jacob stared at his mug, knowing he would need to ask, and dreading the answer. "I'll ask him on Monday. He's always unavailable on Sundays - he's really involved in his church and has made that a day of rest his whole career." He looked up, a bleak look on his face. "But where does that leave us with Finn?"

"With you, Jacob. She's made a connection to you so quickly, I don't know if I've seen anything like that before." Simon studied his friend. "It has to be God, Jacob."

Jacob stared at his friend. They had been through a lot together, those two friends, things not even their other two friends knew about. He finally nodded. "I think so, Simon. But how do I keep her safe?"

"Stick as close as you can. You'll be working through the journals, right? Can you do that at her shop?" Josh glanced at Blackie, seeing his nod.

"I can. She'll be able to tell me about the town and the people." He frowned, sitting back in his chair, and digging his hands into his pockets. He blew out a breath, searching the faces of his friends and then staring across the cafe. "I feel like I'm in over my head, guys."

"You are, Jacob. But you have us in your corner. No matter what happens, remember that God is in control." Simon stood. "Let's get you back to the hospital and see if we can sneak you in to see your lady."

Leaning back in his chair, Jacob's eyes sought to find Finn among the shelving and displays in her store. When he couldn't see her, he rose, stretching, and then meandering slowly to the office. He propped himself against the office doorway, watching her deep in her work. A small sound roused her, and she looked up, blinking at him before she smiled. He winced as he saw the bruising on her face from the accident on the Saturday night.

"How are you feeling, Finn?"

She shrugged. "Like I was run over a truck." She stood, walking towards him. "How is your research coming?"

He shook his head. "I can't concentrate on it. The grief is too fresh for Grand, and I feel like I'm invading Grams' privacy looking at her journal."

"You're not, you know." She glanced back at her desk. "I'm caught up here for now. Let's take a look at them together." She reached out her hand, holding hers steady as he stared first at her and then her hand.

Jacob finally reached and grasped her hand. "Thank you, Finn. Having you here makes it easier. But first, let's pray. I know that whatever is in these books will change my life in a drastic manner and forever."

He sat once more at the desk she had told him to use and she scooted a chair close to him. He sighed as his phone chimed that he had a voice mail. He listened to it, a frown covering his face, before he tucked his phone away.

"That didn't sound like happy news." Finn watched him closely.

"No, it wasn't. I was asked the other night if the police chief lived in one of my buildings. It turns out he does. He tried to buy it years ago and every so often since. Grand refused to sell it to him." He paused, his eyes on her. "The lawyer didn't know why other than that Grand said he would never sell anything to that family."

She nodded. "I can see that. They have never been well liked in this town. We're still trying to figure out how he got to be chief. He had to have had something on someone to make it this far."

"More than likely he does. Simon is looking into that. His chief has asked him to. I turned over the video from the other night to them."

She sat back, before reaching for his grandmother's journal. "May I?"

He nodded. "Go ahead. I'll look through Grand's." He paused, fingering the letter from his grandfather he had never read.

"You need to read that first, Jacob."

He looked up at her, an expression on his face she couldn't read. He handed it to her. "Will you read it to me? It would be too hard reading it, seeing his handwriting. And knowing Grand, it will be written by hand."

She paused, staring down at the letter with just the word "Jacob" written on it. "Are you sure? This is likely pretty personal."

He gave a bark of laughter. "Nothing is so personal with that, I don't think, that I can't share with a treasured friend." He nodded. "Please."

She laid the letter down and rose. "I'm closing up the shop. We're going to go somewhere we can read it and look through the journals where I know we won't be disturbed. Grab your coat and your journals."

He hesitated for a moment, then did what she asked, his thoughts not on what he was doing, but on the lady walking away from him. Lord, I have no idea where this road is leading me, leading us. You are in control. I need to seek You in all things related to Grand's estate. I also need to seek Your will about Finn. I have never met anyone like her before.

Finn stood for a moment, watching him, not realizing her heart was in her eyes when he looked up. A smile creased his face as he reached for her hand.

"Come on, sweetheart. Show me where you want to go with these." He held up the journals.

She nodded. "We need to stop for one of our vehicles. I would say mine as I know where we need to go."

He shrugged. "Whatever. I've had females drive me before." He ducked as she swatted at him.

❀ ❀ ❀ ❀ ❀

An hour later, Jacob stood on the porch of an old cabin, looking around, feeling the peace that came from the area. He saw the bits of snow that had accumulated under the trees where the sun couldn't reach.

"Who did you say owns this?" He turned as he heard Finn opening the door and then walking through, her footsteps echoing on the wooden floor.

"My Pops did. It's mine now. I think it goes back to his grandparents. I would imagine your grandfather was a frequent visitor here."

"I would think he would be." He stopped just inside the door, looking around. "This is nice, Finn. I like it. It's comfortable. It's like coming home."

She nodded, a grin on her face. "I'm so glad you feel like that. That's how I feel about it." She turned to head for the fireplace, when Jacob stopped her.

"Let me, okay?" Jacob crouched, reaching for the newspaper to crumble it and then layer the kindling and logs on it. He watched as the wood caught before he rose, finding Finn sitting on the couch watching him.

"Finn?"

—

"Why do I trust you, Jacob? I don't trust anyone else the way I trust you."
She was genuinely puzzled.

He sat on the couch beside her, turning so he faced her. "I have no idea,
Finn. Given what you've gone through in the last few days, I don't know who
you'd trust in town, other than your family. And they can't be with you all the
time."

She sighed, her head going back on the couch. "I know and they want to.
But they smother me when they do that." She raised her head to stare at the fire.
"You don't. You protect. You care. But you let me make the decisions I need to.
You don't tell me what I have to do and demand I follow what you say."

Jacob shrugged. "You're your own person and have the right to make your
decisions and to follow your heart. No one should ever force you to follow what
they have determined you should follow. That's not how life works. That's not
how God leads us."

She studied him for a moment before she nodded. "Whoever taught you
that was very wise. You're a wise man, Jacob Whitson. I am honoured to be a
friend of yours."

He grinned briefly. "Thank you, Finn. My grandparents raised me. My
parents were overseas as missionaries and were killed in a typhoon when I was
little. I had been left with Grand and Grams as Mom and Dad were only to be
gone for three months. We didn't know they'd never come back."

"I'm sorry to hear that, Jacob." She paused. "Do you prefer Jacob or Whit,
as your friends call you?"

"From you, Jacob." He reached for the letter he had set on the table near
the couch. "I guess we can't put this off any longer, can we?"

She shook her head. "Do you still want me to read it? Or are you okay
reading it?"

Jacob sat, the letter on his knee, his finger tracing his Grand's handwriting,
struggling with the thought of reading his Grand's last letter to him. He blinked
back the tears, praying for the strength and wisdom he suddenly knew he would
need.

He finally looked up at Finn, handing her the letter. "I think you need to."

She nodded, her heart breaking for her friend. She prayed for him before
she untucked the flap and pulled out the letter. Her eyes raised to his before he
lowered his lashes, not willing to look at her. She sighed to herself. *Lord, how do
I do this? I need Your strength to help my friend.*

She unfolded the letter, taking in the script of a scholarly man, turning to
the end, seeing his signature. She raised her eyes once more to Jacob, who sat,
hand covering his eyes. She swallowed hard and flipped back to the first page,
finding it difficult to start.

   "Dear Jacob

"If you are reading this, then the Lord has called me home. I am ready to go, have been for many years, but I don't want to leave you alone, son.

"You never knew my history. I was very careful to keep it from you. Your father knew and we agreed that once you were a man, we would both talk to you. But God had other plans. Your father was called home as was your mother. When I went to talk to you, you were so excited about joining up with the armed forces, I didn't have the heart to talk with you then. I should have.

"You came home and I still couldn't talk to you. I should have, I know that now. I should have talked to you and prepared you for what I fear you are facing.

"You were directed to a small town called Mistletoe. You will find out its history over time but my family was one of the founding families. Over time, we have acquired many of the buildings and vacant land as people moved away, died, couldn't afford to live on the property any more. Anyone who sold us the land and still wanted to live there could, at no cost. That was one of the stipulations my father made. I pray that you will continue that. It's part of who we are as Christians to take care of those in need.

"Now, this is the hard part. I'm sending you back to a town where you'll find a family who has resented our family, the Adams, and a family named Bronagh, another one of the founding families. Another founding family, the Blackwells, left before my grandfather was born. I think your friend, Levi, is one of them. He is the image of a picture I have of one of the founders. There are two other founding families, whose names you'll discover over time.

"If you do go back, please be so careful. Don't trust everyone. If you have questions, call Norman Earl, my lawyer. He'll walk you through whatever it is you're facing. He's been back to Mistletoe for me many times. I was back just a few weeks ago. I needed to go, to leave something for you.

"If you go back, find Finn's. What I left for you is there. Finn, the young woman who owns the store now, is the image of her grandmother and from the little I spoke with her, has her character and love of people. She'll be your guide to what you need to find.

"Jacob, I love you, son. You have been a delight in our lives. You have become a man of God like few I have seen. Keep your hand to the plough that God has set before you. You will face dangers in the days ahead. That is something I regret I can't prevent. But know that you have friends and people who will stand with you. You are never alone.

"Love

"Grand."

Finn folded the letter, placing it carefully back into the envelope. She stood, her hand resting on Jacob's bowed head for a moment before she moved away, to the kitchen where she found a seat at the table, her head on her folded arms as tears flowed for her friend.

Finally raising his head, his hand on the letter, Jacob looked around, not seeing Finn. He had had no idea his grandfather would direct him to her. He thought he had chanced on her on his own. It must be God's hand, he thought. That's the only explanation. I could have gone anywhere, but Grand knew somehow I would end up in her store. Must be my love of old books.

He rose, looking for Finn, finding her sitting at the table in the little kitchen, a mug of tea in her hand. She looked up at him, her lashes still tear stained.

"Jacob?"

"Thank you, Finn. I couldn't have read it on my own." He dropped a kiss on the top of her head on his way by, not catching the stunned look on her face before she schooled her features.

"What will you do now?"

He sat in the chair beside her, his mug cradled in his hands, his face thoughtful. "I have no idea. At some point, I'll need to talk to Norman. He's our lawyer." He stared at his mug. "I have no idea who the family is." He looked up at her snort.

"You don't? You should."

"Tell me, Finn. Who do you think it is?"

"The Adams." Then, she paused. "No, that's too obvious. I have no idea then." She looked at him, fear momentarily crossing her face. "We need to find them and fast, Jacob. They won't want you to find out who they are."

He nodded. "I know, Finn. Grand named a family and I'll have to verify if it's them. And I fear that you're being my friend will bring trouble to you and your family." His face grew grave and new stern lines traced across it. "I don't want you or your family hurt. Maybe this wasn't such a good idea, coming here after all."

"I don't think you had much choice. You were meant to come here, Jacob. You may be the one who can break whatever hold this family has on our town." She sat back, her eyes on her friend. "There have always been undercurrents here, and no one has been able to pin down where the trouble started or who instigated it. Other than that caused by the Adams."

He sighed. "I know. I just don't like it that I brought danger to you." He searched her face, trying to get a sense of what she was thinking.

"You didn't, Jacob. Let me make that very clear. I may face something because of you, but I was already in danger. You walked in on it on Friday. But your grandfather was right. Let me repeat myself. There have always been undercurrents in town, that no one could define or get rid of. I think you're the one who will accomplish that. Fresh eyes and all."

Jacob shook his head. "I doubt that. It will take work and investigation." He rose and returned with the journals, setting them on the table in front of him. "It's getting late, Finn, and I need to get you back to town before it gets dark. I'm going to start with one of these. How be you take Grams' and read through it over the next few days? Make notes of anything that puzzles you. I'll do the same with Grand's. Then, we switch and read the other one. He brought Grams' here for a reason. I want to know why." He frowned as his phone chimed and he pulled it out. "Blackie. He's looking for us."

"Tell him we're on our way back. Twenty minutes should have us home. If we're not, tell him to find Peter and come looking for us at Pops' cabin."

Jacob nodded as he sent the message, then rose to put out the fire. He looked around the cabin, once more feeling the peace it gave him.

❊ ❊ ❊ ❊ ❊

Blackie watched Finn closely, noting the black circles under her eyes, the bruising on her forehead she tried hard to hide, the fatigue that dogged every move she was making and shook his head. She's just as stubborn as Whit, he decided. He rose from where he had been seated at their kitchen table and took the journal from her hands. Gently, he turned her towards the stairs to their upstairs, and hands on her shoulders, guided her to them.

She paused, not quite sure what was going on, but too tired to make a protest.

"Go to bed, Finn. Take a hot bath, a hot shower, soak for a bit. Then go to bed. You were in a serious accident two nights ago, spent that night in hospital, came home, went in to work today when you shouldn't have. You need rest. The journals can wait."

She shook her head. "But they can't, Blackie. They can't. Someone will be coming after Jacob, and the clue has to be in those books."

"Not tonight, Finn. Off to bed or I'll personally take you back to the hospital and have you admitted and placed under guard to keep you there."

She spun, mouth open at his words, staggering a little as the world around her spun. Blackie braced her up with a hand on her arm.

He smiled. "Go to bed, Finn. Jacob will still be here in the morning. I'm sending him to bed shortly too. I know he didn't sleep much on Saturday night, not worrying about you."

Jacob had watched their interaction from where he sat, not daring to rise and add his voice to what Blackie was saying. He watched in relief as she finally nodded and reached for the railing. Mary stood, stopping to hug Blackie, before she followed her daughter up the stairs.

—

42

Timothy watched in silence, waiting until the women had disappeared before he spoke.

"You've read the letter, Jacob?"

Jacob nodded, his eyes on the stairs where Finn had disappeared. "I did, Timothy. Grand mentioned Finn, that I should seek her out, that she would be of help to me." He looked at Timothy. "I don't want to involve her, Timothy. She'll get hurt."

Timothy shook his head, a small smile on his face. "It's too late, Jacob. You won't stop her now. She's like a terrier with a bone. She will not give up." He studied the younger man. "But that's not all, is it?"

Jacob shook his head, his eyes turning to Blackie. "Did your father ever speak of the other founding family?"

Blackie frowned, feeling the tension in Jacob and finding his eyes on him. He didn't understand.

Timothy swallowed the mouthful of tea he had just taken. "He used to talk of a family, but I can't recall the name off hand. It would be listed in the town hall. Why?"

"Because Grand mentioned the name. He told me I know someone who is the image of one of that family. That family moved from here years before Grand did."

Blackie's eyes darted between Timothy and Jacob, finally resting on Jacob. "Jacob?"

"It's your family, Blackie. The Blackwells. Grand said you were the image of one of them."

"Me? No way! We didn't come from here." He paused, trying to remember his family history. "At least, I don't think we did." He pulled out his phone. "I need to call my Mom. She'll know." He excused himself.

They watched him walk away. Then Timothy spoke. "Your grandfather was sure? Then we need to watch Blackie as well. Whoever it is seems to want to get rid of the founding families. They've gone after you two."

"How many families were there?" Jacob was still trying to absorb the fact that Blackie came from the same town his own roots did.

"Four, five, maybe. Finn would be able to find that out for you." Timothy sighed as he shifted in his chair. "We can't stop her, you know, Jacob. She will stay involved. Even if you tell her not to, she'll work away at it. And that will get her hurt."

"I know." Jacob ran his hands through his hair before clasping them together. "I want her to stay safe but I don't know how to."

"Stay with her, Jacob. She's made a connection to you like I have never seen before." He watched the emotions flickering across Jacob's face, emotions he didn't think Jacob had put a voice to yet. "Just watch her heart, Jacob. Don't hurt her that way."

Jacob's eyes shot to Timothy's, seeing the concern of a father in them. "I'll do my best not to. She's too precious to be hurt that way."

"She is. She's my little girl, always will be, even though she's an adult. Treat her as a precious jewel. That's all I ask." He rose, walking away from Jacob on those words.

Jacob watched him head for the stairs and sighed. He stood, pacing, knowing he needed sleep himself, but not willing to go. He reached for his grandfather's journal, but a hand on top of it stopped him from picking it up. He looked up, seeing Blackie's face.

"Blackie?"

Blackie nodded. "Your grandfather was right, Jacob. We were one of the founding families. I hate to tell you this but Mom went back through papers Dad has. We're not the only friends involved in this town."

Jacob sank into a chair. "Simon? Josh?"

Blackie nodded. "Both of them. They don't know it, I don't think. How did we all end up being friends and then back in this area?"

"God. It was His handiwork." Jacob sighed. "I want to read Grand's journal tonight, but I'm too tired."

"Go to bed, Whit. It will be there in the morning. I would suggest you lock them and the letter up somewhere safe."

Jacob nodded, fatigue suddenly setting in. "I will, Blackie. Good night." He dragged himself off to bed, not seeing Blackie watching him.

❀ ❀ ❀ ❀ ❀

Finn rose early the next morning, her body protesting every move she made. She sighed. She needed to be in the store, but today, she would have liked not to have been. She stood for a moment on the porch, eying the steps before she walked down and towards the downtown area. She hadn't seen Jacob yet and hoped he wouldn't show up too soon. She sighed as she reached her shop. Jacob sat on the bench outside the door, reading.

Jacob looked up as he heard footsteps stop in front of him and grinned. "Finn! Fancy meeting you here."

"Jacob. You need your rest."

He stood, looking down at her upturned face. "Not as much as you. Here. Let me unlock the door for you."

She refused to give up the key, giving him a grumpy look before she stopped and then turned to apologize.

———

"It's okay, Finn. Really. I shouldn't be taking up your time." Jacob moved to walk away when her hand on his arm stopped him. He stood, his back to her, a rejected feeling in his heart.

"No. You do need to be here. Let me get through what I need to first, and then I'll work on the journal."

He nodded even as she turned away. Something had changed, he thought, and I'm not sure what or how. He prayed for his friend, then lifted his eyes to search the surrounding area. He could feel someone watching them, someone close, but he couldn't see anyone. He did not like that feeling at all.

He was soon immersed in his grandfather's journal, jotting notes and names down. He finally sat back, glancing at his watch. It was lunchtime and he knew Finn had not stopped all morning.

Finn looked up as she felt watched, her eyes on the doorway. No one stood there. She rose, searching the building, not seeing anyone, not even Jacob. She hesitated beside the desk he had been using, seeing his notes and the journal, but not him. She shivered, her hands rubbing up and down her arms. Something was off in the building and she didn't know what.

She turned as she heard the doorbell and tilted her head to watch the two men walking towards her. One was Blackie. She didn't know the other man. She walked behind the counter, her hands shoved into her sweater pocket, clenched into fists. She felt that this visit was going to change everything.

"Finn? How are you today?" Blackie stopped in front of the counter, head tilted to study her.

She shrugged. "I don't know. How am I supposed to feel?" She shook her head. "I'm sorry. I shouldn't take it out on you. I'm never grumpy and this is the second time I've had to apologize this morning."

Blackie grinned at her. "Not a problem. You've been through a lot. You're entitled to feel beaten up and worn down." He glanced as the man standing beside him. "Finn, this is another of our friends. Simon Gardner. He's a lieutenant with the county force."

She held up a hand to stop him, her eyes on Simon. "The county force? What is it with you four? You meet in the armed forces, go your separate ways, and all end up here."

Simon started to laugh at her, his eyes sparkling at her question and in response to the glint of mischief he saw in her eyes, even as he turned to face the door as it opened, Jacob walking through with bags of takeout food.

"Harassing a store owner, guys? That's not like you." He grinned at his friends as he set the food down on the counter. "Josh said you two were heading this way and sent your favourites." He paused as he peeked into the bags. "At least, what he sent used to be your favourites."

Blackie shook his head at him before he turned to Finn. "Where can we sit and eat, Finn? Jacob called in reinforcements to look at some of the journal entries, but we need to eat first. Growing boys and all, you know."

Finn laughed at his nonsense before pointing towards the desk Jacob had been using that morning. "There, I think. You three have a seat. I have a call coming in that I need to take and then I'll join you."

The three men watched her walk away, Jacob's eyes lingering on her, not seeing the looks his friends were exchanging. Yes, they both thought as they nodded. Jacob's found his lady, whether he realizes it or not. Protect them, Lord, was their prayer.

Simon wiped his mouth on his napkin, his eyes on Finn. She was uncomfortable, he could tell, and kept glancing around the store. He rose, asking Finn to show him something on the other side of the store.

"Finn? You're nervous and keep looking around. Why?" Simon's keen eyes assessed her as she hesitated to respond.

She shuddered once more as she looked around. "I feel like I am being watched, but that's ridiculous. It's just the four of us here. How could I have that feeling?"

"Have you had it before?"

She nodded. "Just before you and Blackie walked in. I don't like it, Simon."

He gave a sigh. "Then there's something here making you nervous. Let me look around. If I don't find anything with a quick look, I'll come back after you close and we'll search. If you have that feeling, then you're not wrong. With what you've been going through, I could see someone sticking in a camera or something." He looked at Jacob standing just behind Finn. "Go with Whit, Finn. Work on those journals. That's where the answer likely lies."

She nodded, turning to walk away and walked right into Jacob, whose arms came around her to steady her. She hesitated, then hugged him, before moving past him to her office. She needed a few minutes to compose herself. Being around Jacob was disturbing her, but in a good way. She needed to try and sort out her thoughts, but couldn't. Lord, please help me. I'm in over my head right now. It's not enough that I have to deal with Adams and their threat. Now you send someone like Jacob into my life. Him and his friends.

Jacob watched her walk away before he turned to Simon. "What was that all about?"

"She's feeling watched. She felt it this morning when you were out getting our lunch." Simon turned in a circle, assessing the store. "There are many places someone could hide a camera."

"And we need to find them, if they're really here." He looked around. "I'd start with her security cameras. There are four of them. Someone could hack into them." He pointed them out. "I'll have her call the company and see what they can find out." He walked away, heading to find his lady.

Blackie watched from where he sat, a finger holding his place in Grams' journal. He had come across something he needed to talk to Jacob about, but it didn't look as it would happen then. He marked the place, and pulled out his phone as it rang. Not now, he thought. I don't need any distractions.

Simon finally turned back to where Finn stood watching him, seated behind her counter, paperwork spread out in front of her. He could see the apprehension on her face. He looked down at the electronics he had found. Someone had definitely wanted to keep her under surveillance, but what they had installed was overkill, he thought.

—

Finn watched as he sorted out the cameras and microphones, sticking each one into an evidence bag and then labelling them before he pulled off his latex gloves. "Don't you have to turn them into the police here? If you do, I can guarantee they'll disappear."

Simon shook his head. He had already talked to his supervisor. "No. This is not a crime scene. You asked a friend for help. Just because your friend is a police officer doesn't matter. I'll take them to our own lab and have them run them."

Finn had been searching his face. "You're not expecting to find out anything, are you?"

He shook his head, his eyes finding Jacob's. "Not likely. But I do know these are not an average run-of-the-mill pieces of equipment. They were likely found on the black market."

Jacob's hand rested on the back of Finn's chair as he leaned in to take a look at them. "They're very sophisticated, aren't they? Somehow, I don't think Adams would have the knowledge of where to find them."

Simon nodded, his stance tense as a thought crossed his mind before he shrugged it off. There was no way, he thought, that man would be here in Mistletoe, not this far out of the way. "I'll see what the lab says. Now, about your journals. Find anything interesting?"

Jacob nodded as he placed Grand's journal down on the counter. "Bits and pieces that I'll have to work through. He gives a lot of names that I'll have to research." He turned as Blackie stopped beside him. "Blackie?"

"I found an interesting reference a couple of years before your Grams died, Jacob. She mentions a man who came looking for your grandfather. She didn't know him, and he wouldn't leave a name. But she did give a description of him." He found the page and read it aloud, stopping as he heard a sound from Finn. "Finn?"

She looked at him in horror before turning to Jacob, her hand on his arm. "That's Chief Adams. How did he find your grandparents?"

"Easy. He could use his resources to do so. But why? Grams didn't say." He looked down at his Grand's journal. "I didn't see anything where Grand mentions that visit, but he does talk about Adams early on. I think he was one of the reasons Grand walked away from this town." He raised his eyes to Simon. "What can we find out about Adams and his past?"

"I can do some digging, but there's a lot buried in this town that people aren't going to talk about. It will take a lot of work, Jacob, and I'm not sure we'll have the time we'll need to do that."

Blackie spoke up. "Let Josh and I work on it, okay? This is right up the line of work I'm taking up."

Jacob leaned against the counter, his eyes thoughtful as he watched his friend. "You have never said what line of work you've gone into."

Blackie shook his head. "No, I haven't. It's no secret. I've taken up investigations, mainly concentrating of past histories of people. That's what Dad does and he's trained me. I can pretty much work from anywhere."

"I had forgotten that, Blackie. That's wonderful. I'm not sure how you ended up here but I'm glad the three of you are." Jacob looked up at the clock. "Time to close up, my love. Your Mom will be waiting for you."

His two friends exchanged glances even as they moved towards the door, Blackie shaking his head at Simon. They realized Jacob's endearment for Finn had slipped out.

❈ ❈ ❈ ❈ ❈

Jacob finally laid his Grand's journal down and rising from the armchair in his room, stretched, his glance going to the clock. It was late night or rather early morning. He needed to talk to Norman that day, to find out what he knew. He didn't want to make the drive the four hundred miles away and leave Finn on her own. He feared for what might happen to her. He still hadn't acknowledged what was growing in his heart, thinking it too soon.

He sat on the edge of his bed, the low light leaving most of the room in darkness. His thoughts drifted to what Simon had found that day in Finn's store and he frowned. He didn't think the police would have done that. But who then?

He finally gave up and laid down, pulling the quilt over him. He didn't think he would sleep but he did. He didn't look out the window, didn't see the figure standing there watching the house, his eyes on Jacob's room and then seeking Finn's. An angry growl came from the person before steps led them away.

—

Jacob slowly laid his phone down on the desk and stared at his notes. Talking to his lawyer, Norman, had given him information that he had not expected. His grandfather had been researching the people in the town and left quite a packet of information with Norman, who indicated he would drive over with it. He told Jacob that once he was in the town, Aaron had not wanted Jacob to leave it, not until he had resolved whatever the underlying issues were. Norman could explain no more than that.

He felt a hand laid gently on his shoulder, and looking up, saw Finn standing beside him, a softened look on her face, a mug of tea being set down beside him. He reached up to clasp her hand but before either of them could speak, a customer called for assistance. He heard Finn sigh as she walked away, still limping slightly from the bruising she had taken from the car accident. He reached for his mug, sipping absentmindedly as his mind once more went to his notes. He knew Finn had his Grams' journal and that it was time he looked at it. He tidied up his papers, slipping them into his briefcase before he picked it up and headed for her office.

Finn's eyes followed Jacob as he walked towards the office before she returned her attention to her customers. Business was picking up as it always did at this time of year, with all the tourists coming in just to say they had spent December in Mistletoe. An underlying sense of danger permeated the air around her and she didn't like it one bit.

She turned back as a question was asked regarding some old tools and her mind once more focused on her work. She would talk to Jacob later.

Finally, the end of the day came and with a sigh of relief and fatigue, she locked the door, turning off lights as she walked back towards the office. She stood in the doorway, finally leaning against the doorjamb as she watched Jacob deep at work, his hair ruffled from running his hands through it, the shadow of a beard on his face, and knew that she hoped he never left that town, never left her.

Jacob heard a faint sound and looked up, his face lighting up as he saw Finn, and then the darkened store behind her.

"It's that time of day already?" He stood, gathering his work and stuffing it into his briefcase.

"It is. I'm all locked up. We can go out the back and set the alarm there." She waited for him to follow her, holding the door as he left and punching in the code before shutting the door and locking it. "Did you have a successful day?"

He nodded. "I did. Norman's heading this way in the next couple of days. Grand had a bunch of material for me, that Norman was only to give me if I asked for it." He sighed. "I have no idea why Grand did it this way."

"Likely he wasn't sure you would come here. He also didn't want to influence you at first."

Jacob reached for her hand, drawing her close to him. "I think you may be right. If Norman hadn't pushed me, I not likely would have come. And I would have missed meeting you."

She tilted her head to study him, and then nodded. "I would not have liked not to have met you." She laughed at herself. "Does that even make sense?"

He laughed as he followed her up the steps to the B&B. "It does, somehow. Let's compare notes after supper, if you're up to it. You're still hurting, my love, and I don't like that."

She stopped walking and turned to face him, hearing the endearment once more from him. Her mouth opened to question him, then snapped shut.

Mary turned as they entered the kitchen, Jacob setting his briefcase down out of the way.

"Did Blackie find you, Jacob? He was looking for you about an hour ago."

He shook his head. "No. And I didn't get a message from him. He'll catch up with me tonight if not before. What can I do to help?"

Mary stood for a moment, her eyes taking in the young man standing in front of her, an engaging grin on his face. "I need the table set. Put on a place for Blackie. I think he said he'd be back for supper."

"I can do that." Jacob headed to the small powder room to wash up, leaving the two woman staring after him and then at one another.

"Is he for real?" Finn's low voice caught her mother's ear.

Mary smiled. "He is, Finn. That he is. I pray he never leaves this house."

Finn stared at her mother, her mouth open before she snapped it closed. No way, she thought. He'll find someone somewhere and be off.

Blackie stood for a moment, assessing Jacob. He could see the stress in his friend, knowing how much this was weighing on him. He prayed for him, even as he wondered at Jacob's grandfather putting him through this. But then, again, he thought, he never got a chance to talk to him, or didn't take a chance he should have. He slid into a chair near Jacob, causing him to look up.

Jacob's eyes narrowed as he looked at his friend. Something was up, he thought. His eyes moved to Finn, who was curled up in an easy chair, a book open on her lap, but she was staring into the open flame in the fireplace.

"Blackie?" Jacob's voice was low as he spoke.

"Jacob. We need to talk, somewhere Finn isn't around. Come up to my room. No, that won't work." Blackie was frustrated.

—

51

"How about going to see Josh? Would that work? Somehow I think what you're about to say involves him too. Besides, I need to talk to you two and Simon about something I found in the journal."

Blackie nodded as he rose and headed for the front door, grabbing his jacket and boots as he did so. Jacob hesitated for a moment, but didn't want to disturb Finn so he walked quietly away.

Josh stood for a moment, staring at the two men standing there, and then at Simon walking towards them. "Come on in. I can see I'm not going to have a peaceful evening."

Jacob nodded. "I'm sorry, Josh. I don't think you will. Not with what I think Blackie has to say or what I have to say."

Settling down around Josh's living room with their mugs of coffee or tea, the four men looked at one another before Simon spoke.

"I can tell this isn't just a social call. How be we spend some time in prayer first?"

Jacob finally looked at Blackie. "What was it you wanted to talk to me about?"

Blackie stared at him. "I know your family was one of the founding ones. I have information as to why your grandfather left. I don't think it's common knowledge or that he would have put it into his journals. I'm guessing you knew his parents died early, in a fire, but not that the fire was deliberately set. Your grandfather wasn't home that night. He had gone to stay with Aaron and his family at their cabin. No one ever told Aaron that they suspected murder." Blackie watched with compassion as Jacob absorbed that. "I'm tracking back through who would have wanted him dead. I'm not getting far, but I do have a couple of names to give to Simon."

"That explains a lot." Jacob was thoughtful. "Grand was always so careful of fire and hazards like that. He never said and I thought it was just him being him."

Simon spoke up. "I can track the name but it may not do any good after all that time."

"It won't but if we can find out who, then we can deal with them." Blackie pulled a paper from his pocket and handed it over to Simon. "These are just some of them. There's someone in the background I haven't been able to identify just yet."

Jacob leaned over to read the names, before nodding. "I've met some of the family. They acted scared when they hear my name. That would be why." He leaned back in his chair, his eyes searching the faces of his friends. "Now, for my news. It's really earthshaking when you think of it. How long have we been friends? And we came from different areas of the country.

—

"I did some research and my grandfather's letter has confirmed the facts as has my lawyer, Norman. All of our families were founding families here in Mistletoe." He sat back, seeing the stunned looks on the other three men's faces.

"How can that be? No one ever said anything." Josh was puzzled. "And how did we all end up here anyway?"

"I have no idea, Josh, and it was God. It had to be Him leading us all here."

Blackie spoke up. "So, now that we're here, what's the purpose?"

Jacob shrugged. "I have no idea. But I think there is someone hidden here that needs to be removed, and we're the ones who will do it. We're outsiders, even though we have history here and can see things others can't. Let me explain further about the journals and what Norman had to tell me."

Four hours later, Blackie and Jacob headed for the B&B, their words quiet in the night air. Despite discussing the situation for hours, none of them had come closer to a solution or a name.

Jacob walked through the downtown area the next morning, his eyes assessing the buildings. He wasn't sure which ones he owned but he did want to know. He could see most were in good shape, well painted but a few had begun to become rundown. Don't let those ones be mine. And if they're not, let me be able to buy them. He turned as he heard his name called and reached to shake Norman's hand.

"Norman. You made good time."

Norman, a man in his late-twenties, grinned. "It helps to have a cousin with their own airplane. We flew into the large city about an hour from here and then rented a car. John came with me. He wanted to see this town and say he was in Mistletoe in December." Norman looked around. "This is something. I've been here in the spring and summer but never this close to winter."

"It is something. It's peaceful and really stirs those memories of being a kid. But there is an undercurrent here, one I'm picking up on."

Norman nodded. "I know there is. Now, where can we talk?"

"How be we head back to the B&B? I left all my information there this morning."

Four hours later, Jacob sat back in his chair, his mind whirling. "That much information Grand had found? How?"

Norman shrugged. "I guess because he knew the families and knew what to ask for. He hired a private investigator to come in and search through records." He paused. "Now, what was the name of that investigator?"

"Blackwell?"

Norman's eyes shot to him. "It was. How did you know?"

"Because his son is a good friend of mine and is in town now. Levi Blackwell."

Norman nodded and then stood. "I'll leave this with you, then. You and your friends need to be very careful. Whoever this is will stop at nothing. You've already seen some of the steps he'll take."

"But the attacks were directed at Finn."

"The first one from that Adams character was directed at her. I think you'll find any additional ones and those cameras and listening devices Simon found are directed at you. You spend a lot of time in her shop. They have to be able to track you somehow and that's one way they can."

Jacob slowly sank back into his chair. "You mean, I'm bringing danger to this family?"

Norman gave a small smile. "We have no idea if that's true or not, but you do need to take precautions. You and your friends and Finn and her family."

He walked away, leaving Jacob sitting there, a stunned look on his face. He didn't hear Finn enter, didn't see her hesitate before she approached him, her hand rubbing against his back before she sat in a chair near him.

He looked up finally, seeing her sitting there, a frown on her face.

"Jacob? Did Norman come today?"

Jacob nodded. "He did. We spent the last four hours going over everything." He sat back, his eyes dropping to the pile of paperwork on the table in front of him. "It's not good, Finn. We can't figure out who is behind it all. And he said you and your family are in danger. But we don't know who all from, other than Adams. And they have gone into hiding."

Finn shook her head at him. "Your head's spinning right now, I imagine. Set it aside for overnight. I want you to come to our prayer meeting tonight. It will do you good."

He nodded, his eyes finally leaving the paperwork in front of him. "I have something else you need to know, and I'm not sure how to tell you."

Her heart sank. Did he already have a lady friend? "What is it, Jacob?"

"It's like this. Blackie, Josh, Simon and I met years ago. We came from different areas of the country, from the four corners of it I guess you could say. The thing of it is, all our families have roots here. All of them were one of the founding five families."

Finn sat back, not quite sure whether to believe him or not. "And none of you knew?" When he shook his head, she rose and began to pace. "Then, they'll be at risk as well, won't they? Whoever this is won't stop until he has chased you four away or killed you. What secret is he or she hiding?"

"That's interesting. You don't automatically assume it's a man."

———

54

She spun, fire flying from her eyes. "Why would I? Women can be just as dangerous as men and more so as they are not expected to do something like this." She reached for his hand, pulling him to his feet. "Come. Mom left dinner ready for us. We just have to heat it. She was over in the county seat today and thought she might be late getting back."

Mary stood for a moment, watching the two work together to put the meal on the table. She sighed, knowing that her daughter's heart had already been caught by Jacob but not sure how he felt. Then, she paused as she caught him looking at Finn without Finn seeing him, his heart on his face and in his eyes, that he quickly schooled away. Lord, don't let either of them hurt the other. They're so good together, bringing out the best in one another. I can see that already. Protect and hide their hearts until Your timing is right.

"Mom! I didn't hear you come in." Finn moved to hug her mother. "Jacob's coming to prayer meeting tonight."

"He is, is he? Then you'd better get a move on. It starts in an hour and we still have to eat. Dad and Peter will eat after, Dad said."

"Oh, okay. I thought they'd be here." Finn moved to remove their place settings even as Jacob slid the lasagna pan onto the hot plate on the table, then waited to seat the ladies before he seated himself, not thinking anything of it.

Finn paced her store, not quite sure what the problem was. It was busy enough, she thought, I need to look at hiring someone, even just to run the cash, and train them to work the store. The online store is so busy, it would take up all my time if I let it.

She turned as she heard an unwanted voice behind her. Gerry Adams stood there.

"You need to leave, Gerry. You're not welcome in this store."

"And you'll leave with me. I checked. Your boyfriend's not in here today."

"But there are plenty of other customers. You won't want me to start screaming, now would you?" Finn looked behind him and saw Josh approaching, a relieved feeling coursing through her. "Josh. Just the person I needed to see. And Simon. He's with you."

Simon stood for a moment, assessing the man in front of him, before removing his handcuffs and approaching Gerry. "He's bothering you again, is he, Finn? That's okay. I can remove him for you. We need to talk to him over at County. It seems as if he's been up to no good over there."

Gerry turned, staring Simon up and down. "You're not taking me anywhere. You have no idea who I am." His voice was loud enough to attract the attention of the customers, who gathered around, peering at the activity and whispering among themselves.

"Yes, actually, I do. Your father can't help you out on this one. What you did wasn't here in Mistletoe." He snapped the cuffs around Gerry's wrists. "I have a car outside just waiting for you. And don't think your friends will help. They won't want to get involved. Finn, I don't think he'll be back for a while. At least I pray he won't be."

"Thank you, Simon." Josh stood at her shoulder as she watched the two men walk from the store and Gerry be stuffed into the back seat of Simon's cruiser.

"Take some time, Finn. I'll run your cash for you. It can't be that different from mine."

"Thank you, Josh. Bless you. Give everyone here a 10% discount for their trouble." She moved away, quiet words of thanks coming to her, words of support coming from the townsfolk.

Jacob walked into the store, staring at Josh behind the counter, before he shot a look behind him.

"Josh? Who's running the cafe?"

Josh looked up, a grin on his face. "Faith is. I came here to speak to Finn with Simon and we found Gerry Adams here. Simon arrested him and carted him off to County."

"Oh, I see. He won't be back?"

Josh shook his head. "Not for a few days and longer if Simon and his chief have their way." He nodded to the office. "Finn's back there. I offered to help for now."

"Thank you, Josh." Jacob headed for the office, stopping back from the door to watch Finn.

Finn had become immersed in her online sales and had almost forgotten that she had a store to run. She knew she was in denial, that she really didn't think Gerry would have appeared as he had, but he did and was now out of the town. For good, she prayed. She looked up at a small sound, fright momentarily crossing her face until she saw Jacob standing there, moving towards her as she looked up, to catch her close in a hug.

"You're okay?" Jacob stood back, his hands on her arms.

"I am, thanks to Josh and Simon. What was he thinking?" She could feel the rage rising within her once more.

Jacob grinned at her and then grabbed her hand, pulling her through the store to the back door. "Come out here for a moment."

"I don't have a jacket, Jacob. I'll freeze."

"It's not that cold today. You won't freeze."

He turned to face here as she stood, back to the door, watching him intently. "I'm glad you're okay. And that Simon and Josh were here. Who knows what he would have done."

She nodded, not able to speak.

"I spent the morning going through town. Then I talked to Norman. There are some buildings that are getting run down. I don't own them but if God is willing, I will and I can renew them. Norman talked to the owners. They should be making a living but they're paying someone for protection."

"Protection? A protection racket in this town? But who?" Finn was shocked.

"I have a good idea who and Blackie is working on that with his Dad. By the way, did I tell you we're all founding family members?"

She looked at him, not quite sure if he had or not. "I didn't know that. Wow! Life is strange, isn't it? So now what happens? Do you all just leave again?"

"I'm not leaving here, Finn. Not until I die. I like it here. And there is someone here to keep me here." He watched her face intently, seeing when she comprehended what he had to say and paled at his words. "Come on. Let's get you back inside. Josh needs to get back to his cafe."

"Josh! I forgot all about him!" Finn yanked the door open, running into the store, intent on finding Josh and apologizing.

Jacob roused in the night, hearing a sound from outside. He rose, pulling on his clothes and reaching for his jacket. He crept down the stairs, pulling on his boots and then opening the door as silently as he could. He crouched down, his eyes searching the backyard, finally seeing a figure hiding in the trees. Breathing a prayer of thanks that it was a cloudy night, he moved through the yard towards the figure, not seeing the man rising up behind him until he heard a whisper of a sound. Turning too late, he crumpled to the ground, eyes closed, blood already streaming from the blow to the back of his head.

The man from the back of the yard approached, his booted foot reaching to shove Jacob over onto his back. The two men stood arguing before one of them stooped, pulling Jacob to his feet and draping him over his shoulder. They made their way to the waiting truck, dumping Jacob into the bed of it before they climbed into the cab, pulling away as silently as they could.

Timothy touched the door the next morning, a frown in place. He knew it had been locked the night before, he had checked it himself. He glanced at the boots sitting by the door and realized Jacob's were missing. He turned, heading for Blackie's room to rouse him. Jacob was missing, he was sure.

Blackie stared at Timothy, then turned to reach for his clothes. "What time do you think, Timothy?" His voice was low.

"It must have been early. It's only five a.m. now."

Blackie nodded as he followed Timothy out the back door, shrugging on his jacket. "We need to call the police."

Timothy snorted. "It won't do any good."

"Then we tell them it's Aaron Whitson's grandson."

"No, that's not our place. Tom will help. Let me go call him." Timothy headed back for the house even as Blackie pulled out his phone.

"Simon. Sorry to wake you so early. Whit's missing. Yeah, sometime earlier this morning. Timothy found the back door unlocked when he came down to the kitchen." Blackie walked through the yard, stopping near a disturbed patch of snow and looking back towards the house and then towards the back of the yard. "From what I'm seeing, he came out, was ambushed, and then carted away. No, we won't disturb anything. Timothy went to call Tom, an officer here he can trust. Oh. Okay. I'll tell him." Blackie pocketed his phone as Timothy approached.

"Tom's on his way. He won't bring anyone else in until he sees what's up."

"Simon's on his way. He's bring one of their lab techs with him. He says the county force will be moving in today to take over leadership of this force. That won't go over well."

"It will go over better than he expects. People have be running scared for months and years now of Adams and his cronies. If they clean up the force, then I welcome their involvement."

Blackie nodded as he searched the area with his eyes, desperately seeking his friend. "He said his chief talked to the town council and mayor and was asked to step in, now that Adams is hiding. And Simon arrested Gerry Adams yesterday in Finn's shop." He stopped at a sound from Timothy. "You didn't know he came back around?"

Timothy shook his head, even as he heard a voice behind him.

"Dad? What are you two doing out here at this time of the morning?" Finn stood watching them.

The two men shared a look before Timothy moved to his daughter, an arm coming around her to lead her back to the house. "I've got some back news, love. Jacob must have heard something or came out here for some reason. We can't find him."

Finn's feet stopped moving abruptly and she spun to look behind her, causing her father's arm to drop away from her. "Jacob? Missing? Oh, no! Who?"

"That's what we'll find out. Tom's coming from our force. Simon's on his way over as well. I have news that you'll like. County is taking over our force for now."

"Well, that's something. It's about time. But it doesn't solve the mystery of where Jacob is, or why, or who?"

"No, it doesn't. But we need you to stay inside. I'll arrange for someone to be with you at your shop. If they've taken Jacob from here, who knows where they'll take you from."

"But I don't think I'm a target, Dad." Finn was digging in her heels, not willing to admit that she might be.

"It doesn't matter. If Jacob gets away or they want to play with his mind, they'll take you to get to him. You've been seen together in town. You're never with a male friend, only with your brother or me. That will tell whoever is watching you two he means something to you." His facial expressions softened. "I don't know what he means to you now or in the future. But we need to keep you safe. He would want that."

She agreed, feeling grumpy and disgruntled that she had to be watched. Then she sighed. *Lord, improve my attitude. I need to stay safe, I get that, but I can't stop living my life. I have a store to run and need to be there. I have a life to live. Protect Jacob, please, Dear Lord. Bring him back to us safely.*

—

Four hours later, Simon pushed open the door to Finn's store and stepped inside, pausing to watch as she worked with a customer. Her head raised as she saw him and then nodding went back to her customer. Simon wandered through the store, searching for evidence of tampering and finding none. He had talked to her security company and they couldn't see where her system had been hacked at all.

"Simon. Have you news?" Finn's voice was quiet behind him.

Simon turned. "Not yet, but we're working on it. We'll find him for you, Finn. Trust us on that." He looked around, seeing no one else in the store. "I need to talk to you about your own safety."

She scowled at him. "I don't need a protector."

He held up a finger, stopping her words. "That's not a decision you can make. It's already been made for you. I'm here for the rest of the day. Starting tomorrow, we have one of our officers who will come in and work with you on a daily basis. We have another one that will take a room in the B&B. That is for your family's sake as well as yours. Your parents have agreed to it."

She scowled at him again and then shrugged. "Then I guess I have help tomorrow. I can close up now, it's close enough." She turned to walk away, stopping to say over her shoulder, "And I suppose you're walking me home."

He grinned at her back. "Actually, driving you home. No walking on your own for the foreseeable future."

Finn's head dropped for a moment, then Simon watched as her shoulders tightened. "I guess that's that then, isn't it?"

Reaching for the back of his head and the pain he could feel, Jacob roused slowly, his body rocking back and forth with the movement of the truck. He shivered, not quite comprehending why he was so cold. He raised his head, his eyes blinking in the near dawn light as they slowly focused on where he was. He groaned as he remembered walking out into the yard and then nothing. He raised his head enough to look towards the front of the truck, knowing he would have to escape somehow and not quite sure how he would. The truck slowed as the driver negotiated a turn, and Jacob took advantage of that, reaching for the side and pulling himself up and over, rolling away from the narrow dirt track the truck was on. He rolled until he came under a tree and stopped, his head on his arms, trying to catch his breath.

He struggled to his feet, knowing he had to get away, but not knowing where he was or where he should go. He stumbled as he blindly walked forward. He had no idea how far from Mistletoe he even was. He had no idea of how long he had been unconscious. He paused, his eyes struggling to focus on his watch. It had been an hour. They could have taken him anywhere in that time.

He paused, his head turned to listen for his kidnappers but he heard nothing. He knew they would be back, would be trying to track him. Stumbling forward, he moved his feet, his head pounding with each step.

Finally, he had to stop. He sank down, his back against a fallen tree, his knees raised as he folded his arms on them and rested his head down. He didn't think he could take another step. His vision faded as he lost the battle to stay awake and alert.

He had no idea how long it was before he felt hands on his arms, on his head bandaging his wound. He didn't hear the call for help or see the officials that ran towards him. He didn't feel himself lifted to a stretcher and then carried back to the nearby road and lifted into an ambulance, that raced away to take him to safety, a police officer in the back with him.

Simon stood with the young couple who had found him, a young couple out looking for a Christmas tree. He took their statement and then turned as he heard the barking of the K-9 unit that had responded. He sighed. He wanted to go with Jacob but he was needed here. He looked around the area, not expecting to find anything, and he was right. So close to town, yet not so close. He thought through the distance. The kidnappers must have driven around for a while. They really weren't that far from the B&B.

Finn looked up as she heard the door to her shop open and saw her father walking towards her, a grim look on his face. She stepped backwards, her head shaking from side to side, even as the female officer braced her arm behind her.

"Dad? Please! Don't tell me!" Tears choked her voice.

"He's found, Finn. Simon called about ten minutes ago. They found him and are on the way to the hospital with him. Let Candy close up for you. Leave your keys and your code. She'll open for you in the morning as well." He looked past Finn at Candy, who nodded.

"I can do that, Mr. Bronagh. I have no problem with that. Finn's so thorough with her research and description of the articles, I don't think I'll have any problems tomorrow. I can always call her if I need to."

Finn turned to hug Candy before she ran for her jacket, shoving her arms in the sleeves as she ran back, her purse slipping down from her shoulder. Timothy stopped her, straightened her jacket and zipped it closed, then pushed her purse strap back on her shoulder before drawing her into a hug. He tucked her into the car and headed for the nearby county town.

Timothy pulled into the hospital parking lot and reached for his daughter's arm, startling her into looking at him.

"Before we go in, Finn, we need to pray for him. Simon said he was unconscious from a head wound. He didn't know how far Jacob had struggled to walk when I talked to him but he thought miles. Just remember that we really don't have any right to see him." She frowned at him when he said that. "We're not family. We may need to contact his lawyer to get permission to see him."

Finn shook her head. "I'll get in, Dad. Trust me. They won't keep me out." She was out of the car and running for the doors before her father could respond.

Timothy searched for Finn when he entered, his eyes not seeing her but seeing Josh and Blackie waiting for him.

"Where is she?"

"She headed back. I have no idea what she said to the clerk but they let her in." Blackie turned to study the doors to the exam rooms. "You don't think she said she was his girlfriend, do you?"

Timothy groaned. "That's exactly what she would do. I need to have a talk with her." He moved to walk towards the clerk, but Josh's hand on his arm stopped him.

"Let her go, Timothy. I think that's how Jacob thinks of her. It's there when he looks at her. If it's okay with you, she'll need to be there and he'll need her."

Timothy nodded. "I know. But she shouldn't be stretching the truth like that."

"No, she shouldn't. Talk with her later. Right now, we need her with Jacob. He has no one else."

Finn regretted running from her father, and she didn't like that she hadn't told the whole truth to the clerk. She wasn't officially Jacob's lady but he made her feel like he wanted her to be. The nurse looked around as she paused in the doorway before she smiled and beckoned her forward.

"Are you family?" The words were quiet.

"No, a good friend. He has no living family. Not any more." Finn's eyes pleaded for understanding and the nurse nodded.

"That's fine. If you're a good friend, then we'll let you stay. Let me have your name and I'll add it to his record." She turned to study Jacob. "He's not from here, is he? He looks familiar."

Finn took another look at the nurse. "Caitlin? Is that you?"

Caitlin turned. "Finola. I didn't recognize you for a moment. It's been a long time. How do you know this man?"

"He turned up about a week ago in Mistletoe and is staying with Mom and Dad. His grandfather was Aaron Whitson."

"Whitson? Oh my! What a greeting to give to a Whitson! Of course, we'll let you stay."

"How is he?" Finn moved forward, her hands gripping the bed rail as she watched Jacob's head twist and turn.

"The doctor's been in and out. We'll be sending him for some imaging to make sure there is no damage other than a concussion. He'll be staying for a day or so. But if he's with your people, then I know he'll be discharged sooner."

Finn nodded, before she turned. "We have a friend of his staying at the B&B as well. Blackie was a medic in the army, so he'll keep an eye on him."

"Well, I must say, you're well prepared for this."

Finn gave a small smile. "God knew what we needed and prepared it all."

Caitlin's smile faltered. She didn't share Finn's confidence in God, not any more. She wished she did. She had become cynical over time and regretted that.

Finn stepped aside as they came for Jacob, moving back towards the waiting room, just hesitating to get a promise from Caitlin to come get her when he was back. She stopped as she saw her father and knew he would be speaking with her.

Blackie reached her first, hugging her, then standing with his hands on her shoulders. "Finn? What's the word?"

"A concussion. Exposure. They've taken him for imaging, Caitlin said."

"Caitlin?" She looked up at Timothy. "Caitlin works here?"

Finn nodded even as she moved into her father's hug. "She does, Dad. After all Mistletoe did to her, she couldn't leave the area."

Timothy wrapped his arms tight around his daughter and then drew her to a chair, looking up as Simon walked towards them.

———

63

"Simon?" Josh rose as Simon looked their way.

He nodded at an acquaintance across the room and then reached for the cup of coffee Josh handed him, grimacing at the bitter taste.

"How is Jacob?"

Finn looked up at him. "Concussion. Exposure. I've been back."

"And we need to talk about that, young lady." Timothy's voice was stern, even though compassion flooded his eyes. "You can't go around saying what I know you said."

"All I said was that I was a good friend and he had no family." Finn stared among the men, a frown in place, not quite sure what their looks meant.

Timothy sighed, a prayer raising from his heart for healing for his young friend and protection for his daughter's heart. He also prayed that whatever it was that Jacob was seeking would be found quickly.

"Finn?" Simon stared at her, not quite sure what he should be asking her.

"All right. Fine. I said I was a close friend and that he had no family. They let me back. Caitlin's coming to get me when they bring him back from imaging." She stared at Simon, a frown on her face. "They didn't say much. A concussion. Exposure. That's all they will confirm."

Simon nodded as he set his cup down and rose. "Stay here, Finn. I'll see that you're banned from there unless you do." He stared her down until she looked away.

Finn sank back on her chair, her eyes following Simon as he walked away, not seeing Josh and Blackie sitting down on either side of her, her father sitting beside Blackie. Please, Lord, let Jacob be okay. And don't let Simon follow through on his threat. Josh and Blackie exchanged looks over her head before their eyes dropped to her face and the worry and devastation they could see there.

An hour later, Simon stood behind Finn as she watched from Jacob's bedside, an arm supporting her. She studied the man lying there, his eyes closed, his head tossing from side to side. She winced as she saw the large bandage that wrapped around his head, knowing it covered the wound he had been given.

"Did they say when they would let him go, Simon?"

"Maybe tomorrow. As long as Blackie is willing to help look after him." Simon drew her away. "We need to get you home, Finn. Josh and Blackie are waiting for you. Your Dad went on ahead."

She shook her head. "I don't want to leave him."

"Once again, Finn, you don't have a choice. You need to leave. We'll get you back here tomorrow." Simon steered her out the door and down to the hospital entrance. "What about your store?"

"Candy said she'd work it, but I can't let her." Finn sighed. "I don't know what I'll do."

"Work your store. I'll have someone let you know when you can come see Jacob. It may be he'll be well enough to go home."

Finn stood, shivering in the cool damp air, lost in thought, before she raised her eyes to Simon, finding him watching her.

"What do they want, Simon? What does Jacob have that they want?"

He shrugged, even as he tucked his hand into her arm to lead her to where Blackie stood waiting. "I don't know, Finn. I don't even know if Jacob knows. But I suspect it is something in one of those journals he's been reading. He tells me you've been reading them too."

She nodded. "I have been, but I feel so lost reading them. I don't know his grandparents, so I'm not sure what level of value to put on different thoughts or people's names. We've been making a list. Maybe I should see if Jacob will let you have a copy."

"We can address that later. I think he's already been talking with Blackie and Blackie's father about just that." Simon tucked her into Blackie's vehicle, then stepped back to where he could watch her.

"She's going to try and get back in overnight, you know that, Simon." Blackie's voice was quiet.

"She will, but make sure she doesn't. It won't do either one of them any good if she gets banned from him. And that's what will happen. Keep me updated on how he is? I'll try and stop in tomorrow at some point. I really need to hear what he has to say."

Blackie nodded. "I'll do just that."

His balance off, Jacob hesitated as he stepped through into his bedroom, Blackie's hand on his arm keeping him upright. He looked longingly at his bed but turned towards the bathroom, staggering sideways as he did so.

Blackie gave a small smile. "You need to get laying down, Jacob. With the concussion and vertigo, you can't be on your feet for long."

Jacob gave his friend a black look, even as his hand went to his abdomen. "No, I need to go in there." He pointed to the bathroom and moved cautiously that way. "I'm going to be sick and I don't want to be sick out here."

Blackie guided his friend to the room, then closing the door, walked back across to the hallway. It was evening and Jacob had just been released into his care. Finn hovered near the door, worry etched on her face.

"Blackie?"

"He'll be fine, Finn. It's to be expected he'd feel nauseous. Now, how be you find us some ginger ale, crackers, water, what have you that will sit easy on his stomach?"

She hesitated, her eyes on the room door, before she nodded. "I can do that."

"Give us about fifteen to twenty minutes. I need to get him settled and it won't be an easy task."

"Is he really okay, Blackie?" Finn watched Blackie's face.

"He is, Finn. He's had harder hits and worse injuries than this and survived."

She stared at him. "Worse than this? Oh, dear. I don't like the sounds of that."

Blackie laughed, turning her towards the stairs. "Go on. Find what I asked. Come back in twenty minutes."

Twenty minutes later, Finn stood outside Jacob's door, shifting from foot to foot, a tray in her hands, watching for the door to open.

Blackie stood for a moment, watching his friend. He had finally gotten Jacob settled, an ice pack on his neck, some painkillers down his throat, and now Jacob had drifted off. He sighed to himself. He had heard the soft footsteps outside the door and knew Finn was waiting for him. He stared at the door and then back at Jacob, trying to make up his mind what actually was going on with those two.

He turned towards the door and as he turned, he saw the papers Jacob had been working on. Jacob had muttered that he couldn't work on them, feeling like he was, and would Blackie take it on. Blackie hated to intrude that way, but he knew he had to. Someone was after his friend and he wanted it over yesterday and the culprit behind bars.

Finn watched as the door opened and Blackie slipped out, the tray shaking slightly in her hands. Blackie reached for it, setting it on the table in Jacob's room, before he reached to hug Finn.

"Blackie?" Finn's voice was muffled against him.

Blackie turned her back to the stairs and with an arm around her, led her back to their living area.

"He's sleeping now, Finn. He needs it. I'll have him awake a few times overnight, and I know that won't go over well."

"Who did this, Blackie?" Her eyes searched his, not seeing an answer.

"I don't know. Neither does Simon." Blackie stared down at the papers in his hands. "Jacob asked me to go over what he had found. I could use your help. You know the people in this town."

She nodded, even as she headed for the counter and mugs she had left sitting there. She filled them with tea and set Blackie's down in front on him before sliding into a chair and reading for Aaron's journal.

"I've gone through his grandmother's but not his grandfather's." She rose and headed back up the stairs, Blackie's eyes following her, before she ran back down, a notebook in her hand.

"Here. These are my notes." She sighed as she looked down at Aaron's journal. "I feel like I'm invading Aaron's privacy or something."

"Don't feel that way. I suspect Aaron knew Jacob would call in help." He pointed to the journal. "Now, read. I'm going to go over all your notes."

Three hours later, Blackie leaned back in his chair and stretched, reaching to gently take Aaron's journal from Finn. At her protest, he grinned.

"It's getting late, Finn, and you need to be in your store tomorrow. No, don't protest. That's where Jacob would want you. He'll likely sleep most of the next few days, and his body needs that."

She finally stood, stacking the papers, notebooks and journals into a neat pile and then handing them to him. "I'm not sure I accomplished anything tonight, but you can look through what I did. We need to find out what is actually going on. I think his grandfather left a clue or cryptic message somewhere in there." She paused, her hands reaching for the journal again, and she flipped through it to a sketched image. "I've seen this or something like it." She paused, her eyes growing round. "I have it in the store. I'll bring it home tomorrow night."

"That sounds like a plan. Good night, Finn." Blackie walked away, leaving her standing staring after him.

❀ ❀ ❀ ❀ ❀

Finn stood in her store late the next morning, staring around. It had been a busy morning and she finally broken down and called in a friend to come and help her. She needed to hire someone to help with the Christmas rush, she decided. She had stood for a while, wrapped in her jacket, outside watching the townsfolk and tourists rush through the day, carrying bags and packages she knew contained Christmas gifts. Her mother, she thought, would soon be baking her Christmas goodies and be after the three of her family to decorate the B&B for the holidays.

She headed for the office, a thought sidetracking her. She searched until she found the globe she was looking for, a small old-fashioned one, and picked it up, carrying it with her. She didn't remember where it came from and she had a good memory as to her stock. She sat, staring at it, realizing that Aaron had likely left it for Jacob just as he had left his wife's journal. It's a wonder it wasn't sold, Lord, but I can see Your hand in that, keeping it here for Jacob.

She looked up at a noise and saw Blackie and Simon standing in her doorway, grinning at her. She frowned.

"Blackie? Who's with Jacob?"

"Caitlin stopped by. She said she's a friend of yours?" At her nod, Blackie continued. "She offered to sit with Jacob for a while, to give me a break." He nodded at her desk. "You found it."

Simon stared between the two of them. "Found what?"

"This globe." Finn reached to hand it to him. "Here, you take it back to my place. I think it's dangerous for me to have." She looked between the two men. "It matches the etching, Blackie. We need to examine it closely."

"Why would that be so important?" Simon was puzzled.

Blackie took pity on him. "Finn found an etching in Aaron's journal last night. This globe matches it. I'm taking it back to the B&B and see if Jacob remembers it."

Simon reached for it, his hands running over it. He frowned. "There's a seam or something here, Blackie and Finn. I won't look at it too much closer until I can see the etching." He looked around. "Isn't it time for you to close up?"

Finn shot a glance at the clock and sprang from her chair. "It is. Just let me ring off the cash and stuff it into the safe." Simon followed her, eyes watchful as she quickly finished off her tasks, sending her friend on her way, and heading for the office with her cash.

"Do you need to deposit that tonight, Finn?" Simon's quiet question stopped her in her tracks.

She stared down at the money bag. "I should. I didn't do last night's either."

Simon sighed, pointing her to her chair. "Do your deposit and we'll walk you to the bank on your way home."

Finn glanced at him, then at Blackie, finding the two men sharing a glance. She rushed to do her deposit, sealing it into the bag and reaching for her coat. She turned to find Simon with the bag in his pocket, reaching for her keys.

"Set your alarm, Finn, and turn off all the lights you normally do. Let's get you home." He grinned at her frown. "Your mom asked us for supper and she said we would enjoy it. Something about stew and fresh bread."

Finn stood a while later at the open door to Jacob's room, her eyes on him, not seeing Caitlin standing behind her. Blackie watched her before he moved up beside her, his hand on her arm drawing her closer to Jacob.

"How is he really, Blackie?"

"He's groggy right now, Finn. It will take a few days until he can sit upright. Your mom has been feeding him when he's awake." He turned her away from the bed, his hand guiding her back out of the room.

She stood for a moment, looking back at Jacob. "Was it because of me this happened, Blackie?"

Blackie shook his head. "We don't know yet, Finn. It may well not have been. Simon and his people are still investigating."

Three hours later, Simon reached for the globe Finn was turning over and over in her hands as she read through Aaron's journal. She looked up, startled, meeting his grin.

"That won't solve anything, Finn." Simon studied the globe. "It has to open somehow, but I just can't figure it out."

Timothy reached for it. He had come in late from his construction work and had been sitting watching them. He examined the globe carefully, finally detaching the base from it. He rose, heading for the kitchen to find a pin or something. That should work, he thought. There's a small hole that if I do this correctly it will open the globe.

Finn could hear her brother and her parents talking in the kitchen, her brother breaking out into laughter at something his mother had said. She smiled, thanking God for her family, and then breathing a prayer for healing for Jacob. She heard an exclamation from Timothy and raised her head, watching as he walked back towards her, the globe in two halves.

"Dad! What did you just go and do?" Finn was shocked, even as she took the pieces of the globe he handed her.

"It's okay, Finn. It was meant to come apart. I think you'll find the contents interesting."

The three men crowded around, watching intently as Finn stared down at the globe before her fingers reached for the paper inside it.

She looked up. "Jacob should be the one reading this first, not us."

Blackie shook his head. "No, he would tell you to. Things like this aren't important to him. People are."

Finn finally reached for the paper, exclaiming as she uncovered a ring laying underneath it. She held up the ring, a ring containing five different gemstones.

"This is unique. I wonder if Jacob knows about it."

"Jacob knows about the ring. He just haven't seen it in years." Jacob startled them all by appearing in the room and then dropping down beside Finn on the couch, his head falling forward for a moment. He looked up, squinting against the light, as he reached for the ring. "This was my great great grandmother's. Grand showed it to me when I was a child but then I never saw it again. Grand, what were you up to?"

Finn handed him the letter, but he shook his head.

"You read it, please, Finn. I can't see well enough to follow any writing."

"You shouldn't be out of bed." She frowned as he gave a half-smile.

"Don't worry so much, Finn. I'll be okay." He jabbed at the paper she held. "Now read."

"If you're sure."

"I am."

Finn slowly opened the page, her eyes scanning it before she looked up, shock on her face.

Chapter 12

Jacob reached for Finn's hand. "Is it really that bad, Finn?"

"I'm not sure what to say, Jacob. It certainly explains a lot of things in this town but leaves a lot of questions as well." She stared at him for a moment, a question on her face, before she looked down. She didn't see her parents and brother edge into the room and sit where she couldn't see them. "Let me read it out loud."

"Charter for the formation of the town of Mistletoe:

"The following families have agreed among themselves to incorporate Mistletoe as a town, with the following stipulations:

"1. None of the land is to be sold to outsiders.

"2. Land possessed by these five families will be passed down to the males of each family. If there are no male issues, then the land passes to the females. If there are no issues for a family, the land will be held in perpetual trust by the remaining families.

"3. Land is to be purchased or acquired as needed for town expansion, with the land being divided among the families.

"Signed by the following families:

"Whitson, Bronagh, Blackwell, Gardner, and Smithson."

Jacob's hand stopped her. "That's all there is, isn't there?"

Finn nodded. "There is. It pretty much tells you what to do with the land."

"It does. If someone found this, they could destroy it, or use it to take control of the land. We would have to trace back the families."

Finn's hand stilled as she followed the paper. "That's what he meant."

"What who meant, Finn?" Blackie looked at Jacob before his glance went to Finn.

"Aaron. In the last few pages of his journal, he documented a visit to his lawyer. He didn't say why, but I would imagine the lawyer was tracing your families." She looked between Simon and Blackie. "How did you come to Mistletoe, anyway?"

Blackie shrugged. "Dad got a letter from a lawyer, suggesting we might want to check out Mistletoe. It didn't say why. I had never heard of the town before."

Simon leaned his head back as he studied the ceiling. "I received an offer of employment with the county force. I thought it was just in response to some feelers I put out." He glanced over at Jacob. "I have a feeling your lawyer was behind it." He looked over at Blackie. "Josh was offered the cafe."

"So it sounds as if all of us were brought back here at this particular time." Jacob rubbed at his forehead. His headache was back and he knew he'd soon have to deal with it.

"Jacob, let's get you back to your bed." Blackie stood, hauling Jacob to his feet. "We can deal with this tomorrow. Right now, we're all in too much shock to think clearly. And it is late."

Jacob nodded even as he wavered on his feet, Blackie's hand keeping him steady. They watched as he moved slowly back towards the stairs.

Jacob drew a deep breath as he contemplated the stairs, knowing he shouldn't have come down them.

"They're not going to bite you." Blackie grinned at the dark look Jacob sent his way. "Come on, friend. Let's get you up them."

Finn slowly folded the charter and then handed it to her father. "We need you to lock this and the globe in the safe, Dad. I don't think we should leave it out anywhere."

"No, that's not likely a good idea, love." Timothy headed for the office, pausing at the door. "You know we'll have to contact Jacob's lawyer. He likely has more information for us." He shook his head. "It's just strange the way Aaron did this. That globe could have been sold."

"I know, Dad. It's only God that kept it from happening." Finn turned to walk away, then spun back to stare at her father. "But the thing is, it wasn't there before. It only showed up after Jacob came to town. Did the lawyer bring it that day he came to meet with Jacob?"

Her father nodded. "That may well be what happened. We'll have to ask him." He glanced at the clock. "Right now, Simon needs to hit the road. Josh needs to get home so he can get up at his usual unearthly hour. You have a big day tomorrow too, Finn, with the sale you're planning."

❀ ❀ ❀ ❀ ❀

Finn looked up from her work the next morning, hearing her friend running towards her.

"Finn, get out of here. Gerry's back. I've locked the door. I hope you can get out the back door without him seeing you."

Finn stood. "Are you serious? He just can't stay away." She reached for her phone. "I'm not leaving. If he damages anything, I'll have him charged with that."

She spoke rapidly into the phone, for the first time getting a positive response. She frowned at her phone as she turned to her friend.

——

"What happened to our police department? They never respond to me." She looked up as she heard sirens and saw Gerry looking around, before he once more began shaking the store door. "If he keeps that up, he'll break something."

Thirty minutes later, Finn walked back through her store, her hands rubbing up and down her arms, a frown in place. The officers who responded had promised her that Gerry would not be out again soon. There had been too many violations of his restraining order. They had talked to the judge who ordered him into custody.

Anna looked around. "Well, at least he didn't scare off all the customers." She grinned at Finn's frown.

"No, thank goodness for that." Finn spun to study the door and then moved away to assess her stock. "Something is different, Anna. What is it?"

Anna finally pointed at the wrapped gifts Finn had placed under the tree. "Aren't there more there than yesterday?"

Finn knelt, sorting through them. "There are. Five to be exact." Her hand froze as she reached for them. "Anna, they have our names on them. All five of us. Simon, Josh, Blackie, Jacob, and I." She looked up, fear etching on her face. "Who put them here?"

Anna shrugged. "I have no idea. Do you think they're safe to open?"

"I don't know." Finn rose, heading for the storeroom, returning with a box. "I'll take them with me tonight and ask the guys."

Finn set the box down on the table in the living room at home and glared at Jacob, who sat in an easy chair near the fire, watching her.

"Why are you up?"

"Finn, back off. The doctor was here and okayed it. I can't stay flat until I recover."

She sighed as she slid down into a chair. "I know you can't. I'm just worried about you."

Jacob tilted his head to watch her. She was becoming important to him and he was learning to read her moods. "What happened today?"

"Why do you think anything happened?" She stared at him, finally giving a sigh. "Gerry Adams showed up today but at least the police dealt with him. Anna managed to get the door closed and locked before he entered the store." She glanced at the box. "After the police left, I felt something off in the store. I found these."

Jacob rose and walked carefully over to the table, peering into the box. "Christmas presents? That's not odd, is it?"

"No, not in itself. It's the fact that there is one for each of us."

"One for each of us?" Jacob carefully removed them from the box, setting the box on the floor out of the way. "They're all basically the same size, wrapped the same." He leaned over to read the tags, his hand balancing himself against the table. He frowned. "I don't get this. Why one for each of us? Who knew who we were and that we were here?"

"Your lawyer." Finn paced the living room, arms wrapped around herself. She was feeling afraid. "You need to talk to him and soon, Jacob."

He nodded, regretting that at the pain he felt. "I will. Tomorrow, I promise. Aren't you curious to see what yours is?"

She snorted. "You don't unwrap Christmas presents before Christmas."

"On the contrary, I think these are meant to be opened now." He reached for his phone laying on the side table by the chair he had been sitting in. "I need to call the others."

"I already have. Simon can't make it tonight nor can Josh. That leaves you, me and Blackie." She paused, her eyes on her father standing in the kitchen doorway. "Dad, what's your take on this?"

"My take on what? And why do you have Christmas presents out already?"

"Your take on these. Anna and I found them this afternoon under the store tree. There is one for each of the four guys and myself."

Timothy stood for a moment, his gaze going between the young couple in front of him before walking over to the table. "Do either of you recognize the handwriting?"

Jacob nodded. "I think it's Grand's lawyer but I'm not sure. No, wait. It's Grand's. Now how did he know all our names?"

"That's something that may be explained in the package, but you may also have to talk to your lawyer." Timothy paused, a thoughtful look on his face. "If it is your grandfather's, Jacob, then there is no reason not to open them. On the other hand, if you feel better having Simon go over them before you do, that's another option."

Finn stared at the box, finally reaching for the one labeled for her. "I'm going to open it. I need to know. I won't sleep unless I do." She carefully peeled back the paper, finding a small box inside. She frowned as she carefully opened it, finding a smaller box inside. She raised her eyes to the two men, her gaze lingering on Jacob who had moved closer to her.

When she finally opened the small box, she hesitated, finding what looked like a jeweled piece of puzzle. "Jacob? What is this?"

Jacob took it from her, turning it over and over, before he began laughing. Timothy and Finn stared at him.

"Jacob? Care to share?" Timothy's grin grew wider as Jacob's look of astonishment turned to wonder and then understanding.

"Let me open mine. I have an idea of what Grand was up to." He opened his box, taking out another piece of puzzle. Laying the two pieces down flat, he

—

74

carefully worked them together. "This is a puzzle that Grand designed by the looks of it. It has to be something in this town. That's why he's drawn us all here."

Finn shook her head. "I have no idea what he would have been thinking. We'll have to wait until tomorrow when the others can make it out here." She looked at her father. "Dad?"

He threw up his hands even as he laughed. "I know. Put them in the safe. If you two keep on, I'll have to buy another safe just for your belongings."

Finn shook her head at her father before turning, finding Jacob watching her, a look on his face she couldn't read. Timothy watched the two of them, his heart raised in prayer. Lord, if this is the man You have chosen for our Finn, bless them. If not, protect both their hearts.

❀ ❀ ❀ ❀ ❀

Simon, Blackie and Josh stared at Jacob the next night before their eyes went to Finn, who stood nodding and grinning at them.

"Puzzle pieces? Seriously?" Blackie reached for his package. "And it was your grandfather, Whit?"

"It was." Jacob nodded at the packages. "Go on. Open them. Then we'll see how they fit with ours."

An hour later, they all stood staring down at the assembled puzzle, no clearer as to its meaning. Finn frowned, a look crossing her face that Jacob wondered at.

Simon excused himself as his phone rang, walking away from them, spinning abruptly to stare at Finn. Josh watched him, then shook his head, looking back to the puzzle and listening to the wild ideas that were being tossed around.

Finn finally turned the puzzle over and stopped, her fingers tracing an etching on the back.

"Did you guys see this? It's a raised etching. Now, I wonder?" She ran for a piece of paper and a pencil, making a tracing of the etching, laying it flat on the table and flipping the puzzle back over. She looked up as Simon laid a hand on her shoulder. "Simon?"

"I have some news, Finn." He looked up at Jacob, who was watching intently. "Gerry Adams was killed last night in custody. We're investigating that. He won't be bothering you any more."

Finn backed away from Simon, stopping as she felt Jacob move behind her. "Murdered? Who? How?"

"I can't give any details yet, but yes, it was a murder. I'm sorry. I'll need to leave. Let me know what I can do to help with this puzzle."

—

Finn stood, stunned, unable to comprehend that the villain who had haunted her for so many years no longer would. She looked up at Josh and Blackie, not able to read the looks on their faces, before she turned to Jacob.

"Jacob?"

"Simon will find out, Finn. Leave it with him. Now, do we continue our research tonight, or do we do something fun?"

"Fun, after that news? How can we?"

Jacob reached to pull her into a hug. "Yes, fun. We need to get your mind off what happened." He turned her towards the lounge area at the front of the house. "Your mom asked if we would decorate tonight. Blackie and Josh will help." He looked over his shoulder, catching their nods. "We'll be done in no time."

"How be we tackle the outside and you two the inside? Bit of friendly competition and all." Blackie laughed at their expression, trying to lighten the mood for Finn.

She shrugged, her mind not on what she was doing. She just followed along behind them, reaching for the garland Jacob handed her for the dark wood mantle of the large fireplace.

She stopped an hour later, her hands clenching the ornaments she was holding before she set them down, a puzzled look on her face.

Jacob watched her walk away, his hands busy hanging the ornaments on the tree she had handed him. He turned as he heard the laughter from his friends as they came in.

"Where's Finn?" Blackie looked around. "We need her opinion on the lights."

Jacob nodded towards the living quarters. "Back there. I'm not sure what's up with her."

Blackie caught Finn up in a hug as she rushed back through the doors, spinning her in a circle before setting her down.

"Finn, you're in a rush. We need your opinion outside."

"It's fine." She didn't move towards the door or even look at them.

Blackie and Josh started laughing. "How can you say that when you haven't even seen it?"

She looked up, bringing her thoughts back to the room. "I've seen what Josh did at his place. He'll have done as nice a job here as there." She headed for Jacob, hooking an arm through his and drawing him away from the tree. She stopped, staring at the tree.

"I don't think we've ever had such a nice tree. Are you sure you three aren't interior decorators in disguise?"

Jacob shook his head, his hand resting on hers. "No. But what was the rush? You took off out of here so fast."

"I figured out what the etching is and where it is." She pointed to the map she now held. "There. About an hour past Pops' cabin. There's a set of hills that match this. There are also caves there. Could something be hidden in one of the caves? Could there be more hints in his journal?"

Jacob stared at her for a moment, then reached for the map she held. "This is the area?" When she nodded, he looked around, then laid the map on a table, the other two men crowding around them. Thankfully, he thought, there were no guests in the lounge at the moment. He stood staring down at the map, wondering just what his grandfather had been up to. He sighed as his phone chimed and excused himself.

"Norman? What's going on?"

Norman gave a soft laugh. "Don't you remember the scavenger hunts you and your grandfather used to dream up? He said this was an adult version of it. You'll have more information tomorrow. I'm taking it you found the gifts."

"We did. When did you put them there?"

"I didn't. Someone in town did for me. No, I'm not saying who is was. But that's not why I called. We need to meet again. You have some decisions to make. You haven't settled down into your work again and your Grand would want you to."

Jacob sighed, thinking of his graphics company he had started. "I know. I'm getting there. It's just, just….." His voice died away.

"I know. It's tough without your grandfather to see and approve what you're doing, isn't it? Just be very careful, Jacob. Someone will try and stop you, even to the point of murder, from finishing off this hunt. I have heard rumours from the town, but no one can or will say who it is. Take care of your lady, too." With that, Norman was gone.

Jacob pocketed his phone, turning to watch Finn interact with his friends. He had to admit it, Norman was right. He was beginning to think of her as his lady, and he couldn't. He didn't have the right to do that. Lord, I have no idea what the next few days will bring, but You do. Protect us please. Keep my Finola safe.

Josh approached him. "I need to get going. Is everything okay?"

"It is, I think. Norman wants to meet. He said someone in town put out the packages for him but he wouldn't say who. Watch your back, Josh."

"I will. You watch yours and Finn's. She's come up with a plan to have her brother watch her store on Saturday and head out to the hills and the caves she says are there."

"I don't like that."

"Like it or not, you're not stopping her, you know." Josh laid a hand on his friend's shoulder and then headed out the door.

Jacob draped an arm over Finn's shoulders as he studied the map, not catching her quick intake of breath or Blackie's surprised look

"When are you planning on this trip, Finn?"

"Saturday, I think. Peter will watch the store, I know, he and Anna. They like working together. From what I can remember, it's maybe an hour or less to the last of the caves, so we should be able to search them all." She looked up at him. "I just have no idea what we're looking for. Do you?"

Jacob shook his head, a thought crossing his mind. "Not off hand. I don't know about this, though, Finn. Something tells me it's too dangerous."

She glared at him as she hurried gathered up her papers. "Too dangerous?" She spluttered for a moment, then turned and stalked away, leaving him staring after her.

"That went well, Whit." Blackie moved to stand beside him.

"I know, didn't it? Norman says we're all in danger from someone but he can't say who. I don't want to put her in any more danger."

Blackie shook his head as he walked away. "It's too late, Whit. She's determined to go, with or without us. Let's make sure we're with her."

Saturday morning, Jacob shrugged into his backpack, his eyes searching the area. He didn't feel like they were alone. It almost felt as if someone was following them, but Simon hadn't said anything about that, and he knew Simon had been watching. He turned to watch Finn as she laughed at the nonsense Blackie was saying, her face alight. He wondered again at how beautiful she was, catching her eye as she turned to find him.

Thirty minutes later, Finn stopped, pointed to an area just off to their right. "There's the first cave. It's not really big, more like a depression. We can take a look at it, though." She had shed her jacket, waving aside Jacob's concern, stating it was warm for that time of year but yes, the weather could change. She had searched the sky when she said that and then shook her head, saying it would likely stay nice for the rest of the day.

Blackie nodded to Simon. "We'll look it over. Anything in particular you would think we should be looking for?"

Jacob shot a look at Finn, then spoke. "Anything out of the ordinary. Maybe Finn should go with you. She's familiar with the caves. You are, aren't you, Finn?"

She nodded. "This is Pops' land, so Peter and I played here all the time. We know those caves well." She held up a camera. "We'll take pictures of every angle we can and have Peter and Dad take a look at them. They may see something we miss."

"Now that's thinking." Josh grinned at her before the three moved away. "How many caves are there, Jacob?"

Jacob shrugged. "Timothy said six. If we don't get to them all today, we'll come back. I want to be out of here before dark."

"I agree with you there." He turned as the three returned. "That was quick."

"Finn was right, it was small." Simon nodded towards the trail. "How far to the next one and is it any bigger?"

"About ten minutes and yes it is somewhat bigger but not as big as the last one. They all seem to increase in size." She looked around, suddenly nervous. "I don't know if we'll be able to explore the last one today. It's large and has some rooms off the main room. We'll likely have to come back to that one."

"Can we do that after church tomorrow?" Josh glanced at the other three men, catching their nods.

Finn shook her head. "I can't. It's the annual seniors' Christmas dinner at the church and I have to serve. Peter could come with you." She paused, her focus on the distance. "That might be the best idea. He's the one who really explored that last cave. I never liked it."

They had reached the last cave and Finn stood, rubbing her hands up and down her arms. She really didn't want to go into the cave, but she knew she had to. Jacob stood beside her, finally turning her so he could hug her.

"You don't have to go in, Finn. We'll take lots of pictures."

She shook her head. "I have to. There's just something about this cave I've never liked and I don't know why." She moved away, pulling out her flashlight and turning it on as she entered the cave, ducking to miss the top of the entrance. The four men followed her, eyes searching for what, they weren't sure of. She wrinkled her nose at the smell of animals and decay and death in the cave. Maybe that's what she hated about it, she thought

Blackie and Josh moved off towards one of the side rooms, leaving Jacob and Simon studying the main room and taking their photos. Finn finally moved away towards a room on the left, tired of waiting for the men. She knew she was leaving them on the other side of the cave and that scared her, but she was determined to overcome her fear.

She stood for a moment at the entrance, flashing the light around, trying to see if something just jumped out at her. This is ridiculous, she thought, now isn't it, Lord? Whatever it is will not just walk over and hit me over the head. She moved forward, her foot catching for a moment on what she thought was a rock.

Sudden sound and light filled the cave as an explosion ripped through the wall near Finn. She was flung forward into the room as the debris blocked off the entrance. The four men were thrown to the ground. Silence gradually filled the cave as the dust and smoke filtered out the entrance. No one moved.

❋ ❋ ❋ ❋ ❋

Four hours later, Timothy, Peter and other members of the town search and rescue group slowly approached the cave. Peter had called his father when Finn hadn't reported in three hours previously. They had decided as a group to go searching and this was the last cave.

Timothy's hand came to rest on Peter's arm.

"I don't like this, Peter. There's fresh debris near the entrance." He looked around, worry etched on his face.

"There is, Dad. I don't think they made it out." He turned to the other five with them. "Let's go, guys. Let's see what we're facing."

Slowly entering the cave, they stood for a moment, shocked at the destruction they saw. Hearing faint moans, they turned to the right, finding Simon and Jacob, and then further back, Blackie and Josh. No Finn.

"Where's Finn?" Timothy spun, trying to find his daughter, his eyes landing on the fresh rock pile. "No! Tell me it's not true!" He ran for the rocks, Peter on his heels.

Ed, one of their team members, was at their side. "Careful, guys. Start at the top. We don't know where she is and we don't want to bring anything more down." He turned as he heard voices behind him. "Peter, go see if one of the men knows where she is."

Two hours later, Peter stood in the room Finn had been entering. They had removed the debris, but had not found her. She had simply vanished. He frowned. There had to be another entrance, he thought, turning as he heard footsteps approaching. Jacob stood there, fear on his face for Finn.

"Where is she, Peter?"

"I have no idea, Jacob. There has to be another entrance here somewhere, but I don't see one. She can't have just vanished into thin air." He turned. "We'll need to come back tomorrow. First, we need to get you four checked out."

"We're fine, Peter. I'm staying at your grandfather's cabin tonight, even if I have to break into it." Jacob stared at Peter, silent communication going on between the two of them before Peter nodded.

"That's what I was planning. Dad's heading out with the rest. He knows that's what I was planning on doing. She has to be here somewhere, Jacob. I just don't see it."

Three days later, Jacob sighed as he signed into his laptop. He needed to work. He had clients waiting for graphics he was to be designing for them, but his heart wasn't in it. He stared at the screen as it flickered to life but what he saw was the cave and the rock pile. Peter and he had gone back to the cave the next day and the next day, searching for a secondary entrance, but finding nothing. Peter thought he had found a crack in the wall in the one room where Finn had been headed but neither one of them had been able to open it. They had searched around outside for a secondary entrance but again had drawn a blank.

He finally shook his head and pulled up his program. His email was overloaded, he thought. He sighed. He really didn't want to be this busy but it seems as if the Lord had other ideas. He was soon immersed in his work.

Mary came looking for him just after noon, having called him and gotten no response. She stood for a moment watching before heading back down for a tray of food.

Jacob didn't stir except to say a quiet thank you when she placed the tray next to him. Her hand rested on his shoulder for a moment before she walked away, her heart raised in prayer for the young man who had become so important to them all and such a part of their lives in so short a time.

Blackie stopped at Jacob's door later that day, finally bringing Jacob back to the present. He rose and stretched, his eyes going to the time.

"Blackie? Any word?'

Blackie shook his head. "We've been out with the search and rescue teams and a couple of dog trackers, but nothing. She's vanished into thin air. The last scent the dogs got was in that room."

"Then, where is she?"

Blackie shrugged, before he held out a shallow tin box. "I found this in the cave today. I think it's what we were looking for. I haven't opened it today. You can see where it was damaged by the explosion."

Jacob took it, turning it over and over, before setting it on his desk. He looked up. "Do we open it or do we wait?"

"I'd say we open it. We can share with the others what we find. I have a feeling time is short."

Jacob nodded, his hands shaking as he pried open the box. He stopped, staring at the parchment within, before looking up at Blackie.

"Blackie?"

"I don't know, Jacob. That looks old."

Jacob nodded, carefully handling the fragile parchment. He opened it and read it several times, his mind not comprehending what it all said. Blackie read over his shoulder, a soft exclamation coming from him.

"That would explain what your Grandfather was after then, wouldn't it?"

Jacob nodded before placing the parchment back into the box and picking it up to head for the stairs. He gave a quick grin. "Wonder if Timothy has invested in that other safe yet?"

Blackie started to laugh. "He'll have to soon, you know."

Her eyes blinking open and closed, Finn slowly stirred, glancing around. She wasn't at home, she knew. She just didn't know where she was. She felt a hand under her head, holding it up to help her drink, then a cloth gently wiping away the spilled water. Her vision faded as she lost consciousness again.

The man stood watching her for a moment after straightening back up. The tin mug clanged slightly as he set it down on the rickety crate beside the rough bunk she was laying on. He looked around. He couldn't let her stay here. He had to get her away. He didn't know that it was Finn the man wanted him to guard, or he wouldn't have agreed to it. He wouldn't leave her here.

He crept to the door of the ramshackle house near the edge of Mistletoe, hidden back in the trees, and looked around. The man had left earlier, saying he would be back by noon. He glanced up at the sky. He had time to get her to his truck and to help. He turned as he heard a faint moan and then a cough from her, creeping back on silent feet before reaching to sweep her into his arms and out of the house, towards the truck he had hidden nearby. He carefully fastened her in and then stood for a moment, head cocked to listen before he slid behind the wheel. Surprisingly, the truck started right away and was almost silent. He had kept it that way.

He pulled to a stop near Finn's home, watching the activity going on around it. He needed to get her in there, but he'd have too many questions to answer if he walked in the front way. He stepped from the vehicle and walked around to the passenger door, scooping Finn into his arms and heading for the back door. He had been there frequently. Finn and her family treated him right, he decided.

Mary frowned at the tap at the back door. No one should be there, she thought. She pulled the door open, ready to tell off whoever was there, then stopped short, astonishment on her face. Old Jack, as he was called, stood in front of her, Finn in his arms. She reached to draw him in.

"Jack?"

"I found her, Miz Mary. I was to watch her for someone, but I just couldn't. You've been too good to me." Tears streaked down his face as he stared at her.

"Jack! Thank you! Timothy!"

Timothy came through the doors on the run at the urgency in his wife's voice, Peter on his heels, both men sliding to a stop as they saw Jack and Finn. Timothy reached for his daughter, tears on his own face, even as Peter reached out a hand and drew Jack to the kitchen table, seating him. Peter watched as his parents headed for the stairs. He knew they wouldn't take her to the hospital. Not now. Maybe later, once Doc had seen her.

Blackie peeked through the door and then came in, his eyes on Old Jack, who cringed away from him. He slid onto a chair away from Jack and just watched, a quiet work of thanks for the mug of coffee Peter handed him.

"Jack, when did you last eat?" Peter looked around from the fridge.

Jack shrugged, even as Jacob walked in, a puzzled look on his face. "Don't rightly remember, Peter. Not yesterday. Maybe not the day before."

"Then, a feast you will have. I remember you like Mom's breakfast casserole and bacon. I have that here for you. Toast as well?" He slid a large mug of black coffee in front of the man, not waiting for an answer.

Jacob stood for a moment, not quite sure what was going on. He could hear hurried footsteps over head and then a new voice speaking from the front area. "Peter?"

Peter turned as he set the plate down in front of Jack. "Jack here found Finn. Mom and Dad are with her."

Blackie laid a hand on Jacob's arm. "Let them be with her. You'll get a chance, Jacob. Sit. Peter had tea for you." His eyes were on Jack. "What part of the service, Jack?"

Jack looked up, a startled look on his face, then fear tracing over it. "Who are you and why do you want to know?"

Blackie held up his hands. "Hey! No reason. I just recognize a brother vet is all. I was a medic in the armed forces."

Jack studied him, then turned his eyes to Jacob. "And you, what were you?"

"An MP." Jacob stopped him from rising. "That part of my life is over. I don't arrest or contain anyone any more. You're with friends here. May I call you Jack? I'm Jacob and this is Blackie."

The three men finally watched as Jack rose without saying a word when he was finished eating and walked out the back door.

"What's his story, Peter?" Jacob turned to watch the stairs even as he asked.

"He lives outside of town. We really need to do something about his house. It's almost falling down. But anyway, he's an army vet. Been living here for twenty years I think. He doesn't say much. Won't say if he has a family or not. Maybe you could check that out, Blackie."

"Why doesn't he live in town? He seems like a nice enough fellow." Jacob turned his eyes to Peter.

Peter shook his head. "Some people in town are real friendly to him, but then he's not real friendly to them. He does odd jobs around town, earning enough for food and whatnot. He has never said anything about his service, but Doc says he lives out there because he has really bad nightmares and doesn't want to scare anyone, especially the little ones. Doc checks in on him every week as do we."

"PTSD?" Blackie's question caught Peter's attention.

"That's what we think. It's never been confirmed though. He refuses all help."

They turned as footsteps sounded on the stairs and Timothy appeared, slumping down onto a chair. He thanked his son for the mug of coffee Peter set in front of him, his head bowing before he reached for the mug.

"Dad?"

Timothy looked up, his eyes on his son. "She's fine, son. Bumps, bruises. Doc says Jack looked after her well the last day or so. He's not sure where she's been before that though. He doesn't think Finn will remember though." He sighed. "He's afraid of pneumonia. She's doing some coughing. But he says all things considered she's in good shape. He doesn't think there are any internal or head injuries. He'll have to wait until she wakes up fully to assess for any memory loss or anything, he said."

Jacob stared at his hands. "If we hadn't gone there, she wouldn't have been hurt."

Timothy shook his head. "Whoever it is takes advantage of where you five are. He's likely watching you. He may even be listening to us without us knowing that. Simon's checked our place and says it's fine. He's also rechecked Finn's store."

Blackie watched the emotions flickering across Jacob's face and shared a look with Peter. "Jacob, any more thoughts on that parchment?"

Jacob brought his thoughts back to the room. "That puzzles me, Blackie. I don't get it."

"What parchment?" Peter hadn't heard about their find.

"We found an old tin box with a parchment in it. It must have been jarred loose from somewhere during the explosion." Jacob looked at Timothy, who nodded and rose, returning with the box. "We can't figure it out though. We're hoping Finn can help." He opened the box and carefully handed the fragile parchment to Peter.

Peter laid it down carefully and then opened it, staring at it for a moment, before he rose and headed for the library, returning with an old volume.

"Pops had this book. I think it was his father's, grandfather's, something like that. This parchment reminds me of something in there." Peter searched through the book, finding laying the book beside the parchment. "There. These almost match. It's the old homestead of the Whitsons, Dad. Out near Pops cabin. Jacob owns that now."

"I do? I didn't know I had property that close to yours." He rose and stood behind Peter, staring at the picture. "What is this?"

"It's an old mill, I think, Jacob. Your property contains a river with rapids and there used to be a flour mill there. Not big, just enough for the community. There is still some of the foundation there."

"There is, Peter. I was out there about a month ago, just checking on the property, like I've always done. There's not a lot of the foundation left, but we can check it out."

Jacob shook his head. "You need to stay here with your daughter. Simon and Josh will be free on Saturday. We'll go then."

"Don't wait too long, or you'll be tracking through snow." Peter grinned at the look on Blackie's face. "Not sure about the snow, Blackie?"

"No. I've always lived in warm climates, although being the armed forces did take me to some colder places."

Jacob started to laugh. "Nothing like here, though, Blackie. Nothing like here."

Timothy nodded as he rose. "Just be very careful wherever you go. Someone is after you four and Finn as well. I've heard rumours in town, but I can't pin them down to anyone in particular. The townsfolk are not too sure about you young men. You're newcomers to town, even though your roots are here. Finn, they'll watch out for."

❀ ❀ ❀ ❀ ❀

Turning her head slowly, Finn roused, her eyes peeping open as she looked around. Surprised to see her own room, she sat up, regretting it as the room spun and she dropped back to her pillow. Hearing movement to her side, she jumped, then relaxed as she realized it was Peter.

"Finn. You're awake. Here. Doc wants you to drink lots." He held a glass of juice for her to sip.

"Peter? How'd I get here? The last I remember was standing outside Pops' cabin."

"Old Jack brought you home. He's not saying much about where he found you." Peter sat on the edge of her bed, leaning back on a hand. "You really don't remember?"

She shook her head. "No. Tell me, What happened?"

"You and the four guys were exploring the caves behind Pops. In the last one, somehow an explosion was triggered and you were supposed to be trapped in one of the rooms. Only you weren't there when we got through the debris." He studied her face. "You really don't remember at all?"

"No. The guys are okay?"

Peter grinned. "Yes, Jacob is." He ducked back as she swiped at him. "They're all fine. Just bumps and bruises. Jacob and I kept going back to look for

———

86

you." He studied her. "I wish you could remember. There had to be another entrance to that room."

"Was it the first one on the left when you walked into the cave?" At his nod, she continued. "Pops showed me the door one time. It leads back to the other side of the hill. About a mile or so I think."

"That's why we couldn't find it then. But you wouldn't have been there anyway. Jack's not saying much."

"What time is it?"

"About two in the morning. One of us has been with you since Jack brought you home yesterday morning."

"What day is it?"

"It's Wednesday morning. Why?"

She groaned. "I have a new client coming in with some objects for the consignment shop. I have to be there today."

"Not happening, sis. I'll meet him. Luke's okay with me being off this week." Peter worked for a local contractor.

"That's not the same, Peter. I need to see the pieces."

"Then, how be I take you down there long enough to meet with him and then bring you back home? Other than that, you call him and postpone."

She finally nodded, her eyes closing. "He's due to be there for 10. Wake me about 8:30. I'll need time to get ready. I'm not moving very fast, am I?"

Peter gave a low laugh. "No, you're not. It's a good thing Jacob had to travel last night to meet with his lawyer today. He'd have something to say about your plans."

"Really? I don't think it will matter to him what I do." Her breath evened out as she slept.

Peter sat for a few minutes, watching his sister, just one year younger than him. They had always been best friends, never a real argument between them. He finally shook his head as he rose and then dropped a kiss on her cheek. "But it will, Finn. It will. You don't see the way he looks at you, his heart in his eyes. Please, God, don't let her get hurt by a guy again. But somehow, I think you brought Jacob into her life for a reason. Please, let him stay. She needs him and he needs her.

He turned as he felt an arm around him. Mary stood there.

"She's been awake?"

"She has, Mom. She's planning on going to the store tomorrow. She has a new client to meet."

"I don't like that, but it is her choice, Peter. One of us will be with her."

"I told her I would take her and then bring her home." He stooped to kiss his mother on the cheek. "I'm off to bed then, Mom, if you're here." He stopped on his way to the door, turning to find his mother watching him. "What's Jacob going to say?" He grinned as she shook her head.

"He's not going to be happy, I know, but he's just a friend. So far, anyway."

Chapter 15

Jacob stared at Mary, not quite sure he had heard her right. "She's where?"

"You heard me, Jacob. She's at her shop. She had to meet a client this morning. No matter how sick she is, her clients come first. This is a new one to her, with antique documents that she wants to put up."

Jacob shook his head. "It's that important to her? More important than her health?"

Mary's anger grew and she drew Jacob to the table, shoving him down in a chair. He looked at her in shock as she sat beside him, her hand on his arm.

"You need to be very careful how you treat Finola, Jacob. She looks strong but she has a very fragile side, one she has shown you. She doesn't show this to very many people, other than the ones she loves, and that would basically be her father, her brother and me. Pops and her had a special relationship. You also need to understand that when she was about twelve, she was beaten severely and left lying in an abandoned house. She can't remember who did it or if she does, she's buried it too deep to bring out. Pops is the one who found her. She hadn't come home and we started to look for her. I'll never forget the look on his face the day he walked in with her in his arms. It crushed him, Jacob. She's been afraid to let people close since then. That tells us it was someone she knew well who did it."

"And you have no idea who?"

Mary shook her head, compassion for the young man in her eyes. "We don't. We might suspect someone but we have no proof." She pointed at him. "Today, this was her way of claiming back her life. She wasn't ready to go to the store, far from it, but she had made a commitment to someone and she always keeps her word. Anna has taken up a lot of the slack for her. Peter and Anna are a couple, if you missed that, and Anna really wants to go into the store with Finn, if Finn will have her. She's been learning a lot, taking courses over the internet, with that in mind. It was God's way of having someone prepared to take over for Finn."

Jacob nodded, his mind slowly digesting what Mary had told him. "I'll be careful with her, Mary. I don't want to hurt her."

"We know you don't, Jacob, but you didn't know her history. She wouldn't have told you, not thinking it necessary. That would have left you doing or saying something that would have frightened her deeply and chased her away from here."

"I can see that. In ways, we're both walking wounded, aren't we? I lost my parents when I was young, and then Grams when I was ten, eleven, something like that. I lost buddies overseas." He paused, his eyes on his folded hands. "Believe me, I don't want to hurt her."

Mary stood, hugging him, and then dropping a kiss on his forehead. "We know you won't. Just don't tell her I told you. She needs to trust you enough to tell you herself. It will come with time."

She looked up as the door opened and Finn and Peter walked in. Finn stumbled as she tried to take off her boots. With an exclamation, Peter swept his sister up into his arms and headed for the stairs, shaking his head at his mother, Finn's arms around his neck, her head on his shoulder, eyes closed.

"I'll be right back. She overdid it, I think."

"I'm sure she did. There's fresh water and juice in her room, Peter. Make sure she takes some pain meds."

"I will, Mom. Be right back."

Jacob slowly sat back down, his eyes on the stairs, not knowing that his heart was showing to Mary. She gave a sad smile, knowing that Finn may well never think of Jacob that way and she hated to think that Jacob's heart would be broken.

Peter hugged his mother on the way by to the fridge. He pulled out sandwiches she had fixed and then reached for juice.

"Peter?" His mother stood beside him as he sat, her arm on his shoulders.

"She shouldn't have gone out, Mom. She couldn't even speak to Anna, she was that tired and in pain. I think we'll need to take her to the hospital. Doc thought we might have to."

"But what happened today, Peter?" Jacob's quiet voice broke into the silence that followed.

"She didn't meet with the client. Anna and I wouldn't let her. He was bizarre. He didn't have any antiquities, just a bunch of garbage. Anna looked at it and sent him on his way. Do you know when she set up the meeting?"

Mary shook her head. "No, I don't. She hadn't mentioned it. You don't think….." Mary's voice died away.

"They were trying to nab her again, weren't they, Peter?" Jacob had to tamp down his anger. "When will they leave her alone?"

"Not until we figure out who it is and what they want. And that answer I think lies on your property, at that old mill." Peter shared a look with Jacob. "Did your lawyer have any more information?"

Jacob shook his head. "Not really. He had no idea Grand was going to do this. He would have talked him out of it if he had. He doesn't want any more of us hurt. The thing is, we don't know what the answer is or why someone is after us if we don't follow through."

"I can tell you what they're after." Finn spoke from the bottom of the stairs. Her face was white and Jacob noted the dark circles under her eyes. "That

---

man today, Peter? He used to live here. I don't think you know him, though. His son was in some of my classes during high school."

"That's why he looked so familiar then." Peter's hand steadied his sister as she sat. "You shouldn't be up."

"I need to be. I can rest when we solve this. You said something about the old mill?"

"Blackie found an old tin box with a parchment in it. It leads us to the old mill on Grand's property. We're planning on going out there on Saturday. And no, you're not coming." Jacob watched her closely.

Finn glared at him. "You can't keep me away, Jacob. I've as much invested in this now as you do. Someone tried to kill us all and that someone kidnapped me."

"Finn!" Jacob's voice was firm

"I'm not one of your prisoners, Jacob. Get that through your head. If you are all going, so am I. Peter? Are you in?"

Peter quickly hid a smile, seeing his mother doing the same. "I can't, Finn. Anna wants me to help her with the store."

"That figures. Copping out, aren't you?" She stood, wavering for a moment, waving off the hands that came out to steady her. She turned to Jacob, a hurt look on her face. "At least with you, I thought I had a friend and an ally. You're just like all the rest, aren't you? See a female and think you have to protect, regardless of the circumstances or even if the female is able to protect themselves." She stopped herself from continuing, glaring at him. "Stay away from me, Jacob. I don't need any more people like you in my life." She turned and walked away, leaving him standing staring after her.

Jacob's eyes never left the stairs as he sank back into his chair, Mary's and Peter's eyes in turn on him. Peter shook his head as he met his mother's eyes and a small smile appeared on her face.

"This is what I meant, Jacob. She's begun to trust you and doesn't understand that you care too much for her to see her hurt. You need to talk to her." Mary's hand rubbed his back. "She'll come around. Just don't shut her out. We've never coddled her, wrapped her in cotton and stuck her on a shelf because she's female. She won't accept you doing that." Jacob had turned to her. "I have no idea who is after you five, but someone is. And one of you right now is in real danger. I sense that. It's you or Finn, I can't determine which one of you it is."

"And Mom usually can do that." Peter picked up their dishes and headed for the sink. "Talk to her, Jacob. But first, spend time in prayer. Decide exactly what she means to you." He turned to face his friend. "I'm getting the sense that she's important to you. Tell her that if that's the case. She won't throw it back into your face. She treasures your friendship. I've seen her let you do things not even we can do for her."

Jacob nodded, his eyes flickering between the two and then to the stairs. "If I go up there now, will she talk to me?"

Mary spoke up, her hand on Jacob's arm keeping him in his chair. "Not just yet. Give her a couple of hours. You need to spend those hours with God. Talk to her then. You also need to deal with your business. You can't let it slide."

Jacob looked down, blinking rapidly to clear his eyes. He had never had a woman talk to him like that, not even his own mother or his Grams. "Thank you, Mary. I'll do just that."

❀ ❀ ❀ ❀ ❀

Finn looked up later that afternoon as she felt the couch sink beside her. Jacob sat there, his eyes on the fireplace, not on her. She tilted her head to study him and opened her mouth to speak but didn't when he reached for her hand.

Jacob entwined their fingers, his eyes on her neat nails, before he frowned. "You have presents on your nails."

She laughed. "I do. It's my one extravagance every once in a while. I get my nails done, particularly near special holidays. I'm sorry, Jacob. I shouldn't have said that to you."

"No. You were right when you said what you did. I want to protect you and that's me. Your mom talked to me and explained how it is with you, from their standpoint. So did Peter." He finally shifted to watch her face, finding her eyes on him. "I've begun to think of you as someone special in my life, Finn, and that scares me. I've never had a special lady before, just never found one, or had God direct me to one. You're that one."

She sighed. "I know, Jacob. I find it difficult to get to know people. I keep things in. It goes back to something that happened when I was young, when I was beaten up and left by myself. I can't remember who it was, but they think it's someone I trusted. I wish I knew who it was." She stopped at the pressure of his fingers on hers.

"That doesn't matter, Finn, not with me. You've shown you've trusted me right from the first moment we met."

She nodded. "Can we say we had the rest of this conversation and be done with it?"

Jacob began to laugh even as he pulled her into a hug. "We can. But I reserve the right to come back to it at some point."

She nodded, her hair brushing against his cheek. "I'll grant you that. That's something I never do either. Once a conversation is over, with me, it's over."

"Now what, Finn? You are really determined to go with us on Saturday?"

She stared at the fireplace. "I need to, I think, Jacob. Part of me is afraid to go, afraid of getting hurt again. Part of me is angry that we were in that explosion

—

92

and all of us suffered to some extent." She looked back at him. "Part of me wants to run as far from this town as I can, and I know I can't do that. Does that make sense?"

"It makes perfect sense. It's how I feel." He settled back against the couch, his arms still cradling her to him. "I want this over, Finn. I never dreamed when I walked through this town that day how my life would be changed by it, how it would come to feel so much like home. I'm going to find one of Grand's properties and fix it up to live in. I can work from here."

"That would be nice, Jacob." She settled down against him, not seeing her father standing in the doorway behind them, watching intently before he moved on to find Mary.

They sat in silence for a while before Finn spoke, asking him about his lawyer.

"Norman? He's been Grand's lawyer for the last ten years or so. He took over for his uncle. Why?"

"Just how much do you trust him? How well do you know him?"

Jacob stilled, catching what she wasn't saying. "I see what you mean. I'll need to look into him, won't I? I'll call Blackie's Dad. He'll look into it for me, without letting Blackie know. The fewer of us in on this the better."

—

Saturday found Jacob standing on his grandfather's property, looking around. He walked towards the cabin, finding it in surprisingly good shape. He tried the door, finding it locked, disappointed he couldn't enter. He felt Finn's hand on his, closing his fingers over something. He looked down as he opened his hand. A key. He looked up, seeing her smile and then her nod towards the door. He unlocked it, and shoved it open, still hesitating. He didn't see the looks of his three friends. Instead, he reached for Finn's hand, drawing her with him into the cabin. He sighed. He was just as he pictured it would be. His grandfather had built this dream cabin for him as a bedtime story when he was tiny. This was the cabin. He felt like he had come home.

Finn reached to wipe the tear from his face and he caught her hand again as he turned in a circle.

"You've kept it up for him, haven't you?"

Finn nodded. "Pops made us promise to do just that, just in case Aaron ever came back. He missed his friend so much." She looked around, seeing the other three men standing just inside the doorway, compassion on their faces for their friend. "Do you think he left anything here?"

Jacob shook his head. "I have no way of knowing. I think we need to look for the mill first and then come back here." He turned, stopping to study his friends. "I can't contact Norman. He's not answering his phone and his secretary has been taking my messages. I find that strange."

"It is strange, Jacob. Do you trust him?" Blackie spoke up.

"Finn asked me that the other day. I had your father research him. It's not what I expected to hear from your dad, what he reported. Apparently Norman is just one complaint short of being charged by the authorities. I don't know how Grand trusted him."

Blackie nodded. "I thought you'd check him out at some point. Now, where do we go from here, Finn?"

She pointed behind them. "Out the door, for starters." She smirked at their collective groan. "Lock up, Jacob. We sometimes have people coming through who shouldn't." She led the way across the clearing and stopped. "If we follow the path, it will take us to the remains of the mill. It's about a half mile, I think."

Simon moved to the front. "We want you between us, Finn. Blackie, you're on the end, Jacob, Finn, and then Josh behind me. No arguments, Finn, or we turn around and leave."

"I wasn't about to argue. I was going to say I appreciate your attention to my safety."

Simon shot her a suspicious look, finding her looking at him with understanding. He shrugged. "Okay, then. Let's move. I'd like to be out of here before dark." He glanced at the sky. "Those are snow clouds."

Finn shook her head. "Maybe, maybe not."

They stopped as they reached the river, hearing the rapids before they saw them. Jacob turned in a circle, studying the area. "This is on Grand's land?"

"It is, Jacob. He has about 30 acres of woodland here. This used to be the flour mill." Finn walked towards some of the large stones that had formed the mill. "I guess there was an explosion from the flour and that destroyed the mill. After that, they took their wheat to a neighbouring mill."

"Why would Grand send us here? I don't see anything that would have him doing that."

"Let's separate and look around. Finn, stay with Jacob." Blackie headed off to his left, his eyes searching for anything that looked suspicious. Then he groaned. How would he know what was suspicious, anyway? He shot a glance around him and saw the other four moving around, searching as well.

Jacob moved towards the river, his eyes on a large section of wall. He traced the stones with his hands, Finn keeping step with him. He finally stopped, his hands brushing away debris and light snow, his fingers tracing lettering.

"Did you know this was here, Finn?"

"What was here?"

"This." Jacob drew her to him, an arm around her. "Look. It's a verse. 'Seek the Lord while He may be found.' Grand used to quote that to me at least once a day." He looked up, blinking away tears. "I think we found the treasure, Finn. Let's go find the others."

Finn looked around. "But where are they? They can't have disappeared."

Shards of stone flew through the air, and Jacob caught Finn in his arms, taking her down and shoving her against the stone, covering her as best he could with his own body.

Finn struggled to get away from him, but he only pressed her tighter to the ground. "Jacob! Let me up!

"Ssh, Finn. Someone's shooting at us."

"Shooting at us? But who? And why?" Finn still shoved against him but he refused to budge, his head up listening. "Jacob?"

He shook his head. "Finn! Stop now!" He turned his head to listen. "Okay. This is what we're going to go. See how the foundation follows along to the trees. We need to crawl that way and get under better cover. We can hide there until we find the others."

"Crawl? Are you serious?" Finn stared at the face so close to hers.

—

"We have to, Finn. There's no other way to stay low enough." He ducked more shards of stone. "Now! Let's move." He shoved at her and she finally moved, staying as low as she could, Jacob right behind her.

Jacob finally reached for her hand and pulling her with him, ran the few feet to the trees, ducking as splinters of bark flew around them. He searched the woods, finally seeing Blackie, but not Josh or Simon. He pulled her deeper into the woods, then headed towards Blackie.

"Jacob! Finn! Thank God you're okay." Blackie had turned as he heard their quiet footsteps, ready to do battle with an attacker. "Josh is fine. He's pinned down to our right. Simon's trying to work his way around to where the shooter is."

Jacob settled Finn down behind a large fallen tree, making sure she would stay, before he turned back to Blackie.

"I don't get this, Blackie. Who knew we would be here?"

Blackie shot a look at Jacob, then shrugged. "The only one I can think of would be your lawyer. I think he's been playing you all along. It's just never felt right, the clues and what we've found." He searched the woods, finally catching sight of Simon entering the clearing from the other side. "I have asked around. No one remembers your grandfather being here in the last year. But they do remember Norman."

"So you're saying he did all this? Arranged all this." Jacob sank back on his heels. "You're right, you know. This has never felt like Grand. He wouldn't have us running around like this." He peered through the trees, feeling Finn's hand on his back. "He must have left, whoever the shooter was."

"And I don't like that." Simon spoke from the edge of the clearing, Josh at his side. "We need to get out of here."

"But first, I want to show you something. I found the treasure Grand left me." Grasping Finn's hand, Jacob led them over towards the rock. He pointed. "There. That's the treasure he left me."

The three men stood and read the inscription, then nodded. "That's the only treasure worth having, Jacob." Blackie spoke up. "Now, let's get back to the cabin. I could use a hot drink. I don't know about you."

Finn moved around the tiny kitchen, open to the rest of the cabin, as she listened to the four men discuss the events from earlier. She finally set the sandwiches and hot drinks in front of them, then pulled up a chair beside Jacob.

"So, if it wasn't your grandfather, Jacob, who was it? The lawyer?"

Jacob shrugged as he bit into his sandwich, chewing slowly as he thought through the events. Swallowing, he opened his mouth to speak, then closed it, his eyes on Blackie.

"Blackie? What're your thoughts?" Jacob turned to his friend, knowing he would be honest with him.

Blackie stared at the table, his finger pushing a crumb around as he thought. "I think your grandfather sent you here for this purpose. To remind you of your treasure in heaven. To find your past." He nodded at Finn and Jacob got his message, a slight smile on his face. "He probably said something in passing about a treasure he wanted you to find, and the lawyer decided it was money or jewels or something monetary. I think you'll find some of the letters you've been given have been written by him, not your grandfather. I called Dad earlier. He's talking to the police in your hometown. They have enough to obtain warrants and seize his computers at home and work, and any other documentation related to your grandfather and his estate."

Jacob sat back, not having expected that, but realizing that Blackie had been thinking it all through. "I think you're right, Blackie. Some of the wording just wasn't Grand. I put it off to how he was feeling."

Finn reached for his hand, hers putting pressure on his. "You never said, Jacob. How did your grandfather die?"

"They thought a heart attack. I didn't do an autopsy. I was in too much shock." He looked at her, seeing the look on her face. "You're thinking he didn't die naturally, aren't you?" He stood, running his hands through his hair, deep in thought before he turned back to the table, his hands turning white as he gripped the back of his chair. "Blackie, call your Dad. Find out how we go about doing an autopsy at this point, if it's not too late."

"Already done. He's talking to the authorities. He said he'd call you when he had the details of what needs to be done. The police were already thinking that way."

Tears gathered in Jacob's eyes. "Why didn't I see this, guys?"

Simon shook his head. "You were too close, Jacob. It was too sudden. You said your Grandfather was going to talk to you that night. That couldn't be allowed to happen, now could it?" He stood. "Let's head back to town. It's getting late. Jacob, I suggest you come back here at some point and go through what's here. I don't think you'll find anything other than what you would expect to find. Your lawyer knows he's been found out and can't get away with sending you on a wild goose chase any more."

Finn rose, reaching for the debris of their lunch, but finding Josh's hands ahead of her. He nodded towards Jacob and she turned, seeing the devastation on his face. She approached him, suddenly hugging him, drawing his attention to her. His arms came around her and he laid his head on hers. She could feel the wetness of his tears. She drew back to look up at him.

"Let's go home, Jacob. It's late."

The next morning, Finn sat in the back pew at church, the four men on either side of her, her parents, Peter and Anna in the pew in front of them. Not much had been said about the events of the day before and she was glad. That was not something she was keen to repeat.

Her attention on the bulletin she had opened, she didn't catch the look Jacob threw her and it startled her as his arm came around her and pulled her tight to him. She looked up, a frown in place, seeing the mischief in his eyes and the smile he was trying to hide.

"Jacob. We're in church." She waited for him to move his arm. It stayed in place. "Jacob? Do you think you could move your arm?" By this time, the other three men were watching them, biting back grins. "Jacob? If you hold me any tighter, I'll be on your knee. That wouldn't do at all."

Jacob took a look around, then leaned over, his breath wafting her hair from her ears as he spoke quietly. "You know, I kind of like that idea, keeping you close to me, maybe sitting on my knee. Think we can take up this conversation later?"

Finn stared at him, open mouthed, as a blush spread across her face. She could feel the pew shaking as the other three tried to control their laughter, knowing from her face that Jacob had been flirting with her.

"Jacob!" She went to continue when Timothy turned around, a frown on his face, at the slight noise.

Timothy studied his daughter flushed face, the smirk on Jacob's and the barely controlled grins on Blackie, Josh and Simon's faces before he shook his head and turned, bending over to say something to Mary, who in turn had to control her own laughter. Peter and Anna looked back, an open grin on Peter's face.

Finn turned her head into Jacob's shoulder, wishing she was anywhere else but there. Then the music caught their attention and they were immersed in the service and the sermon

Jacob listened intently, thinking it was only God who would have chosen that very scripture for that morning. Seeking Him and finding the true treasure, he thought. Grand was right. That's what he was pointing me to and reminding me of.

After the service, Finn stood talking with an older lady in church, Jacob's arm tight around her as he held her at his side. She was having trouble following the conversation with him that close, but then something the woman said caught her attention and Finn nodded, finally understanding what she was being asked.

Jacob looked around at the small church and decided he had come home. This was family, even thought he had only started attending there. He nodded and spoke to the church family, not minding the speculative glances thrown his way as they caught sight of his hold on Finn before they smiled and nodded at him.

Timothy stopped beside him, his head tilted as he studied first Jacob, then Finn, and then Jacob's hold on her.

"We need to talk, Jacob." His eyes caught Jacob's, who nodded, knowing that the conversation was already overdue.

"We do, Timothy. Do you have time this afternoon?"

———

98

"I was planning on having an afternoon-long nap and then visiting friends. I think I can work you in somewhere there." Timothy grinned at the look Jacob threw him.

"You had me going there, Timothy." Jacob grinned in return. "I'll come find you."

"You know where to find me. I'll be in the study more than likely. I have to work on the men's Bible study for Tuesday night. I'd like it if you could join us."

"I'll plan on that. Thank you."

Finn had turned just as her father walked away, a satisfied look on his face. Her brows lowered, she glanced between him and Jacob, finding Jacob watching her.

"Where to now, love?" Jacob caught her hand as they walked out of the church.

Finn stopped, her face tilted up to the fat lazy snowflakes floating down from the sky, the sound of the church carillon filling the air with Christmas hymns. She felt content and happy, a strange combination for her, she thought.

"I don't know, Jacob. We usually just spend Sundays relaxing or visiting with friends."

He nodded, drawing her with him. "Let's walk through the downtown area. I know the stores are open, but I don't shop on Sundays, not unless I have to. I'd just like to play tourist for a few hours."

"We can do that. Lunch will there when we get home, or Eddie has his hotdog cart set up in the town square."

"That sounds like a plan. I don't think I've ever eaten a hot dog in a snow storm before." He dodged the elbow she threw at him. "Let's pretend today there's no one after us. We're just friends out to spend some time together."

She studied his face once again, catching the softened look on it as he looked down at her, even as he tugged her hat lower on her hair before doing the same with his, catching her hand in his once more.

They didn't see the man who followed them all through the town, waiting for an opportunity to approach them, but not finding one. He cursed to himself. He wanted this over. Once Jacob was out of the way, he would have the Whitson fortune and own this town. That's what drove him.

Jacob turned from warming his hands over the fire and faced Timothy, who sat, open Bible on his knee, watching the younger man, remembering how it had felt when he had faced Mary's father.

"Jacob, sit. I won't bite. We've already told you how glad we are you're in Finn's life. That's not changing, is it?"

Jacob shook his head. "Not if I can help it, Timothy. She means too much to me, already. It's just this danger I'm in. I feel like I'm bringing it to her and to you."

"In a way you are, but Finn was already in danger. Thanks to you and your friends, that danger is over for her." Timothy studied the younger man. "Talk to me, Jacob. What are your feelings for my girl?"

Jacob stared at the floor, not quite sure how to respond. "I want to get to know her better, Timothy. She's precious, a treasure. One thing I do not want to do is hurt her. She's given me her trust and I don't want to break that. If it wasn't for what I'm going through."

The two men talked for a while longer before Jacob rose. He had to spend time in prayer, he knew, and today was the day he had to do that. He felt that the culmination of what he was going through was close and he needed to be prepared for that.

Chapter 17

Blackie came looking for Jacob three days later, knowing it was going to be a tough day for him. His father had called, letting him know that he had talked to Jacob, that Aaron's body had been exhumed the day before and that the autopsy would be that day. Jacob looked up from the table in the study. Timothy had told him to start using the table there for his work, he would be family soon anyway, and had just laughed at the look Finn threw her father.

"Jacob?"

"Blackie? Aren't you working?"

He nodded. "I am. Right now, my work is to be with you. Dad called."

Jacob looked down, blinking rapidly, sorrow on his face. "I hate this, Blackie. I hate having to do this. I should have done it back then."

"Not necessarily, Jacob. Who would have thought this would have come up? I know your Grand had health issues." Blackie paused, seeing movement at the door, and watching as Finn slipped into the room and into a chair near the door. He motioned for her to come closer but she shook her head, tapping her watch. He nodded, knowing she had slipped home for a few moments, just to see how Jacob was.

"But I still should have."

"Did the authorities suggest it?"

Jacob nodded. "They gave me that option, but I just wasn't considering that it was anything but natural causes."

"Who suggested that you not do it?" Blackie waited, his eyes on Jacob, even as he heard Finn rise and come towards Jacob, pulling up a chair beside him and reaching for his hands as she sat.

"The lawyer!" He raised his head, his eyes on first Blackie and then Finn. "The lawyer told me it wasn't necessary. Now I know why. He wanted to hide what he did." His fingers gripped Finn's tightly. He paused as he heard soft words from her and realized she was praying, praying for him, for the medical examiner, for the detectives, for his friends. Then he heard her pray for the lawyer and was puzzled at that until he realized that she was right to do so. That's what we're supposed to do, isn't it, Lord, pray for those who despitefully use us? And I haven't been.

Blackie raised his head when Finn was done, watching the couple in front of him, knowing that Jacob would soon know if it was a natural death or murder.

Jacob reached and hugged Finn, listening to her speak to him before she kissed his cheek and slipped away, back to her work. He watched her go, not wanting her to, but knowing she had to. He turned back to his work, struggling to

———

101

concentrate but praying that he could, that what he was creating in graphics for the churches would bring a message with them.

Hours later, he was vaguely aware of Blackie rising and leaving the room and then coming back, moving to sit beside him, just waiting for him to look up.

"Jacob? Are you at a point you can stop for the day?"

Jacob looked at him, then back at his computer screen. "Five minutes, maybe? Why?"

"We need to talk but you need to finish that first. I'll be back."

Jacob watched him walk away, then turned back, his heart sinking, knowing Blackie likely had an answer for him and he wasn't going to like it.

He finally rose, seeing Finn standing in the doorway, and went to her, welcoming her hug. Blackie stopped behind her, just waiting, a look on his face Jacob was familiar enough with. It would not be good news.

"Blackie?"

Blackie nodded at the question in Jacob's voice. "Let's sit. I spoke with Dad and we need to talk."

Jacob nodded, even as he dropped to the couch, Finn's hand tight in his. He looked down, not wanting to acknowledge Blackie, then sighed.

"Blackie? You have news?"

"I do, Jacob." Blackie bit his lip, not wanting to continue.

"He was murdered, wasn't he? The lawyer?"

"He was. I'm sorry, Jacob. The police will be calling you with the official report, but Dad got permission for me to tell you. The medical examiner found traces of trauma to the head. How it was missed, we don't know. The police have issued a warrant for the lawyer's arrest for murder. He's not in your hometown. They suspect he is here in Mistletoe and that he's been the one planting what you've found."

Finn finally spoke, her cheek resting against Jacob's shoulder. "That would make awful sense, now wouldn't it? How do we keep Jacob safe?"

Blackie's eyes searched first hers, then moved to Jacob, seeing his nod of comprehension. "We need to keep you safe, Finn. It's obvious to everyone you two share a bond with one another. He'll use you to get to Jacob."

"That's what I was afraid you'd say." She sighed. "I'm not giving up my life, though. I can tell you that right now."

"We don't expect you to. Dad has asked that I shadow you as much as I can. You're likely safe here at home, but at the shop, when you're out, even with Jacob, I'll be there." He looked at Jacob, making a face. "Sorry, buddy. I don't want to cut in on your budding romance."

Jacob shook his head, his eyes on Finn's head. "That's okay, I think. Is it, Finn? This is all new territory to me. I've never really dated before."

She looked up at him, a frown in place. "Is this what you and Dad talked about, what he won't tell me, just says ask you?" At his nod, she laid her head back down. "Then, yes, it's fine. Not how I ever expected to date anyone though. Stop laughing, Blackie. Your turn will come."

Blackie tried to control his chuckles but had difficulty as she frowned at him. "Sorry, guys. Finn, you're too funny for words at time."

"Stop insulting my lady, Blackie." He hugged Finn tighter. "Now what, Blackie? What does your Dad recommend we do?"

"He's going to head this way along with a couple of his operatives. They'll help by being in the background. He's trying to pull information and records but has hit a dead end on your lawyer. Norman Earl doesn't seem to exist before ten years ago."

"Norman Earl?" Finn sat up, a look of horror on her face. "No. It can't be."

"Finn? Talk to me?" Jacob reached for her hands, finding hers cold and clammy. "What about the name bothers you?"

"Blackie, tell your Dad to look for Earl Norman. It just can't be."

"What can't be?" Jacob stood and watched as Finn ran from the room, her hand to her mouth. "Blackie?"

Blackie shrugged. "I have no idea, Jacob. Let me talk to Dad." He paused, a thought crossing his mind. "Didn't you say she was assaulted when she was young and couldn't remember who it was? Did this fellow she named live here?"

"I have no idea. I'll find someone and ask." He headed for the kitchen, knowing Mary would be there. He dreaded having to bring up old news.

Finn walked slowly through the downtown area. Jacob had asked her to meet him near the Christmas tree that noon, and she had readily agreed. It had been two days since Blackie had broken the news about Jacob's grandfather and he had been really quiet. She searching, finding him watching her approach him, a large smile on his face. She walked into his hug, relishing how cherished he made her feel.

She tilted back her head to look up at him. "Jacob? You wanted a hot dog from Eddie's cart?"

He laughed as he hugged her tighter. "Not really. I just wanted to see you. We need to talk at some point about where we see us going, but today, let's find somewhere we can just sit. Your mom sent a picnic lunch if you want."

"Mom did? Wow! She's really wrapped around your finger, isn't she?"

He laughed as he reached for the pack he had set down. "No. She's just helping out a budding romance. She told me she remembers how she felt when she and your dad were dating, how the little things were more important than anything else."

"Mom said that?" Finn turned to walk with him, her hand in his. "Is that what we are? An 'us'? A budding romance?"

"I would like to think so. That is, if it's okay with you." He watched her face intently.

"It is, Jacob. You make me feel so different from anyone else. I've prayed about this and I know God's hand is in it." Her words faded away even as her steps slowed until she had stopped walking, people bumping into them, some walking around them with glares, others with words of apology.

"Finn?" Jacob looked around, not seeing anything to be concerned about. "Finn? Why did you stop?" He felt her hand tighten on his. "Finn?"

"Well, well, well. Look who we have here. Finola Bronagh. I thought you had died that day."

Jacob could feel Finn shaking in fright, but couldn't see the speaker. The voice was familiar but he couldn't place it. A movement to his left caught his attention and he watched in horror as a man emerged from the crowd and ripped Finn's hand from his. An arm snaked around her waist, holding her arms tight to her body, and a knife appeared, held to her throat. His eyes raised, he saw the man they had all been looking for standing in front of him, holding the love of his life literally in his hands.

"Norman? Put down the knife. Let's talk."

"There's nothing to talk about. You ruined it all. You should have just let sleeping dogs lie, or in this case, left your grandfather buried." He tightened his hold on Finn, the knife waving towards him, even as the crowd realized there was an armed man in their midst and they moved back, some almost running to get away. They kept Blackie and his father's men from getting to Jacob and Finn.

"There is always a reason to talk. I just want to know why?" Jacob moved forward slightly, determined to get to Finn.

"Your grandfather had a fortune, one you never knew about. I deserve it. I was chased from this town years ago. Partly her fault." The knife headed for Finn's face and she ducked even as she gave a small scream, startling the crowd into moving back into a tighter mass, blocking Blackie where he had managed to get closer to his two friends. "You don't deserve it."

"No, this is not about money, is it? It's about power. That's what you want. You want power and think by trying to take over this town you'll get it. You'd never get that, even if you got Grand's fortune. The town charter precludes that."

"That can be changed. We all know that." He shoved Finn forward, the knife now waving at Jacob. "You can sign over your share to me."

Jacob shook his head. "Sorry, but I can't. The charter is very clear. I've had someone look into it, someone well versed in that kind of challenge. It's iron clad. If you kill me and get control of Grand's fortune, that's all you get. The portions of town land and buildings he owns goes to the other four founding families. Even if you got rid of us all, you'd never get the town. That's been taken care of." He reached out a hand. "Come on now. Let me have the knife."

"Not happening." He turned his attention to the crowd and then back to Finn. "She'll die first. You'll watch her die before you do."

Jacob shook his head in sorrow. "That's not going to happen, Norman. Or should I call you Earl?" He saw Finn's recognition of the name. "It wasn't bad enough that you beat Finn up years ago, leaving her to die? Now, you want to finish it. That won't happen. Finn, now."

Finn allowed her body to suddenly relax, dropping away from the knife even as Jacob sprang forward. She felt herself released and then pulled away from the men, safe in Blackie's arm. He turned her from the fight, handing her off to Josh, even as he moved forward.

A groan from Jacob caught his attention and he sprang forward, taking Norman down, even as Jacob collapsed, a hand to his arm.

Blackie shoved the man at Tom who had appeared through the crowd and handcuffed him, dropping to his knees beside Jacob, hands reaching to assess him.

"Whit? Are you okay?"

Jacob nodded. "He caught my arm with the knife, but I don't think he did much damage." He looked around, his face white. "Help me sit up. I don't want Finn to see me on the ground."

"Too late for that, Whit." Blackie looked up as Finn moved into Jacob's space, tears on her face, her hand helping to remove his jacket. "Just a flesh wound. You're fortunate, Whit. I thought it was worse. I thought he got you in the stomach."

"His elbow did. That's what threw me off and let him slice me." He looked at his arm, then at Finn. "Help me up. Please. I want away from this crowd."

Blackie's hand steadied Jacob and then led him to Finn's shop, where she shoved him down in her chair and fetched the first aid box for Blackie.

She stood, watching Jacob's face. "It was really Earl Norman, Jacob?"

"It was. I wasn't sure, Finn. No one knew where he went when he left here. It's finally over for you." He watched as she struggled with the knowledge.

"And it's over for you as well, isn't it, Jacob? You have the answers you were sent here to find?"

Blackie took a look at them, then moved away, letting them have privacy. Jacob nodded to him, then reached for Finn, drawing her down on his knee. "I did, Finn. I found the treasure Grand wanted me to find. My faith. But more than that, I found a more precious treasure than I ever dreamed of finding."

She looked at him, her hands captured in his, not sure what he was saying. "And that is?"

"You, my love. I found you. Please don't shove me away."

Finn shook her head. "I couldn't even if I wanted to. And I don't." Her last few words were quiet, but loud enough that Jacob caught them.

His arms drew her close as his mouth found hers, capturing her lips in their first kiss. He leaned his forehead on hers finally. "I talked to your Dad. He's welcomed me to the family. But it's up to you, love, where we go from here."

Finn nodded, glad Jacob was the man of God he was. "We'll take it slow, Jacob. You've been through a lot and you need to heal from that first. I'm not going anywhere."

"Neither am I, love. Neither am I."

❀ ❀ ❀ ❀ ❀

Blackie approached them later at the B&B, finding them sitting on the couch in the living room, staring at the fire.

Jacob raised his head, not knowing if he would like what he had to hear.

"Jacob? Finn? You're both okay? Good." Blackie looked at his hands. "Simon will be by later, but I have news. Chief Adams has been found and charged. I'm not sure what all he's facing. Simon can tell you that. Dad had more information on Norman. He was in this town and has admitted to being the one who attacked you, Finn. He won't say why but speculation is that he was jealous even then of the ancestry you can trace back. His family was never great, into crime for years. He's facing a number of charges.

"He has admitted that he planned to take over the practice of your old lawyer, Whit. He had no relation to him, making that up. He had never been to law school, his certificates and diplomas are forged. We speculate that your grandfather had suspicions about him and was ready to pull all his legal work and take it elsewhere. Norman didn't want that. As to why he killed your grandfather, he's not saying."

"I suspect he thought if Grand was out of the way and he could get rid of me, he'd bring forth a new will, forged of course, leaving everything to him. Have them search for that, if you will." Jacob sat back, his hand held tight in both of Finn's. "It doesn't really matter now, does it?"

Blackie shook his head. "It doesn't. Your Grand sent you back here to find your roots. I think Norman took it one step further, sending you on that hunt, something I don't think your grandfather would have done."

"No, I don't think he would have. He would have left a letter directing me back here and who to talk to about the town and my ancestry and that never happened." He looked down at Finn. "But somehow, Blackie, I don't think we're done. There's still something out there that's unresolved, and I can't determine which one of us four that it involves. We're the newcomers to town. It has to be one of us or Finn would have solved the problem years ago."

"I think you're right, Whit." Blackie sat back, his eyes on the fire as well. "God kept you safe. You may have felt like you were hunting in vain, but you weren't. You found your treasure." With that, he rose and walked away, leaving Finn and Jacob together.

———

Shedding his suit coat, Jacob moved through Finn's store six months later, his eyes searching for his love. Anna waved at him. Finn had taken Anna on as a partner, pleasing both ladies.

"She's upstairs in the apartment, Jacob. She didn't think you'd be back yet." Anna grinned as he dropped his briefcase and coat in the office and then headed for the stairs.

"I didn't expect to be either but the meetings went well and quickly. You're sure she's upstairs? She's been known to disappear a time or two."

Anna started to laugh. "I'm sure. She just headed up there with some flowers or plants or something, I think. She said she wanted it ready for us before the weekend." Peter and Anna had married about a month ago, and Finn had had the apartment upstairs remodeled for them as a thank you.

Jacob grinned as he took the stairs two at a time, searching for his lady love in the apartment. He found her in the room she had designated at the office. He leaned against the door jamb, hands in his suit pants pockets, a smile on his face as he watched her move around the room, a smile on her face, humming a worship song from the Sunday before.

Finn paused, sensing eyes on her, turning, her face lighting up as she saw Jacob standing there, running towards him. He caught her close, a kiss dropping on her lips, as he hugged her

"You're back early!" Finn leaned back. "How come?"

"The meetings went well. I've gotten some new contracts. That new office in my house will come in handy. Thank you for designing it."

She hugged him again. "I'm so glad." She grabbed his hand. "Come look through the apartment. Tell me what you think and if I missed anything."

They wandered through, their voices quiet as they discussed it, ending up in the living room, near the large bay window. Jacob watched the afternoon light play across her face, falling further in love with her.

Finn looked around. "Have I missed anything, Jacob, that you can see? I don't think I have but it's been a crazy few months."

Jacob's eyes were on her face. "I think you've covered just about everything for them, Finn. If not, you can also add to what you've done after they move in. Peter and Anna are so happy with the apartment."

"I know. I think they'll be happy here." She turned in a circle. "But I still think I've missed something." She took a step to move away, stopping as he caught her hand. "Jacob?"

He moved in front of her. "I think you did miss one thing, love."

"I did?" She turned in a circle. "I don't see what. What did I?" She turned back to find him on his knee, a beautiful ruby ring held up in his fingers. Her hand went to her mouth as he reached for her left hand, holding it tightly.

"Just this, love. Over the last few months, I have come to love a beautiful, sensitive, caring, God-fearing, God-following woman who makes every day a joy for all around her. She cares for her family and her friends, works tirelessly to make life better for those around her who have less than she does. Finola, I love you more than I thought I could ever love anyone. That love has grown each and every day. You are a treasure that Grand didn't see coming, I don't think, even though he prayed for you every day of his life. Will you marry me, grow old with me, help me to find the treasure in life that God has for us?"

Finn nodded, unable to speak as tears flowed down her face. She finally found her voice. "I will, Jacob. I will. You are my treasure as well. I love you deeper each day. God has prepared you just for me."

He slid the ring on her finger, then stood, sweeping her into his arms and sealing their vow with a kiss. Thank you, Lord, was his thought. You have provided a lady for me to love, whose worth is far about the rubies You created.

Dear Readers

Thank you for picking up the story of Jacob and Finola, his Finn, as she's called by those who love her. Jacob had no idea when he walked into Mistletoe what God had in store for him. He certainly didn't expect to own part of the town.

He found his town, his ancestry, and more importantly, a lady to love, whose worth he decided was far about rubies. Finn found the love of her life, despite the search and trouble they both faced.

My father often quoted Proverbs 31 when describing godly woman. He never said, but I suspect this is how he viewed my Mom. As I write this, his 92nd birthday is fast approaching as is the sixth anniversary of his graduation to heaven. I miss his words of wisdom and his quiet dry humour. I miss his "you did a wonderful job" when I've accomplished a renovation around the house. Dad is how I pictured Jacob's grandfather, a quiet man of few words but with a great love of family and a deep love of God.

Where is your treasure? Here on earth or up in heaven? I know where mine is. In heaven. God has given that confidence of that. He has also promised that if we seek him with all our hearts we will find Him.

Jacob was sent on a hunt for an earthly treasure, instead finding the reminder of where his greatest treasure is. My prayer for you, my readers, is that you find that great treasure God has for you.

Blessings.

Ronna

Mistrust and Medicine in Mistletoe

Mistletoe Treasures

Book 2

By

Ronna M. Bacon

Lamentations 3:25 The Lord is good to those who wait for Him, To the soul who seeks Him.

Psalm 9:10 And those who know Your name will put their trust in You; For You, Lord, have not forsaken those who seek You.

Deuteronomy 4: 29 But from there you will seek the Lord your God, and you will find Him if you seek Him with all your heart and with all your soul.

New King James Version

Table of Contents

She crouched in her closet, praying he didn't find her that night. She hated him but was too young to leave home. Why, Lord, was her constant cry. She could hear him calling her and tried to make herself smaller. She knew when he found her, he would beat her and that she didn't want again. Her brother wasn't there to protect her. He said he was coming back for her, but he hadn't come. She hadn't seen him in three years and missed him.

The closet door was yanked open and the clothing roughly shoved aside as her arm was grabbed and she was hauled from her hiding spot. She saw the murder in his eyes and knew tonight, it just might happen. She could hear her mother talking, but she wasn't trying to help her. She was talking about how bad she was, how ungrateful, that she should be sharing her fortune with them. The girl, teen, young woman, for she was in her early twenties by now, didn't know what she meant.

Twenty minutes later, she lay in a broken heap, her back bruised and battered, blood seeping from numerous cuts. She lay there, unable or unwilling to move, knowing if she did, he'd only return. She missed her real daddy, she thought. Why, God, did you take him and bring this monster into my life?

She finally crept to her bathroom and into the shower, tears falling as the water from the shower stung and then soothed. She couldn't dress her wounds, not where they were. She slipped into her night clothes and then into her bed, her eyes red but dry, her tears all fallen. She stared at the window, praying for death, praying for relief, but knowing she'd have to rise early the next morning, put on her dress clothes and go to the job she hated but one that she had no choice about. He had almost broken her that night. It was only a matter of time, she thought. Lord, I don't know why, but I'm in Your hands. Protect me. Help me to find somewhere I can run to. Help me to get away from this monster they want me to call father, but that I can't. You know I can't do that.

She shuddered at the thought, her eyes finally closing as she slept. She didn't see the dark form move away from the house, anger burning inside him. He had heard her cries and pleas to stop but knew the police wouldn't interfere. He needed to find her help and soon. His eyes raised to the sky as he prayed as he had never prayed before. Please, dear Lord, protect this child of Yours.

Chapter 1

Levi Blackwell, or Blackie as he was known to his friends, studied the form in front of him and finally tossed it aside, running his hands through his golden blond curls. He wasn't interested in becoming a paramedic, he knew that for sure, but just what he wanted to do, that was the question. The town doctor has asked, no, he thought, had begged him to stay and become a paramedic for the town. That was something he knew he just couldn't do. He had had too many nights of awakening, drenched in sweat, at the dreams he experienced after his eight years in the armed forces. He knew he just couldn't do that any more. Right now, he was seated at a desk in the small town of Mistletoe, brought there by a letter from a lawyer, a lawyer for his friend, Jacob Whitson. Only the lawyer had been arrested for the murder of his friend's grandfather and was behind the adventure his friend and his lady had drawn him into.

He raised his head as he heard voices from the reception area, one he recognized as Jacob's. The other, a female voice, he didn't know. He scooted his chair back enough he could see out the door, but could only see Jacob. He could hear Jacob's laughter as he teased whoever it was out there and her quiet response and laughter.

He listened as he heard Jacob thanking her for the food she had brought and then his laughter at her comment that Josh told her she had to hand deliver the order to Blackie. Jacob told her he was in the back office and to head that way, but before she could reply, her phone rang.

Then, a sharp exclamation came in her voice, and he was on his feet, heading that way, catching the grim look on Jacob's face. He watched as the woman turned back to face Jacob, concern etched on her face as she spoke into her phone.

"Give me ten minutes to change and I'll meet you at the entrance to the trail. The only thing is, we don't have a medic to go with us. Paul's out of town this week." She pocketed her phone, turning towards the door, as Jacob's hand came out to stop her.

"Julia? What's the problem?"

She spun, her long dark brown hair sparking with red highlights as her hazel eyes turned to him. "The Evans' youngest girl is missing. She's six. We're heading out to search for her. I guess from what Donald said, she's been missing since earlier this morning and no one realized it."

"Do you need help on the search and rescue?"

She nodded. "We can use the help. But what we need is someone with medical training."

———

116

"The concern being?" Jacob's eyes met Blackie's amber ones, a question in them.

"She's deaf, Jacob. She's not going to hear us calling her. Donald will have his dog, but we need someone who can assess her when we find her. The weather's to change this afternoon for the worse."

"Blackie? Can you help?" Jacob turned back to his friend, a plea in his eyes that Julia couldn't see.

Blackie started to shake his head, then caught the look of fear on Julia's face. He shrugged. "What all you do need?"

Julia spun at the new voice, startled, a hand going to her throat. "Excuse me?"

"I asked what you needed." Blackie sighed. As much as he hated to admit it to himself, he couldn't walk away from anyone in need, particularly a young child. "I was a medic in the armed forces."

Julia's face lit up. "You were? Do you have some time that you can use to help us search? I can't guarantee how long it will take."

Blackie shook his head. "That's not important. It's important that we find this young girl. I need to swing by the B&B and grab some gear. Where are we meeting?"

She frowned before looking at Jacob, who grinned at her.

"This is my friend, Levi Blackwell, or Blackie as we call him. Blackie, this is Julia Whittaker."

She nodded at him, then tilted her head. "Are you sure?"

He nodded. "Just let me know where to meet you and I'll be there."

Thirty minutes later, Blackie stood watching at the search and rescue team sorted itself out. He studied the ground, a frown in place, not seeing the small footprints in the bits of snow that he would expect. He raised his eyes to the sky, seeing the gray clouds, and knew that with only two weeks to Christmas, they would likely have snow today.

Julia approached him. "You're with me. Have you done search and rescue before?"

He gave an abrupt nod. "In the armed forces."

She paused, a look crossing her face he couldn't read, before she pointed to one of the trails. "We're taking that one."

"I don't see any small footprints." Blackie looked around once more.

"I know. That's bizarre. I would think there would be. But her father insists she came out here. I don't know the reasoning. We have to check this out, then move on."

———

117

Blackie nodded as he shouldered his pack, tugged his knitted hat down lower on his ears and forehead and pulled on his gloves. "I'll follow. You know the area."

They didn't see the man standing back in the shadows, watching the search teams move out, or see him head after them. He had been hired to get Julia in any way he could. Having a man with her complicated things.

Snow began falling about an hour after they set out. Blackie finally pulled Julia to a stop.

"We'll never find her in this."

She nodded, fear on her face. "I know. And because she can't hear us, that makes it worse." She turned as she heard a noise, heading towards it.

Blackie's hand reached out. "Let me go first, please?"

She shook her heard. "You're not trained in this type of search and rescue. I am." She pulled away, even as she heard the roar of an ATV approaching.

Blackie spun, then dove for Julia, wrapping his arms around her and throwing them both away from the trail. A glancing blow from the machine sent them off balance and tumbling over the edge of a ridge, to roll and slide down to the bottom. The man on the ATV stood, trying to spot them through the snow and unable to. He finally left, hoping that what he had been hired to accomplish had been done. If not, he'd have to try again.

Looking around as he heard his name called, Jacob waited for his friends, Simon and Josh, to catch up with him. He didn't like the looks on their faces.

"Whit, have you seen Blackie since this morning?" Simon Gardner was an officer with the county police.

Jacob shook his head, a small grimace crossing his face. "He headed out with Julia on that search and rescue."

"What search and rescue?" Simon studied the area around them, always on alert.

"Something about the youngest Evans girl? She spoke with Donald and then Blackie volunteered as they needed someone with medical training."

"I don't like that." Simon pointed back at the office building Jacob had just locked up. "Can we go inside out of the snow?"

Stamping their boots as they entered, Jacob motioned to the chairs in the reception area. "We can sit there or head for my office."

"Your office, I think, Whit. We may need the computer and your phone." Simon headed that way. "What time did they head out?"

"Around 10, maybe? It was just after you sent Julia here with the food, Josh." He looked over at his friend, sitting at his computer, and booting it up.

"That would be about right. It's now 4? And you haven't seen them since?" Josh shared a look with Simon.

"We received word this morning that a hoax was being played out here in Mistletoe, Jacob. We've just been able to sort it out. Someone is after Julia and staged the disappearance of the Evans' girl."

Jacob stilled, his hand resting on the coffee pot he had reached to fill. "There was no disappearance? They're out in this weather for nothing?" At their nod, he replaced the coffee pot and reached for his jacket and gloves. "We need to go find Donald and see what he has to say."

Josh started at the computer. "I'm going to stay and see what research I can do for you, Simon. I may need to call Blackie's father and I don't want to do that until we know for sure what's going on."

Simon shook his head. "No, not a good idea. I'll call as soon as we find out anything at all. You have the names of those on the search team?"

Josh looked up, his eyes meeting Jacob, and then quickly scrawling them done, handing it to Simon. "I do, Simon. I've gotten to know them over the last year and I can't see one of them being involved." He sighed. "But then Jacob didn't see it coming with his lawyer, so who knows the name of the culprit this time."

Simon agreed. "Before we move off, let's spend some time in prayer. We need God's guidance on this one, I'm thinking."

Raising his head slightly, Blackie tried to move, finding himself unable to do so. He groaned as he stirred, his eyes blinking open to snow, the flakes large and soft as they tickled down on his face. He blinked again, trying to orient himself and unable to do so. He could feel his pack digging into his back and sharp pain in his left shoulder. He tried to reach for it and couldn't, for a moment unsure why. Then, becoming more alert, despite the cold and the pain, he looked around him and realized he had a lady wrapped tight in his arms. He frowned through the pain, not remembering who she was or even where they were. He finally raised himself up enough to move away from her, laying her gently down, before he stood, staggering a bit before he caught his balance.

Lord, where am I? I don't remember where I am. I think I know my name, but even that is a blur. He turned, pain driving him to his knees as he clutched his arm to himself. He groaned once more, knowing he had to move, had to get them both to safety, but knowing he was unable to. He tried to reach his phone and realized he didn't have it with him. Where was it, he thought?

He turned to his pack, pulling out a scarf to fashion a makeshift sling, and then reaching back in for some thermal aluminum blankets he had stuck in at the last moment. Moving very slowly and cautiously he scraped snow away from the shelter of the rocks and draped the first blanket down the rocks themselves and across the ground as much as he could. He stood, head bowed, as he gathered breath and strength to move once more.

Shifting the packs to make a windbreak, he crept on his knees towards the lady, stopping once more to study her. He shook his head, pain wracking through him at that. He didn't know her, did he? As carefully as he could, he gathered her close and crept slowly back to the shelter he had erected, sitting with his back to the rocks, cradling her close to keep her warm and drawing the remaining two blankets over them, tucking them in as best he could.

I've done what I can, Lord. Lead someone to us. I can't get us out of here, and this lady can't help either. He tilted his head for a moment to stare down at her before his eyes slid closed.

Simon looked around at the trail, watching as Donald searched for tracks.

"They did come this way, Donald?"

Donald, a local contractor, looked up at Simon's words, his eyes catching his, before he looked past him at Josh and Jacob. "They did. Julia started off on this trail." He looked around again. "With the snow, it's hard to catch their tracks. I have Betty bringing in her dog to help track them." He glanced up at the sky. "It's clearing and that means the temperature will drop."

"In other words, we need find them and now, before night totally falls." Simon paced the area, his eyes searching the ground, a frown on his face. He shared looks with Josh and Jacob, who nodded and then moved to each side of the trail, both searching even as Simon moved back to the middle of the trail, Donald watching them before he shook his head and moved away. His thoughts were that they had no clue what they were doing and they would just destroy the scent trail.

Simon looked up as he heard Josh call quietly to him from where he stood near the edge of the trial.

"What did you find, Josh?" Simon stood, his eyes on his friend before he looked over the edge of the ridge, a frown in place.

"Someone went over the edge, I think, Simon. I'm afraid it was Blackie." Josh looked around. "It's not that far down. I see a spot further along where we can get down to that area."

"Lead the way." Simon turned to find Jacob standing with them, ready to head over the edge as well.

They had disappeared by the time Donald had returned with Betty. He was angry, and Betty could get no reason for it from him. Her dog headed for the same area where the three men had stood.

"They were here, Donald, and for some reason have disappeared."

"They can't just have disappeared, Betty. You know that."

"What I know is that I think you've been leading us on a wild goose chase and caused harm to someone." She spoke to her dog and followed the men's footsteps, finding the trail they had taken.

Simon stood for a moment, his eyes searching the area before he felt Jacob's hand on his arm. He turned to where Jacob pointed, even as he heard Josh give a cry and drop to his knees there, pulling out the backpacks Blackie had stacked against the wind.

"Simon! Jacob!" He turned, his arm waving at them. "I've found them. Pray they're still alive."

The two other men scrambled through the snow, their feet slipping as they rushed forward. They could hear a woman's voice behind them, calling for them to wait.

Josh had dropped to his knees besides the two, carefully pulling back the blankets.

"Josh?" Simon was on the other side of them, bending over even as Jacob reached for the blankets.

"They're alive, Simon. I don't know how but they are. It looks as if Blackie's hurt in some way. I can't tell about Julia, though. Help me move them."

Hands reached for both Blackie and Julia. Blackie's arm tightened on Julia, refusing to give her up. Simon shook his head before he leaned over to Blackie and spoke.

<hr>

"Blackie, it's us. Come on, now. Let us have the lady. We'll take care of her for you."

Blackie roused slightly, his eyes flickering open and closed, before he sank back into blackness. Jacob reached for Julia, turning to lay her on one of the blankets even as Betty dropped beside him.

"She's alive?"

"She is, Betty. How, I don't know. Blackie seemed to do what he could to keep them both that way." Jacob looked around, his eyes on his three friends, then back on Betty. "Can you have the ambulance meet us at the beginning of the trail? We're not that far away."

"No, we're not. They can have the stretchers up top." She stood, her hand shading her eyes against the setting sun as she searched for Donald. "Now, where did he get to?"

"Who? Donald? Didn't he wait?"

She shook her head. "Doesn't look like it. Something's been off with this whole thing, Jacob. We'll need to look into it." She turned. "I'll head up where I can get some cell service and make the call. Can you three manage to get them up top?"

"We can. Go." Jacob watched as Betty ran as fast as she could through the snow, her dog on her heels.

"Jacob? How's Julia?"

"Not as cold as I thought. But she has a nasty cut on her head." Jacob turned to watch Blackie. "How's Blackie?"

"Dislocated shoulder, I think. And he seems to have taken the brunt of the cold." Josh stood for a moment. "Where's Donald? I thought he'd be here."

"That's what Betty asked. She's heading up to call for help. Can we manage to get them up there?"

"It will be easy for Julia. With Blackie, no matter how we carry him, it will hurt."

"He's not up to walking out, that's for sure." Simon stood for a moment. "I've swing him over my shoulders and carry him out. Can you to manage the packs?"

"We can. Let's get them out of here."

The three friends stood watching as the paramedics worked on the couple before Simon walked towards the ambulance, climbing aboard and finding a seat. He nodded at his friends as the doors shut and the vehicle moved off, gathering speed as it hit clearer roads.

Betty spoke from beside Jacob. "How are they?"

Jacob shrugged. "They didn't really know. Blackie's shoulder is hurt, that's about all." He looked around. "Where's Donald?"

Betty shook her head. "I have no idea. I haven't seen him."

Josh nodded. "Find him. I want to talk with him. So will Simon, not just as a friend of Blackie's, but as law enforcement. Something tells me this was all a set up." He turned and walked away with Jacob, leaving Betty staring at them, her mouth open before she snapped it shut and silently agreed with them. This was a set up, she thought. But which one was it? Julia who had lived here all her life? Or Blackie, new to town but a descendant of the founding families?

Chapter 3

Shaking his head in disbelief, Blackie shifted on the bed, grimacing slightly at the pain from his shoulder, dislocated in the fall but now repaired.

"There is no way I'd be out in a snow storm, guys. You know me better than that." He glared at Josh and Jacob as they laughed at him.

"You were, trust us on that, Blackie. You volunteered to help search for a young girl." Jacob stopped, his eyes on the doorway where Simon stood. "Only thing is, we can't figure out how you two ended up where you did."

"Two? There were two of us?"

Josh nodded, a grin on his face. "There were two. You headed out with Julia, then never came back. We went looking for you and found you."

Blackie shook his head again, sitting up to the side of the bed and reaching for the bag of clothes Josh had set on it. "I still don't see me doing that. You know me and search and rescues now."

"We do, but you went anyway." Jacob's hand steadied him as he stood, heading for the bathroom to change.

"How'd we end up where we did?" His voice came through the door.

"That's what we're working on, Blackie. From what the physician said, it looks as if you were struck a glancing blow to the side, likely from an ATV, and sent over the side of the ridge. Until we find the driver or either of you remember what happened, we won't know for sure."

The door popped open and Blackie stood there, sling in hand. "Doesn't this Julia remember?" He allowed Jacob to adjust the sling for him.

Simon shook his head. "I haven't had a chance to talk with her. She was unconscious when you came in last night. I'm heading that way now."

"Not without me, you're not." Blackie reached for his jacket and wallet. "I don't have my phone with me."

Jacob stared at him. "You don't? You never go anywhere without it."

"I know. That's what's so strange." He walked towards the door, as Simon's hand came out to stop him.

"Blackie, we need to pray over this. Someone likely tried to kill one of you yesterday. I don't know which one. I've talked to the force here. They can't figure it out, but there's something they are not saying about Julia, and I have no idea what it is."

———

124

Blackie stood for a moment in the hospital room door, watching the young woman who stood near the bed, folding her hospital gown, before she looked up. He winced as he saw how white she was, the dark circles under her eyes.

Julia had sensed someone watching her and glanced up, her gaze locking with Blackie's. Her eyes searched his face for a moment before she gave an inward sigh. Not someone else to walk in and walk out of my life. Lord, I need someone to protect me. I know You do, but it would be nice to have someone here, to stand between me and the harassment and brutalities I face.

"Hi." Blackie walked towards her, stopping abruptly when he saw fear flicker across her face and a slight withdrawing. "You must be Julia. I'm sorry I don't remember us meeting before today, but I sure wish I did."

Julia frowned, her head tilted as she watched his face and saw the honesty and something else she couldn't read on it. "That's right. I'm Julia. You were kind enough to help search yesterday." She sighed. "Only I hear tell we didn't get too far."

"Do you remember what happened?"

"I do, unfortunately. I saw something off the trail, went to look at it, heard you yell, and then we were falling. I remember an ATV there." She looked up, fear in her eyes. "Who was it, Blackie? May I call you that?" At his nod, she continued. "Who did that? They left us for dead, you know."

"I know. I have no idea. Simon is working on that with the Mistletoe force." He looked at the door and then back at her. "Do you have a ride somewhere?"

She shook her head, even as the door slammed back against the wall and a tall hulking man entered. She gave a stifled scream and moved back, her face full of fear.

Blackie watched the man, ready to step in if needed.

"You just had to go and do that, didn't you?" The man stood, fists clenched, staring down at Julia.

"Do what?"

"Be found like you were. Always chasing after some guy, aren't you?" The man's hand raised and struck Julia across the face, knocking her into the bed.

Blackie gave a cry of rage and jumped towards the man, his right hand catching his arm and spinning him around. No match for him with only one arm, Blackie tumbled backwards as the man's fist connected with his jaw, slamming into the door frame and then crumpling to the floor, to lie in a still heap.

The man turned back to Julia, curses raining down on her as his hand came back to once more strike her, this time drawing blood from her mouth.

Simon slid to a stop in the doorway, instantly assessing the situation and together with Jacob, approaching the man and taking him to the floor, holding him there despite his struggles. A lucky blow from the man's hand caught Simon's across the eyes, temporarily blinding him as he felt for his hand cuffs. He blinked rapidly and snapped the cuffs in place, hauling the man to his feet and to the door. Tom, one of the town officers, stood there, ready to take control on Simon's prisoner.

"I would be quiet, man, if I were you." Tom read the man his rights, finally getting through to him that he was under arrest.

The man struggled to turn, his eyes seeking Julia, hatred and murder in them, before Tom hauled him away.

Jacob was on his knees beside Blackie, even as Blackie righted himself and leaned back against the wall. Blackie's eyes sought Julia, wincing at the red hand print on her face and the blood on her mouth.

"Help me up, Jacob." Jacob helped Blackie, despite protesting such a move.

Blackie moved towards Julia, stopping as she cringed back from him.

"Julia? We need to get your face looked at."

She shrugged. "Why? They won't do anything. They never had before, so why now?"

"This isn't the first time?" Simon stood beside Blackie, a dark look on his face. "The police did nothing?"

She shook her head. "Why would they? He's Chief Adams' brother-in-law. Unfortunately, he's married to my mother." She held up a hand at their protest. "No, he's not my father. Thank God for that." She looked past him at the older physician and sighed. "All right, Paul. You can look and take pictures, but it won't do any good."

"It will this time, Julia. Adams is out of being in control as are a lot of his cronies. Simon here is helping out to restructure our force. He'll listen." Paul, the physician, shot a look at Simon's face. "And it looks as if Hal has assault on an officer added to the charges today."

"He's done that before and it's always been shuffled under the rug." She stood, gathering the bag she had been given. "Why does God let this happen, Paul? We've discussed this before. No one can tell me that."

Paul nodded towards Blackie. "Ask him. He's not from this town. He may have an answer for you we don't."

Her gaze shifted to Blackie, catching that expression on his face again and she frowned even as Paul set her down on the bed and assessed her face. She winced as he touched the mark.

"It's going to bruise, Julia. How many times has this happened to you?"

She shrugged, her eyes still on Blackie. "Too many, I guess. But you know. I've tried to report it and been told it's my fault." The men heard the pleading and the tears in her voice even as she blinked rapidly. "No one, except you, has ever believed me. Jonathan took off as soon as he could, and that was fifteen years ago, when he was 17, to escape this. And Hal usually didn't hit where it showed."

"I know, Julia. That still doesn't make it acceptable or right." He looked up at the men standing there, catching the look on Blackie's face, and nodded. Good, he thought. God has finally brought in a rescuer for Julia. It's about time. Thank you, Lord. Protect them both. Hal won't take the arrest quietly.

Julia finally stood, reaching for her bag, to find Josh had already picked it up, grinning at her as she frowned. Jacob and Simon had already headed out for the vehicle, Josh following them. Blackie hesitated for a moment.

"Where do you want to go, Julia?"

She shrugged. "I can't go to Mom's. She's always stuck up for him and having had him arrested, she'll be as livid with me as he was." She sighed. "I have no idea, Blackie. It doesn't look as if I'm wanted in this town."

Blackie wrapped an arm around her, feeling her stiffen and then relax against him as he walked her towards the door. "Finn's parents have a room available, I know. Or they did. If they don't, you can have mine and I'll bunk in with Jacob. That won't be the first time we've done that."

She shook her head. "They won't do that."

Blackie grinned, even as he tucked her into Jacob's truck and slid in beside her. "They will. I'm sure you know Finn."

"Everyone in town knows Finn. And yes, I do. We had classes together." She stared out the window. "I need to stop by Mom's and collect some clothes. I'll also need to pack up my stuff on another day and find somewhere else to live. I can't go back there."

"We'll take you today, Jewel, and then back again on whatever day you want. And we'll find you somewhere you can live. Between the four of us here and Finn's family, we own quite a few buildings in town." Blackie shared a look with Simon and then Jacob. Josh had headed back to his cafe to make sure all was set for Monday

She spun, surprise on her face. "How is that possible? None of you are from town? Other than Finn."

"We're all descendants, believe it or not, of the town's founders. We've been brought back here for a purpose, what purpose we're still working on." Blackie watched the emotions flicker across her face, hope rising within her.

Blackie stood just inside the house door, listening to the abuse and berating that Julia was facing from her mother. His heart broke, knowing he would never hear those words from his own mother, and wishing desperately he could just pack Julia up and take her to his home. He knew his mother would just sweep her into her arms and give her the biggest hug as would his father. His two sisters would just take her over and make her part of the family.

He looked up as he heard her footsteps coming towards him, rapid, almost running. He caught her into a one-armed hug and pulled her out of the house, the abuse continuing as he tucked her back into the truck. He stood for a moment, staring back at the open door and then shaking his head, a prayer raised for protection and healing for his Jewel, he crawled in beside her, reaching to cradle her against him, sharing a long look with Simon, who nodded and then pulled away from the curb.

She turned her face into Blackie's shoulder, surprised that she didn't fear him, in fact, welcomed his arm around her. She felt cherished, something she hadn't since her own father had died when she was five. She finally raised her head, to find Simon pulling up in front of Finn's parents' B&B. She hesitated as Blackie slid out and reached for her hand, not letting go as he walked her up and into the house and then back into the private living quarters, despite her protest that she didn't belong there.

Finn's mother, Mary Bronagh, looked up, a smile of greeting on her face. Her hands were deep in pastry as she prepared desserts for her guests.

Jacob walked around the counter and dropped a kiss on her cheek. He was family as far as they were concerned, now dating their daughter, Finn.

"Blackie, who do you have here?" Mary's face was alight with her smile, no censure seen at all.

"This is Julia Whittaker. I'm not sure if you have ever met."

Mary brushed the pastry from her hands and then washed them, dropping the towel she had dried them with on the counter.

"I have. At church. I have so wanted to get to know you better, Julia, but you have been gone before I can find you. Welcome to our home. Please have a seat. These boys just take it for granted they can help themselves to food and coffee or tea. Which would you prefer? Or I have hot chocolate and hot cider on the stove."

Julia hesitated as Mary stood, her hands on her arms after having hugged her. She had never had a greeting like this before.

"Oh, whatever is easiest, I guess."

Mary directed her to a chair. "Now, that's not how it works in this house. Which do you prefer? That's how it works. And I have some Christmas baking here, if the boys haven't eaten it all."

Blackie slid into a chair beside Julia. "Not yet, we haven't." He reached for a cookie from the plate he had set down and then shoved the plate towards Julia. "Here, Jewel. You need something. Hospital food is not fit to eat."

Julia gave a surprised laugh, her look questioning as she once again caught the name he was using for her. He stared at her, then winked, causing her to blush.

Josh handed Blackie his phone. "Mary found this on the table in the hall yesterday. She said your dad called here looking for you."

Blackie nodded, as he slipped the phone into his pocket. "I'll call him later. He'll understand."

Julia stared at him. "He'll understand? Just like that? You don't have to call him and apologize over and over for not calling him sooner?"

Blackie blinked at the vehemence in her voice before he shook his head. "No, I don't have to. Dad knows I'll call when I can. He understands. He always has. And with me having been in the armed forces, he knows there are times he'll call and I can't answer for a day or so."

Julia's hand dropped from the mug she had been reaching for. "You were in the armed forces? What did you do there?"

Blackie sighed, not wanting to say it out loud but knowing he had no choice. "I was a medic. And no, I'm not going to become a paramedic just because this town has need of one. That's not where God is calling me. And I have to follow that calling, not my own."

She shook her head, not quite believing what she was hearing. The four in the kitchen with her exchanged looks before Blackie reached for her hand. She started, then stared at his hand gripping hers before she raised her eyes.

"My family understands what it's like for me to be away from home and unable to call them. Even my two sisters are allowed a certain amount of leeway but they know when to call our parents and when not to. Mom and Dad have drilled it into our heads. They allow us the freedom to come and go." He paused, biting at his lip, not quite sure how to proceed.

"I never ever had that, Blackie." Her voice was so low, he could barely catch her words. "I had to report at designated times. I wasn't allowed to move around freely. If I did, I paid for it." She raised her eyes to Mary, finding compassion and understanding there. "I need to break away from them but I don't know how. I have never had anyone who would stand up for me. If I tried to leave, I got dragged back. Even as an adult, my life was controlled." She brushed at the tears rolling down her face. "Hal or his buddies made sure of that. They seemed to think they owned a portion of the town, but I know better." She looked at Simon. "Simon, I have documents hidden away that I need to give you, You'll need them. Hal and his buddies are involved in something here in town, but I'm not sure what. I hope you can find out."

Simon nodded, even as he lifted his mug to have a drink. "Just let me have them when you get them. The important thing now is that you're out of that house. Mary, can she stay here for at least tonight? Until we can make other arrangements for her?"

"She can stay here as long as she likes. You know how we're set up. There's the empty room beside Finn's that she can have, with the shared bath and door opening to both rooms. Finn will love that. She always wanted a sister, but God didn't choose to let us have any more than the two."

Blackie reached for Julia's hand, clasping hers in his, his eyes on her face, his heart raised in prayer. Lord, there's something special about this lady, and I'm not sure where I'm headed but I know I'm in for an adventure, at the very least. Protect her please. Help her to find the treasure she's seeking and doesn't know she is and doesn't know how to find.

Julia's eyes searched the faces watching her and didn't find what she expected. She didn't find dislike, hatred, censure. Instead, she found compassion, love, warmth, and something else she just couldn't put into words. She felt welcome. Tears gathered in her eyes and her head went down on her hands. Mary rose and came around the table, her arms around the young woman, even as she heard movement from the men as they stood and walked from the room, to let Mary have time with the young woman, time to show her what a mother's heart was like.

Finn stood for a moment in the doorway, watching her mother. She frowned, then her face cleared. Julia! Wonderful, she thought. I want to know this lady better. We've had contact, Lord, but not enough. Help us to help her.

Mary looked up as she heard footsteps, and greeted her daughter. "We have a guest for a while, love. Julia has come to stay. Is the room next to yours ready for our friend?"

"It always is, Mom. I'm so glad she's here." Finn had questions that she would ask later. "Hi, Julia. Let's get you upstairs and settled before supper. I can smell the chicken potpie Mom has in the oven. It will be ready soon."

Mary nodded as Finn linked her arm with Julia's and led her up the back stairs.

Julia stood for a moment in the doorway of the room, taking in the canopy bed, the oak furnishings, the warm peach and cream colourings, and shook her head. "This is too nice for me, Finn. I can't stay here."

"You can and you will. See, Mom has already designated this as Julia's room. Please?" Finn knew she was begging and wasn't about using her mother as a bargaining chip. "It looks as if the guys had put your belongings in here. That door there, it leads to my room. It's unlocked and open to you at any time of the day or night. Come find me if you need me." Finn led her to the other door.

———

130

"This is your bathroom. I hope it's okay." She watched in compassion as tears rolled down Julia's face.

"I have never had anything so nice. You wouldn't want to see the room I have been living in, or the shabby, broken down bathroom I've had to use."

"No more. Not if Blackie has anything to say about it."

Julia spun to stare at her. "Blackie? Why would he care?"

"Because he cares what happens to you. I can see he cares for you. He wouldn't have brought you here if he hadn't." Finn pointed to the bathroom. "Go on. You've time for a shower if you want. I'll lend you some of my clothes for tonight if you like." Finn almost danced across the room. "This is going to be so much fun. I always wanted a sister to share things with and now I have one." She disappeared through the door into her room.

Julia stared, open mouthed, after her before her jaw clamped closed and she shook her head. She stepped into the bathroom, awed by the colours and the design and the cleanliness of it. No matter how she tried, she couldn't get her bathroom this clean. It was just impossible.

Finn searched her clothing, finding just the right peach sweater and grey cords for Julia. She knew her mother would agree that Julia needed some new clothes. Her clothes were neat, but worn and faded.

Blackie turned to face Simon as he paced the office. They were alone for the moment, Jacob and Josh heading out to shovel snow.

"Simon? What is going on with Julia?"

Simon shrugged. "I have no idea, Blackie, but something is. We've been watching her stepfather for a while now, from what I can tell. He's involved in something here in town. Maybe that's why you've been brought to town. You're likely the one who can get through to Julia. She's responding to you like she doesn't with anyone else. Just like Finn did with Jacob."

Blackie stopped his pacing, turning once more to Simon. "There's something about her. She looks fragile but she has an inner strength in there." He sighed. "I heard that her boss fired her, likely on the instructions of Hal. We need to find her something to do."

Simon nodded. "Her boss is a crony of Hal's. That's how he controlled her."

Blackie nodded. "We have to watch her. He'll try and take her again. He's not the type to let her just walk away. It's a matter of life and death with her."

"That it is, Blackie." Simon turned as Jacob and Timothy, Finn's father, entered the office.

Timothy spoke. "I heard what you said, and you are correct, Simon. We have tried for years to get her away from him and never succeeded. Not until

Blackie here." He paused, lost in thought. "But Blackie's right, we need to find her something to do."

Jacob spoke up. "I could employ her. My business is growing to the point I need a secretary. If that's what she has been doing, I'll gladly offer her work."

Blackie turned to his friend, before nodding. "That would work. With both of us in the office, that would help to keep her safe. But we need to find out what it is she has hidden away and how it affects this town. I just know it does."

His friends laughed at his tone of voice, knowing he would be investigating until he found the answer.

Julia turned in a circle, studying the reception area of Jacob's business office, before nodding. She looked up to find Blackie watching her, a small smile on his face.

"Do you think you could work here?"

She sighed. "I suppose. It's too nice, though. I'm not used to this."

"It's not as nice as some offices I've seen. Jacob has only set up the bare bones of it. We'll need your help to expand what he started." He pointed to the counter. "That's there for your protection. No one comes past it without an appointment with either Jacob or myself. Make sure you follow that directive, please?"

She once more nodded, fear flickering across her face. She came around the counter and stood staring at her work station. "I've never had such a nice work area. I don't think I'll get anything done."

Blackie linked his arm with hers. He had discarded the sling, much to her protest. He turned her towards the rest of the office.

"Now, Jacob's office is right behind yours. He's there most days. Sometimes he'll have to travel, but on those days, if I can't be here, you're not here. The office will be closed. Understood?" He waited for her nod. "Now, this is my office, right across from Jacob's. I can see your work station if I move back from the desk and I will if I hear anything I don't like. I don't have to travel. Not yet anyway. My investigations are done on the internet and I communicate back and forth with my father. I work for him but can work from anywhere. Back here is the lunch room. It has a secondary exit to the back of the building. We've also put in a strong door and lock. If you're concerned or scared, head here and lock the door. There is a cell phone kept here at all times. It has all our numbers programmed into it for you."

Julia stood for a moment, staring around the room, before looking at Blackie.

"Why?"

"Why what?"

"Why go to all this for me?"

"Because you're worth it, Julia. Whether you believe it yet or not, you are definitely worth it. Now, about your work. Let's head back to the desk and get you started. I don't have a lot right at the moment, but I know Jacob's work is taking off. You will be busy. And as for dress code. Don't dress up. You don't need to. Jeans are fine."

She spun to stare at him. "Jeans?" She managed to choke out the word.

"Jeans. We're not fancy and we don't expect many clients to come in. Jeans are just fine with both of us."

She was upset, he could tell. "I've never been able to dress like that for work, you know? Most of the little pittance I made had to go for fancy dress clothes, even though there were very few people through the office."

Blackie reached to hug her, waiting until she finally hugged him back before he spoke. "I know. Part of the control he wanted over you. That's in the past. I suspect he'll try and get to you again, but we'll do our best to protect you. And we need to find that paperwork you have to give Simon."

"It's at the house. I have it hidden there." She turned away from him, her shoulders slumping. "I just don't know how I'll ever get it or the rest of my belongings."

Blackie sighed, before reaching to place his hands on her shoulders. "We'll take Simon and Tom. As police officers, they will protect you and help you claim your belongings. Hal and your mother cannot get rid of anything of yours nor can they prevent you from taking it. Let me call Simon and set it up for tonight. He said Hal would be held in jail until at least tomorrow."

She turned, a troubled look on her face. "It's too much bother."

"No, it's not. Not for a friend. Not for someone who needs us. It's what we do, Jewel. It's who we are." Blackie watched as she thought that through, her head shaking.

"I've never had that, you know, not that I can remember. Jonathan tried before he left but Hal was so hard on him." Tears pooled in her eyes before she blinked them away. "I just wish I knew where he was."

"That, maybe, I can help you with. Let me have his full name and date of birth and I do some research."

She studied his face once more before she told him. "What time today, Blackie? Mom works until 5. If I can get in and out before then, I'd like that."

"Let me call Simon and see if we can go about three. How many boxes will you need?"

She gave him an incredulous look and a broken laugh before she ran for the rest room. She needed time to compose herself.

Blackie reached for Julia's hand that afternoon as they sat at the curb outside her home, waiting for Simon and Tom

"I need to pray for you, Jewel." He reached for her hand.

She stared at him. "Really? You think God cares that much about us?"

"He does, Jewel. I know He does." Blackie closed his eyes as he prayed for their safety, wisdom in dealing with the situation, and for Julia, to know God's love for her.

———

She stared out the window, not responding when he was finished. He desperately wanted to reach her but didn't know how. He heard a vehicle and looked, watching as Simon and Tom each climbed from a cruiser.

"Are you ready, Jewel?"

She turned to eye him. "Not really, but let's get it over with. Mom will likely accuse me of theft, knowing her."

"That's why Simon and Tom are here. They will watch everything you pack, and verify that it is yours and that you're not taking anything that doesn't belong to you."

Simon reached for a couple of the boxes Blackie pulled from the back of his vehicle and nodded towards Julia. "How is she?"

"Broken. Hurting. Wanting this over with. I can't reach her, Simon."

"You have, Blackie." He walked towards the house, eyes watchful, and followed Julia into the house. "Where's your bedroom, Julia?"

"At the back of the house. That's all they'd allow me." Julia headed that way, not seeing the looks the three men shared.

Blackie noted the opulent look of the house and shook his head. It was not what he expected.

Simon spoke from behind him. "Tom will stay here by the door, just in case. You go help Julia. I'll be at the bedroom door. I have a bad feeling about this, Blackie."

"You and me both. Let's get her packed up and out of here. I'm sure the neighbours will have something to say."

Simon watched for a moment as Blackie headed for Julia before he followed.

Blackie stood watching Julia before he spoke.

"What can I do to help, Julia?"

She spun, surprise on her face before she shook her head. "I'm almost done, Blackie. I don't have a lot. Those two boxes can go. I have a duffle bag here with my clothes." She spun and almost ran for the closet. Blackie followed as she pulled at the trim on the inside of the closet door. She pulled on a packet of rolled paper and stuck it into the duffle bag. She looked around, sorrow on her face but also relief. "That's all, I think. If not, it can stay."

Blackie stopped her for a moment, his hand cupping her cheek. "You're sure?"

She nodded, then flinched as she heard a strident voice from the front of the house, chastising Tom, who stood in the doorway

"Is there a way we can get out back?"

She shook her head. "No. Hal made sure of that. I have to go back out through the front."

Blackie stopped her. "Stay behind Simon, as tight to him as you can. He'll take your boxes. Let me have your bag. I'll be right behind you. Don't stop and talk, just keep moving. Tom will keep your mother away from you, as will Simon."

She nodded, blinking rapidly before she moved towards Simon. Sandwiched between the two men, she walked away from the room that had been hers for so many years. She knew she would not be back, not unless something drastically changed.

Her mother stood on the porch, Tom standing in her way, as the three made their way from the house.

"Of course, you'd come when I wasn't home, wouldn't you? Hal said you would. I want to inspect those boxes and bags to make sure you're not taking anything of mine." She reached past Tom, who caught her arm and stopped her. "What's the meaning of this?"

"The meaning of this is that Julia has taken only what is hers and hers only from her bedroom. She was watched by an officer of the law." Tom kept stepping in her way to stop her from moving towards Julia.

Blackie tucked her into his vehicle and slid behind the wheel, nodding at Simon as he waved them away before he headed back to the house.

Julia leaned her head back, drawing in a deep breath, flinching when Blackie's hand touched hers.

"Jewel?"

She finally nodded, raising her head and staring at Blackie. "Can I ask you something?" At his nod, she sighed. "You keep calling me Jewel. Why?"

"Why Jewel? Because that's how I see you, a precious jewel, an undiscovered treasure, something so precious and loveable that God sent His Son to die for you. I'm not sure where you stand on that, Jewel, but that's how I see you. You're important to me and I can't call you Julia when I think of you as that."

She shook her head. "This is all new, Blackie. I've never dated. Never been allowed to, even as an adult. Hal kept so tight a control I couldn't get away. His friends watched and tattled on me no matter what I did. I did try and escape a few times but paid the price in beatings."

Blackie drew a deep breath. "No more, not if I can help it, Jewel. Now, what about those papers you dug up? What's so important about them."

"I'm not sure. There are papers that Hal had as well as some limited research I did. It has something to do with land willed to descendants of the original founders. I have no idea who they are but maybe Simon can figure it out."

———

Blackie started to laugh, drawing a frown from her. He gave a small smirk before he spoke. "Seeing as I'm one of them as are Simon, Josh, Jacob and Finn, I'm sure we'll figure it out."

She gasped, a look of horror crossing her face. "You are? That must be what he meant."

"Who meant what?" Simon pulled into the B&B and turned off the ignition before turning to face Julia.

"Hal. He said something on the phone two weeks ago about needing to rid the town of the founders' descendants. Oh, Blackie, what have I done?"

"You done? Nothing. You didn't know. Now that we know, we can take precautions. Come on, let's get you inside."

Simon looked up from the papers, a thoughtful look on his face, before he turned to Julia.

"You really don't know what you have here, do you?"

She shook her head. "No, I'm sorry, Simon. I don't." She paced Timothy's study, her arms wrapped around herself. "I just grabbed a bunch of papers one day that Hal had left out. I'm not sure if he's even aware that he did that. It was about a year or so ago."

"That's about the time I was sent that letter and directed to the cafe." Josh leaned back in his chair, his eyes on Simon. "So, who really directed us all here?" He looked back over his shoulder at Jacob and Finn, who were researching on her father's computer.

"That's what I'd like to know. The lawyer Grand had, that Norman fellow, isn't talking. He has to know who it was." Jacob looked over at Blackie, who sat, his eyes on his laptop as he worked away. "Blackie?"

Blackie roused, his eyes raising to find them all staring at him. "What? Did I miss something?"

"You miss something whenever you don't hear what I say." Jacob smirked and ducked the crumpled ball of paper Blackie lobbed at him even as he laughed. "No, we were trying to figure out who set Norman up to get us all here."

Blackie nodded. "That's what I want to know, too. Someone gathered us all here for a reason." He rubbed his forehead, his eyes going back to his laptop and then he was lost to the rest of them as he delved back into his work.

Josh shook his head. "What did you find out, Simon?"

Simon raised his head. "I'm still not sure, Josh.   There's something different about this that I need to study. There seems to be two or three different people involved in whatever it is Hal has become involved in." His eyes focused on Julia and he frowned, catching Blackie's eyes once more as Blackie looked up. Simon shook his head at Blackie, who nodded.

Blackie's eyes focused on the email he was sending his father, telling him what was going on and attaching what he knew about Julia's brother and asking for him to search for Jonathan. He knew his father would search until he found something. A tone sounding on his laptop let him know that he had an email. His father had responded quickly, letting him know that he would search for the brother. Then a sentence at the end caught Blackie's eye, causing him to shoot a quick look at Julia, before he re-read it. "Have you found your princess?" his father asked. Blackie smiled, not quite sure if he had or not. Julia had issues that she needed to work through and finding freedom for the first time was one of them.

Simon finally packed the papers away into his briefcase. He needed to talk to his lieutenant and that would have to wait until tomorrow. First, he needed to get Blackie off on his own and find out what his thoughts were, and he knew that was going to be difficult, given how close he was staying to Julia.

Julia looked up as Finn dropped to the couch beside her and handed her a cup of hot chocolate. Finn studied her new friend, not quite sure how to ask what she wanted to. Julia finally sipped the chocolate, looking away from Finn. She wasn't quite comfortable with her, not knowing her. She sighed to herself, wished Blackie was there but he and Jacob were shut up in the office on a conference call of some kind and had been for at least an hour.

Finn finally spoke. "I have to go do shopping for presents. Do you want to come?"

Julia's head whipped around. "You're asking me to go shopping with you?"

Finn nodded. "I am. I know Mom wants to but she's busy right now trying to get all the baking done for the Christmas party for the kids at church."

"She's the one that does that?"

Finn stared at Julia. "You never knew?" When Julia shook her head, Finn reached for her hand and squeezed it. "Mom has done it for years. She just loves coming up with new designs and treats for the kids. We keep telling her to cut back but she always adds something new and takes away something."

Julia finally nodded. "I guess I can. I just don't know though. Blackie probably won't let me."

Finn looked behind Julia, catching the look on Blackie's face as he heard her words and then shifting her gaze to Jacob, who shook his head at her.

Julia jumped as she felt someone touch her arm and then shift her over enough so that he could sit beside her. She stared at Blackie for a moment, trying to read his face.

"I'll take you shopping with Finn, Julia. I won't stop you. You get to decide what you want to do and then we assess the risks and make it happen. You're not a prisoner." He nodded towards the door. "If you want, the door's always open. You can leave at any time you want. I just pray that you don't. We don't want to lose you, now that we've found you." Blackie met her eyes, finally reading her acceptance of his friendship there. She had always held something back, he felt.

"Okay, so when, Finn?" Her focus returned to the other woman, sitting with Jacob's arms tight around her, wishing it was that way with her, that Blackie's arms were around her. Now, where did that come from? Lord, I'm not too sure about You or about Blackie. I don't have a good father figure and that's what they say You are, a Father to us. You'll have to teach me, please, Lord.

"We'll make sure you stay safe, Julia." Jacob spoke up, his eyes on Blackie. "I suggest we go over to Merryville instead of shopping here. I've

———

wanted to wander those shops." He laughed as Finn dug her elbow into his ribs. "You don't believe me?"

"No, I don't. I know how much you like shopping." She smirked at him before turning her attention back to Julia. "Tomorrow's Saturday. I have Anna working the shop and Peter said he'd help. Can we go tomorrow? We only have a couple of weeks left and I'm usually done my shopping by now."

Blackie nodded. "That works. Now, how be we head out to Josh's for dinner?"

Compassion filled Blackie the next day as he watched Julia wander through the shop, her fingers touching various objects and trinkets, but not buying anything. He realized she likely didn't have money to do any shopping. He approached, his hand on her arm.

"Julia, you can help me out here." She looked up, a question on her face. "I need to shop for my parents, my sisters, and then Finn's people. I have no idea what to get them."

She shrugged. "I have no idea either, Blackie. I was never allowed to shop. Mom always did that. She said I had no clue as to what to buy." She gave a harsh laugh. "It's hard to shop for people who hate you, especially when you have no money to do so." She blinked rapidly to clear her eyes.

Blackie looked around, feeling someone watching him but not seeing anyone that stood out. He gently drew Julia aside, his hand on hers as he stood for a moment watching her.

"Then, we'll shop together. I'd like to hear your ideas. Then the gifts can come from both of us."

Her gaze shot to his as she shook her head. "I can't do that."

"I can and I will." He grinned at her. "Now, my sisters are 20 and 16. What would they like? I was out of their lives for the eight years I was in the armed forces and am just getting to know them again."

She shook her head even as he dropped a kiss on her cheek, her eyes going towards the door before she sighed. "I just knew he'd have someone following me."

"Who? Hal? Where?"

"There by the door. That short man. He's a good friend of Hal's." She glared at him. "Now he'll go running to tell him you kissed me in a store."

Blackie laughed in an unrepentant manner as he hugged her. A couple with white hair and matching canes stopped, grins on their faces.

"I hope you two lovebirds have as long and happy a life as we have." The woman spoke, her eyes on the younger couple before she looked up at her husband. "Right, Frank?"

"That's right, Mae. Sixty five years that feel like we're just starting out. God bless you two young people."

Julia stared after them as they walked away. "But…". Her voice died away. "They think we're a couple."

"That's what I would like, Jewel." He watched the couple walk away, not catching the look on her face.

Blackie led her towards some scarves. "So, tell me. Would Rachel and Rebecca like these?"

She fingered them. "They're beautiful, Blackie. I'm sure they would. But what colours? They have such an amazing selection. And they're so soft." She held up a pale peach patterned one and Blackie knew somehow he had to sneak that into the pile for her.

"For Rachel, something soft. Blues, yellows, greens. Yes, that one. She'd like it. For Rebecca, something gaudy." He laughed at her expression. "She's 16 and is in that gaudy phase." He watched as she sorted through the scarves, tucking the peach one into the pile he held before she saw him.

"This one, maybe?" She turned to him, holding up a scarf with a pattern of many colours.

"Oh, yeah. She'll like that one." He reached for it. "Now, my Mom."

"What's your mother like, Blackie?"

"She's sweet, compassionate, a neat freak but she has a wonderful sense of humour. She used to make up stories for me at bedtime and did the same for the girls. Always with a moral to them or based on a Bible story. I missed that when I grew too old for those." He watched her, compassion on his face for what she had missed. "I'm really sorry you didn't have that." His eyes raised as he felt a watcher and saw the man following them. He pulled out his phone, quickly snapping a picture and sending it off to Simon.

"He's behind me?" At his nod, she sighed. "I'll never had a normal life and I was so hopeful with you helping me get away from that house and providing me with a job."

"It will come. It may take us a bit, but we'll win your freedom from them." He tucked her arm into his and led her around the store. "Now, for Mom. She loves trinkets, collecting various objects." He stopped as she did, her hands reaching for a figurine of a mother and three children, a boy and two girls, the mother seated with a book in her hands. "Just perfect, Jewel. I would never had found that without you."

"Sure you would have. What about Finn and her mother?"

"That's a good question. What would you suggest?"

"Let's try another store. I think finding Mary something for her kitchen might work. Finn loves to read, so maybe something in that line?" She stopped. "What am I saying? You likely have your own ideas."

He shook his head. "I don't. The guys and Dad are easy to buy for. And then there's you."

Her eyes shot to his. "I don't need anything, Blackie. It's a gift enough that you got me out of that house."

———

142

He shook his head, his eyes on the man following them. "No, it's not. Come on. Let's pay for this and then ditch our shadow. Think we can?"

She stared past him. "I doubt it, but we can always try. Where are we meeting the other two?"

Jacob looked up from where he had stood, waiting for Blackie to catch up with him. Finn and Julia had already gone ahead, Finn intent on finding something for Julia without her knowing it. Jacob glanced back at the store and smiled. It would be an antiquities store, he thought. Only my beloved Finn would do that. His head shot around as he heard squealing of tires and screams and searched for Blackie, not seeing him. He was torn. He needed to find Blackie, but he didn't dare leave the women on their own. This would be the perfect opportunity for someone to snatch Julia. He headed into the store, finding the women, heads bent over a selection of old-time kitchen gadgets, their laughter wafting around them.

Blackie appeared at his shoulder, brushing off his clothing.

"Blackie?" Jacob shot a look at him, then at Finn and Julia.

"Later, Jacob. Someone just tried to run me down. I'll give you the details when we're alone. Have they found anything yet?"

Jacob gave a forced laugh, his eyes on Blackie's face. "I think they have. You may need deep pockets in this store, my friend, if Finn has her way."

Blackie shook his head at Jacob's teasing. "If it loosens up Jewel more, then it's worth it." He walked up behind them, his voice so close causing them to jump. "What did you find?"

"Blackie! Look at this! Old fashioned cookie cutters! Finn says her mother would love them. What do you think?" Julia turned, her face alight with laughter and enjoyment.

"They're perfect." His eyes never left Julia's face.

"You haven't even looked at them." She shook a finger at him.

"If you like them and Finn says they'll work, then we take them." He took them, then looked around for a basket, saying a quick thanks when Jacob handed him one, watching as the two women moved away.

"Blackie, what happened?" Jacob searched the store, looking for what he wasn't sure.

"We've been followed. I sent the picture of the man on to Simon. Here, this is him." He stuck his phone back into his pocket. "I think it was him that just tried to run me down out there. A quick thinking bystander pulled me out of the way in time." He looked around, finding the women just ahead of them. "We need to be very careful. It looks as if he'll do anything to get to Jewel."

"That sounds familiar, Blackie, and I don't like it. Come on. Let's stay with them."

Julia sat back, her eyes on Blackie as he watched the road around them, faintly hearing Jacob and Finn's conversation and laughter from the front seat. She reached to touch his hand, bringing him around to face her.

"What happened, Blackie? I know something did."

He sighed. "Someone tried to run me down after I put the parcels in the vehicle. I'm fine. I just didn't see who it was."

"It was likely Hal's friend. They'll try and get you out of the way, you know."

Blackie's hand turned over and he grasped hers in his. "It won't work, you know. It just won't work."

"That's what you think, but I've always heard rumours around town. Of people they've gotten rid of. People who were there one day and gone the next."

Blackie caught the look Jacob threw him and shook his head. "We'll survive, Julia. We'll make it through, no matter what we face. Together. That I promise you. I won't let you face this alone."

She shook her head, not believing him, not wanting to at any rate. She thought back to when Hal had first started to threaten anyone who helped her and knew she was fighting a losing battle with keeping Blackie safe. But what was it that Hal was trying to hide? It had to be something big for him to go to those lengths.

"Blackie, how far can we trace back my family?"

He shifted to look at her, a concerned look on his face. "Why?"

"There has to be something there that Hal wants to hide or wants to find. I have no idea what it is." She caught the look Finn gave her. "What if I'm related to one of the founding families and have something that he wants, something that would give him ownership of something or some place in town?"

"That makes weird sense, Julia." Jacob spoke up. "We can start searching tomorrow after church. I would suggest you call your dad too, Blackie, and see what help he can give."

"I'll do that tonight. I have to call anyway. Mom wants to talk to me, she says." Blackie thought back over the day and then he began to pray as he never had before. His heart lifted to God, knowing that they were facing some dark days and hours but also knowing that they wouldn't walk them alone. God had already gone before them, he knew. His eyes searched Julia's face in the darkness of the car, catching sight of it in the dimness of the light from the dashboard and the occasional flash of passing headlights. Lord, she's been through so much. She doesn't understand that You are a loving father, who loves her deeply and without end. She needs to understand that and find her place in Your family. I sense she does believe in You, has placed her trust in You already. Just walk with her through this valley and cover her with Your hand. Please, dear Lord, don't let anything happen to my lady.

Hours later, Blackie raised his head as he heard a mug set down beside him and someone move towards the desk in the study. Finn's father sank into his chair, his head in his hands for a moment before he looked up at Blackie.

"You should be in bed, Blackie. It's late."

Blackie nodded. "So should you."

Timothy gave a short laugh. "I was and couldn't sleep. That's when I get up and do some studying. I'm working through the Minor Prophets right now."

"I haven't studied those in years." Blackie hesitated, his eyes going to his laptop before he looked up to find Timothy watching him. "Timothy, you know the people in this town. Tell me about Julia's people."

"Hal has always had a very mean streak in him, all his life. He didn't get it from his parents, I can tell you that. We weren't surprised when he married Julia's mother. She's had a mean streak as well."

"She has? I can see that, but why?"

Timothy shrugged. "She wanted more than she could get in this town. Her parents wouldn't leave. She married Julia's father right after high school. Now that was a match no one saw coming. She really hid her true character from him, I would think."

"She must have." Blackie sat back. "How did her father die? She's never said."

"Car accident. But there was something strange about that. I can't remember all the details but I know there were rumours around town that he had been killed."

Blackie nodded. "That's what I was finding. The only thing I'm not finding is much of a family tree on her. It's just not there or it's hidden." He looked up at a sudden sound from Timothy and caught the distressed look on his face. "Timothy?"

"Oh my, I'm so sorry, Blackie. I had forgotten. Lord, forgive me. Her paternal grandfather and mine were cousins. That means she's family. She goes by Whittaker but that's not her name. That's Hal's."

"That also means she related to one of the founding families, yours. Did she ever legally take Hal's name, I wonder?"

"No, I never did."

Blackie shot to his feet as he spun and stared at Julia before reaching to draw her to his side and then down to the couch where he had been sitting.

"You didn't? But you go by it, don't you?"

"Not any more. I've always hated it, but he didn't give me much choice. You don't want to know the abuse I suffered until I gave in. I want my father's name back. That's the same as yours, Timothy." She hid her face against Blackie's arm. The two men shared a look before Timothy spoke.

"You're our family, Julia. I wish I had realized that before. We would have gotten you out of there."

She looked up, no tears in evidence, not what they had expected. "He would have killed you or your family, Timothy. Even now, just having me here, puts you in danger."

"So, how do we mitigate that?" Blackie's mind was racing with ideas and questions. He knew there would be no sleep for him that night.

Timothy rose, heading for his filing cabinet and pulling out a folder, re-seating himself as he leafed through it. He glanced up, his keen gaze on Julia.

"Julia, how old are you?"

"Twenty-seven. The same as your Finn."

"That's what I thought. According to the old will that is honoured even today and it is legal, you had an estate coming to you when you turned twenty-five as did your brother. Did you get it?"

She shook her head. "If I had, I would have left town. What would have been the estate, Timothy?"

"I'm not sure. I can talk to my lawyer on Monday. In fact, I think you should come with me. With Finn and Peter, they got a number of buildings and stocks, bonds, and a bank account. They get more when I go. With you and your brother, Jonathan, you would split your father's. It would be similar to what I got from Dad. You don't need to worry about working, young lady, I can tell you that. You just can't sell the buildings in town."

"Wow!" Julia sat back, stunned before she turned to Blackie. "Did you know?"

He shook his head. "No, I didn't. I know Dad has an estate that he didn't know he had coming to him and he's made arrangements to split it between my sisters and I."

Julia shook her head as she stood. "I need to think this through." She walked towards the door, spinning around to find the two men standing, staring after her. "Is this what he was after, then? Dad's estate?"

"I would suspect so. He likely married your mother, thinking it came to her, and found out it didn't, that it went to you and your brother." Blackie shared a look with Timothy. "Did he ever try to get you to sign any papers around the time you turned 25?"

She stared at him, thinking through the years, and then her face paled. "He did, and I refused. They were legal looking and I just didn't feel comfortable with signing them without a lawyer explaining them to me. Is that what they were?"

"Probably. He would have tried to get your portion of the estate, but legally it would not have held up in court." Timothy watched as her face cleared. "You have nothing to worry about that way, Julia. Your father's estate from the town goes to you and your brother. It's structured in such a way to provide a perpetual income for you both."

"And Jonathan left without knowing. How do I find him? Blackie?" She turned to him, tears on her face. "This isn't it all though, is it?"

Blackie shook his head as he walked towards her. "No, I don't think it is. Neither does Simon. We're looking into Hal and his friends, trying to determine what he's all involved with."

Blackie walked back through the town of Mistletoe, his eyes on the buildings, picking out the ones his father had said belonged to him. He smiled as he realized that Hal was paying rent to his father for his office. Now, that was something he could talk to his father about. He was sure his father would come up with something creative there to keep tabs on him.

He turned as he heard his name called and frowned, not recognizing the man walking towards him.

"You're Levi Blackwell, aren't you?" The man was tall with brown hair and brown eyes. He seemed familiar. "You don't remember me, do you?"

Blackie shook his head. "No, I'm sorry to say I don't, but I should, right?"

The man laughed and Blackie realized who it was he looked like. "Jonathan Bronagh?"

"That would be me. We met years ago on a base overseas and spent some time together. You and your three friends. Your friends who I understand are now in this town."

"They are. But you haven't been." Blackie looked around, then pointed at Josh's cafe, The House. "Josh has that cafe. We can find a booth where we can talk or he'll let us use his office."

"I would suggest his office. Less conspicuous that way. I know there's a back way in. I'll meet you there." He was gone before Blackie could say anything more.

Blackie stood for a moment, watching for anyone watching him and then headed for The House. He waved at Josh as he headed through the cafe towards Josh's office, knowing he was welcome there without a question.

He turned, closing the door behind him, and stared at the man he knew as Joe White. "Joe White's not your real name, is it?"

Jonathan shook his head. "No, it's not, and from what I understand, neither is Jonathan Whittaker. I've been doing some research. Help me out here, Levi. I hear you've been protecting my sister."

Blackie leaned back against the door, crossing his arms and then his ankles. "How'd you hear that?"

"A friend in town. She's been watching out for Julia and let me know that you had come to town, you and your three friends. I was never so glad to hear anything as I was to hear that. I had to leave when I was 18. He'd have killed me and then killed Julia. I had to keep her alive. I've been back and forth from town over the years, making sure she's safe."

Blackie snorted. "Safe is a word I would not use for her. How many beatings could you have spared her if you had taken her with you? How much abuse?"

Jonathan paled. "He beat her? I didn't know that or I would have gotten her out of there after the first one. Why didn't someone tell me?"

"Probably because they didn't know. He's crafty, Jonathan. He's hidden what he's done. Julia is just starting to open up to me, to tell me what's been going on." He sighed as he moved to where Josh kept a coffee pot and poured himself a cup, raising the pot to Jonathan and then pouring him one as well. He sank into Josh's chair for the moment, pointing with his mug to one of the other chairs. "We need to talk and talk long and hard, Jonathan. They have already tried to kill both of us."

Jonathan's hand shook enough he had to place the mug on the corner of the desk before he buried his head into his hands. Blackie watched with compassion, realizing the other man had not known what his sister had faced. Josh cracked the door open enough to enter and then, shaking his head as Blackie went to rise, slipped into the other chair by Jonathan.

Jonathan looked up, devastation on his face. "I never knew. He used to beat me, until I finally left. I would have taken Julia with me when I left if I had ever thought." His eyes found Blackie's. "I'm guessing the letters I sent her she never got?"

Blackie shook his head before he sipped at his mug of coffee. "Not a one. She never knew where you were or I think she would have taken off to find you, somehow getting to you."

Josh finally spoke, his words a prayer as he prayed for his friends and for Jonathan, knowing they were facing dark days ahead.

They sat for a while, Josh finally having to go back to the floor. Blackie eyed the keys he was turning over and over in his hands.

"How do you want to handle this? Do you want to see Julia?"

Jonathan shook his head. "Not yet. I need to get a better handle on what Hal has been up to."

Blackie gave a bark of laughter, causing Jonathan to stare at him. "Sorry. I was just thinking of how Julia's going to react when she finds out you've been in town and not gone to find her. I don't want to be the one who tells her that."

Jonathan stared at him for a moment longer. "How serious are you?"

"Very, but that's something I discuss with Julia first. She deserves that."

Jonathan nodded. "I agree. Now, I need to get out of here. Here's my cell number. Call me if you need me. I'll be around town somewhere."

"Before you go, here's my Dad's number. Call him and talk to him. He'll want what you know. He's been looking into this town for about a month and finding some interesting items he hasn't shared with me yet."

Jonathan took the card, programmed in the number and then handed it back. "It's better I not have that on me. No one can get into my phone but me." He looked at Blackie for a moment. "I know your father, have talked to him over the years. He has never said but I have done work for him before. That's what I'm up to right now, why I'm back here. Not to keep an eye on you. He assures me you can take care of yourself, but I wonder, now that you told me Hal tried to kill Julia and I suspect you were involved in that." He held up a hand. "Don't tell me. I'll find you when I need." With that he was gone, leaving Blackie staring at the doorway, surprised when he saw Jacob and Simon standing in it behind Josh.

"Called in reinforcements, did you?" Blackie moved away from the desk, back towards the coffee pot, before he stared down at his mug and set it down. "We have a problem, guys, and I have no idea what the solution is."

"Talk to us, Blackie. That's how we resolve things." Simon shoved the door closed. "Can we talk here, Josh, or do we need to move to somewhere more private?"

"I would say we meet tonight and talk. I'm going to be on and off the floor all day. How about my place around 7?"

Blackie found Julia later that afternoon, curled up in a chair in the family living room, her eyes on a book, but he could tell she wasn't reading it. He slid down into a chair near her and waited. She finally looked up, a smile growing on her face.

"I didn't hear you come in, Blackie."

"I just got here. I don't think you were reading though, were you?"

She shook her head. "I've had too much to think about, I guess. Have you talked to your father?"

"I did. He confirms what Timothy said, that your Dad's share would have gone to you. The buildings are shared between you as is the bank account. Your mother didn't get anything from the estate at all. Your father left everything, including his life insurance, to you and your brother."

"So, if Hal thought he was getting a fortune by marrying Mom, he didn't." Her eyes strayed to the window, not seeing the wreath hanging in it. "That would explain why he's been like that with me. I just wish I knew for sure if that's why."

Blackie reached to draw her to her feet and into his arms. He felt her relax against him and then her arms came around him, under the plaid flannel shirt he was wearing as a jacket. Her head came down on his chest even as he tightened his hold on her.

"He's playing mind games with you, Jewel, trying to wear you down. We won't let him win. I promise you that. I will do everything in my power to keep you safe."

Her head came back so she could look up at him. "I know you will and that scares me, Blackie. I don't want you hurt and he will hurt you if he can, particularly if he knows you're important to me."

"And am I?" He watched as she nodded. "I'm so glad, Jewel. You're so important to me, important enough for me to take a chance and ask that you be my best girl for life. I love you. I also believe in love at first sight. Will you?"

She moved back a bit more, her eyes on his, her mouth rounded in surprise, before her features softened and she nodded. "If you'll be my best beau, as my Dad used to say."

"That's good enough for now. We'll talk more as we go along." His head bent as he kissed her gently, the first kiss leading to another and another.

A chuckle rang through the room and Julia felt Blackie's body start to shake in laughter even as he raised his head to smile at her.

"Really, Levi?" A male voice had a tinge of laughter in it.

"Yes, Dad. Now go away. Let me kiss my best girl in peace."

Shocked, Julia stared at him, even as he shook his head and kissed her again. Moving back a bit, he whispered, "It's okay. It's my father. We'll be getting some teasing, I suspect."

"He lets you talk to him that way?"

Mischief sparkled on Blackie's face. "He does, within reason and with respect." He groaned as he heard a teenager's voice.

"Levi? What are you doing?" The words were cut off abruptly as the speaker protested having her eyes covered and then there was silence.

"You're too young to see this, Rebecca." They heard a squeal of protest from the second speaker even as laughter rang out again and the voice was silenced.

"And so are you, Rachel."

"Samuel, behave yourself. Take your hands off Rachel's eyes and mouth. Rachel, you do the same for your sister. Girls, Mary has something for you in the kitchen. Your brother will be out shortly to see you. Behave yourselves now." Laughter tinged the woman's voice.

Julia stared at Blackie as he began to laugh harder and swept her back into a hug. "It's okay. My family's here. A surprise or I would have warned you."

"You would have warned me?" Julia hugged him tight. "Do you know how long I have prayed for a family like yours? For Jonathan and I?" Tears sparkled on her lashes as he hugged her back.

A warm hand rubbing along his back had him turning, his arm still around Julia even as he stooped to give his mother a kiss on the cheek and reach to shake his father's hand. Samuel took one look at Julia and then nodded. Thank you, Lord. She's what he needs. I don't understand how You bring people together but You do.

Miriam greeted her son, and then stood, hand on his arm for a moment before her hands came up to cover her mouth in a surprised gesture and tears brimmed in her eyes. Samuel's arm was around her shoulder as she stared first at Julia and then up at her oh so tall son. When did he grow up on me, Lord, she asked? It just seems like yesterday I was tucking a toddler into bed and here he is, on the brink of starting a life of his own in a new way.

Blackie stood watching his mother, a smile on his face, seeing the look Julia was shifting between mother and son.

"You found her, Levi. I really didn't think she existed. But she does and you really did find her."

"I did, Mom. I really did." He took pity on Julia and hugged her tighter to him. "Mom used to make up stories for us at bedtime. Did I tell you that? I can't remember. Mine were of valiant knights and men of honour. There was also a lady in them, a beautiful lady. The knight and the lady would fall in love after he rescued her from some predicament." He stopped, sharing a look with his mother. Then a beautiful smile broke on his face. "She described you, Julia. Almost perfectly."

She was shaking her head by the time he finished. "She can't have. It's just not possible. We've never met before." Her words were almost panicked, her eyes flying to Miriam.

"It's true, Julia. It is so true. God was in that, preparing us for you, for us to welcome you to our family." She reached to hug the younger woman, who clung to her as sobs shook her body. Miriam's arms tightened around her, hugging her as only a loving mother could.

Samuel drew his son away. "Let the women be for now, son. She's perfect for you, I can see that." He nodded towards the kitchen. "She won't have a moment of peace once the girls get a hold of her."

Blackie gave a short laugh. "I know. I need to prepare her for that."

"Don't. Let her find her way with them. Your mom will keep the girls in line." He looked back. "I'm glad you found her, you know." He turned back to Blackie. "You haven't asked yet why we're here."

Blackie started to laugh harder at that. "I really haven't had a chance, now have I, Dad? Why are you here?"

Samuel laughed with his son. "Let's find us some coffee and Timothy. He said you'd tell me where his study was."

"That I can do." He stopped before he reached the kitchen. "Do I really have to go in there?"

Samuel laughed hard at that, slapping his son on his shoulder as he moved past him. "You do. The girls have been anxious to see their big brother."

Blackie took a moment to absorb what had just passed, thanking God that Julia had been receptive to his question. His eyes slid shut for a moment, popping open when he heard his name said from in front of him. He reached to hug Rebecca.

"When did you grow up, Rebecca?"

She laughed at him. "When you've been away. Was that Julia?" She looked up at him, similar eyes and features to his staring back at him.

"That she is, squirt. That she is. Now, do we have coffee and cookies, or did you drink all the coffee and eat all Mary's cookies?" He wrapped her into another hug, reaching for Rachel as she appeared in the doorway, heading for her brother.

"Levi? Who was that?" She hugged her brother tight. They were best buddies when together and she feared someone taking her place with him.

"That's Julia, love." He sent Rebecca back to the kitchen, but Rebecca kept shooting glances over her shoulder until she was out of sight. Then his attention turned to Rachel and he drew her away from the doorway. "As I said, that's Julia. She's special to me, Rachel. Do you remember the stories Mom used to make up for us?" When she nodded, he continued, "She's the lady in mine. But no one will come between you and I. Life will change for us. It already has, Rachel, but you are my sister and very precious to me. Do you understand?"

She nodded. "I do, Levi. I really do. I can't wait to meet her." She moved to walk past him but he stopped her. She frowned at him.

"Let Mom have a chance to talk to her. She's had a really rotten life so far, her mother has not been like our Mom. Let's share ours with her for a bit."

She shrugged. "Sure. Whatever. Mary has the best cookies, you know?" She linked her arm with his and drew him laughing to the kitchen.

Blackie watched his father pace Timothy's study later that day. He hadn't made it to meet with his friends but they had willingly come to meet at the B&B. They were glad to see Samuel, always glad for his teasing and his words of wisdom.

Simon finally spoke from where he stood, arm on the mantle, eyes on the fire burning in the fireplace. "Josh says you met someone today, Blackie."

Blackie nodded, his eyes on his father, who had stopped and turned to face him, nodding at his son before Blackie spoke. "We did. Julia's brother." He shot a quick glance at the closed door, the first time he had seen it closed since he had come to stay there. "He says he knows you, Dad."

"He does. I really didn't know he was from here. I had Stephen research him and approve him for employment with us. You know me. Where someone comes from is not the important thing. It's who they are."

Blackie agreed with his father but was puzzled. "He said you had him watching people in this town. Not on our account, though."

"That's correct, son. I can't say much as the investigation was handed to me as a confidential one, my eyes only and only those who I chose to bring in know some of what I know. Jonathan didn't tell me he was from here but he has been invaluable to the investigation because of that." Samuel stopped, his eyes on Timothy. "You've been in our church at home, Timothy. You spoke at a men's retreat once."

Timothy nodded. "I did. I had the privilege of sharing a dinner table with you, Samuel. I never knew we'd meet again this way, or that our families would be connected in this way."

Samuel smiled. "God works in ways we never understand. I think He laid the burden for this town on my heart that day. I have prayed for you and this town since then."

Timothy nodded once again. "Of course you have. You have been in my prayers as well. Now, where do we stand?"

They stared at Blackie as he suddenly laughed, mirth brimming in his eyes. "Sorry. I just remembered something." He turned to his father. "Julia's stepfather, Hal Whittaker? He rents office space in one of the buildings you own."

Samuel grinned. "He does? Wonderful. I think there's an empty office right beside his, if I remember correctly. I didn't know that was him though when the lease came up for renewal two months ago." He shook a finger at Blackie. "No, we don't. We can just not renew in when it comes up in ten months."

Blackie grinned at his father. "Maybe it won't take that long." He sobered, eyes on his friends. "So, what have you all come up with?"

Josh spoke first. "I've had feelers out about Hal's businesses. They are all illegal - drugs, gambling, protection money. I can't say if it's gone any further, but people aren't talking a lot about him. They're running scared. He has a vicious group working for him."

"And how much did they demand from you?" Timothy spoke up, knowing Josh would have been approached as a newcomer to town.

"Enough that I would have had to shut down the cafe and that would seem to be their plan. Shut it down, take it over, and open it up again." Josh shook his head. "I hear rumours this is what he's done over the years."

"I've heard the same rumours. He tried that with me years ago, but he quickly learned he had approached the wrong man." Timothy sat back in his chair, his eyes on Blackie. "Blackie, what more has Julia had to say about what's been going on?"

"Not a lot, Timothy. I think she's buried it all way down inside her and I don't know if it will ever all come to the surface or if it does it will come in one great rush. That's what I'm afraid of. I think she's seen or heard something she shouldn't have heard." He paused, his thoughts on his lady, wondering just how to reach her. "She needs a lot of prayer, Timothy. She really does."

"We are doing just that for her, son." Blackie looked up at his father as he sat on the couch beside him, his hand going to his son's shoulder. "Your Mom will reach her. She has that knack of pulling things out that people can't or won't share. Just stay close to your lady."

"She will. Rachel and Rebecca will do her good. I could hear the four of the ladies giggling from the girls' room. I have no idea what they're planning but I'm sure we'll be in trouble, Jacob."

"Only a quarter of as much as you will be." Jacob smirked at it took Blackie a minute to figure out what he meant. The other men laughed at Blackie's expense even as he grinned at Jacob.

"So now what, Dad? Simon? Where do we go from here? I'm out of my league here. This is nowhere what I am used to."

"We wait. We investigate. I'm learning more and more about Hal every day, Blackie." Simon looked at Samuel, who nodded. "I'm not even sure if Hal Whittaker is his right name."

"And if it's not, then who is he?"

"That the question we're trying to answer. Leave it with us for a few more days. Stay close to Julia. Don't let her out of your sight when you are away from here. If needed, my supervisor has agreed to pull some officers from here and put her into a protective custody situation."

Blackie shook his head. "She'll never go for that, Simon. Not after how she lived all her life. She's tasted freedom and wants to stay that way. Even a day would break her again. And I won't have that."

Simon nodded. "I get that, Blackie. We all do, but we have to consider that might be a possibility, even for a few days. I pray it isn't." He looked at the clock. "I need to leave. I'm on call starting at midnight and need to catch as much sleep as I can." Simon walked away, leaving Josh to follow shortly after him. The four remaining men sat in quiet until Mary came looking for Timothy.

"Timothy, James is on the phone. Something about the worship team for tomorrow not being available due to illness?"

"On it, love." He walked away, his arm around his wife, leaving Jacob to follow after him looking for Finn.

Samuel studied his son for a few minutes, seeing how lost in thought he was. His hand tightened on Blackie's shoulder, drawing Blackie's attention to him.

"Dad, where do I go from here with Jewel? She's not used to living like you raised us. I know that's going to create issues."

"It may and it may not. Be open to her. Let her have her privacy and her space if she needs it. Let her know you understand she's hurting and broken and needs God to heal her. Pray for her and with her. That's the important one, Levi. Pray with her. I know your heart is entangled now but don't lose sight of how much she needs healing and shelter that only God can provide." He paused, not quite sure how to proceed. "I get the sense that you're not quite satisfied working for me."

Blackie looked at his father. "I am, Dad. I love working with you, but there's something I feel I should be doing. Some kind of ministry. There are kids here out on the streets after school and on weekends that have no place to hang around."

"Well, you do have your psychology diploma. You did manage to get that while in the service. Use it here. Take one of our buildings, fix it up as a youth centre. I'll take to the town council for you. Give me a business plan and a diagram for what you plan to do. Tomorrow's Sunday, but we can walk through town, and see which building would suit."

"Thanks, Dad. I'll plan on that." Saying good night to his father, he walked through the door to find Julia standing just outside the door, not wanting to disturb the men. "You could have come in, Julia. We don't bite."

She smiled at him as he took her hand. "I know, but you haven't seen your dad in a bit."

"That's not the point. If you're going to be part of our lives, and I pray you will, he'll welcome you to any conversation we're involved in, unless it's a private one. Those he pulls us aside into a room with a closed door and talks. He always has."

She nodded, stopping suddenly in the hallway. Blackie reached to hug her, finding her stiff and unresponsive.

"Julia? Julia, what's wrong?"

She didn't respond and he swept her into his arms heading for her room, calling for his mother as he went. Miriam and Mary ran behind him up the stairs, watching as he laid her on her bed and then began assessing her.

"Levi?"

"Don't know, Mom. She all of a sudden went stiff and hasn't responded. Mary, do you know a doctor who will come and see her?"

"I do. From the church. Levi, come with me. Let your Mom get her settled and then we'll come back. I want you to talk to Allan. You can tell him what happened."

He followed Mary from the room, taking the phone from her as she put in the call to their friend from church and describing rapidly what had happened. He breathed a sigh of relief when Allan gave him some directions and offered to come over if needed, and then handed Mary the phone as he heard Miriam calling quietly for him.

"Mom?" He stood in front of her, eyes search her face.

"She's awake, Levi. I can't get her to settle into bed. She just won't." Tears sparkled in his mother's eyes in the dim light. "Oh, Levi, son! What has he done to her?"

"What do you mean, Mom?" He was getting scared, not knowing what his mother was talking about.

"I helped her into a fleece suit, Levi. That's what she wanted. Her back is scarred, Levi. She flinched when I lightly touched her."

Blackie hugged his mother. "She was abused, Mom, by her stepfather and either no one knew or no one did anything. Let me talk with her." He paused, his hands lightly resting on his mother's arms. "She needs a mother, Mom, just like you. Hers wasn't. Thank you." He moved past her to stop in the bedroom doorway, watching Julia pace the floor.

Julia heard a slight noise and spun, fear on her face that vanished when she saw Blackie. She launched herself at him, feeling safe in his arms.

"Jewel? Can you tell me what happened?" His voice was kept low and calm, even though his heart was racing with fear and concern.

She finally nodded. "I can. Can we go downstairs? I need to be on a first floor tonight."

"We can do that." He swept her into his arms and carried her back down to the dimly light living room area, settling down into a chair and cradling her close. "Do you want to talk about what happened?"

"In a bit. Just let me be for a few minutes." Her head nestled down on his shoulder as she stared straight ahead.

Blackie felt hands on his back tucking a blanket around his shoulders and then a blanket was tucked over Julia. His mother dropped a kiss on his head before she moved away. He heard quiet voices and then felt his father's arms around them both, his voice sounding out quietly in prayer for them before he too left.

Finally, Julia's head tipped back and she looked up at him. "Thank you, Blackie. Everyone else would have tried to make me talk right away."

"You weren't ready. You would have just shut down even further if I tried to force it."

"You're right. I would have." She sighed. "Do I have to leave my town to get peace?"

"No, you don't. God will grant you His peace right here and now. It's yours for the asking. But talk to me. Tell me what happened."

She shuddered. "He heard that the descendants of the original settlers were coming back. He plans to kill all of you and take over the town." She tilted her head back to look up at him.

"That's not going to happen. First, he's not going to kill us. Secondly, he can never take over the town. It just can't happen. The founders made sure of that." His arms tightened around her. "Now, what else did you remember?"

"How did you know I did?"

He shrugged. "I don't know, love. I just do. And it's not because of the psychology diploma I have."

"You're analyzing me?" She pushed to get away, but wasn't able to loosen his arms enough to do so. Anger settled on her face.

"No, I'm not. I would never do that to you. I had to do something with my spare time and that's what I did. I wasn't even sure I would ever use it. So you're safe with me."

She shook her head before she calmed down. "Just make sure you never do." Her eyes stared towards the closed windows. "Do you think someone is out there, prowling around, trying to get to us?"

Blackie shrugged. "There might be, but I doubt it."

They talked for a while longer before her head went down on his shoulder and she slept. He tugged the blanket up higher over her and settled back himself, his head resting lightly against hers, his heart raised in petition to God for peace and   safety   for   his   beloved.

Blackie looked up the next morning, raising his head from his Bible as he heard footsteps stop outside his bedroom door and then a light tap at the door. He rose, looking longingly back at the passage he was reading before he opened the door to find his youngest sister standing there. He stepped back, letting her in.

Rebecca's arms hugged her brother and then held on, not willing to let him go.

"Rebecca? What's the problem?" Blackie gently stepped back, a hand on his sister's cheek.

"I don't want you to get hurt."

"And who says I will?"

"I heard Mom and Dad talking. Dad doesn't want to leave you here on your own."

"Rebecca, what did we talk about when I went into the forces? Didn't we say God was in control and only He could really protect me?" When she nodded, he continued, "It's the very same right now. God is in control. He will protect."

She finally turned to the door. "I know that in my head, Levi, but I can't convince my heart of that." She faced him again. "Please stay safe. Mom says Rachel, she and I are heading home tomorrow for a few days but that Dad's staying. Is that true?"

"I have no idea, Rebecca. I haven't talked to them this morning." He watched as the door closed, sighing to himself. *I need this over with, Lord, and soon. All of my loved ones are hurting.*

Blackie turned as his father approached him later that afternoon. They had spent the morning in a worship service that both challenged and calmed them, Blackie though, if those words could be used in the same sentence.

"Blackie, I've asked your Mom to take the girls home for the week. They have to finish their classes before the Christmas break, and then they'll be back here for the following weeks. I'm at the point in my investigation that I need to be here in town."

"Rebecca's a little put out that she has to go home, you know." Blackie grinned as he remembered the look on her face.

"I know she is, but it's necessary. And no, I'm not staying because you're in trouble, but I sense that what you two are facing is all tied up in what I've been asked to determine." Samuel paced, wanting to share more openly with his son, but constrained from doing so by the confidentiality agreement he had signed.

"Listen, Dad, I know you can't talk about it. That's fine. But I do have a question for you." Samuel had turned to face Blackie as he spoke. "Can we go for one of our walks? I would like to take a look at some of those buildings you own."

Ten minutes later, the men approached the first of the buildings and circled it, coming back to stand staring up at it.

"It's in good shape. I thought it would be more rundown." Samuel reached his pockets, coming up with a key. "I brought keys with me this weekend, hoping to look through some of the buildings."

Blackie followed his father through the first floor, liking what he saw. "This is great, Dad. It's got great bones. It would make a good youth centre. The rooms are large, so we wouldn't have to knock down any walls."

"Let's check upstairs. Of all the buildings, I think this is the one that would suit you best."

They finally returned to the first floor, Samuel watching his son closely and knowing his thoughts were not totally on the building. "Talk to me, son. What's really going on?"

Blackie shook his head. "I'm really not sure, Dad. It's all this with Jewel. I know Hal isn't finished with her yet and that her life is likely in danger. I just want to protect her, but I need to let her have the freedom she's never had. Even if it means she walks away from me." He blinked rapidly at that thought.

"Love hurts, son. That's what happens when we care so much. I almost lost your Mom before you were born." Blackie's head shot around. He had never heard that. "She was really sick. The doctors never did figure out what it was, but they only gave us a couple of days for her to survive. Our church prayed, hands were laid on her and she was anointed. She rallied and survived."

"Is that why she has to take care when she's around someone that's really sick?"

Samuel nodded. "It is. Since we don't know the trigger, we can't prevent it from happening again. Now, about you four boys. What can I do to help you with your investigation? And I know you are. You've told me what transpired with Jacob."

Blackie nodded. "I will, Dad, but can we go back to the B&B? I feel unsafe here today, for some reason, and I shouldn't."

Samuel searched his son's face and then nodded. "We can. I have that same feeling. How was Julia this morning?"

"She seemed okay, embarrassed at what happened last night. I don't think she realizes Mom saw her scars."

Samuel's steps slowed and stopped even as his hand came out to stop Blackie's forward motion. "Scars? What are you talking about?"

Blackie looked at his father, shock on his face. "Mom didn't tell you? Hal beat Julia and she has the scars to show for it." He paused, a thought crossing his mind. "Just how far will he go to get possession of their inheritance?"

"As far as he can, likely. Money and power drive some people to do unconscionable things. And I think he's one of them."

Blackie turned and headed for the B&B, almost on a run, his father on his heels. "Finn and her family are gone for the day. Mary said all the guests were headed out. The girls have gone to a youth event at the church. That leaves Mom and Jewel on their own."

Blackie ran through the B&B, desperately searching for his mother and Julia. Hearing a sound from off the kitchen, he tried to open the pantry door, finding it stuck and not able to move it. Samuel lent his weight but it still didn't budge.

"Miriam, are you in there?"

"Samuel? We are. Wait. I have to move some stuff. You can't open the door. We barricaded ourselves in here." The door finally flew open and the women emerged.

Samuel caught his wife in his arms, not caring about anything but that she was fine. Disheveled, but fine.

Blackie stood for a moment, seeing the fear on Julia's face before she ran the few feet separating them to throw herself at him. He caught her, feeling the shudders shaking her body. He wrapped her tight in his arms, finally turning and pulling out a chair to sit and cradle her close.

"Jewel? What happened?"

"They came looking for me, Blackie. They tried to take me with them but your mother hit them with something. I can't remember what." She leaned around Blackie to look at Miriam. "What did you use again?"

Miriam started to laugh. "First the broom and that broke. Then the vacuum hose until they grabbed it from me. By that time, I had you in the pantry. I think… Now what did I grab up?"

Samuel straightened up from picking an object up off the floor, trying to control the laughter that threatened to break out. "This?"

"That? That whatever it is?" Miriam stared at him in shock as he held up something she couldn't put a name to. "I have no idea what that is. Do you?"

Finn had entered the room without them hearing her. "You mean the old-fashioned corn popper? You defended yourself with that?"

"I guess I must have. It kept them away long enough to shut the door." She looked up at Finn and then past her at Mary. "I'm sorry, Mary. I think I made a mess of your organized pantry."

By this time, the men had open smiles on their faces, barely controlling their laughter. Finn was not as generous. She was bent almost double as gales of laughter pealed from her and she had to wipe her eyes. "Oh, I would have loved to have seen that. I never knew you could use that for a defense weapon."

Miriam shared a look with Julia even as she smirked. "Well, now you know. It's very useful. Know where we can get some more to carry with us?"

That sent the men off in fresh peals of laughter, imagining the four women walking down the street, each carrying a long-handled corn popper.

Blackie finally sobered enough to look Julia over, satisfying himself she was fine. "Who was it, Jewel?"

"Hal's cronies. One was the man from yesterday, who followed us." She held up her wrist and anger burned through him at the red fingermarks that showed. "When your mother hit him with the broom, he let go of me." She paused, wonder coming over her face. "He really does, doesn't He?"

"Who really does, love?" Blackie had an idea of what she was going to say but waited.

"God! He really does protect us, doesn't He? He must have sent your parents here this weekend. If your mother hadn't been here with your dad, I would have been on my own. I don't think I could have protected myself that well."

Blackie breathed a sigh of relief and wonder. Thank you, Lord. You're working there, showing her You really do care.

"He does, Jewel. About everything. I'm so glad you're realizing it. It doesn't mean we won't have trouble or face danger, but He has promised us He's there. When we seek Him, He will be found. That is a treasure you will never lose."

She nodded. "I'm finally getting what you've been saying. Your youngest sister helped me to see that."

"Rebecca? How?"

"She remembers how she felt when you went off the first time and she didn't know if she'd see you again. She said she tried praying but didn't think she was getting through to God. Then one day she found a little sparrow on the ground. It let her approach it and pick it up and hold it for a few minutes before it flew off. She quoted that verse about how much more important we are to God than even a sparrow." She glanced at him, finding his eyes fixed on her face. "That got through to me. No one else ever has, but your sister did. She's so precious, Blackie. We need to keep her here."

"Ssh. Don't tell her that, or she'll never leave."

Blackie looked around the building he had decided would work as his youth centre and sighed. It was the next day and he was on his own. Today, it didn't look so bright for him to design this. Yesterday, he had been full of plans and dreams. Until that is he got home and found out what had happened to Julia and his mother. That scared him. It angered him as well and that was something he was working on leaving with God.

He paced through the building, his mind finally on the decisions he needed to make. His father had told him to do what he wanted with the place, he'd fund it. He knew friends who would be glad to chip in as well. His father was already working on a business plan for him and setting up a trust fund and board of directors for him. Things Blackie hadn't even had a chance to think about, and he was glad his father had taken that step. Samuel wasn't trying to take over but he knew that Blackie's mind wasn't on that part of the plan yet. He would make no decisions without Blackie's input, that he had guaranteed Blackie.

Blackie heard a whisper of sound behind him as he turned from the kitchen area and felt the blow to his back, driving him to his knees. He came up, facing around to his assailant.

"It's you, is it?" The man who had followed them on Saturday stood in front of him, a pipe in one hand, a sharp long-bladed knife in the other. "Which are you planning on using on me? The pipe or the knife? I hear you didn't fare that well with Mom."

"She's lucky." The man's voice was guttural, as if he was hiding the real sound of it. "You won't be."

Blackie circled around, trying to remember how far it was to the front door, and praying he'd have time to reach it and get through it before the man attacked. His eyes fastened on the man's face, watching for the slightly movement that would show him which way the man planned to go.

The man lunged at Blackie, who deflected the hand with the knife and then ducked the swing of the pipe. Blackie knew he had to get the man to drop one or the other of the weapons but wasn't quite sure how.

A misstep on his part had him sliding sideways, the pipe crashing down on his shoulder and sending him to his knees. He reached for the pipe, leaving his abdomen open to attack. He felt the knife as it sliced into him and he dropped to the floor, hands reaching for the wound even as the man knelt on his chest and leaned close, telling him he was done for and that they'd have Julia now. No one could protect her. And that as one of the founding family descendants, he would be the first of his family to die, leaving it open to them to take over the funds.

Blackie's vision blurred and swirled as he sank into darkness, blood dripping to the floor. He lost sight of the man and didn't feel the shove on his chest from the knee as the man rose and then stood over him, glee on his face, as he thought he had won.

Fifteen minutes later, Jacob and Finn came looking for Blackie. He had failed to show up at the cafe as promised and they were afraid, afraid something had happened to him.

Jacob had stopped to search in one of the rooms when he heard a cry from Finn and ran to where she stood, hands to her face, before he rushed past her to drop to his knees beside Blackie, hands reaching for him, even as he yelled over his shoulder for Finn to call for help.

Hands shaking, he rolled Blackie over onto his back and reached to tear away his jacket and then the flannel shirt and T-shirt. He gave a cry and took the scarf Finn handed him, shoving it against the wound, desperately trying to stem the flow of blood.

"Check his pulse and breathing, Finn. I need to know he's still alive."

Finn dropped on the other side of Blackie, hands reaching of his chest and then his neck. "He's still breathing, but it's so shallow. His pulse is very slow." She looked up at Jacob, horror and hope intermingled. "Will he live?"

"I pray he does. Watch for the paramedics, Finn. We need to get him out of here. Call Josh or Simon. One of them was going to be with Samuel today. Warn them to bring him to the hospital. And to bring Julia. He needs her there. Blackie dropped hints last night that they had come to an agreement, but he didn't say to what."

She nodded as she rose, phone in hand, and ran for the door, hearing the sounds of the sirens screaming through the air and then the shrill screeching of brakes as the emergency vehicles slid to a stop.

"In here! He's been stabbed! We're not sure how long ago." Finn pointed to where Jacob has still on his knees, hands pressing against the wound. Then she heard Simon's voice in her ear and turned away, sobs wracking through her voice to the point she could hardly tell him what had happened

Samuel ran through the doors to the Emergency Room at the Merryville Hospital, looking for his son's friends. Jacob was there, drawing him aside. Samuel saw Finn sitting with her arm around Julia. Good, was all he could think.

"Jacob?"

"He's alive, Samuel. They're assessing him now but are heading to surgery with him right away. He was stabbed in the abdomen, how severe they haven't said yet. The physician will be out shortly. They know you were on your way."

"I have to call Miriam. This is not something I want to tell her over the phone."

"Simon called the police department in your town. He found a friend working there who will take your pastor with him to go tell her. If that helps?"

Samuel gave a sigh of relief. "It will, but I still need to talk to her." He nodded towards the women. "How's Julia?"

"In shock." Jacob turned to stare at her. "How serious are those two?"

"Serious enough that Levi asked for his grandmother's ring to come back with his mother on Friday."

"Wow! I didn't think it had gone that far." Jacob turned as he heard steps behind them. "Here's the physician, Samuel."

———

Julia rose and was at Samuel's side before the physician had reached him. His arm came around the lady he knew would be his daughter-in-law. That is, if his son survived.

"Doctor?"

"He's alive and very lucky. The thick jacket helped to slow the knife and kept it from going as deep as it should have. We're taking him up to surgery to repair it. We'll assess if there is any further internal damage, but from my look, I don't think there is. Someone was watching out for you son, Mr. Blackwell."

"God was, Doctor. Now, can we see him before he goes to surgery?"

The physician nodded, looking askance at Julia.

"This is his fiancee, Doctor. She's going in."

Julia stared up at Samuel, dumbfounded at his words, but he shook his head at her.

"We'll talk later, Julia, but I know that's what Levi is thinking, isn't it?"

She gave an abrupt nod, then followed the nurse along the hallway, stopping for a moment at the curtain before Samuel's gentle hand on her back urged her forward.

She paused, her eyes going up to Samuel's, finding him whispering a prayer even as she stood, waiting, not sure what she'd find in the room. She finally moved forward to where the nurse was waiting, her eyes seeking Blackie.

She stood, one hand on Blackie's cheek, the other on his arm as she studied him, seeing the paleness of his face, before her eyes raised and traced the IV lines and other lines running to him. She watched the monitors, a frown on her face as she realized she really didn't understand them. Samuel stood beside her, an arm around her, his hand on Blackie's shoulder. She could hear his whispered prayer once more.

Blackie's movements stilled as he felt Julia's hand on his face, and his eyes flickered open. He strained to focus, finding first his father's face.

"Dad?"

"It's fine, son. You're in the hospital."

"It hurts." His hands shoved at the blankets before Julia's hands reached to stop him. "What happened?"

"You were hurt, son. Now, they'll need to take you to surgery."

"No, I need to get up and out of here." He struggled to rise, his hands shoving once more against the blankets and then fumbling at the side rail of the bed.

"Stay put, son. They'll be coming for you soon."

Blackie's head went back and his eyes slid closed. "I can't. You don't understand, Dad. I need to find Jewel. They'll be after her. He threatened her."

———

165

Samuel's eyes found Julia's, seeing the fear lurking in hers. "Who threatened her?"

"I don't know his name. He's been following us. He's going to come and get her. I need to find her and save her."

Julia's hands reached for his, clasping his tightly. "I'm right here, Blackie. I'm safe."

"Jewel? You're safe? But he said they were coming for you." Blackie's eyes flickered open, he looked up at her, and then his eyes slid closed again as he lost the fight to keep conscious.

Samuel drew Julia away as the nurses approached, ready to head off with Blackie. Julia stood, hands to her mouth, eyes sparkling with the tears she refused to shed, before she turned into Samuel's hug. He gently led her to the waiting room and then followed Simon to the surgical waiting area, seating her and then turning to Simon.

"Levi was awake, Simon." Samuel had moved away from where Julia sat, Finn and Jacob on either side of her. "He didn't see Julia at first and tried to get up to find her. He said whoever attacked him was after her and he thought they had her already."

Simon paused his hand as he lifted the cup of coffee to his mouth, his eyes on Julia. "Did he recognize the man?"

"He said he had been following them? I hadn't heard that." Samuel ran his hand through his hair, pulling it back as he stared at it, willing it to stop shaking. "I never felt like this when he was in the service, but today? I could have lost him, Simon, so easily, with me right in the same town."

"God was watching out for him, Samuel, that you can depend on." Simon turned as he heard footsteps and saw Josh approaching. "Josh? Who's minding the cafe?"

"I called in extra help for the next two weeks. I want in on this, Simon, and if you say no, then I work on my own. Someone pulled us all back to this town. Jacob went through something. Blackie is in the midst of something and could have easily died. We need to find out who is back of this, because I can guarantee you he's not finished. You and I will be next, don't you think?" Josh stood, hands jammed into his pockets, staring around, determination flowing from him.

"Simon, I know who he meant." Simon looked up to see Julia standing at the edge of their group. "It's Hal's best friend. He's the one who has been following us. I think he's likely the one Hal used for doing whatever he needed done. Hal would keep his hands clean, except where it came to Jonathan or I. He let Benny do the dirty work." Her voice faded away for a moment. "Samuel, did you say you own that building?" At his nod, she sighed. "I think if you look either in the basement or in the attic, you'll find some evidence you need. But I wouldn't wait too long, or it will be gone. I vaguely remember Hal and Mom talking about something like that." Her voice faded once more as she stared past the men, then brushing by them, walked into the hallway and towards the elevators. "Jonathan?" Her voice was quiet, so quiet they weren't sure they had heard her right.

The man turned, his eyes on the men before they fell to Julia. Julia stopped for a moment before she began to run, throwing herself at the man, whose arms swept her into a tight hug.

"Julia, you shouldn't be out here. I didn't mean for you to see me. Not yet."

Simon had been right behind Julia, sweeping Julia and Jonathan into an empty room and closing the door behind them, standing guard outside.

Julia clung to her brother, sobs wracking her body. Jonathan's own tears flowed, holding his sister after so many years. He finally released her enough that he could step back and see her face.

"Julia? Look at me." When she did, he winced, seeing the pain and sorrow on her face. "I'm so sorry, Julia. I should have taken you with me when I went but I had no money, nothing for us to survive on. I tried coming back a few years ago but Benny found me and beat me up, dumping me miles away. I've had someone watching you, though."

Julia hit at his shoulders with her closed fists. "Not close enough, Jonathan. No where near close enough. Do you know how many beatings I took over the years?"

Jonathan froze, realizing for the first time the real danger she had been in. "Oh, Julia! If I had only known."

"No one knew. That's the thing. No one knew. He made sure they didn't." She watched her brother's face, seeing the conflicting emotions crossing it. "Did you ever know we are related to the Bronaghs that have the B&B? As in cousins? Our grandfathers were cousins."

"That is our last name, but I didn't realize we were related that close." He groaned. "That's why he's after us. We're part of the legacy of the founding families."

He turned to pace. "I don't like this, Julia. Not at all. That's why Hal has been like he is. He wants what we have."

"But he can't get it. Samuel and Timothy have been checked into it. He will never get it. If one of the founding families die out, their portion goes into trust for the other four."

A tap at the door interrupted them, and Simon slipped into the room.

"The nurse is looking for you, Julia. Blackie's in recovery but not cooperating with them. He wants to get up to find you. The surgeon has asked that you come there and calm your boyfriend down." Simon grinned at the frown she threw him. As she started for the door, his hand on her arm stopped her. "I'm going with you. I know the nurse but we're not taking any chances. For now, someone is with you. At least until we find these guys."

She shook her head. "That can't happen, Simon. You can't pull your men to do that."

"We're not. Samuel has called in people."

"Samuel? But why?"

Jonathan shared a look with Simon before he nodded. "Because to him, you're family and he takes care of his family. Now, let Simon take you to Blackie. I'll be around, sis. I'm not walking out of your life ever again."

She nodded, giving her brother another long hug before she followed Simon from the room, her hand tight in his as he led her after the nurse. She finally stood beside Blackie, watching as he tossed restlessly, picking at the covers and then trying to rise. Her hand came down on his, and he stilled, his hand flipping over to clutch at hers.

"Jewel? You're here? You're safe?" Blackie's eyelids flickered but didn't totally open.

"I am, Blackie. Now, you need to lie still. You've just had surgery."

"I have? No, that's not possible. I need to get up. I need to find Julia. She's not safe." He shoved at the blankets, staring at the IV line before he pulled it out and reached up and pulled the cardiac monitor leads from his chest, sending the machine into a wild beeping.

The nurses hit the room on a run, heading for Blackie. They tried to get him back into bed but he fought them, calling for Julia. Finally, Julia moved in front of them, her hands finding Blackie's face and she kissed him. He stopped, his eyes sliding closed, as his hands grasped her arms.

"Julia, it's you?" Eyes opened part way as he stared up at her. "You're here? They didn't get you?"

"No, Blackie. They haven't. Now, do what the nurses are asking you to do. We need you to lie back down. They have to put the IV back in and the leads back on you."

Blackie stared up at her, a frown in place, and shook his head. "No, I need to get out of here. I need to keep you safe." His eyes slid closed as his body sagged.

"No, what you need to do is to lie back down, okay? Here, put your head on your pillow. There, comfy? Tuck your feet in. The nurses have to do some stuff for you." Julia tried to extricate her hand from his grip but his only tightened. She looked up at the nurses, consternation on her face.

"It's okay, dear." The older nurse spoke, a gentle smile on her face. "He must really love you."

Julia shook her head, her eyes thoughtful. "I guess."

"What do you mean, you guess? I would say he does. How long have you two been going out?"

The nurses' glances held shock when Julia started to laugh. "Um, just a few days? Maybe a week?" She grinned, suddenly comfortable and safe in Blackie's love. "Do you believe in love at first sight?"

The nurses paused for a moment, exchanging glances, before the first one spoke. "I never did before, but I guess I do now. He's settled back down. Let's see if we can keep him that way. Don't leave his side, if you can help it. He'll be here for another hour or so and then we'll take him to a room." She paused to touch Julia's shoulder. "He'll be fine, dear. The wound wasn't as bad as it initially looked."

"Thank you." Julia looked around for a chair, finally perching on the side of the stretcher, her hand still tight in Blackie. "Will I be in the way here?"

The nurses started to laugh. "Not likely, seeing as he won't let go of you."

Blackie nodded to something his father asked, pain evident for a moment on his face, as he sat on the couch in the B&B living quarters. He had refused to stay in hospital any longer than a day, against everyone's wishes, but he saw the look Julia gave him and knew she understood. He had to find this fellow, Benny she called him, before he hurt Julia and he wasn't sure how to go about it.

Julia sat beside him, her hand on his for a moment, before she tucked the blanket around him. He reached to hug her close to him, pressing a kiss to her temple.

Simon paced in front of him, trying to make sense of what Blackie had finally told him. Samuel had gone through the office building as Julia had suggested and had legally obtained the material stored outside of Hal's office. He and Jacob were spreading the documents out on the coffee table even as Simon watched. There had to be something there.

"What was it you said again, Blackie? What did he actually say to you?" Jacob sat back on heels, his eyes on Blackie.

"I can't really remember, Jacob. He muttered it as I was going down. Something about getting Julia." He looked over at Julia, who had sat forward, her eyes on the paperwork. "Julia?"

Julia didn't hear him, her fingers sorting through the papers, before they stopped. She drew in a sharp breath. "There. That's what you need." She handed a paper to Simon before gathering all she had sifted through and putting them in order of date. She handed these to Jacob. "Now, you go through these and see if you recognize any names, events, etc. Simon, do you have that paperwork I gave you earlier? I need to go through it as well. I think we'll find we'll match dates and names."

Simon was to his car and back with his briefcase almost before she stopped speaking, opening it and handing her the sheaf of papers.

"Here, you go through it and then we'll match it with what Jacob and Josh are working on." He looked over at Blackie, whose head was back and his eyes closed. "I think we lost Blackie somewhere along the way, Julia."

She turned, her hands coming out to tuck the blanket tighter around him. "He shouldn't have left the hospital yet. But he was determined to. I couldn't say no when he begged me to help him leave."

"None of us could, Julia." Samuel stood watching the couple. "Now, what have you come up with?"

"This. These are all in chronological order. Jacob, have you found anything yet?"

He nodded. "I have. There are names that recur. I think he was running a protection racket and Timothy was right. But there's more than that." Jacob sat back, his eyes on Finn. "Finn, when we were looking back through all the information on the founding fathers, did we go back just to them or did we get back any further?"

"I think with yours we got back further, back to England or Ireland if I remember correctly. Why?"

"Because Hal seems to have connected with a gang from over there and brought people here to town. I can't determine who or if they are still here in town."

Samuel paused in his pacing, his eyes on Julia. "Julia? Did you know anything about this?"

She shook her head. "He was careful not to let me see who he was speaking with. That was guaranteed. Jonathan may know more than I do, but if I remember rightly, Hal changed how he did things after Jonathan left. He became much more secretive than before."

She turned to face Samuel. "How long has Jonathan been around?"

"For years, Julia. He had no idea what you were going through. Trust me. He would have gotten you out of there had he known. He has had someone watching out for you." He nodded at the paperwork she held. "Sort through that and then we'll compare the two piles." He turned and walked away, leaving her staring after him

She felt a hand on her arm and looked around. Blackie was watching her and then reached to draw her close to him, taking the papers from her hands.

"Dad's right, you know. Let it go, if you can. We can't change the past. God will provide us the wisdom and the resolution we need for you."

She nodded, her hair brushing against his chin. "I know that in my head. It's my heart that's having the trouble figuring it out." She reached and took the paperwork back, staring at it for a moment before she thrust it back into his hands and was up and out of the room, the men staring after her. Finn had been standing watching and followed her friend.

"Julia?" Finn tapped at the door to Julia's room. When invited, she cracked the door open, to find Julia standing in the centre of the room, her eyes on the picture above the bed.

"Finn? Where's that picture from?"

"The picture?" Finn shrugged. "I have no idea. We've had it for as long as I can remember. Why?"

Julia walked towards it. "Can I take if off the wall?"

"Sure. Why?" Finn moved to help.

Julia laid the picture of an old house and barn down on the bed before flipping it over. "Hal talked about a picture like this one time with Mom. He accused her of getting rid of it." She ran her fingers along the edge of the backing, before frowning. "There's something about this picture. I feel it, Finn. Would your mother object if we loosened the backing on it?"

Mary stood at the door. "No objection whatsoever, Julia. If it helps. Let me see, how is it fastened?"

"Staples, Mom. Just a moment." Finn was off the bed and back in a moment with a nail file. "Here. We can work this under the staples without damaging the backing."

Working carefully, Finn did just that, handing the staples to Julia. Mary stood, interest on her face. Finally pulling gently on the loosened backing, Finn moved it away and set it down, staring at what was there.

"Julia, how did you know?" Finn and Mary both stared at her.

"I have no idea. That picture has been bothering me all along. Now I know why. Who put those documents there? And what exactly are they?"

"Here, take them out, and then we'll go find the men. Maybe they'll have an idea of what we've found. Finn?" Mary realized she had lost Finn's attention.

"Julia, do you know what this is?" Finn looked up, her eyes on Julia.

Julia shook her head. "I have no idea about old papers. That's what you do."

Finn sat back down on the bed, carefully searching through the papers she had in her hands. "There are deeds here, a will, a court document, jail records. What did we find?"

"What are the names on them?" Julia sat beside her, leaning over to look. "Oh no! Those are Hal's parents. What did they do? Theses can't be legitimate documents. Well, maybe some of them, but not the deeds. They can't pass the land or buildings on, can they?"

"It depends on where they're located." The three women looked up to see Timothy standing there. He entered the room, reaching for the papers Finn handed him, flipping through them. "From what I can see, they can't on these properties. They belong to the founding families. Now, this jail record. It's not for his father, Finn. It's for Hal himself, as a young man. Well, well, well! What do we have here?" He looked up, compassion on his face as he faced Julia.

Julia stared at him, not quite sure what his look meant. "Timothy? You're scaring me." She glanced behind him to see Blackie and Jacob standing there. She sighed. "I came up here to be alone. That's not working so well. Can we go back downstairs now and Timothy, you can explain what you mean?"

Timothy gave a light laugh, his eyes not showing his mirth as he shared a glance with Mary. "We can do that. Mary, you need to be putting out the tea items anyway. Finn, you can help. The rest of us are going to go through these and compare them to what we have already. I think we're finally getting somewhere. And Julia, dear, you will tell us how you knew about that painting."

Blackie found Julia the next morning standing in the backyard, her arms wrapped around herself, her eyes on the sky. He came up and wrapping his own arms around her, drew her back against him.

"Jewel?"

She turned her head and looked up at him. "Just thinking, Blackie. Do you really think Hal had something to do with dad's death? I know Timothy does by the questions he has asked."

Blackie shrugged. "He's looking at any and all possibilities as is Dad. Come on." He tucked her tight to him and walked towards the storage barn at the back. "Mary was looking for something and she said you'd know where it was."

"And what was that?" She waited as he unlocked the door, reaching around him to turn on the lights. "Something for the kitchen?" When he didn't answer, she turned, finding his eyes on her, a slight smile curving his lips.

"You. She sent me after you." He reached and pulled her to him, his lips covering hers in a kiss before he hugged her tight. "She knew I just needed some time with you."

Julia pushed away. "We can't do this, Blackie. Not right now. Not while we're in danger."

He refused to let go of her hand, pulling her back to him. "We can. No one knows how long they have on earth. That's in God's hand." He watched as she mulled that over before he sighed. "I'm not rushing you, Jewel. Just think about it, okay?"

She finally nodded. "It is, Blackie. Just let me take my time. I've never had freedom before and I need to get through that before I jump into anything else."

"That's what God has been saying to me, Jewel. I won't rush you, but please, don't walk away from me." He realized he was begging and sighed, regretting his words as soon as he said them. "That wasn't fair. I shouldn't have said that."

She stood for a moment, staring at him. "Are you for real? You really just apologized to me. No one does that in real life." She turned to walk away, her footsteps slowing and then stopping as she heard his sigh and then his words.

"My family does, Jewel. It's how I was raised. If your words hurt someone, you make it right. That's life. Not everyone can do that. Sometimes the hurt goes too deep and words are said in hurt and anguish. I've seen it happen."

Blackie felt the blow that hit him, driving him to his knees and then to the floor, not seeing his assailant but hearing Julia's scream. His body hit where the wound was, pain flooding his body, darkening his vision. He didn't hear Julia's screams as she fought to get to him, restrained by men's hands, hands that clutched her arms and dragged her away from him. Blackie was hauled to his feet and dragged after her, not able to keep to his feet on his own. They were shoved through the back door and into the pastures that lined the back fence and then through the snow to a waiting vehicle. Shoved inside, Blackie's vision faded and he lost the fight to keep himself awake and alert.

Julia had fought her abductors, trying to get away, to reach Blackie. She had more bruises, she knew, and raised a hand to her face, to touch the soreness where she had been backhanded. Her eyes sought Blackie, wincing as he was manhandled and then shoved into the vehicle, sinking into stillness. She moved to go to him, but stopped as the weapon the one masked man was holding on Blackie turned to his temple. She sank back, fear coursing through every cell of her body. She wouldn't, couldn't help him, not right now. She blinked back tears of fright and then jumped as a blindfold was drawn over her face.

She listened intently, but couldn't hear any words from the men. She raged inside, knowing that no one would have known they were gone, not until they didn't show up for a meal or unless someone came looking for them. And who knew when that would be.

She laid her head back on the seat, knowing she had to relax and listen. Maybe she could figure out where she was by the sound, but she knew better. That only worked in books or movies, not in real life. One thing she knew for sure what that she would do everything to keep Blackie alive, even giving up her own life, and try to find a way for them to escape.

She felt the vehicle stop and she was dragged from it and shoved forward, stumbling as she tried to walk, fighting to keep her balance and losing, falling forward on her hands and knees, the impact jarring through her. She was hauled to her feet and the hand kept on her arm to draw her towards a building. She was shoved inside, this time just managing to keep her feet. She heard the sound of a body being dumped near her, then the slam of a door and the clicking of a padlock.

She waited, for what she wasn't sure, until she sank to her knees, feeling trapped once more. She could feel the panic rising inside her and struggled not to give in to the despair she felt. It was a losing battle and she curled forward, her arms wrapped around her head as the sobs came. This is not where I wanted to be. I thought You had given me my freedom, Lord, so what I am now a captive again? She sobbed until there were no tears left to fall but stayed curled up, not wanting to face anything or anyone. Who knew how long it would be before they were either free or dead? She had no doubt that was the plan, and she knew exactly who had arranged it.

Finn was on a mission. Her mother said she had told Blackie where to find more of the Christmas cellophane she needed for her packages but he hadn't come back. Finn searched the storage shed and then the house, not finding either Blackie or Julia. She grew afraid.

She turned as she heard her name called and walked into Jacob's arms.

"Aren't you working, Jacob?"

"I was, but God told me I needed to be here. Why?"

She looked up at him and then around. "I can't find either Julia or Blackie. Mom sent him to the storage shed but he's not there. They're not in the house either. They wouldn't just walk away."

Jacob's arm swept around Finn and he rushed her into the house, his phone coming out as he called for reinforcements. Finn stared at him, fear on her face.

"Jacob? What do you think happened to them?" She didn't see Samuel appear in the doorway behind her, concern on his face.

"I don't know, Finn. Stay here. Samuel, come with me." Jacob ran for the storage shed, Samuel on his heels.

"Jacob?"

"Blackie and Julia have disappeared." He paused at the door to the shed, not entering, knowing that he couldn't, not until the police had been through it.

"No, not that!" Samuel looked around, stepping to the end of the building. "There. Tracks leading to the pasture at the back." He turned, his eyes fearful but determined. "Tell Simon that. Maybe they can track them, somehow."

Jacob had his phone out, speaking rapidly to Simon, who was on his way from Merryville.

"He'll be about twenty minutes. He's sending officers around to search. He wants us to stay away from the area and from the shed if we can."

"That we can do. Lord, please, bring them home."

Jacob watched with compassion as his friend's father stood, eyes raised to heaven in prayer before he spoke. "They're in God's hands, but that's little comfort, now isn't it?"

"We have to trust that, Jacob." Samuel turned, his keen eyes on the younger man. "What did you four discover with the paperwork?"

"I really don't know, Samuel. I had to go take a call from a client and never got back to the others. Blackie was working through it today, I think. He may have come up with something I don't know about."

"He'll have left notes, I know that." He turned as he heard men moving towards him. "Let's talk to the officers. Then we'll get out of their way so they can investigate and you and I will go look for Blackie's notes."

Blackie stirred, his hand going to his abdomen where pain shot through the wound. He felt it, not sure if it had opened up again. He groaned as he rolled to his back, his eyes opening to darkness and cold. He pulled himself to a sitting position, shrugging deeper into his jacket and pulling it tighter around him. Somehow, he needed to get to his feet and wasn't sure if he even could.

He felt a hand on his face and turned, barely seeing Julia's face in the dark. He could make out the track of the tears on her face, mingled with the dirt.

"Jewel?" His voice came out as a croak. "Are you okay?"

"Okay? That's relevant isn't it, considering we locked up in some building who knows where. And they hurt you again." She reached for his jacket, pulling down the zipper and pulling up his shirt and sweater. "There's no blood on your T-shirt. That's good. But it had to have hurt."

He shoved her hands aside and pulled his sweater and shirt back down, zipping up his jacket. "Help me up." He stared as she shook her head. "Help me up, Jewel, or I swear, I'll crawl over to a wall and drag myself up, probably tearing the incision open."

She sighed. "Blackie, please. You've just come back to me."

"Now, Julia." He met her eyes and nodded. "Please? I need to see what I can find out about where we are."

"I've searched. I didn't see anything we can use as a weapon or any way we can get out."

Blackie gave a quick grin. "You weren't in the armed forces, love. We learned all kinds of tricks. Now, please, help me. I already know it's going to hurt."

He stood for a moment, his arm around her shoulders, catching his breath against the pain. He knew it had only been a few days since the attack and he shouldn't have come home, not yet. But something had made him and now he knew why. God had prompted him to come, to be there for his Julia when she needed him.

"Do you have any idea where we are?"

"None. They blindfolded me. I think there were four? Two had you and two had me. Oh, and a driver." She paced, anger emanating from her. "It has to be Hal. Will he never leave me alone?"

"When I get my hands on him, he will." Blackie paced the building, his hands running over the walls and then the doors. He frowned as he found the windows and tried them.

"Jewel, did you see any sign of any cameras?"

She moved towards him. "No, I didn't but they could have hidden them."

He shook his head. "They wouldn't go to that extreme. I think we're out in the country somewhere, just where I have no idea." He shoved at the window, stopping to hold his side. "This one is loose. I need to get it up and then you can climb through. When you get out, find some shelter and run for it."

She shook her head. "Not without you."

"I'll be right behind you. I need to know you're safe, so please run."

She finally nodded, reaching to help him push at the window. Cold air rushed in, stinging their faces. Blackie's hands were on Julia's waist as she jumped for the window, her legs sliding through and then she was dropping to the ground, her eyes searching the blackness, see another building behind the one they were in. She ran for it, knowing that she had to. If Blackie didn't make it out, she had to get to help. She paused, her back to rough wood siding, her breath coming in pants. She started as she heard a sound, then relaxed as she felt Blackie's hand reaching for hers and pulling her away from the area and onto the road.

"We'll follow this for now. I don't think they'll be back before dawn." He glanced at the sky, knowing he would have to find them shelter somewhere. Those were snow clouds, he thought, shivering at the thought. He wasn't used to snow.

They slugged through the debris on the road, Blackie's eyes following the tire tracks before he lost sight of them as clouds covered the moon. He shivered, drawing his coat closer around him, praying they could find help soon. He stumbled, barely keeping his balance, as Julia gave a cry and reached for him, her arms around him the only thing holding him upright.

"Blackie, we need to rest. You can't go on." Her voice was desperate as she searched for a place for them to rest. She thought she recognized the area and with sinking heart, realized they were miles from the B&B, miles from Mistletoe, a town going on with its Christmas celebrations, not realizing the danger some of its inhabitants were facing. She knew tomorrow would be the annual parade through the down town, where the children would be welcomed into each business and given small gifts and treats and that the carolers would be making their rounds tomorrow night.

She finally saw what she was looking for, a small rutted laneway leading away from the road. She directed Blackie that way, staggering under his weight as he slumped for a moment, her arms feeling weighted as she held him upright.

"This way, Blackie. There's a cabin down here. I'm not sure if it's still occupied or not, but there will be shelter either way. Just hold on to me, please. Don't fall. I'd never get you on your feet again. Blackie!" The tears lacing her voice reached him and he nodded.

"I'll make it, love. Head us in the right direction."

Julia stopped at the edge of the clearing, dismayed to see a dim light in the cabin and smoke rising from it. She had prayed that it would be empty, but it wasn't. Now her prayer was that they were friends and would help her. Blackie seemed oblivious to her concern, his only thought to stay upright and not fall, taking Julia with him. That he couldn't do.

Julia tapped at the door, waiting with apprehension as she heard shuffling coming towards the door and then the door cracking open. She sighed. She knew the man there. Old Jack, she thought. What was he doing out this far?

"Julia?" Jack pulled the door open and then reached to take part of her burden. "What are you doing out here? Who's this with you?"

"It's Blackie. I think you've met him, haven't you?"

Jack stopped, staring at Blackie. He knew of him. "He's that medic fellow, ain't he?"

"He is, Jack. I need your help. He was stabbed two or three days ago and today we were kidnapped. We were left way up the road. I need to get him laying down so I can check his wound."

Jack nodded, even as he helped Julia walk Blackie over to the second bunk in the cabin. Blackie sank to the bed, his head bobbing forward before Julia gently forced his shoulders to the bed and then helped Jack lift his feet up to rest there as well. She tore open his jacket, her hands frantic to find his wound.

"Oh, no! Jack, he's bleeding. I can't tell if he's broken open any stitches or not."

"Go, grab the lamp, Julia. Let me take a look." Jack's gruff voice had changed and strengthened, as if looking after Blackie had given him a purpose. He set the boots he had removed neatly under the end of the bunk and reaching, pulled a small table over close.

"Set the lamp here, girl, and then go get me some hot water. The kettle had just boiled. There's a clean basin by the sink, and you'll find towels in the second drawer." He peered around at her, his light gray eyes troubled. "Go. Do what I've asked."

She finally nodded, flying to do what he asked, and finding the first aid kit where he called to her to find. She flew back to his side, her hand to her mouth as she watched him pull the bloodied T-shirt back.

"You ain't going to faint on me, are you, girl? Cause if you are, go sit down somewheres. I can only look after one of you at a time."

"I'll be fine, Jack. Just let me help." She handed him the cloths and then the bandages as he called for them.

"There, that should do it. Thank you, girl." Jack stood, heading for the small kitchen to wash up and get rid of the debris. "I ain't seeing that he ripped open more than one or two stitches. I think what I did will help." He turned, his eyes suddenly hardening. "Who did this to you, girl?"

She shook her head. "I have no idea, Jack, but I think it was Hal's friends."

"That no-good Hal? Up to his tricks again, is he?"

She could hear Jack muttering under his breath and went towards him. "Jack? What do you know about Hal?"

"More than most people. He's the reason I lost my home. He stole it from me, just like he stole from others." He peered at her. "I know your mom is married to him, but she knew what she was doing and walked into it with open eyes. Your father wasn't so lucky."

"Jack? Whatever do you mean?"

"You never knew?" He watched her keenly, seeing the distress in her face and the questions. He sighed. He didn't want to be the one to tell her but it looks as if it was his story to tell. Thanks a lot, Lord, he muttered. I'm not the one to be doing this, but for some reason, You seem to think so. You'll have to give me the words. You know I ain't much of a one for talking.

"Sit, girl. Here. I only have tea. Hope that suits." He slid a tin mug in front of her, his eyes rising to check on Blackie.

"Anything hot works today, Jack." She wrapped her hands around the mug, relishing the warmth, her eyes on the liquid in it. "What was you need to tell me? Please? I need to know and it doesn't look as if anyone else is able to tell me."

Jack sat, his own tin mug in front of him as he rubbed at the back of his neck. Where did he start, he wondered? No matter what he said, she'd be hurt, and he decided she'd been hurt enough. He sighed, finally ready to tell the story that he had kept in his heart for so many years, a story he knew would hurt those around him and that he didn't want but couldn't help.

"Jack?" A soft hand closed around his, bringing his eyes to it and then to her face. It had been years since he had felt a female hand on his. They usually ran away from him, and he couldn't say that he blamed them.

"Julia, what I am about to say goes back many years, years you'll never get back with your daddy. I wish I could have stopped it, but I couldn't. I didn't have proof until now of what actually happened."

Julia stared at him, wonder on her face, not sure what he meant but knowing in her heart that his word would change her life dramatically, not necessarily for the good. She prayed for them all, her heart raised in a petition like she had never done before.

Chapter 13

Samuel turned as he heard steps behind him and Simon, Josh and Jacob approached him. He looked back down at the paperwork he had spread out on the dining room table, sorting it out by date and event.

"Samuel, where do we stand with what you have there?" Simon stood for a moment, his eyes on his friend, and then on the paperwork.

"It's a mess, that's what, Simon. How did he get away with what he did for all these years? You won't believe all I'm finding. I don't believe it myself." He stared at the paper he had in his hand, a list of deeds Hal had been guilty of. "Assault. Robbery. Blackmail. Extortion." He shot a look behind the men. "Jonathan's not here?"

Josh shook his head. "No. Were you expecting him?"

"I was praying that he wasn't." He handed Josh a paper he had picked up as he spoke, watching keenly as he read it and paled, before passing it to Jacob and from Jacob to Simon.

Simon's hand stilled as he read before he raised his head. "This changes everything, now doesn't it? I'll get someone on this. I'm too close, I know my lieutenant will want someone else to investigate this."

"Talk to Paul in my office. I've had him working on this. He may have some information for you that will help." He sighed, his hand rubbing the back of his neck. "I don't like this, not with Levi and Julia missing. Hal must have them."

Julia watched as Jack rose and paced over to the bunk, checking on Blackie and as she suspected, gathering his thoughts. He stood for a moment, his eyes on the younger man's face, knowing Julia had found the one God had planned for her. She was fortunate. He had thought he had all those years ago but lies and deceit had driven her away, not on his part. He had motive for revenge but chose not to go that route.

He sat once more at the table, sipping at his tea for a moment before he finally spoke.

"You'll need to let me say it in all one go, Julia. If you stop me, I just can't continue. It's been building in me for far too many years. Can you do that for me?"

She nodded. "I can, but it will be hard. Jack?"

He watched her face before he finally nodded. "All right then. I have no idea where to start."

"The beginning is usually a good place to start, isn't it?"

He shook his head at her levity, then began to speak.

"Years ago, I loved someone dearly. We had planned to marry but someone went to her, telling her lies about me, that I was dishonest, that I stole and assaulted people. No matter how much I protested my innocence, she walked away, taking part of my heart with her. She left town and I lost contact with her.

"The person who did this was Hal. Even as a teenager and young man, he was thoroughly dishonest. But he hid it so no one could prove anything, no matter their suspicions. I couldn't prove he's the one who said what he did, she refused to talk about it. Hal has continued as he was, getting worse and worse.

"He is not one of the descendants of the founding families, thank God for that. I'm not sure how long his family has been in town but I think his father was the one to move here. There were rumours about what he was mixed up in." He paused to sip at his tea.

"Now, about you. You have no idea how glad I am that you got away from Hal. He would eventually have killed you, and will continue to try unless we put him away. Unfortunately, your mother doesn't or won't see what he's doing. That I can't figure out.

"Your daddy was a wonderful man, caring, compassionate, loving. He loved you and your brother so much." He paused for a moment, as if to say something, then shook his head.

"I don't know if you know the real way your father died. It wasn't a sudden death as you've been told or how it was spread around town. Your father was held hostage and starved, finally having a heart attack. Your mom tried to put out that it was a car accident. He was found in a wrecked car but that's not how he died. He was way too young to have died. And it was Hal who did this to him. He caused your daddy's death."

Julia stared at him, horror and shock on her face, her hands over her mouth, before she began to shake.

"It was, Julia. I just now have the evidence I need to take to that Simon fellow and have him track down Hal and his cronies. But you're not safe until we find him."

"But if we're not safe, where do we go, Jack? I can't bring any more danger to Finn and her family."

"No, you can't. I have a place you two can hide out in. No one knows about it. It's not this place but it's not far. If I can get your fellow there early this morning, the snow will wipe out the tracks and they won't find you. I have a way of keeping in touch with you."

She finally nodded, rising and walking over to Blackie, slipping to her knees, an arm under his neck to raise his head to sip at the glass of water. She watched him as she stood for a moment before turning back to Jack and sitting near him.

"There's more to your story, isn't there, Jack?" She tilted her head to watch him, frowning at familiar movements of the head and hands.

"There is, Julia, and I'm not sure if I should even tell you."

"You're related to Dad, aren't you?"

He finally nodded, his hands reaching out to cover hers. "People in town have forgotten. Jack's not my real name. It's a name I chose to use when I came back here." He paused, his eyes taking on a faraway look. "Your daddy was my brother. I was away, overseas when he died and couldn't get home to the funeral. Your mom made sure I didn't find out for long afterwards."

Julia stared at him, her mouth suddenly widening into a huge smile. "Uncle Ben. It's you. No wonder I always felt a connection with you."

He held up a finger. "You can't tell anyone, girl. It would mean both of our deaths, if you do. You can't even tell your fellow over there until Hal and his cronies are behind bars. It's too dangerous."

She nodded even as she rose to hug her uncle. "I've missed you. I had almost forgotten about you. Mom made sure of that."

She sat beside him, her hands clutching his. "Why, Jack? Oh, I should call you Uncle Ben!"

"Not yet, girl. We need to keep that between us, at least for now. Don't even tell your fellow over there. He doesn't know Hal like I do. He'll use that against you and against him."

She nodded. "I know he will. I won't let him. He's taken enough of my life."

They talked for a long while before she sighed, then rose, walking over to drop on the floor by Blackie, her arm crossing his chest as she laid her head beside him, her heart praying as she had never prayed before. Her eyes closed and she slept.

Jack watched her for a while before he rose and gathered her up, placing her on his bunk and covering her up. He had watched from afar as she had grown. His heart broke to know the abuse she had told him about, that he hadn't had the evidence he needed before to prevent this. He drew up the blanket, tucking it around her, just like he used to when she was a toddler and he had gotten to watch her. He thought of Jonathan and knew he was in town but that he had to avoid him. Jonathan would know who he was. He was that keen, that young fellow, he thought.

He walked over to check on Blackie, finding the bleeding had slowed. He was worried that Blackie would develop an infection and he didn't have what he needed to give him. He couldn't even get what he needed from the forests at this time of year, and he didn't want to walk away from these two to go get the medications. He knew the physician in town, that he would gladly give him the antibiotics and treatments he needed. For you see, Jack too had been a medic in the navy, and Allan knew this. He trusted Jack in a way few had. Allan also knew exactly who he was and helped him in ways most people wouldn't.

Blackie stirred in the early morning, finding hands helping him sit up and drink. He nodded at a question and then slipped back into unconsciousness, pain evident on his face as he did so. Jack stood over him, fear warring with concern. He turned to look at Julia, knowing he had to get her up and get them moved.

Julia stirred as she heard Jack's voice and nodded, even as she sat up, her eyes flying to Blackie.

"How is he, Jack?" She pleaded with him to say he was better.

"He's hurting, girl, and I have to hurt him even more to move him. Come on. Let's get you two out of here."

"But how? We don't have a vehicle."

Jack smirked at her. "I do. It's a little ramshackle but it runs real smooth. Let's get your fellow out the back door."

Jack lifted Blackie in his arms, grunting a bit at his weight, then nodded for Julia to open the door leading from the kitchen. She stood, open mouthed, staring at the old truck there.

"This is yours? I've seen it around town and never knew."

"Not too many people do. That's a blessing right now. I don't think Hal or his cronies know. Here, you climb in the middle and hold on to your fellow real tight."

Julia's arms surrounded Blackie as Jack pulled away from the cabin, heading back to Mistletoe and then through the quiet early morning streets. He chose a street near the edge of town, heading for the quarry and then beyond, finally pulling in beside a small house and parking behind it. He ran around the truck and once more gathered Blackie into his arms, handing Julia the keys.

"It's all ready to use. There's a bedroom just off the kitchen. We'll put him there. It's the easier spot to look after him."

Jack stood back, his eyes assessing Blackie and knowing he had to go for help. Blackie was starting to run a fever and he couldn't treat it without supplies. His hand on her arm drew Julia back to the kitchen.

"The kitchen is well stocked with canned and dry goods. Keep him warm and get as much water down him as you can. Broth if possible. There are some cans of that here." He looked at her, concern on his face. "Are you able to do that for me?"

She nodded, her eyes fearful, but determination on her face. "I can. But I need you to do something for me. You need to find Simon and Samuel, Blackie's father. You need to tell them what you know and today. I don't think we'll have much longer."

"No, we don't. Hal's been released, I hear, and is on the hunt for you two. You should be safe here. No one knows about this place. It's not in my name and the name it is in no one knows."

"Jack?"

He shook his head as he reached for his keys and then the door handle. "No, I won't say. Just take care of your fellow. I'll be back as soon as I can." He paused. "Your father was a real Christian, and Lord knows I've tried to live that way. Pray like you never have before, Julia. I know you believe." He was gone before she could respond.

Jack watched as Simon walked back to his vehicle. He suspected he had been in the B&B all night. He approached carefully, eyes watchful in the dim morning light, before he paused beside Simon.

"Simon, you and I need to talk and talk now. Where can we meet? I don't want to be seen talking with you."

Simon's fingers continued to turn the key in his vehicle lock as he listened. "You sound like you could use a good meal, my friend. I hear tell the back door of The House is unlocked at this time of the morning. Josh will feed you."

Jack shuffled off, back into the character he had lived for so many years. Simon slid into his car, his eyes watchful, before he drove a circuitous route to Josh's cafe, parking down the street, and making his way quickly to the back door. Josh looked up from his prep table and nodded towards his office. Simon raised a hand in greeting, then snagged some muffins and tea. He knew that was Jack's preference.

He set the food down on the table by Jack, shrugging out of his jacket and turning to hang it on the coat rack before he sat himself, picking up his cup of coffee and inhaling the aroma. He waited as Jack ate, knowing Jack well enough to know that he would speak when he was ready to. He needed a break and a break soon. He feared for Blackie's life and that of his lady, Julia. He had no idea where they were.

"They're alive, Simon." He almost missed Jack's low voice and spun in his chair to stare at him. Jack's keen eyes peered at him, eyes Simon suddenly realized were clear and calm, not what he had been led to expect from him.

"What did you just say?" Simon kept his own voice low.

"They're alive, Simon. I have them tucked away somewhere safe. We need to keep them there for as long as we can." He took another bite of muffin, his eyes on it. "Does Josh bake these himself? They're good."

"Yes, he does, and yes, they are." Simon breathed out a sigh of frustration. "Explain yourself, Jack."

Jack reached for a napkin and wiped his fingers, then sipped at his tea. "I said I have them tucked away. Somehow they escaped from where they were locked up. Julia helped get Blackie to me and we've dressed his wound. It was broken open again." He tilted his mug towards Simon. "She's a wonder and good for him. Doc will get me some supplies and I'll dress it again when I see them."

"No, when we see them."

"Not happening, Simon. If you go with me, Hal or his people will see you and follow us. He's watching each one of you now, including Blackie's father and also the B&B. There is no way to get you to them without being seen."

Simon sat back, frustrated, knowing the truth in Jack's words. "I guess. But what did they tell you?"

"Blackie's been out of it for most of the night. Julia finally slept until I woke her early this morning to move them. No one should be able to find the house where I have them. And no, I'm not saying where. I trust you men, but who's to say someone hasn't bugged this office or anywhere you gather."

Simon nodded, looking around as he heard Josh saying something outside the door before he cracked it open and slipped in.

"Simon, I don't have long before the breakfast rush starts and I'll likely be called out. What's the word?" Josh watched Jack closely, knowing something was different about him.

"Jack has them tucked away. Blackie's wound opened and Julia's fine. He won't say where though." Simon was not happy about that.

"Makes perfect sense to me. We need to keep them safe and we can't tell what we don't know." Josh studied Jack closer and realized who he looked like. Jack was watching him and nodded, a finger coming to his lips. "Jack, what can we get you to help out?"

"Doc's getting me supplies. I have food stashed there. Just need some fresh stuff and some bread. That will keep us for now."

"You're heading back there? Ask Amy in the kitchen for what you want. It's on the house. Tell her that."

Josh's question had him shaking his head. "Not until this afternoon when it gets dark. If I feel a real need I'll head back." He dug into his pocket, pulling out the papers he had prepared the night before and handing them to Simon. "Here. This is what you can do. I know for a fact that Julia's father was tortured and killed, why I'm still working on. Hal was behind it." He tapped the papers Simon held with a long forefinger. "Work through that, son. I think you'll find the evidence you need to finally put him away." Jack stood, his eyes shifting between the two men before he shook his head and slipped out the door.

Josh stared after him, then back at Simon, who was leafing through the papers, horror growing as he realized the implications of what Jack had just handed him.

"Simon?"

Josh's voice brought his head up and he shook it. "This is worse than I ever imagined. Jack, there, he found evidence that Hal had Julia's father killed, because he wanted what he had in property. I don't think it would have been a very pretty picture when he found out he got none of it."

Josh's shocked look stopped him. "Murder? That's what he's saying?" Josh's hand ran through his hair, before he rose and paced. "That just changes everything." He spun. "You'll need to talk to Samuel. Their lives are in more danger than we ever thought."

"I know. I just wish I knew where Jack had them stashed."

"He won't tell, I can guarantee you that." Josh rose. "Keep me in the loop and if I need to I'll cut myself free from here." He paused. "I don't like this, Simon. We need to make this a matter of prayer and strong prayer at that."

"We do and we have. Mary said the prayer chain had set up in the church prayer room, opening it up 24/7 until these two are home."

"That's good." Josh paused, not sure if he should admit he knew who Jack was related to, but knew Jack has his reasons for not saying.

Julia stood for a moment in the late afternoon, her eyes on the door, wondering when Jack would come back. Blackie's fever had worsened and he was fighting her when he roused, wanting to get up and go and find her, to protect her. She had only just been able to keep him still, but she knew eventually the fever would drive him to his feet and out the door, and she would be unable to stop him. She prayed as she hadn't prayed in years, fearing the worse and hoping for the best.

She paused in her walk as she heard footsteps and then voices. Her eyes flew to the door. Yes, all the locks were engaged, and she had kept the drapes and blinds closed, a suggestion of Jack's she was now glad he had made. Her hand at her throat, she crept towards Blackie's room, praying that whoever it was would leave.

She listened to the voices, two men, she thought, discussing the house and whether someone was in there. The doors were tried but didn't open. The doors shook as they were tried harder. Her head dropped in fear as she silently slipped into Blackie's room and shut the door, looking for anything to defend herself and finding nothing. Finally, she heard the voices moving away.

Jack, don't come back just yet. Not until they're gone. She turned towards the door, opening it once more and sneaking through the house to the front, where she peeked through the window on the front door. She didn't see anyone. She lowered herself back to the floor and leant against the wall. She couldn't take much of this, she thought, but then the determination not to let Hal win coursed through her. He was after a treasure that wasn't his. She wouldn't let that happen. She had never heard how the actual wills from the founding fathers worked, that only the founding families' descendants got what was in them. Even if she had, it was doubtful it would have eased her worry.

Hours later, dark had descended. She was careful to keep a light low, hoping if anyone saw it, they would think it was just a light on a timer. She heard quiet footsteps outside and grabbed up the fireplace poker she had found and kept near her. The locks opened and Jack stepped in, his eyes on the deck for a moment before he turned and saw Julia standing there, poker raised.

"Had some visitors, did you, girl?" Jack grinned as she shook the poker playfully at him.

"We did. I was so scared they would get in."

"Did they see you?"

She shook her head. "No, I had everything shuttered like you asked and then hid in Blackie's room. I recognized one of the voices. It was Tad, Hal's brother."

Jack nodded. "They're searching for you two, and it makes sense they would search every outlying building." He set his parcels on the table and shrugged out of his jacket, hanging in on a chair back. He nodded towards the bedroom. "How is he?"

"His fever has gone up. I've given him what I can, but it's a fight to keep him there. He keeps wanting to get up and find me." She sighed. "That's what he was like in the hospital that day. He kept forgetting I was there."

Jack grinned at her again. "That boy in there is in love with you, girl. That's as plain as the nose on your face." He watched with compassion as she nodded. "Now, let me have a look at him and dress his wound." He sorted through the parcels, finding the one that he wanted. "Doc sent out some medications and more dressings for me."

He paused at the doorway, his eyes on his niece as she moved to put away the food he had brought, his heart breaking for her. This was not how he had wanted to introduce himself to her again, but it seemed that was how God had it planned. He shook his head, not understanding the workings of the Lord, and headed into the bedroom.

He drew in a breath as he saw the wound, knowing they had a fight on their hands. It was no wonder he had a high fever. He hurried back to the kitchen, searching for a bowl and filling it with hot water, his words quiet and calm as he talked with Julia. She followed him, knowing what he had found. She had seen it earlier herself but hadn't touched it, not wanting to make it worse.

Blackie flinched and groaned, his body twisting as he fought the pain of the wound being cleaned. He finally laid still, Julia's hand on his cheek, her other hand holding his. They had gotten pain medication and antibiotics down him, but not without a fight. Jack watched the IV drip, adjusting it as necessary, giving Julia instructions on what to do if he wasn't around. In his heart, he knew he wouldn't leave, not unless he absolutely had to. And the only way that would be was if Allan reached out to him by phone. He was the only one who had Jack's number.

Julia finally sagged down into a chair, her arms folded on the table, her head on her arms. Her uncle rested his hand on her back for a moment before he moved to the stove, coming back with the tea she needed. A quiet thank you, muffled by her arms, was all he got.

"Julia. Look up, please." Jack waited until she did, seeing the fatigue in the whiteness of her face and the dark circles under her eyes. "I talked to Simon and that Josh. Simon has everything I know and he'll look into it." He grinned briefly. "He was a little put out that I wouldn't bring him out here."

"It's better that they don't come. It was too close a call today, Jack. If they had got in, I couldn't have stopped them."

"No, you couldn't have. That worries me." Jack sipped at his tea, eyes thoughtful as he worked through what had to be done. "Pray that what we've done for your fellow works. Because if he isn't better by morning, I'll have to take him to Doc, and they'll find us for sure. They'll be watching him too, and likely have someone at the hospital in Merryville."

She nodded. "I know that." She rose, dropping a kiss on her uncle's cheek. "Now that you're here, I'm going to get some sleep. Wake me in a couple of hours, will you?"

Jack didn't respond, knowing full well he wouldn't be doing that. He sighed, taking their cups to the sink and rinsing them out, setting them upside down on the drainboard, before he turned, crossing his arms over his chest, deep in thought. A groan from Blackie had him heading that way, concern wafting through him.

Chapter 14

Blackie roused towards morning, his mouth dry and feeling like it was full of cotton balls. He felt the hand under his head, holding it up so he could sip, water he thought, but he wasn't even really sure of that. He groaned as his head was lowered, his hand going to his abdomen.

"Blackie, boy. Are you awake?" A rough voice reached him, kindness in it.

"No, not really. Why? Do I need to be? What day is it, any way? I need to find Julia. She's in danger." Blackie's eyes flickered opened and then closed, he was just too tired to keep them open.

"I need to look at your wound. It may hurt."

Blackie nodded, steeling himself for what he knew would come. He gritted his teeth, then relaxed, drifting off to sleep again.

Jack tucked the blanket up around Blackie's neck, feeling his forehead, glad to feel the coolness there. Blackie's fever had broken, but Jack knew only too well it could go up again. He was not out of the woods, yet, he thought. He reached to check the IV drip and then sat back down in the rocking chair he had placed near the bed, a light kept low the only illumination in the room, and reached for his Bible. He had just turned to a favourite passage when Blackie had roused, a passage about touching the hem of the Master's garment. It was a passage he had claimed many times over.

He turned as he heard soft footsteps as the dawn light cracked the morning sky. Julia stood in the door way, her hair still tousled, wearing what he suspected was a sweatshirt of Blackie's over her jeans. He had slipped unnoticed in the B&B and found Blackie's room the day before, carefully taking only a few clothes that he didn't think would be missed.

"Jack?" There was both dread and hope in her voice.

"He was awake, girl. The fever's broken for now, but we're not out of the woods yet. I'll have to go back to town to scout out the area again, but I won't leave for now. Maybe tomorrow."

"Tomorrow? Do we have until then?"

Jack nodded. "I suspect we do. We'll make sure we do." He rose and stopped beside her in the doorway. "He'll make it, Julia. Trust God on that."

She nodded, her eyes on Blackie. "I pray he does. He's been talking to me about treasures that we need to find. He tells me I'm his treasure. I don't see that, Jack. I'm broken, that's what I am."

Jack turned her to face him, sorrow filling him at her words, then anger at how she had been treated. "No, you are a treasure, Julia. God sees that in you.

———

189

He is your treasure, first and foremost. Seek Him, and you'll find Him." Then he pointed at Blackie. "Next, that young man is there is a treasure God prepared for you. Don't chase him away." He paused, not quite sure how to continue. "Pearls are just grains of sand until the oyster coats them, making a gem that people pay a lot for. That happens with a lot of precious gems. Hardship and beatings and what have you make them what they become. Don't let anyone put you down.'"

She finally nodded. "Thank you. I forgot to ask. Has Simon found them yet?"

Jack turned her towards the kitchen, seating her and then reaching to fill the kettle, setting it back on the stove and turning on the burner, watching it for a moment as he thought. He finally shook his head. "No, he hasn't. He's getting close, but there's still a lot he has to work through. Hal is staying one step ahead of him, and I need to find out why."

Julia shook with fear at the thought of what lay ahead of them, her mind blanking out, not hearing the concern in Jack's voice as he called to her. A groan from Blackie reached through the darkness, bringing her to her feet and into his room, her hand on his head, finding it warm again

"Jack? His fever's back. What do we do now?"

"We fight it, girl, with everything we have. We'll keep him alive for you."

Chapter 15

Samuel stood in Josh's office, his eyes on the younger man.

"Who did you say was here?"

"An old fellow from around town. He does odd jobs for people to earn an income. He says he has Blackie and Julia stashed somewhere but won't tell us."

"I want to talk with him. Now, if possible."

Josh shook his head. "He's not in town. I've looked, knowing you would. I have no idea where he goes when he leaves town. No one does. He just comes and goes." Josh sank into his desk chair, rubbing a hand down his face. "He says they're safe. He also says Hal has people watching each one of us, the B&B and also Doc."

Samuel paced in the small area that was clear. "He would. I have documentation back that I need to go over with all of you. I guess it will have to be you, Jacob and Simon for now. I'll have to pretend to be Levi, I guess."

Josh started to laugh at that, bringing a welcome grin to Samuel's face. "I don't know about that, Samuel. Looking at you is like looking at Blackie in a few years."

Samuel just shook his head at Josh's jesting. "Are the other two heading this way or do we go theirs?"

"Here, I think. They're planning on showing up after I close. Simon has some things as well, he said." He turned as he heard the men's voices, Simon teasing Jacob about something, Jacob's voice raised in protest.

Simon stuck his head in the door. "Your staff are gone, Josh, but Amy said she left our meals in the warming oven. Let's go eat. I didn't have lunch and I'm starved."

Josh shook his head at him. "You're always hungry." He shoved himself upright, groaning to himself. It had been a long day, with two staff off sick, and tomorrow promised to be just as long.

They settled around the counter in the kitchen, Samuel's keen eyes watching his son's friends as they joked and teased one another. He knew they were deliberately doing this, to hide their worry from him. He finally pushed his plate away, wiping his mouth on his napkin, catching Simon's eyes as he did so.

"Samuel? You found something?"

"I have. David in my office did a real good in-depth search, finding information that we didn't know about." He paused, gathering his thoughts, and then reaching for his jacket to pull out the papers he had stuffed in there. "Now, let me think for a moment.

"Okay, so this is what he's found. Hal is not related to any of the founding families. That we knew. Nor is Julia's mother. Where she is from is not relevant at the moment but may become so. Julia's father was related to Finn's family, a cousin I think Timothy said. That we have confirmed. Because he is deceased, whatever he left goes to Julia and Jonathan. That has been what Hal has been after.

"David did find an interesting wrinkle. Julia's father, John, had a brother, Benjamin, who disappeared a number of years ago. He was in the service, came home after he found out John had died, returned to the service, mustered out and then disappeared. David wasn't able to access any further information on him because it suddenly became classified and unavailable. We haven't been able to find out why."

Simon nodded. "Do we have any idea where he ended up?" He turned as a sound from Josh. "Josh?"

Josh sighed, knowing he would have to tell what he knew. "I know where he is, but he really doesn't want it told about."

"And just how do you know that?" Jacob stared at him. "You can't leave us hanging like this, you know."

Josh nodded. "I can tell you, but we can't let anyone know we know." He groaned as they laughed at his choice of words. "Not quite how I meant to say that." He paused, his eyes on Samuel, knowing Samuel would really want to talk to the man. "It's Old Jack. He confirmed it this morning when we were meeting."

A flurry of talk broke out at that before Simon turned to Josh. "But he never said a word. Not that I heard."

"No, he didn't. He caught me watching him and realized I had figured out who he looked like. Julia and Jonathan do look like him."

Samuel nodded. "I've seen him around, just didn't realize he was so involved in this." He sighed. "He won't let us near him, I know that now. He'll look after Blackie and Julia."

Simon nodded as Jacob and Josh agreed. "That helps to make sense of what I found then. I knew there was someone in town watching them, but I didn't know who exactly. We've been digging into Hal's background. There is an officer on the way in from a town four hours away, with an arrest warrant for murder. Hal has been charged in a man's murder from there. That will take him out of here but that doesn't solve the problem of his friends watching for Blackie and Julia."

"We'll find them, Simon, and bring them to you. I have some of my men coming in this weekend. They're bringing the family back. They've wanted to be here, but I talked them into waiting."

Blackie's head turned restlessly as his eyes opened and stayed open. It was early the next morning. His body ached and he didn't know why. He felt for his ribs, finding the bandage just below them, but not knowing why he had it. He felt a cool hand feel his head and he looked up, a frown on his face. He didn't know the man.

"You're finally away, Blackie. That's good. Here. Take a sip of water." Jack raised Blackie's head to help him sip and gently lowered it once he was through.

"You've been through a lot, young man. There's a lady out there real worried about you. Here. Let's get you cleaned up some and then I'll go get her."

Julia looked up from the chair she had been sleeping in, not willing to head for her bed as she heard Jack's footsteps heading her way.

"Julia, girl. He's awake. At least he was. Come, see your fellow."

Julia scrambled from the chair, her feet tangling in the blankets, fighting until she was free, Jack holding her arm to help her stay upright.

"Did he speak, Jack?"

Jack shook his head. "Not yet." He watched with a small smile as she headed for Blackie.

She paused in the doorway, her eyes on Blackie, watching for him to rouse again. She walked quietly across the room, sitting on the side of the bed, causing his head to turn towards her and his eyes open.

"Julia? You're okay?" His voice was rough and not above a whisper.

"I am. I can't say the same for you, though. You scared me."

He reached for her hand, squeezing hers gently. "I'm sorry. I didn't mean to." He looked around. "Where are we?"

"Jack's place. He brought us here to keep us safe. We've been here for a couple of days. You won't remember that though. You've been pretty much out of it."

Blackie nodded, his eyes sliding closed, before he asked. "You'll stay, Julia? You won't disappear on me, will you, love?"

"No, Blackie. I won't. Not for the rest of our lives, if I can help it." She knew he didn't hear that, he was already asleep.

Jack stood in the doorway, his eyes watchful, a sad smile on his face. Her father should be here for this, he thought. But then if he was, maybe these two would never had met.

"Jack, when do you head back into town?" Julia's question caught him off guard later that morning.

"Likely mid afternoon, seeing as your fellow is now sleeping. Why?"

She shrugged. "I just wondered. I want to know what's going on. Can you find one of the fellows and ask them?"

Jack gave a soft laugh. "Oh, I guarantee you I'll find them. They'll be on the look out for me."

She shook her head at him. "Just come back with some news." She turned back to the broth she was heating, not seeing the speculative look on his face.

Jack tapped at Josh's office door later, bringing Josh's head up and then entering, closing the door behind him.

"He's alive, Josh, before you ask. It was a struggle, but he's pulled through."

Josh was relieved to hear that, pointing at the chair for Jack to sit. "And Julia?"

"She's tired, worn out from nursing her fellow." He studied the younger man. "Where does the investigation stand?" His voice had lost the croak that Josh associated with him.

"Simon's arrested Hal for a murder in another town. The officer headed off with him around noon. His friends are still in town, but laying low right at the moment." Josh looked down at his desk, not seeing the paperwork he had been immersed in. "When will you bring them back into town?"

"Blackie needs two or three days to get some strength back. He's not got much left to fight with right now." Jack stood and stretched. "Did Simon take a look at the paperwork I left?

"He did. He's following up on a few leads. You had some interesting facts there for him. Facts that Blackie's father has confirmed."

Jack nodded. "I know Hal had Julia's father killed. I still have to prove that."

"And we will. With Hal gone, his friends may talk now. He'll be put away for a long while. The judge there said there would be no bail set, given his past history and what he is up to right now."

"That's good news, but he can still control his friends' movements from there."

"Not if we can help it, and we're trying our best to make sure that he can't."

Josh stood for a moment, watching the door swing closed behind Jack as he walked away. He sighed, knowing he would not be finishing his paperwork now. He had to find Samuel. He turned, hearing a noise behind him but not seeing the man who struck the blow, knocking him into his chair, slamming his head on the desk and sending him to the floor unconscious. The man stood over him for a moment, cursing at the turn of events. He needed Josh to talk and know he wouldn't be able to. He followed Jack, unaware that Jack knew he was there and had stopped to ask someone to go back and check on Josh.

Jack finally ducked into a doorway, listening to the footsteps and watching as the man passed him, darting out and taking him down. Twisting his arm up behind him, he yanked him to his feet and shoved him back towards The House, finding Simon running his way.

"You caught him! Great!" Simon slid to a halt, his balance off for a moment as he hit a patch of ice. "He's knocked Josh out, but Jacob's with him. Let's get him to the department." He peered closer at the man. "Well, well, well! Just who did you catch, Jack?"

"Hal's brother and his partner in crime." Jack shoved the man forward, his voice quiet as he talked to Simon.

Josh looked up, pain in his eyes, as Jack walked back through his door.

"We caught the man, Josh. Hal's brother."

Josh went to nod, then decided against doing just that. "Good! Now how many more do we need to find?"

Jack grinned for a moment, then sobered. "I think you'll need to find five or six. That should do it. Also Julia's mother. She's not innocent in any of this."

"No, she's not. Simon's looking for her but she's disappeared."

Jack nodded. "Thought she would. She has family back in her home town. They'll hide her."

Josh stared at him for a moment. "You seem to know her well."

Jack sighed. "I do, unfortunately." He paced again. "I need to get Blackie and Julia back, but it will be a couple of days."

"Whenever. Just keep them safe."

Blackie stood for a moment, his hands braced against the door frame, his eyes closing as he caught his breath. It was two days after he had finally woken up, and Julia had protested that he shouldn't come out to eat in the kitchen. He just stared her down and told her to leave the room, he was getting up and getting dressed. Jack had bitten back a grin at that, as Julia brushed by him, a thunderous look on her face.

Sliding down onto a chair, Blackie rested his arms on the table, his side burning from the exertion of getting dressed and then walking the few feet to the kitchen. Lord, I can't protect myself or Julia, not just yet. How do I do this?

Jack's hand rested for a moment on his shoulder and Blackie nodded. He looked up at Julia, seeing the concern in her face.

"We'll need to get back to town, Jack. I need to talk to the others." Blackie winced as he looked up and moved slightly.

"We will, Blackie, but not today. Today, I'm heading in. You two are staying here."

"Jack, it's only a few days now to Christmas and my family will be here. I need to see them." Blackie protested.

"Blackie, please. Let Jack go today. Maybe tomorrow he'll let us go. I know Hal and his brother have been arrested, that Mom has disappeared, but he still has men out there that will keep after us. Next time, we might not be so lucky. They almost killed you this time."

Blackie nodded. "I know. I want justice, not revenge. I need to be there to see it done."

Jack looked between the young couple, wondering which one of them would prevail, and saw the moment Blackie decided it wasn't worth the fight. Blackie reached for Julia, drawing her close to him and arm around her waist. She wrapped her arms around him and laid her head down. Jack could see her lips moving and knew she was praying.

Blackie finally reached around, pulling Julia down onto his lap, wrapping his arms around her. How do I keep her safe, Lord, when I'm so sore?

Jack paused in drawing on his jacket, watching Blackie. "How be we head into town tomorrow, you two? Your Dad should have everything set up enough to keep you safe."

Blackie snorted, drawing a frown from Julia. "Likely. I'm sure he's working on it. But I don't think all the precautions we're taking will work. They'll find us, somehow, I know."

Jack nodded before he walked away, knowing that Blackie was likely right and that scared him. He didn't want someone close to his niece hurt again, and that was sure to happen.

Julia paced the house later that afternoon. She was bored and didn't know what to do. If they were leaving tomorrow, she would need to make sure the house was tidy and clean. She sighed, shooting a look at Blackie where he sat, engrossed in a book he had found on the shelf. She wouldn't disturb him, she knew. Finding the cleaning supplies, she worked away, ending up in the bedroom she had been using. Jack had mentioned that he wanted to redo it at some point and asked for her opinion. She didn't realize that he had bought the house for her and had intended to give it to her when she turned thirty, a couple of years from then. But that had changed when he saw how she and Blackie cared for one another.

She moved to the window, finding a crack to peer through, as she heard a vehicle. She froze, terror racing through her, as she saw the men who climbed out. She ran for Blackie, pulling him from his chair and with her towards the spare room.

"Julia? Is that Jack out there?" Blackie was bewildered, his book still in his hand.

"No, it's not. Stay here. I'm going after our jackets and boots." She was gone and back in a flash. "Here. Get yours on. Jack told me of a way out of the house and I think we'll have to take it. I don't think they'll know we were here. Jack's made sure of that." She grabbed the book from his hand and placed it on a table, then shoved her feet into her boots and her arms into her coat before heading for the closet and kneeling. "He said there's a trap door here somewhere. It leads downstairs. There are flashlights down there. We can lock it from underneath."

Her scrabbling fingers finally found the latch and she pulled, the door rising easily. She looked up at Blackie. "I need you to go down first. Please, Blackie! Don't be a gentleman at this point."

He nodded, his feet finding the ladder and he scrambled down it, his eyes seeing a flashlight before Julia's movement blocked the light. Partway down, she reached and pulled the door closed, shoving the latch home and then dropping the few feet to stand beside him. They listened to the sound of the door crashing in, the heavy hurried footsteps above them, and the angry shouts and accusations and curses. The sounds finally ceased.

Julia leant back against the ladder, her eyes adjusting slowly to the darkness. Blackie moved to stand beside her, his hand on her arm.

"When do you think it will be safe to go back up?" His voice was low.

"I don't know. Jack didn't say when he would be back. I hate putting him in danger."

"He's done it willingly and I would like to know why." Blackie's hand kept her from moving away.

Julia finally sighed, her chin dropping for a moment. "He's my uncle and I never knew it. My Dad's brother. He's trying to prove Hal and Mom had Dad killed. He said he had proof and was going to talk to Simon."

They heard hurried footsteps overhead and then a low voice calling for Julia and Blackie. They waited, not knowing if it was Jack or not. Finally, the voice raised to a normal level.

"That didn't work. I guess they're not here after all."

"And who said they were? We don't have time to follow false leads." The voice was hard and coarse and Blackie felt Julia tensing under him.

He leaned over close enough to whisper in her ear. "Hal?"

She nodded. "He was supposed to be back in jail." Her voice was equally low. "How'd he get out?"

They waited, Julia making sure that Blackie was not standing, but sitting as much as he could given the small space. They listened, finally hearing new footsteps and quiet voices.

Julia jumped as a tap came to the floor above them and the door was tried.

"Julia, girl. Open up. It's me. I've got Simon with me."

Julia stared at the door for a moment before she felt Blackie's hand on her.

"Go on, Jewel. It's Jack."

She finally nodded, heading up the ladder and sliding the door bolt back, letting Jack lift it up and then reach to help first her and then Blackie from the space. Jack hugged Julia, then stood, hands on her arms and studied her.

"You're okay? They didn't find you, I gather."

She shook her head. "I heard them coming and pulled Blackie down there." She turned to study the hole, watching as Jack closed it up again. "I wouldn't have known it was there if you hadn't told me."

"That's the whole purpose of it. It was here when I bought the place. I have no idea what the original purpose was for it."

Simon had been speaking quietly with Blackie and now turned to Julia. "Blackie says it was Hal?"

Julia nodded. "It was. I recognized his voice. I think it was his cousin with him." She shivered. "If I hadn't heard them, they'd have taken us, and you would never had found us."

"We know, Julia girl. Now, let's get you back to town. That's what we came for. Simon's made arrangements for a place in town for you."

Julia nodded, her eyes going to Blackie, who was watching her closely. His face was white and she could tell he was in pain. "Let's get going then. Blackie needs to be laying down somewhere."

———

Simon turned at that and saw what Julia saw, catching his friend as his legs gave way.

"Sorry, guys. I think I did too much." Blackie shook his head.

"That's okay, friend. We need to talk too. I have information that your Dad's dug up that we need to go over."

Blackie nodded, heading for the door. "Then let's go do just that."

Julia watched later as Simon stood, his eyes on Blackie as he slept before he left the room, pulling the door closed behind him.

"Did I hurt him more, Simon, taking him down that ladder?"

Simon shook his head. "No, Doc said you didn't. In fact you probably saved both your lives. Now, we need to talk, Julia. They've proven they will not stop until they find you. We're still trying to determine how they knew you were there. Jack was careful coming and going."

"I know. I think you'll find a lot of homes broken into around the area, with nothing gone. They've been searching the area looking for us and that would have been a logical step."

Simon agreed, before pointing towards Timothy's office. "Let's head there. Jack is waiting for us."

Samuel turned from the window and was at her side before she barely made it into the room, wrapping her into a hug that tightened with feeling. He finally stepped back, blinking his eyes, unable to speak before he led her to the couch and made her sit. He sat beside her, his eyes on Jack, a puzzled look on his face.

Jack turned to Simon. "Any word on Hal or his cousin?"

"We've found the cousin, just waiting on a warrant to arrest him. Hal has disappeared again." Simon was frustrated. "Hal shouldn't have gotten out. Some clerical error they're trying to remedy. He's to go back into custody, if and when we find him."

Samuel turned as he heard a sound from the doorway and then rose, walking towards one of his men, speaking with him for a few minutes before he returned, handing Simon the paperwork he had been given.

"Take a look at that, Simon, and see what you think."

Simon reached for it, his eyes scanning it quickly. "This is great. I'll have one of our detectives verify it, of course, and then we can start making arrests. It should be over soon, Julia."

She stood, pacing, her arms wrapped around herself. "Not soon enough, Simon. Not soon enough." She turned, a hard look on her face. "I want to find him. I want it to all come out what he's done over the years to me and to Jonathan. I want you to say he's a suspect in Dad's death."

Simon nodded. "We can do that. But we have to be careful. He'll come after you. He's mad and he really doesn't care."

She sighed. "I know. I'm trusting God to protect me. We're standing on the edge of bringing him down and returning what should belong to the founding families' descendants. I don't care about that for me, but you four fellows and Finn deserve it."

Simon closed his eyes. She was really going to do that, wasn't she, Lord? "Julia, promise me you won't make a move without talking to me." He finally got her to agree, but knew if she had the chance, she'd go out on her own.

Julia watched as Simon headed out, knowing he wasn't happy with her, but also knowing that she wouldn't put lives at risk. He didn't know though that's what she planned to do, put her own life out there and draw Hal out, once and for all.

She moved away from the other men, not seeing them watching her, Jack following to the hall to see where she was heading. She slipped into the room she had been using and searched for her backpack. It was time she moved on and did what she had to do. She didn't realize that in doing so, she would hurt Blackie in a way that she never dreamed of. She quickly packed what she wanted and then slipped out the window, shoving the screen back into place and heading around the house, watching for anyone who was around. Her footsteps led her away from the house and to the downtown, to a building she knew well. She had hidden there many times. She drew a deep breath. Now would come the hard part. Staying out of sight until she could determine where Hal was and draw him out. She needed to do this. Lord, forgive me. Don't let me hurt Blackie too much. He's just not in shape to fight for me and he will. I don't want him to die.

Tears fell as she moved into the darkness of the building, her hand finding the familiar wall and knowing she was almost to the hidden room she had there.

Blackie stirred later, his eyes opening as he stared around before he sat up, scrubbing at his face. He needed to clean up but first he needed to see Julia. He searched the house for her, finally standing at her closed bedroom door, Jack behind him. He tapped. When there was no answer, he reached for the knob, dread filling him.

She was gone, he thought, as he turned a slow circle in the room, his eyes finally resting on Jack, who nodded.

"She slipped away on us, didn't she, boy? Well, I have ways of finding her. She's in hiding somewhere, trying to protect you. That's what she does."

Blackie sighed. "I know. I just wish she hadn't gone. I shouldn't have slept."

"Wouldn't have made any difference, son. She'd have gone anyway." Jack sat on the edge of the bed, pointing Blackie to the easy chair. "You need to understand. When someone is abused, they will shut down. They will try to protect those they love as well by drawing the abuse and attention away from them. That's what she's doing with you."

Blackie nodded, his eyes thoughtful. "I thought we had worked past that. I guess not." He waited but Jack didn't respond. "Now what? I can't just sit here."

"You can and you must, at least until tomorrow. You're still not strong enough to be out there looking for her."

Blackie grew determined. "I will if I have to. If you don't bring me back word tomorrow you've found her, I'll go searching myself. I need her here with me."

"I know you do, son, and we'll find her."

Blackie's face grew bleak. "I know what you're saying but it doesn't bring a lot of comfort." Blackie rose, his balance off for a moment before he headed towards his bedroom. He stood for a moment, eyes on the bed, knowing he should be laying down but not willing to. His father was in the study and he should go talk with him but was reluctant to. He knew his mom and sisters were in town, but he didn't want to see them. They would smother him. He reached for his shoes and then his winter outwear, bundling up and heading for the door, not seeing Jacob watching him.

"Blackie just went out, Simon."

"He did? And just where does he think he's going?" Simon moved towards the door, shrugging into his coat and pulling on his gloves. "Come on. We need to find him."

The two men stood, searching the area, but not seeing Blackie. Blackie had heard the door open and close and slipped behind a tree just down the street. He didn't want them to find him and bring him back there. He was determined to find Julia and find her that night.

Blackie watched as Simon's vehicle headed for the downtown area before he approached the sidewalk once more. He still couldn't believe that his father owned property in this little town. He had grown to love it in the short time he had been there and had no plans to return to his hometown. He knew his mother would have something to say about that.

He approached an abandoned building searching the ground for any footprints and seeing none. He sighed. He moved on, searching over and over again, growing more and more weary. He finally fell to his knees, his arms wrapped around his abdomen, pain staring to course through him. This wasn't such a good idea after all, he thought.

He didn't hear the footsteps approaching him from behind, but felt the hands on his arms, yanking him to his feet and dragging him towards the building he had collapsed in front of. He was shoved inside, falling to his hands and knees, not hearing the coarse loud voice thundering questions at him. He was yanked back to his feet and shoved forward, only a hand on his arm keeping him upright. He drew a deep breath, knowing he had blown it in his determination to find his loved one. He fell facedown on the floor, as the men taunted him and then walked away, leaving him in a crumpled heap, unconscious.

Hours later, a scurrying sound came as quick movements approached him. He was turned over, his pulse felt for, and then he was picked up, the two men carrying him from the building towards a waiting car. He was placed gently inside and then driven to another building. The first man shook his head at the other one's question before they gently lifted Blackie and once more carried him into a building, this time one filled with light and warmth. He was carefully placed on a cot, a blanket pulled over him and the younger man of the two running for the physician that was on site that night.

Julia raised her head from where she lay on a cot near the doorway, hearing the whispers and then rising to follow the men. She stopped in the doorway and as one of them moved caught sight of Blackie. Ignoring their voices as she moved closer, she dropped to her knees, her hand reaching for him.

"Oh, Blackie! Why did you come here? Why aren't you still at home?"

A hand touched her shoulder and the physician spoke to her. "Do you know him?"

She nodded, tears on her cheeks. "I do. He was hurt trying to protect me and I thought if I walked away he would be safe."

"He must love you a lot to have come looking for you. He wasn't hurt again, just collapsed from what Fred here says. They were searching abandoned buildings and found him."

She looked up, pleading on his face. "Is he really okay? He was stabbed and then ran a fever."

"He's fine, child. You can stay with him here in the infirmary. We'll not make you leave." He peered at her again. "You're Julia, aren't you?"

She froze in fear, not sure if she should confirm it or deny it.

"It's okay, child. Old Jack asked me to look out for you. He described you well."

Her eyes slid closed in relief. "Please don't tell anyone I'm here. My stepfather has tried to kill both me and my friend here."

"We'll tell no one. We'll keep you here tonight and then get you somewhere safe tomorrow. I have some place that I think will work. Are the police looking for your stepfather?"

"They are and for his friends." She drew a troubled breath. "No one is safe though. He'll find us and hurt anyone who gets in his way."

"He'll not get in here. We have guards at the doors who will prevent that. You can trust us. Here. Up on your feet. You can use this cot tonight for your rest. I'll be in and out to check on your friend."

He stood just outside the doorway, his eyes on them as he spoke quietly to Fred, who nodded and headed out. He knew Fred would find the man they needed. He turned once more to watch Julia and saw the resemblance to a photo from years ago, one of the founding family's ladies. Then he turned to Blackie and saw something similar to another founding family. Well, he thought, what do we have here?

Jack looked up from where he had slouched in a dark alleyway, hearing cautious steps approaching. Fred stood there, his eyes wandering around the area.

<hr>

"We have them, Jack. Both of them. Doc'll move them tomorrow before dawn."

Jack nodded. "Good. I was hoping they had found their way there."

"The girl did. Joey and I found the young man. It looks as if he had just been dumped in one of the buildings. If we hadn't seen the footprints, we couldn't have found him."

"God was in this, Fred. Thank you." Fred nodded and walked away, leaving Jack to head the other way.

Jack drew a deep breath, knowing they were safe, but also knowing he couldn't tell anyone, not even Simon. It was almost Christmas and he needed to get this over with so those two young people would be safe. He had a plan, a plan that might mean his death, but if it saved sweet Julia, he would offer his own life for her.

Julia stirred in the early morning as she felt a hand on her arm. Doc stood there, watching as Fred and Joey carefully helped Blackie to his feet.

"Come, child. We're moving you two. We need to. I have somewhere to put you for the day. Old Jack has been in touch. He knows you're safe. He said for you to do what we asked, that he had a plan."

She shook her head. "We can't be together. It's too dangerous."

Doc looked at her. "No, it's dangerous if you split up. If you're together, I can get both of you to safety."

She finally rose, her eyes only on Blackie. He turned as he heard her footsteps and then reached for her, pulling her to him.

"You shouldn't have run, Jewel."

"And you shouldn't have come after me, Blackie."

They were ushered forth building and towards a vehicle. Sudden revving of a motor in the early morning quiet startled all of them and caused them to spin. Doc shoved at the two, yelling at the men to get them out of there, but he was too late. The vehicle was upon them and the men inside flooded out, their hands reaching for Julia and Blackie, shoving Fred, Joey and Doc down and away from them. Bundling the young couple into the vehicle, the driver yelled for the other men to come. The doors were slammed and the vehicle raced away, careening through the streets towards the edge of town.

Doc hurriedly picked himself up, reaching for his phone and calling in the abduction. Frustration grew in all three men as they realized they had been watched, likely all night, for just such an opportunity.

Jack stood watching the men before his eyes lifted towards the distance. This was what he had feared would happen. Now, he had to find them and he had a good idea just where. He turned, surprised to see Simon standing beside him, his breath coming in quick gasps.

"Just missed him. I got word he was here." Simon was getting angry. "Do you know where they are?"

Jack nodded. "I have a good idea. Come with me, Simon. We'll find your friends."

"Let me call in Jacob and Josh first. They'll want in on this."

"And Samuel."

Simon shook his head. "No, not until we find them."

Shoved down into a chair at a table, Julia stared at the papers spread before her and knew Hal was just going to try and make her sign away what she had. She wouldn't and couldn't do it.

Blackie stood against a wall, directly in her line of sight if she raised her eyes. He kept his eyes focused on her, not on the men holding his arms. He was in pain, but not as much as he had been. Whatever the physician had given him, he thought, had finally worked. Or maybe he was just getting better. Or maybe it was the adrenalin coursing through him.

They waited, for how long they never really knew. Julia cringed as she heard heavy, familiar footsteps heading her way. She refused to look up, refused to acknowledge Hal's presence.

Hal stood, anger emanating from him. He hated it when she refused to look at him. A bully through and through, he wanted acknowledgement of his power and she refused to give it. She always had. This time, he decided, she would or she would die.

He approached her, leaning his hands on the table across from her, waiting for her to cringe back and try to hide from him as was her usual demeanour with him. This time, it didn't happen. She sat, quiet, composed, her eyes on the paperwork, refusing to let him know she knew he was there.

Julia's heart was pounding with fear as she saw Hal's hands come into her vision. She knew only too well how hard they could hit and she just knew they would hit her today, more than likely kill her in Blackie's presence. Lord, why? Why couldn't Blackie have just stayed away? I don't want him to see what I'll go through. Yes, Lord, I know he's seen a lot worse, but this is different. I really thought You had brought him into my life.

Hal's coarse voice broke the silence. "Sign, Julia, and I'll let you go." He waited, but she sat, not responding to his words. "Not saying anything? That's not like you." He knew she never said a word in all the beatings she had taken, knew she never would, but he still taunted her.

He walked around the table, a hand roughly raising her chin. She still refused to look at him.

"Sign the papers, Julia, and I'll let you and your friend here go." When she refused to speak, his hand moved quickly, leaving redness on her face and blood on her lip. He heard movement from behind him and laughed, knowing Blackie was trying to get away.

"Sign, Julia. The next blow goes to your friend."

Julia's eyes raised to Blackie, seeing his love for her in his, and signaling hers back. The strength of character she had always found in him shone through and she drew from that, knowing that if this was the end for them, he loved her in a way no one had ever.

She shook her head. "That's not happening , Hal. I can't sign those. It's not mine to give away. If you knew the town history, you'd know that."

He flicked his fingers in the air. "Just an old piece of paper. Not legal any more." He slammed a hand on the table, expecting her to jump. When she didn't, he stepped back to assess her. What had changed, he wondered? She is refusing to behave like she always had. He turned his eyes towards Blackie and found steady eyes on him.

He pointed at Blackie. "You're the reason she won't sign."

Blackie shook his head, sorrow for the man in his eyes. "No, actually, I'm not. I have no say in what she does or doesn't do. She's free to make her own decisions, likely for the first time in her life." That comment earned Blackie his own blow across the face.

He straightened, his eyes on Julia, finding her steady in her determination not to cave.

No matter the threats, the blows, the beatings they took, both stood firm in their determination not to give in to a bully. They drew strength from one another.

Hal was angry, angrier than he had ever been, and that anger drove him to make a mistake. He walked away from the two for a moment, rage coursing through him, blinding him, absorbing everything in him. He had murder plotted in his heart, murder of those two. It would mean he would never get what he wanted, but he just couldn't abide someone standing up to him and winning.

He didn't hear the footsteps approaching quietly as he turned and raged back towards the two, a hand reaching for his revolver and pulling it out. Blackie looked up with blurring eyes, seeing that and drawing strength to wrest his arms from the two men holding him and throwing himself at Hal. They struggled, each fighting for control on the revolver, the weapon gradually being forced between them. Julia watched in horror, praying, begging for God to spare Blackie. A sudden jolt of sound and the men froze even as footsteps were heard running towards them.

Julia screamed as she saw Blackie falling. She threw herself towards him, drawing him away from Hal, searching for blood and finding none. He raised himself to a sitting position, pulling her to him and just held her as tight as he could, his head down on her hair as she clung to hm, sobbing. His eyes focused on Hal even as he heard voices and confusion around him.

A gentle hand on his shoulder finally raised his head. Samuel crouched beside him, tears on his face as he realized his son was finally safe.

"Dad?"

"I'm here, son." Samuel's arms reached to hug the couple, knowing that Blackie would not let go of his lady. "You're safe, son. Both of you. Simon says they've found everyone involved. The police just have to sort everything out, but he thinks it will be after Christmas now when that happens." He looked up at the approaching paramedics. "Let's get you looked at, okay?"

Blackie finally nodded, his hand going to Julia's cheek, frowning as she winced. "Jewel, we'll get checked out and then head home. We're not going to the hospital. That I can guarantee you." He looked at his father. "Mom and the girls are here?"

"They are, Levi. They are so worried, I'm not sure you'll want to come back to the B&B." He gave a low laugh at Blackie's frown and then quick grin.

Two hours later, Julia turned from where she had been brushing her hair. She had showered and taken the clean clothes Finn had handed her, brand new ones she noted, with a quiet word of thanks. It was finally over, she thought. I am finally free of the monster.

She headed for the kitchen, suddenly hungry, knowing Mary would have food ready for them. She stopped as she saw Blackie standing in the study, staring out the window, hands shoved into his pockets.

She paused in the doorway, not sure if she should approach him or not. He turned, his hand reaching for hers.

Cradling her close to him, Blackie thanked the Lord she was here, was safe, and finally could move on with her life. Whether that included him or not remained to be seen.

"Blackie? Thank you for all you did. I don't think I could have made it through without you."

He said nothing, knowing that words were not needed. She tilted her head, reading his face correctly.

She finally spoke. "It's almost Christmas, Blackie. I will enjoy it this year for the first time since before Dad died. I want to know what happened, but that doesn't change anything about you. You are the one I want to spend Christmas with."

Blackie studied her face, knowing she was speaking the truth. "You're sure? I don't want us to commit and then have you decide you need to walk away. I'll give you the time you need now."

She shook her head. "I know now, Blackie. God has shown me without a doubt. I never dreamed that I would ever be free, that I would meet someone like you."

Blackie finally nodded and reached into a pocket, pulling out a ring with a ruby stone in it. "This was my grandmother, on my Mom's side. Grandfather bought it for Grandmother, always saying she was more precious than rubies. That's how I feel about you."

Tears sparkled as she held out her hand. "I love that, Blackie. That's how you make it feel."

He swept her close, his blond head lowering as he sought her lips. He didn't see his mother stop in the doorway and then retreat, her own tears close as she sought out Samuel, who just gave her a look and swept her close to his own heart. All was right in their world for once, and just in time for the Christmas they wanted to have.

Christmas Day passed, full of laughter, fun and tears. Blackie and Julia had taken a lot of teasing, as had Jacob and Finn, leaving Josh and Simon wistful for ladies of their own.

Simon had worked hard up to Christmas Day and then was back at it a couple of days later. It would take weeks of investigations and serving warrants to determine exactly what all Hal had been involved in, but he was determined to do just that.

Simon was on a hunt. It was near the end of January and he knew Blackie and Julia were at his place, making their final plans before their wedding to take place three days from then. He needed to see them. He had, he thought, the final investigation done and he wanted to inform them of the results.

He paused at the door, a frown appearing as he heard a raised female voice, raised in anger and accusation. That's not Julia, he thought. He tried the doorknob, finding it turning under his hand and entered, his feet as silent as he could make them, slipping from his jacket and throwing it on a chair. He moved forward, stopping before he would be seen. He listened and realized that here was the piece he thought was missing and hadn't been able to discover. Julia's mother. She was part of this and they had not been able to prove it. Now they could, by her own words.

Simon finally stepped into view, catching Blackie's eyes as he stood, his arm around Julia as she faced her mother. Julia was not backing down at all from her, taking the accusations and guilt thrown at her and letting it roll off her.

Simon finally reached for the woman's arm and pulled it behind her, cuffs slapped on her wrists, placing her under arrest. He led her from the room, his phone out to make the call he had dreaded but knowing it was necessary. A few words with the responding officers and he approached Blackie and Julia again.

"Julia? Are you okay?" He was concerned. This was her mother, after all.

She nodded, a light on her face he had not seen before. "Thank you, Simon. I am. I finally am. She has no control over me any more. Thank you, Lord, that happened before we married, Blackie." She turned in his arms, her own arms going around him. "That would have cast a huge shadow on us."

"It would have, love, but we'd have worked through it. I know you're still going for counselling with the pastor and will for months to come. But you're finally healing." Blackie's arm tightened on her and he looked at Simon, a frown on his face. "Simon? How did you come to be here?"

Simon laughed, even as he shook his head. "That's a story in itself. I never expected to find her here, but it does wrap up any loose ends. I just wanted to let you two know that Hal's brother and cousin have talked, taking a plea deal, as have some of the other men. They've been sentenced and will spend time in jail.

"Hal has refused to confess, refused actually to talk with us. He asked for a lawyer as soon as we arrested him and that meant he said nothing. But we have enough evidence to put him away for the rest of his life. The charges include extortion, assault, and murder. We haven't even got to you yet, Julia, and what he will face for that." He held up a hand at her protest. "I know you don't want to, but you need to, as part of your healing process." He paused, sorrow flickering across his face.

"We did find evidence that, as you suspected, he had your father killed. Old Jack helped out that way. He said he had a vested interest in that, but that you would have to be the one to explain."

"I'm glad that is finally settled. Now that I know, I can accept it and move on." She turned in Blackie's arms, her head resting against his strong chest, feeling the love he had for her in how he held her. "Old Jack." A smile spread across her face. "Yes, Old Jack, as he wants to be called. I think it's time the town recognized him for who he is. He's been here, back in his home town, giving an impression that he's homeless, but he's not. I'm sure you found that out, Simon." She paused, her face tilting as she looked up at Blackie, getting his nod, before looking back at Simon.

Her voice was low and full of love as she continued. "You see, Simon, he's not homeless. He is a vet, but he's not homeless. And yes, he does have a vested interest in finding out who killed Dad. He's my Uncle Ben, my father's only brother."

Simon's movements stilled. Whatever he had expected to hear, this was not it. "Your uncle?"

"My uncle. Josh figured it out, Uncle Ben said, weeks ago."

"And he never said a word. It was hinted at, but I never picked that up. Or if I did, I forget. Now, I'm not sure which it is." Simon was shaking his head.

"Uncle Ben asked him not to, just to keep it quiet until this was resolved. Now, Jonathan can come home too." Her face lit up at the thought. "I can't wait for that to happen. It will be so good to have him around again."

"I'm sure it will. Listen, I'm out of here. I'll be in touch, Julia, about the charges against your mother." He waved as he walked away.

Blackie stood, his love in his arms, his chin on her head. "Did you ever decide who's walking you downtime aisle on Saturday?"

She shrugged. "Last I heard, I had both Uncle Ben and Jonathan doing the honours. It will be interesting to see how we manage that."

He turned her to face him, his eyes searching her. "And you're okay with all this?"

She nodded. "I am. I love you so much."

Six months later, Blackie looked up from his work as he heard laughter from the kitchen and smiled. Rachel and Rebecca had dropped in and insisted that Julia needed to go shopping with them. Blackie's family had relocated to town, and he was glad. They fit so well into the town and were loved by many. Miriam had become part of the work Blackie had stared for the youth and become a grandmother figure to many. His father continued to run his business from there and was also part of the church family, reaching out to help anyone who needed it.

Julia appeared in the doorway, her hand reaching for him. "Come on, sweetheart. We need you out here. We're trying to get a lunch ready for the family and need your help."

He gave an exaggerated sigh and rose, smiling as she grinned at him, stopping to gather her close and steal kisses from her until she pushed at him.

"Come on. The girls really do need our help."

He laughed, even as he kissed her again. "Really? I like where I am right now."

She blushed, something he often caused just by teasing her. "So do I, but come on. I really do need you to come to the kitchen."

He took her hand and followed as she pulled him forward, stopping in the doorway as he saw the decorated room and his family and friends standing there. He was puzzled, not sure what the occasion was.

"Julia?" He turned, finding her in tears. "What's going on?"

Samuel moved forward, his arm going around his much loved daughter-in-law. "This was Julia's idea, Levi. She finally got word that her book has been accepted by a small publisher, who wants to use it to forward the cause for help for abuse victims. We're so proud of her, Levi."

Blackie's eyes sought his wife's, seeing the uncertainty there. "Your book? I didn't realize you had finished it."

"I did, about a month ago. I didn't tell you because I didn't think it would be accepted anywhere. The publisher has been great. We're setting up a trust fund to help with counselling for those who need it. I hope we can work it through the centre as well."

He hugged her tight, feeling her tears soak his shirt. "I think this is just wonderful. Just like you, love." Tears blocked his sight until he blinked. "And what title did you come up with?"

She started laughing, bringing laughter from those around him. "Mistletoe Medicine. Subtitle. Healing from Abuse."

"I like that, Julia. It's so you."

They moved away, mingling with the group, laughter and tears part of their afternoon, all part of a healing process started when Julia had been freed so many months ago from the cycle of abuser and victim.

Dear Reader:

Thank you for picking up the story of Blackie and Julia. It is not the story I imagined for him. She was not the lady I pictured for him, but she was what he needed. An abuse victim and a hero, a medic who had seen horrible things, but survived and who could understand her trauma.

Abuse, unfortunately, is prevalent in society today, a lot of it hidden. My admiration goes to the women, children, and yes, men, who make the decision that they will no longer be a victim and seek help.

But, and there is always a but, God sees what is happening and is there, even in the darkest days. He sees what man does not. It is my prayer that people will turn to Him, especially in these dark days.

Blackie and Julia - what a couple! Thank you for sharing their story. And sigh, I can see Jonathan and Old Jack wanting their stories told. Old Jack, or Uncle Ben, was not to be such a strong character in the book, but these characters have a way of making their way into a book and building their stories. Demanding characters, they can be, and throwing in plot challenges and side roads is all part of it.

God bless each one of you. May you seek His presence daily.

Ronna

Misfortune and Mystery In Mistletoe

Mistletoe Treasures Book 3

By

Ronna M. Bacon

Joshua 1:9
Have I not commanded you? Be strong and of good courage; do not be afraid, nor be dismayed, for the Lord your God is with you wherever you go. (NKJV)

Table of Contents

The little girl's cries split through the night as she wept for her parents, for her own bed, for her stuffed dog. The woman in the front seat stared at her dispassionately before she turned around once more, her conversation with the male driver uninterrupted.

The little girl finally slept, not knowing where she was or why she was in that car, taken from her home and her parents. She didn't hear the car stop and the woman ordered out and into a forested area. She didn't hear the woman's pleas for mercy or the shot that reverberated through the forest, ending the cries and sobs.

The man stood for a moment, staring down at the body, before he turned and walked away, not caring that she wasn't buried. He would never know that hunters found her the next day and that the authorities would spend years trying to identify her.

He slid behind the wheel of the car, not paying any attention to the little girl behind him, intent on reaching his destination. Three days later, he pulled to a stop near a police department, hesitating only for a few seconds, before he yanked open the car door, pulled the little girl from her seat, and sticking an envelope into her coat. Looking around, he walked to the steps of the department and set her down between the doors, not seeing anyone at the front desk. He turned, walked back to his car and drove away, not looking back, not caring that he had disrupted lives. He would stay in the area and make sure his plans were followed, that was a given.

A police officer returning to the front desk hesitated as he heard sobs and catching movement at the front doors moved quickly that way, picking up the little girl and comforting her as best he could. He pulled out the letter and handed it to his sergeant.

They tried to find her parents but couldn't. They never did determine how she got there, turning instead to the foster care system for her. Years would go by and every once in a while the file would be opened and then closed, no closer to a resolution.

The little girl sobbed for her parents for days, finally settling down in her foster parents' home, but knowing inside her she was missing people important to her.

Ducking his head to see out the pass-through window from the kitchen of his cafe, The House, Joshua Smithson stared across the floor and out the large front window, one Amy, his head server, was working to decorate for Christmas. It was the last few days of November and the first of December was a big day in the town of Mistletoe. He shook his head at his thoughts. This year, he just wasn't in the mood for Christmas. His eyes dropped to the food he was preparing and then shot back up as he heard Amy yell and then three or four men in the cafe run for the door, yanking it open before they hit the sidewalk, heading across the street.

"Amy? What on earth?" Josh dropped the knife he held in his hand and headed for the door.

Amy was standing there, shaking. "Someone just ran up on the sidewalk. I'm not sure what's going on. It looks as if they were cut off." Her hands covered her mouth as she stared out, fear for the pedestrians in her mind.

"Stay here with the other ladies and children. I'll be right back."

Josh stood for a moment, his eyes searching the area, feeling something off but not quite sure what it was. He finally shook his head and headed back to his cafe, the food not cooking itself, he thought.

"Josh?" Amy quiet voice came to him as he stood for a moment, lost in thought.

"Yeah, Amy?" He looked up, his face clearing of his thoughts, black as they could be at times.

"What happened out there?"

Josh shrugged. "I have no idea. Mrs. White said she was cut off by someone, who hit the front fender of her car and sent her towards the sidewalk. Thank God, no one was hurt."

Amy shuddered. "It could have been so much worse. Still, there had to be a reason for this. Things like this don't just happen in Mistletoe. At least, they didn't until you and your friends moved here." She smirked at him as she walked away.

Josh gave a shout of laughter, then stopped in his movements as he heard the soft click of the back door. He dropped his head enough to look out front again. No, he had everyone who was scheduled to work out there and the students who worked the kitchen were with him. So, who had just entered? He turned slowly, his eyes searching, stopping when he saw the young woman standing there, her eyes on the floor, shaking and not just from cold, he thought.

He walked slowly towards her, finding her shrinking back from him. He stopped, a hand going out, as he murmured soft words, words he didn't even know he was uttering. She finally reached a tentative hand out to his. Your hand's ice cold, girl, and not just from the weather. You're frightened of something, Josh thought, his heart automatically sending up a prayer. No, he amended his thoughts. Not frightened. Terrified is more like it.

"Are you okay?" When she didn't respond he sighed. Now what?

"Josh?" Amy's voice came from behind him. "Who's this?" She stopped short as he raised his free hand.

"I don't yet, Amy. She's not looking at me or talking. I'm going to try and talk her into sitting in my office. Can you call Tom for me? I think we need the police here for this."

The woman's hand jerked back as Josh's words and she stepped backwards, stopping when she hit the wall behind her, her shaking increasing. Josh frowned. Whatever was going on, she needed help and needed it now.

"Amy, can you find Old Jack or Blackie for me? I need one of them for their medic experience." Josh knew both men had served in the armed forces as medics, Blackie one of his good friends. He finally reached and gently grasped the woman's arm, trying to turn her towards the hallway that led to his office, but she pulled free and ran for the door, shoving it open and running through it, Josh on her heels.

He caught up to her, surrounding her with his arms even as she struggled with him, her hand catching his cheek, leaving it smarting. Josh sighed to himself. This was not how I planned my day, Lord. Why me? Then the thought changed. I know, Lord, I know. Why not me?

He looked over his shoulder at his restaurant, knowing he was never going to get the lady back inside there. He reached for his keys, clicking the fob to unlock the doors and pulling open the passenger door on his SUV. He gently tucked her inside, waiting for her to do up her seatbelt. She sat, her eyes finally raised to his face, clear gray eyes that held terror and something else he couldn't place. He pulled out the seatbelt, reaching across her to fasten it, feeling her shrink back from him.

Shutting the door and locking it, he stood for a moment, his eyes on her through the window, seeing she had lowered her face again. He turned, keys still in hand, to walk around the back of his vehicle, hearing the whisper of a sound and raising his arm enough to ward off the bat heading for his head. His arm dropped, numb in feeling, and he wasn't even sure that it hadn't been broken. He dodged as he saw the bat heading his way again, hearing it strike the vehicle. He raised his head enough to get a glimpse of the man, tall, overweight, hat pulled down enough to shade the upper portion of his face, scarf wrapped around the bottom of the face. Well, that's that, he thought. The bat raised again, the man hesitated, his head turning before he ran away from Josh, heading towards the centre of the town, the bat swinging from his hand.

Josh leaned back again his vehicle, his breathing ragged, his arm supported by his other hand. He turned to look back into the vehicle. She was still there, her face white as she stared back at him, fear flowing from her.

Josh moved to walk back around, but hands on his arm stopped him.

"Josh?" His friend, Levi Blackwell, stood there, concern colouring his face.

"I'm okay, Blackie. The arm? I'm not too sure about."

"Let me take a look at it." Blackie's hands reached to feel the arm, stopping when Josh shook his head.

"Not right now. Grab my jacket from the cafe and follow me home, will you? I have a lady in the car that I need you to assess for me."

For the first time, Blackie realized that Josh wasn't on his own. "A lady? Who is she?"

"I have no idea. I hadn't gotten as far as introductions yet. Maybe…". His voice died away. "Is Julia free?"

"She'll make herself free." Blackie ran for the back door, meeting Amy standing outside the back door with Josh's coat in her hands and having a few words with her.

"Here. You're not going to get that on, though."

Josh grabbed his jacket and dumped it into the back seat. "I won't even try. See you in a few."

Blackie stood, watching as his friend drove away, concern on his face before he turned, heading for his office and his wife. Julia would definitely be needed.

She stood in Josh's kitchen, afraid to look around, afraid to look up, not knowing what was going on. Her head was pounding and making it difficult for her to think clearly, and she needed to do that. She felt gentle hands helping her out of her jacket and then on her arms, leading her to a chair when she was gently shoved down, and the man knelt to remove her boots, rising to set them near his on the boot tray.

She listened to water running, then the beep of a microwave before a cup of peppermint tea was set in front of her. She couldn't make her hands reach for it and then his hands came into her line of sight, reaching for hers and wrapping them around the cup.

She listened to his steps moving away and then whispering back across the floor behind her. She jumped as she felt his hands on her shoulders and realized he was tucking a warm blanket around her. He didn't speak, just was there if she needed anything.

Josh watched her from where he was setting coffee to perk. He shook his head. What had God just led him into, he wondered? And was he ready for it? He rubbed at his arm, feeling the pain. Not broken, he thought, but bruised.

He walked towards the front door as he heard a light tap and then the door opening, hugging Julia, Blackie's wife, before he nodded to the kitchen. Julia headed that way, an exclamation coming from her.

Blackie's hand on his arm kept him in place.

"Josh? What's going on? You didn't explain earlier."

Josh shrugged. "I'm not really sure, Blackie. She ended up in my cafe kitchen. She needs medical aid but I don't think I'll get her to the hospital. That's why I asked for you to come, you or Old Jack. She's not saying anything at all but she's terrified. I can see that."

He looked up as Julia came towards them, a troubled look on her face.

"Blackie, I have a bag in the back of the truck. The one from Emily's. I need it. I've talked our friend into a shower and there's some clothes in there I think will pretty much fit her."

Blackie reached to kiss his wife before he turned to head back outside.

"Josh? Your spare room is ready, isn't it?"

He nodded. "It is. There are towels in the cupboard just outside it if you want to change them, but I just put fresh ones in the bathroom yesterday. There is shampoo and what not that Joy left under the sink." He looked towards the kitchen even as his thoughts went to his sister, who was due to visit in a day or two. "How is she?"

"She's not talking. I don't like that. Let me get her into the shower and changed and then see what we can do. I'll have Blackie check her out then for us."

Josh paced his kitchen, his heart lifted in prayer, even as he waited for the women to return. Blackie heard Julia's soft call and walked towards her, staying for a few minutes before he returned, a troubled look on his face, the women following after him.

Josh stood for a moment, his eyes on the lady as she sat once more in the chair, before he approached and crouched down in front of her. He winced as he saw the bruising and cuts on her face. His gaze shot to Blackie, who nodded.

"There's one on her temple that concerns me. We need to get her in and get it checked out but she's refusing to go." He looked around. "I called Doc. He's agreed to come over in a bit."

Josh nodded, his dark brown eyes back on her gray ones. Her dark red hair was still wet from the shower but he could see the curls in it.

"Can you talk to me? Tell me your name?"

He could see her hesitating and wasn't quite sure why. He barely heard her response.

"Leah. My name is Leah."

"That's good, Leah. Do you have a last name? Most of us do." Josh gave a quick grin as Julia slapped him lightly on the shoulder as she walked past him, bringing Leah's eyes to him and then to her, fear briefly making an appearance.

"I don't remember." Tears gathered, making her eyes dark murky pools. "Why can't I remember?"

Josh reached for her hands. "It's okay, Leah. It will come back to you. I have a friend, a doctor. He's going to come and talk to you." He saw her look of fright. "It's okay. He's not going to hurt you. I just want him to check you over and make sure you're okay. Blackie here was a medic in the armed forces but isn't in that field any more."

She finally nodded. "I don't remember what happened. I just remember someone walking towards me in a building and I froze and ran." She looked at him, seeing his nod. "That was you, wasn't it?" She snatched her hands back, bringing them to her mouth. "He went after you. Did he hurt you?"

Josh shrugged off her concern. "Nothing broken. Just a bruise. But why would he be after you?"

"But who was he? And why was he after me?" Her fright was palpable as she stared at him, then raised her eyes to study Blackie and Julia.

"We don't know that. Yet." Blackie spoke up. "Josh said you ran when he mentioned the police. Any reason why?"

She shook her head. "I have no idea. I'm sorry." She looked up at the three of them, distress and something else they couldn't read in her eyes. "I just don't remember."

Josh stood and moved to the kitchen doorway as he heard the front door open and close, giving a quiet hello to Simon Gardner, another friend.

Simon dropped his coat on a chair in the living room, kicked off his boots, and moved to the kitchen, his socked feet quiet on the floor, greeting his two other friends, taking a look at Leah, and then reaching for the coffee pot. He had dropped in on his way home from work as a police officer, his badge and weapon still on his belt. He spun as he heard the stifled scream from Leah, coffee spilling across his hand and he grimaced, reaching for a wet cloth to wipe it off.

Leah's jump had shoved her chair back hard enough that it toppled over as she moved way from Simon, her hands to her mouth. They could feel the fear coming from her but didn't understand why.

She stopped as she ran into Josh, whose arms encircled her from behind. She struggled against his grasp, finally hearing the soothing words he was murmuring and her fight stopped as she leaned back against him.

Simon's startled eyes sought Josh before a frown came over his face. He had a good memory for faces and something about the lady Josh was holding seemed familiar.

"Leah? Are you okay now? Simon is a good friend of ours. He will not hurt you in any way. Do you understand?" Josh's words were quiet in her ear, his blond hair so close to her own head making a sharp contrast.

She finally nodded, letting him release her, her hand swiping at the tears on her cheeks.

"I'm sorry. I have no idea why I'm scared of the police."

Simon nodded. "It's understandable. Josh let me know what was up when he called earlier. I gather you don't remember your full name?"

She shook her head even as she heard Josh righting her chair and gently shoving her down into it again. "I don't. I have no idea. And I'm not even sure Leah is my correct name." She looked around at them. "How do I find out?"

"First, we can take your picture and run it through our system, to see if there are any warrants, etc, out for you. Fingerprints too." Simon held up a hand as Josh went to protest. "I know, Josh. It sounds as if I'm treating her as a criminal, but I'm not. Then we check for missing persons reports that would match you."

Josh walked Simon out to his car later, deep in conversation with his friend.

"What now, Simon? How do we keep her safe if we don't know who she is or who she's running from?"

"You're sure she's running?" Simon shot a quick look at the house before turning to his friend again.

———

Josh nodded. "I'm sure. The fear that came from her after the attack was real. I didn't see enough of the man to get a good description. That's frustrating."

"It is. We'll work with what you've given Tom and see where we go. Stay safe."

Josh stood for a moment, his face turned to the clear night sky, the stars twinkling white against the blackness. He started as he heard a voice beside him.

He spun, startled to see Old Jack, a well-known figure in town, standing beside him.

"Just where did you come from?" Josh demanded.

"I've been waiting out here for a while. Knew you'd come out sooner or later. That lady you have in there?" He nodded towards the house.

"What about her?" Josh demanded. "Do you know her?"

Old Jack shook his head. "No, I don't. Not really. Saw her around town for the first time yesterday. She holed up in one of the abandoned buildings near your cafe last night. Word on the street is that she's running from someone, only no one knows who. If your friend there looks outside of town, he'll likely find her car off the road somewhere."

Josh nodded. "I'll give him a call." He turned to the house for a moment, then turned back to see Old Jack walking away from him. He sighed, frustrated that the older man had just left like that.

"Was that Old Jack?" Blackie stopped on the porch, watching as Josh walked towards him.

"It was. I guess Leah hit town yesterday at some point. He saw her. He thinks her car is outside of town somewhere, wrecked."

"That makes sense. The nicks on her face could have come from flying glass." Blackie stood for a moment, his hands jammed into his pockets, shoulders hunched against the cold. "Where is she spending the night? She can't stay here with you."

Josh sighed. "I know. I have no idea. Unless…". Josh backed away, taking a look at the detached garage. "She could use the apartment there."

Blackie shook his head. "That won't work. People will still talk, Josh, and we can't have that." He turned as Josh walked up the steps. "Julia and I can stay here tonight and then we can figure something out in the morning. Right now, this is where Leah feels safest. We don't want to change that on her."

Hands running through his hair, Josh stared at Leah in frustration, not liking that she wanted to walk away from the town or walk away from him. He didn't want that for her. He wanted to find out why she was so scared and of whom. Please don't let her leave me, Lord, he prayed, not quite sure what all he meant.

"I have to, Josh. If someone is really after me, they'll go after you too." Leah was terrified of just that, without knowing exactly why.

"I can handle them, Leah. It's you I'm worried about." He pointed to the kitchen. "Come on out here and sit. You didn't even have your breakfast yet and you need that."

She finally brushed past him and dropped into a chair, not happy with him, but knowing he was right. She needed to eat. She just didn't want to be there. But where she wanted to be, she didn't know either.

Josh stared at her for a moment, then shook his head as he followed her, watching as Julia turned from the counter to speak to her. He froze, his eyes shooting between the two women before he spun and headed for his office. Blackie had been standing watching Josh and Leah and now followed his friend to his office.

"Josh?" Blackie's question had Josh putting up his finger in a wait motion.

Josh searched the internet, putting in Leah's first name and Julia's maiden name, before he sat back, sighing in relief but troubled as well.

"I know Leah's last name, Blackie."

"You do? And just how do you know that?"

Josh beckoned Blackie around to where he could see the computer monitor. Blackie stopped, frozen in place for a moment.

"She's related to Julia and that means Finn as well. How'd you know?"

"When Julia turned in there, there was a similarity. I wasn't sure until I checked." He reached to draw up his email program, sending off a quick message to Simon and then to Blackie's father, Samuel. "I'll get your Dad to look into her and see what he can find." He spun in his chair, his eyes on the door. "How do I tell her?"

"Tell me what?" Josh drew a deep breath as he saw the two ladies standing there.

He rose and walked towards Leah, catching her hand and drawing her across to his desk chair. "Sit for a moment. I found out who you are."

"You did? How?"

Josh nodded towards Julia at her question. "You looked like Julia there for a moment when she turned." His eyes raised as he heard a sound from Julia and saw that she had her hands to her mouth even as Blackie had his arm around her.

"She looks like Finn, Josh. Blackie. Why didn't I see that last night?"

"Because we were too concerned about how she was feeling. I think we did see it, we just didn't recognize it." Josh perched on the corner of his desk, reaching to turn the chair slightly so that Leah could see the monitor. "This is you. I've asked a friend to research you." He held up a hand as she went to protest. "No, it's Blackie's father. He will not tell anyone at all, not unless you agree to it. I also sent your name to Simon. He needs to know. Again, he will be very careful as he searches for whoever may be after you."

She finally nodded, her eyes still on his face, not on the monitor. She started as he pointed at the screen and she finally turned, her hand reaching out to touch her face on the screen.

"Leah Bronagh. That doesn't sound familiar, but that is me. Could I have been using another name?"

"That's what we'll find out." Josh shared a look with Blackie, knowing the fight had just begun and once again they had no idea who they faced or what it would all involve. He grew fearful, knowing that Leah was in danger and he didn't like that, not one bit. Lord, protect my lady, he prayed, without being conscious of how he had prayed.

Blackie excused himself as his phone rang and he walked away to answer, standing where he could see both Josh and Leah. Simon was on the other end, having receiving Josh's email and wanting more information. Blackie finally pocketed his phone, walking back towards the other three, his eyes on Leah.

"Josh, Simon's confirmed Leah's identity. He also say that an abandoned car was found just outside of town. Someone did a number on it, he said, likely with a bat."

Josh rose to his full height. "A bat? Like our friend from last night?"

Blackie nodded. "That's what he's thinking. Old Jack was right, you know. How does he know these things?"

"I asked him one time." Julia's voice was quiet. "He says God talks to him and tells him things."

"I suspect that is what happens." Blackie looked at Leah, seeing once more the fear on her face. "We'll keep you as safe as we can, Leah. That's a promise." He wrapped an arm around his wife. "Julia and I had an adventure ourselves as did another couple, Jacob and Finn." He looked at Josh, seeing his nod. "Now, I suggest we take you to Finn's parents. They have a B&B and I know they'll put you up."

"I can't." Leah was almost in tears. "I can't put anyone else in danger." She turned to Josh, her eyes beseeching him to let her stay.

"We'll talk about it, okay, Leah? My sister's due in sometime today. That would work if you stay here."

Blackie tilted his head towards the living room and Josh hesitated, his eyes on Leah. He felt Julia's hand on his arm and looked down at her, nodding as she motioned him to follow Blackie.

Julia turned to Leah, wondering how they were related after all.

"Josh, just what are you thinking?" Blackie had a good idea of his friend's thoughts, having served in the armed forces with him for eight years.

Josh shrugged as he paced his living room, hands jammed into his jeans' pockets. "I don't know, Blackie. I really don't know. I just can't let her walk away from me. You know that."

"I know. It was like that for Julia with me." Blackie sighed. "Is Joy coming in on her own or are Jeremiah and the girls with her?"

"She didn't say, but I suspect that Jeremiah will be with her. He did say the church here had asked him to fill in for the pastor while he's on sabbatical. I never heard what his answer was."

Blackie nodded. "That would make sense. If they're here, Leah would be able to stay. You know how small towns are. If they're not here, you'll have to find somewhere for her to stay."

Josh nodded, a troubled look on his face. "I know and I have no idea where that would be. She won't go to Finn's people, I know that."

Blackie shot a look at Josh before turning to where Julia stood in the office doorway. "Let us know what you decide. We have to run. Don't do anything abruptly."

Josh shook his head. "I don't think I'd get away with that." He grinned for a moment as Julia shook a finger at him. "I'll watch out for your cousin or whoever she is, Julia."

Josh stood for a moment, his eyes following Blackie and Julia as they walked out the front door, his mind racing as to where Leah could stay. He finally turned back to the office, knowing he needed to head for his cafe, but hesitant to take her with him. His phone ringing stopped him in his tracks.

Amy was on the line, letting him know she had called in staff and he didn't really need to show up today. They had it covered. He thanked her, knowing the cafe was in good hands, and that he had a day to make plans. Or rather, a day to find out God's plans.

Leah looked up at him, a frown on her face.

"It doesn't make sense, Josh. Why don't I remember?"

"That happens. Remember what Doc said. Sometimes we block things that are so traumatic we can't deal with them at the time." Doc had dropped by the night before, looked Leah over and basically told them she was fine, that she had a concussion but was blocking something and he had no idea what, or when her memory would return.

"Now what, Josh? I can't keep you from your work." Leah shoved herself from his chair and paced, heading for the living room, fatigue suddenly overcoming her.

"I don't have to be there today, Amy called. She's arranged for staff to come in for me. We're good that way." He watched as she stumbled slightly in her walk, seeing the deep-rooted fatigue and knowing it wasn't just from the last few days. "Here, sit on the couch. You're going to fall down if you don't."

She finally nodded, sinking down on the soft material of the couch and then stretching out. "Don't let me sleep, please, Josh. I can't handle the dreams if I do." Her eyes closed, her breath evened out and she was asleep.

He watched for a moment before heading for the bedroom she had used and snagging one of her pillows. He tucked it under her head and then reached for the soft blue blanket that one of his nieces had left the last time his sister was in town. He tucked it over her, brushing back the hair from her face, wincing at the dressing Doc had placed on her temple. She was hurting in more ways than one, he thought, and he had no idea how to help her. Silent prayers rose from his heart. What were the dreams she can't handle, Lord? Grant her a peaceful sleep this day.

Josh raised his head mid-afternoon, his finger marking his place in his Bible. He had wandered the house, caught up on his office paperwork, answered all the emails he had waiting, searched the internet for more information on Leah, and then reached for his Bible, turning to his favourite book of Joshua. He needed to be reminded that he had to be strong, to have courage, that God was in control. His eyes sought Leah, seeing she was still sleeping, and glad for that. He rose, setting his Bible down and hearing for the door as it opened and feeling a rush of cold air that entered. He shivered for a moment as he stood, watching his sister as she carefully shut the door and then shrugged out of her coat and boots before she turned, seeing him standing there.

Joy Williams reached for her brother, drawing him into a tight hug. Something was going on with him, she just knew, she just didn't know what. Both she and her husband, Jeremiah, had felt the need to be there, that Josh needed them. They had planned the trip anyway but made it two days earlier than planned. Somehow Josh had known that.

She stood back, her eyes on her brother, younger by ten minutes, seeing the fatigue and stress there.

"Josh?"

He lifted a finger to hush her and then nodded to the kitchen. "There's hot water on the stove. I just boiled it." He looked at his watch. "Scratch that. We'll need to heat it. That was some hours ago I did that."

Joy shook her head at him as she walked past him, seeing the disarray in his kitchen and knowing that wasn't him. She moved to clean it, Josh leaning a shoulder against the door frame as he watched, their conversation quiet, picking up with they had left off months ago. It was like that for the twins.

"Where're Jeremiah and the girls?"

"Outside. They were fascinated with the snow you have here. We don't have any. He's letting them run off energy." She turned, her cup of tea in her hand. "What's going on, Josh? I know something is."

Josh studied her for a moment, before he shot a look over his shoulder, and then stared at the floor. He wasn't quite sure how to respond to that, not when he really didn't know himself. He turned as he heard the door open, and a man's quiet voice admonishing his daughters to be quiet, that Uncle Josh might be sleeping. He was up early, he reminded them.

Josh grinned at the exaggerated steps the two little girls were taking as they walked towards the kitchen, trying hard to be quiet, before they saw him and raced towards him, confident in his greeting. He dropped to the floor, arms reaching out to hug the two little ones, taking the hugs and kisses they showered him with.

"Uncle Josh! You're not sleeping!" Three-year-old Heidi was thrilled. "Daddy said you were." She threw a dark look at her father.

"Not today, sweetheart. I didn't have to work, so I'm already rested. How come you're here?"

"It's a surprise." She looked up at her mother. "Can we tell Uncle Josh?"

Her mother nodded, even as two-year-old Holly reached hands to her uncle's face, turning it towards him.

"Unca Osh. Can you play with us?"

"It's Uncle Josh." The superior tone in Heidi's voice had Josh's body shaking with suppressed laughter even as he heard the parents laughing out loud.

"What I said. Unca Osh."

Heidi slapped her forehead in despair, a movement that had become common for her in the last few months. Where it came from, no one was quite sure.

"It's okay, Heidi. I'll answer to either one." He hugged the two girls before he set them down and rose, his hands on their heads. "What brings you to town so early?"

Joy shared a look with Jeremiah, even as he walked past her to reach for the coffee pot and pour both himself and Josh a cup. It was home, Josh's house, to them.

"It's like this, Josh." Joy's voice held worry for a moment. "Jeremiah's taking over as interim pastor for yours for now. And Blackie has asked if he'd consider counselling at his youth centre. We've prayed about this long and hard, and here we are."

Josh had listened, happiness growing inside him, knowing his beloved sister and her family would be moving to his town. He reached to hug her, and then Jeremiah, the two little ones demanding their share. As the adults settled down in the kitchen, Heidi crawled up on her mother's knee. Holly headed for the living room, knowing her uncle had books there on the shelf for her.

Sensing she wasn't alone any more, Leah slowly awoke, her eyes flickering open and closed, until they finally stayed open. She felt the pillow under her head, frowning as it hadn't been there when she fell asleep and then touching the blanket that covered her. She smiled slowly, warmth filling her as she realized Josh had made her comfortable, in herself knowing that she was almost a complete stranger to the comfort he had provided her. Scratch that. She was a complete stranger to it lately, she thought. Her eyes searched the room, not seeing him, but seeing his well-used Bible on the table by his chair. Well, Lord, it looks as if You led me to a Christian man. Now what? I can't stay here, that's a given.

She sat up, reaching to fold the blanket and set it neatly on the couch before pushing the hair back on her face. She sat, lost in thought, before she heard a small squeal and jumped, searching for the sound. She spotted the little girl, on her knees near the bookshelf, her eyes on her, a startled look on her face that changed to joy before the little one was on her feet, running towards her, a squeal of happiness coming from her.

"Leah - you here? At my Unca Osh's?" Holly threw herself into Leah's arms, her own arms tight around Leah's neck.

"I'm sorry. Do I know you?" Leah was hesitant to move, not sure what was going on.

Holly sat back, her hands still locked around Leah's neck as she nodded vigorously. "You do. You teach me. At Sunnay."

"I do?" She looked up, puzzled as Josh hit the room, almost on a run, not quite sure what was happening, Joy and Jeremiah on his heels, Heidi running past them, overjoyed to find a friend at her uncle's.

Josh slid to a stop, his eyes astonished as he watched Heidi throwing herself on Leah as well.

"I take it you know these two?"

"Apparently, I do. Unfortunately, I don't remember that I do." Her eyes held his for a moment, seeing understanding in his before they slid to Joy, who stood beside her brother, a hand on arm, surprise on her face.

"Leah MacLeod? What are you doing here, in Mistletoe and at my brother's at that?"

Leah shook her head. "I'm sorry. I really don't know." She looked down at the two little ones cuddling close to her before she looked back up. "You know me?"

Joy approached, sitting beside Heidi, her hand going out to touch Leah's shoulder. "We do. You're the girls' favourite Sunday school teacher. I don't know you as well as I would like to. But that doesn't explain why you're here." She turned as she heard a sound from Jeremiah, who watched Leah, a frown in place.

"Girls, I think I heard Uncle Josh say he had some new toys for you two upstairs in the playroom. Now would be a good time to find them." At their protest, their father held up a hand. "Now, please, girls. Leah will be here for a while. She won't leave without saying goodbye, but somehow, I don't think that's happening." He had caught a look on Josh's face that he had seen on others, and knew Josh had no intention of letting Leah escape from him, not if he could help it.

The two girls slid to the floor, reluctant to leave Leah's side, but obedient to their father's request. With one final glance backwards, they headed upstairs, quiet chatter flowing back to the adults.

Josh sat down across from Leah, his eyes on her, even as she studied first Joy and then Jeremiah. "Leah? Do you remember these people at all?"

She looked back at him, sadness in her face and her voice as she responded, her head shaking. "I don't, Josh. I'm sorry. The littlest one, I almost do, but it's so shadowy I can't be certain."

Josh sighed, knowing that she was correct. His eyes caught Joy's look at Leah, puzzlement on her face, even as he heard Jeremiah cross the floor and sit in a chair near the couch.

"Joy, you say you know Leah?"

"We do. From church. What, about two years now, Jeremiah?"

He nodded, a look on his face that made Josh want to question him. "About that."

"Your name's Leah MacLeod." Joy stopped at a sound from Josh and then saw Leah shaking her head. "Yes, that's what we know you as. It's not correct?" Her eyes flew to her husband's, seeing compassion and relief there. "Jeremiah?"

"That's the name she was going by, but it's not her real name. I couldn't say anything, Joy. You know that."

"I know. This is so hard." She turned to Josh. "What is her name then?"

"Leah Bronagh." All eyes turned to Leah as she spoke. "Josh figured it out this morning. A friend and his wife were here. Apparently I looked like Julia and he searched under my first name and her maiden name."

"Blackie's wife? They're related?" Joy's hands went to her mouth. "That means Finn as well. Josh, what did you just go and walk into?"

Josh laughed at the expression on his sister's face before he sobered. "We have no idea, Joy. Jeremiah, now that it's out in the open what Leah's name is, did she tell you anything that might help?"

Jeremiah's eyes sought Leah, who nodded, giving him permission to speak. "Not really. She just said she needed to hide from someone but wouldn't tell me who or why. That's all she said. She asked if she could be known by a different name, a relative's I think she said." He paused, not quite certain what was going on. "That doesn't explain how she ended up here, of all places."

Josh started to laugh even as Leah shook her head at him. "She wandered into The House yesterday, ran from me, I was attacked by a bat-wielding man who was after her, and then I brought her home."

Joy frowned. "That sounds like you brought home a stray dog, Josh."

The three others broke out into laughter, even as Leah agreed that was exactly what it sounded like. Jeremiah rose as he heard Heidi calling for him, returning with the girls in his arms, before settling down, his daughters cuddling down beside him. Leah watched them, seeing the love between father and daughters, and somehow knowing that had not been her lot.

Josh's head turned as he heard a tap at the door and then the door opening. Blackie and his father, Samuel, stood there, waiting to greet Joy and her family.

"Blackie. Samuel. I take it you've found out something."

"We have. Dad wanted to talk to Leah in person, so we headed over here. Julia's still at the office. Jacob needed her assistance on something." Julia worked in the office Blackie and another friend, Jacob, shared. Blackie walked forward to hug Joy and then reach to shake Jeremiah's hand, picking up Heidi who reached up for a beloved friend.

Samuel greeted the others, then sat, watching Leah, seeing movements that reminded him of his beloved daughter-in-law. *What now, Lord? What have we walked into?*

"Samuel? You've found out something?" Josh's quiet voice broke into his thoughts.

Samuel turned to answer Josh, his eyes on Leah. "We have, Josh, and it's not at all what we expected. Leah, you have remembered nothing?"

She shook her head. "I have flittering memories, but nothing that stays long enough for me to recognize or even see clearly. Why?"

Samuel sighed. *How did he even begin, Lord, he asked?* "Leah, we've been able to track what we can of your life. You entered foster care at age 3, as to why, that we can't find out. You were raised in one foster home, a very loving one at that. They tried many times over the years to adopt you but each attempt was turned down. That, we can't find out why, but I'm still looking into it.

"You left there abruptly as soon as you turned eighteen, not because they asked you to. You didn't give a reason, but they suspect you were scared of something or someone. They have tried to get you to open up over the years but you wouldn't. You broke contact with them about two years ago and haven't seen or talked to them since. They want you to contact them, when you're ready.

"Now, as to why you're running. We think we have an idea, but we're not sure. Your foster sister remembers you receiving a letter just before you were eighteen that she says seemed to terrify you. You wouldn't tell her what was in or who it was from, but she says you changed after that. You were always watching around you for someone."

Leah stared at him, not quite sure if what he was saying was true or not. She finally shook her head. "I'm sorry. I really don't remember. And I should, I know." Her eyes traced to Josh's and stayed there, seeing the concern and compassion there as well as something else she just couldn't read.

"I'm sorry. I just don't remember." She leaned forward, her face buried in her hands. They could barely hear her. "How much danger am I bringing here?"

"We don't know that you are." Blackie watched as her head shot up at his words and he held up a hand. "I know. You're thinking of yesterday and the man with the bat. And then there's your car. Someone has come after you and we need to find out who."

She rose and began to pace, her arms wrapped around herself before she spun. "So, then, how do we do that?" Her eyes went to the little girls, who were fascinated with the conversation, even though they couldn't really understand what was being said. "I can't bring danger to those two."

Jeremiah nodded. "And we won't let you. We'll guard both them and you. If I feel they are in danger, Joy's parents will be here and will take them to safety."

She finally agreed, then turned and walked away. They heard the faint click of her door closing before they looked at each other.

"Now what, Samuel? How do we find out what is going on? She's not faking this, forgetting who she is." Joy watched her brother closely.

"I know she's not, but I have no idea how to reach her." Samuel watched as Josh finally rose and walked away, hands jammed into his pockets. His eyes held compassion as he exchanged a glance with his son. Josh's heart was involved, he thought. Please protect my friend, Lord. Bring this to a quick and safe ending.

Josh stood in the centre of his office at The House, his eyes on Amy as she talked to him, but his thoughts on Leah who was in the kitchen with his prep staff.

"So, it looks as if we're in good shape for the rush later this week and for the weekend." Amy watched her boss and friend closely, seeing stress on his face she had never seen. "Josh?"

"Yeah, Amy?" He brought his mind back to her. "Was there something else?"

She shook her head. "No. I just wondered if everything was okay with you." She was older than him by ten years and looked on him as a younger brother.

"I really don't know, Amy. I'm trying to figure out what's going with Leah and that's not going well."

"We're praying for it, Bill and I. Let us know if we can help in any way."

She walked away, her voice already teasing the prep staff and he heard their laughing answers. He dropped into his chair, knowing he should be in the kitchen with them, but knowing he had paperwork to do and cheques to sign.

"Josh?" Leah's quiet voice raised his head an hour later.

"Leah? I'm sorry. I just got involved here." He stood and walked towards her, seeing something different in her face. "What's up?"

"Why does everyone always ask that? My foster mother always said the sky." She stopped, hands going to her mouth in surprise. "I remembered something."

"Yes, you did." Josh grinned at her. "Doc said you'd remember. Looks like he was right, after all. Just don't tell him that." He laughed at the expression on her face. "But you wanted something, didn't you?"

"I did. Do you have time to walk around downtown with me? I don't want to go on my own, but I think I need to. I was heading here for a reason. Maybe that would trigger something."

Josh shot a look at the clock and sighed. It was coming up to his busy time of the morning, but he couldn't say no to Leah.

Leah caught the look on his face and turned away. "It's okay. I know you don't have time."

"Leah. Wait." He watched as she stopped, shoulders slumping in defeat. "Can you give me an hour or two? Then the rush will be over and I can walk with you. It usually slows down for a couple of hours after the breakfast crowd leaves."

She finally nodded, not wanting him to see the tears on her face. She walked away, heading for the staff break room and dropped to the couch there. She looked around. Josh had taken care to provide well for his staff, she thought. She didn't see him stop just outside the door and watch her, his heart in his eyes, before he turned and headed for the kitchen and the rush he could hear already starting.

Amy stopped by him. "Is Leah okay?"

"I think so. She's in the staff room. Could you check on her in a few minutes?" He reached for the next order that needed preparing, not seeing Amy's look or the look she shared with one of the other staff, before she headed for the staff room.

"Leah?" She sighed as Leah jumped at her voice. "I'm sorry. I didn't mean to startle you."

Leah gave a half laugh. "Everything does these days and I have no idea why." She swiped at the tears, stopping as she saw the warm wet cloth Amy held out for her. "Thank you." Her voice was barely audible.

Amy sank down beside her, her hand going to Leah's arm. "I know it's a strange time for you. A strange town. Strange people. And you don't have anything you remember to base your feelings or reactions on, do you?" She waited until Leah nodded. "Josh out there? He's one of the good guys. So are his friends, Simon, Jacob, and Blackie. Never hesitate to go to one of them or Finn or Julia. Now, what can I do to help you?"

Leah shrugged. "I have no idea, but thank you for caring."

Amy patted her arm and then stood. "Sitting here moping won't help. Come on out when you're ready and we'll put you to work."

Leah stared after her, wonder in her thoughts that these people would just open up to a stranger and take them in. But then, she didn't feel like this town was a strange town to her. She felt like she had come home and she had no idea why.

Josh tucked Leah's hand into his arm an hour later, when, as promised, he headed out with her to walk the downtown area. He could tell she was nervous, and he couldn't say that he blamed her. She was in a new town, didn't know hardly anyone, and had already come under attack before she even reached the city limits.

She looked around, interest on her face, at the decorations that had been placed and those workers finishing off the large tree in the centre of the town square. Her footsteps slowed and she pulled Josh to a stop with her. She could feel someone behind her, but she wasn't sure if it was a friend or a foe.

Josh watched her glancing around, seeing the fear lurking in her eyes, and pulled her off to the side.

"Leah? What's going on?" His own eyes searched the crowd, but he couldn't distinguish if someone was out there after Leah or not.

———

238

"I don't know. I just feel someone out there." She shuddered from fear, not willing to let him see how deeply she was affected.

Josh shot a glance around and then, taking her hand, drew her into an antiquities store. The lady at the counter looked up, waved and then went back to her customer. Leah protested as Josh pulled her with him into the owner's office.

"We can't come in here, Josh. This is employees only."

He grinned. "It's okay. This is Finn's place. We're allowed." He pointed to a chair and waited until she finally sank down, with a mutinous look still on her face. He perched on the corner of the desk, his foot swinging idly as he watched the door, knowing Finn would be along as soon as she could and that Jacob would be there as soon as she called him, likely bringing Blackie and Julia with him. That would be good, he thought. Maybe we can come up with a plan.

He rose as he heard light footsteps heading his way and greeted Finn, who then turned to face Leah, a gasp coming from her.

"Who is this, Josh? She looks like Julia and I." Her glance shot between Josh and Leah.

"This is Leah Bronagh. Did Julia talk to you?"

"Just briefly. So, this is Leah. Welcome to town. I'm Finnola, also known as Finn. Jacob and I are married." She paused as a frown appeared on Leah's face. "You haven't met Jacob yet, I gather. He's another good friend of Josh, Blackie and Simon. I know you've met Blackie's wife, Julia."

Leah finally nodded even as a frown appeared once more. "Forgive me. I can't remember much, even as to why I was coming here to Mistletoe. Who names a town Mistletoe, anyway?" She looked up in surprise as the two with her laughed.

Finn chortled in glee. "That's what no one has ever been able to figure out, but it really does draw in the crowds in December."

Leah nodded. "I would like to look around your store, if I may. It looks fascinating."

Finn jumped up from the chair she had been sitting in and grasped Leah's hand, pulling her to her feet. "Come on. It's quiet right now. Besides, my sister-in-law, Anna, is here and she'll handle things for me."

Josh trailed along behind the two ladies for a while before he stood near the front window, his eyes watching the crowds passing by. Something was off, but he just wasn't sure what. He turned as he felt a hand on his back. Finn stood there, a troubled look on her face.

"Josh? What's her story?"

He shrugged. "No one knows, Finn. She can't remember." He sighed. "Apparently Joy and Jeremiah know her. She's taught the girls in Sunday school. But even Jeremiah doesn't know much. She just never shared." He glanced around, seeing Leah standing talking with Anna. "Someone is after her, Finn, and

239

I don't know who. I want to stop that, get her memory back, and then see what happens."

Finn smiled. "Your heart's involved, isn't it, Josh?" She waited until he gave a reluctant nod. "And you can't say or do anything until you know she's free. We'll pray for you both."

Josh dropped a kiss on Finn's cheek. "Thank you. That is appreciated." He turned as he saw Leah approaching him. "Ready to go?"

"I am." She thanked Finn and then headed for the door, Josh reaching it ahead of her, grinning at her protest that she could open her own door.

Finn watched them walk away, Anna at her side.

"They make a great couple, Finn. What's her story?"

Finn shrugged. "Right now, she doesn't even know. She was injured a few days ago and can't remember."

"Oh, no. And Josh has lost his heart. I can see that." Anna turned to Finn. "Now what, Finn, other than praying for them?"

"That's about all we can do, Anna." Finn watched the couple until they were lost from sight, a heaviness weighing her down.

Glancing around, Leah shuddered in fear once more. Why, she had no idea, and she did not like that one bit. She wanted to remember but just couldn't. Maybe she should just leave town, but then, where would she go? She didn't know where she had come from. She had not asked that of Joy or Jeremiah. Not yet, anyway, but that would come, she knew.

Josh directed her to the town square and then past it, towards an area that held small buildings and decorated trees as well as a large gazebo. He stopped at a refreshment stand for teas for them and then pointed to the buildings.

"These are some of the older buildings from the original settlers, I think someone told me. They keep them closed all year but at Christmas they open them up for a few days. It's fascinating walking through them."

Leah stared at the buildings, a frown in place. "I know those buildings, Josh, but how?"

He stared at her for a moment, then sipped at his tea. "You know them? That's interesting. Come on. Let's walk closer to them."

Leah finally dumped her tea into a garbage bin, not really in the mood to drink it all. She stood watching the few people around them, a sense of doom overcoming her once more but she couldn't see anyone who threatened her. Josh watched her and then did his own watching of the crowds.

Turning as he heard his name called, Josh hesitated at leaving Leah but she urged him to go, that she would be all right. There were people around, weren't there?

Josh stood for some time speaking with Blackie until a loud snap and crashing broke shattered the air, as screams split through the sounds. Josh and Blackie spun, horror on their face as they saw one of the buildings had collapsed.

"Leah? Do you see her?" Josh's feet dug into the ground as he ran forward, not seeing her anywhere.

"The lady that was with me?" He slid to a stop near the older lady Leah had been talking to. "Do you know where she went?"

"No, I'm sorry. I think she went that way." A shaking finger pointed towards the collapsed building.

Josh's heart beat harder as he realized that Leah wasn't to be seen anywhere. He saw the man standing watching him and realized who was after Leah. He then heard cries that someone was trapped and knew it was Leah. His feet dug in once more as he started to run towards the building as Blackie tackled him, taking him to the ground.

———

"Let me go, Blackie. Leah's in there." Josh struggled against his friend's hold.

"We don't know that. The firemen are here. They'll check it out." Blackie's hold slipped on Josh and Josh was up and away, Blackie springing to his feet.

"Jacob!" Blackie saw their friend watching the men working. "Stop Josh!"

Jacob raced towards Josh, taking him down, Blackie lending his weight to try and hold him to the ground. Josh fought them, struggling to get away, to reach the building. The two men's weight could barely keep him down and then Simon was there, aiding them.

Josh continued to struggle, almost getting away, his agonized eyes on the building, his body twisting and contorting under his friends as they tried to keep him still and safe.

"Let me up. I need to get to her." His cries reached his friends' ears but they still managed to keep him down. "Let me up. Please. Let me go."

Josh's struggles to escape almost succeeded until a team of paramedics arrived. Quickly assessing the situation and hearing his cries, they knew they had to restrain him.

"Who's he trying to get to?" The older paramedic was reaching into one of the boxes even as he asked, even as the other paramedic lent his aid in an attempt to keep Josh on the ground.

"A friend. We think she's in the building that collapsed."

"But they're closed. She can't be." He shook his head at Blackie's comment.

Blackie drew in a ragged breath. "Josh thinks she is. We can't see her anywhere." He shoved down on Josh's arm, just missing getting hit in the face. "Josh! Stop! We'll find her. You need to stop!"

Josh continued to fight against the men holding him, almost succeeding once more in getting free. Blackie gave a grumble of concern, his hand reaching to pull the jacket and sweater sleeve back as he saw the syringe in the paramedic's hand, then struggled to hold Josh's arm still and to the ground, the tendons in the wrist corded and tight under his hand. The second paramedic leaned on Josh's upper arm and even that was a struggle. It took two of them to hold Josh's arm still enough for the injection to be given.

The paramedic sat back on his heels. "He's a fighter, isn't he? That's a sedative. It will knock him out for a while. We'll transport once he's no longer fighting us."

Blackie nodded as his eyes went back to his friend's face, seeing the agony there, the terror. He frowned as he heard Josh's voice whispering, the sound getting lower as the sedative took effect.

———

242

"I need to get to Leah. I need to find her. She's not safe. I know who's after her. Let me up." The last few words, or sobs rather, were barely audible as the sedative took effect and Josh lost consciousness, his body going limp, his head dropping to the ground.

His three friends shoved themselves away from him and rose, their eyes first on him, then each other.

"What did he just say?" Simon stared at Josh, and then at the collapsed building. "Does he really think she's in there?"

Blackie nodded. "He does. I don't see her." He spun in a circle, not seeing her, and then froze as he heard yells from the firemen at the collapsed building. "Simon?"

Simon nodded, his eyes on the Mistletoe Police Chief, Ed Waters, who stood watching them. "Ed?"

"Come on then, Simon. We'll check it out. One of your friends is riding with Josh?"

Blackie nodded. "I will." He froze. "Joy!"

Jacob held up his phone. "Already on it. Mary and your Mom are headed to Josh's. They'll watch the girls for Joy."

Blackie nodded. "I'll ride with him. Jacob?"

Jacob nodded. "I'll let the ladies know and then meet you there."

Simon walked away with the Chief, their conversation on Josh's words and the question that had been raised. Did he really know who was after Leah, and who was it then?

Watching Josh walk towards Blackie, Leah stood for a moment, uncertain in what to do, frightened to be on her own, knowing someone was after her, but determined to stand on her own two feet. She finally turned and walked slowly towards the buildings, her eyes taking in the solidness of them, a wonder in her mind that buildings still stood after all those years, beaten by the weather to a soft gray. She stood for a moment, her eyes searching the area around her, before she walked towards one, stepping up on the small porch and approaching the window. She stood, hands cupped around her face as she stared inside.

Hearing a soft cry, she jumped back and looked around, a frown on her face. She heard the cry again, a mew, she thought, and searched for the kitten. Not finding it, she once more approached the window, looking inside and hearing the mew from inside the building. This is strange, she thought.

She tried the front door, finding it locked, more puzzled than ever. She stepped from the porch, searching for Josh and seeing him still talking with Blackie, his back turned towards her for a moment. She couldn't leave the kitten to go and get him. She walked around the building, searching for an entrance, stepping up on the back porch and heading for the door, hearing the mewing sounding louder. She tried the door, finding it unlocked, and hesitated, not knowing if she should enter or not. The cries of the kitten grabbed her attention once more and she slowly shoved the door open, stepping inside, determined to find the kitten and then get out before someone questioned why she was in a locked building.

She caught her breath at the beauty of the building in its simplicity. A school room, she thought. How I would have liked to have attended this school! She turned as she heard the cries and slowly walked forward, her eyes searching. She stopped as she heard a popping sound and then shrugged, moving forward. A second popping sound stilled her movements and she looked around, not quite sure what was going on.

The kitten's cries drew her forward as she searched for it, finally finding it crouched under a desk. She knelt and reached for it, cradling it close to her. As she stood, she heard a third popping sound, and looked up. The building seems to be moving, she thought, and turning, she began to walk rapidly towards the back door, the kitten cradled against her.

Snapping and cracking caught her attention, and this time she felt the building shudder. A low scream broke from her and she tried to run of the door, only to find beams and roofing falling in her way. She flung herself towards the wall, curling up in a ball, one hand over her head, the kitten tight in her other arm, praying for protection. Her head smacked against the old black iron stove, and she collapsed to the floor, darkness falling over her as the ringing in her head intensified. Josh, she thought. I need your help and I can't get to you.

Shouts rang broke through the air as the building slowly crumpled in on itself. For a moment, everyone outside froze. Then men began to run towards the building, not sure what had happened. Sirens rang through the air as emergency personnel rushed to the scene, spilling from their vehicles, and heading for the buildings.

Calls went out, asking if anyone was inside. At first, the responses were negative, until one of the firefighters crouched down along the back wall and caught sight of Leah's jacket. Shouts for help rang through the air, catching the attention of the men with Josh, who were still fighting to keep him down and away from the building.

Working the men working carefully but quickly, the building was stabilized enough that the smallest of the firefighters, a younger woman, could slide inside and reach Leah. She quickly felt for a pulse, her heart thankful there was one. She felt Leah over, stopping as she saw the head wound. She frowned as she heard a mew and saw the tiny tip of an ear over Leah's arm. She tried to free the kitten, but Leah's hold was too strong. She turned at a question from outside, acknowledging that she needed the backboard and collar, and that she also needed help inside.

A paramedic joined her, glancing cautiously at the building as it still creaked and groaned, then helping to stabilize Leah before she was moved carefully to the opening and then outside.

The fire chief stood, eyes watchful, then disbelieving as he heard the kitten.

"She has a kitten in her arms?"

The young firefighter nodded. "She does, and she will not give it up. And we need her to do that. Her grip is too strong for me to release the cat."

Simon had moved closer and listened intently at the conversation going on around him, finally speaking.

"I know her. Maybe I can get the kitten from her." He moved towards Leah, his hand resting on her arm. "Leah. It's Simon. Can you let me have your kitten?" He waited, then moved his hand further on her arm to where the kitten was struggling to get free. "Come on, Leah. Let me have the kitten, please. I'll take care of it for you." He watched her face, then turned his attention to the little calico kitten, seeing her arm relax just a little.

He heard a whisper from her and bent close. "What did you say, Leah? Let me have the kitten, and then we'll get you some treatment for your head."

"The kitten was in the building. I had to get it. Josh needs it for the girls. I can't let it go." Her voice was barely audible and he could hear pain in it.

Simon gave a small smile, then finally managed to get the kitten from her. "It's okay, Leah. I'll take care of it for you. I'll make sure Josh gets it. Let them look after you now." He stepped back, unzipping his jacket enough to tuck the kitten in to keep it warm, his eyes on Leah's face, and his mind on her words.

Ed stopped beside him. "She went in after a kitten?"

"It appears that way. She wants it for Josh, she said. Why, I have no idea." He turned to look at the building. "But her going in there should not have brought the building down. They're monitored all the time for safety, particularly coming up to when the buildings will be opened for Christmas."

"I know. That concerns me. And who unlocked it, I would like to know." Ed walked away to speak with the fire chief as Simon turned to follow the stretcher bearing Leah.

Simon jumped up and took a seat, his eyes still on Leah, his thoughts puzzled as to what was going on with Josh and Leah. Now what, Lord, he asked. Only You know the outcome for this.

The paramedic looked askance as he saw the kitten peeking from Simon's jacket. "You know, they won't let the kitten in there."

"Ssh!" Simon grinned at him. "It's a therapy animal, isn't it? Leah wants Josh to have it for comfort. Isn't that what she said?"

The paramedic shook his head even as he grinned. "Not quite what I heard, but the intent was there. If you want to try it, it's your game. I'm staying out of it." He reached to adjust the IV, then assessed her pupils once more. "You said you know her?"

"Not well. She's just new to town. But she was injured somehow and lost her memory. Another concussion this close to that one won't help her any."

The paramedic looked up at him, then back at Leah. "No, it won't. But it may bring back her memory or drive it deeper. The docs will know best."

Simon waited until the stretcher was offloaded from the rig and then jumped down, his hand holding the kitten in place. He saw Julia heading his way and waited, greeting his friend.

"Where's Blackie?" Julie turned to enter the hospital, stopping as she heard a mew. "Simon?"

"I know. Leah rescued a kitten and I can't let it out of my sight." He grinned as she stared at him, finally shaking her head.

"I think you could." She looked around. "There's Anna. Let her have Leah's kitten and she'll take it over to Josh's."

The kitten quickly transferred hands, Anna agreeing to drop off the kitten, with a promise from them they would let her know how the two were.

Hours later, Joy stood in Josh's hospital room, watching as he moved restlessly, the sedative finally wearing off. Jeremiah's arm came around his wife.

"He's still not awake totally?"

Joy shook her head. "He's not. The doctor's not concerned though. He said they had to give him a lot and that with his fighting them at the time, it likely had an exaggerated effect. What have you heard about Leah?"

"She's in a room, still unconscious. They're concerned about her head injury, not knowing how it has affected her, on top of her previous one." He sighed. "I never expected this when we decided to move here."

"No, but I'm glad we're here." She took another look at her brother and then turned back to Jeremiah. "I need to go home to the girls." She groaned. "Did I just say home? Right now, we don't have a home."

"We do. Josh made that clear. Right now, we're where we need to be, just as you said." He kissed her, then helped her into her coat. "Go. Take care of the girls. I'll call if there's any change." He watched her walk away before he turned back to the bed, finding Josh's eyes flickering open and closed.

"Josh? Can you hear me, buddy?"

Josh finally focused on Jeremiah. "Jeremiah? Where am I?" His mouth and throat was dry and he had trouble getting his words out.

Jeremiah's hands went out to hold Josh's head up and the glass of water to his mouth, before he set the glass back on the table and reached to raise the head of the bed.

"You're in the hospital. Josh, do you remember anything?"

Josh went to shake his head, then stopped. "I can remember not seeing Leah. Where is she?"

"She's in another room here, Josh." Jeremiah paused, not quite sure how to continue.

"Is she okay?" Josh tried to push the covers back, but didn't have the strength. "Tell me."

"She's unconscious right now, Josh. And no, they will not let you in to see her. The chief has posted a guard at her door."

"A guard? Why?" Josh struggled to sit up, Jeremiah's hand on his chest preventing that.

"Someone sabotaged one of the buildings. She went in after a kitten and the building collapsed around her. They think she hit her head on the stove in the building and knocked herself out." He watched with compassion as Josh's head went back and his eyes slid closed.

"How does this affect her?"

"They don't know yet. They're waiting for her to wake up." Jeremiah paused, a smile lurking in his eyes. "Did you really want a kitten? I'm sure there were easier ways for Leah to get you one."

"A kitten? Who says I want a kitten?" Josh stared at Jeremiah, not quite sure if he was serious or not.

"Leah apparently does. She rescued a kitten and told Simon it was for you. That you needed it. For my girls. Shouldn't you have talked to me first?" He laughed at the expression on Josh's face. "Didn't know that, did you?"

Josh shook his head even as he yawned. "I don't remember us talking about animals at all. How do you know she said it was for me?"

"Simon. He had to talk her into giving it up. She told him it was for you." Jeremiah gave a small smile at the look that crossed Josh's face even as Josh lost his fight with sleep. He turned his head as he heard the door open and Simon walked in. "Where's Josh's kitten? He didn't know he needed one."

Simon gave a low laugh. "I hear tell your girls are fussing over it and Joy had to rescue it once again. What was she thinking, Leah, to go into a building?"

"None of us would have expected the building to collapse like that. It was planned, wasn't it?"

Simon nodded. "That's what we think. The fire chief has called in building inspectors and contractors to see what happened." He pointed with his chin towards Josh. "How is he?"

"Sleepy. He was awake just before you walked in. He tried hard to get up to go to Leah." Jeremiah paused, not quite sure how to proceed with what he needed to say.

"And you're concerned that his heart is already taken by her and you have no idea if she's free or not." Simon smiled in sympathy as Jeremiah finally nodded.

"That's it exactly. I heard how he fought you three. That's not him."

"No, it's not. But I can see him doing that for Joy and the girls."

Jeremiah nodded. "Yeah, I guess. Have you heard how Leah is? He asked."

"She was awake but not really doing much talking. I popped in to see her. She didn't recognize me, but the nurse says the doctors feel she's had another concussion and on top of one just days earlier, they are quite concerned. We'll have to talk about where she's to go when she's released." He nodded towards Josh. "He'll want to be close to her."

Jeremiah sighed. "I know he will. But how do we let him, when we don't know her history?" They both turned as they heard steps behind them. Blackie and his father, Samuel, stood there, greeting the two before Samuel moved to the side of the bed, his eyes on Josh who had just awakened again.

"Josh? How are you feeling?"

"A little groggy. What did they give me?"

Blackie moved closer, laughing at his friend. "A sedative, Josh. You were fighting us too hard to do anything else."

Josh finally nodded, his memory coming back. "Leah? Where is she?"

"She's here on your floor and no, you're not going to her." Samuel's hand rested on his young friend's arm. "I need to talk to you first." He glanced as the other three men. "It would be better if you all heard this now. That way, I don't have to repeat myself. The only missing is Jacob."

"And he's just outside. I heard his voice." Simon headed for the hallway, coming back with Jacob in tow. "Okay, Samuel. What did you find out?"

Samuel's eyes studied the five younger men, lingering on Josh's face, knowing what he had to say would be disturbing but necessary. He sighed to himself, then prayed for wisdom in what he had to share. It should be shared with Leah first, but he wasn't able to, and he needed these men's help to keep her safe, if what he had uncovered was true.

"Dad?" Blackie's voice cut through his thoughts. "You have news?"

"I do, Levi. That I do, son. I'm not sure though how to explain it all so you understand." He held up a hand at their protest. "Just keep in mind that I should be talking with Leah first, and I just can't do that, not given her medical issues at present. I will as soon as the doctor gives me clearance." He studied each one, his eyes lingering on Josh the longest, knowing what he had to say would affect him the most.

Dad?" Blackie's voice once more caught Samuel's attention.

"Sorry, son. Okay. So, I guess I should start." He still hesitated, not quite sure what to say, and that was so unlike him. He prayed again for wisdom and words, and knew then that God was with him.

"Josh, you figured out your lady's name. She really is Leah Bronagh, one of the descendants from this town. That also makes her related to Finn and Julia. This is where her story becomes complicated and I'm still not sure how far back it goes, whether it goes back past her parents or not."

"What do you mean, Samuel?" Josh's eyes were stead on his friend.

"Her parents disappeared when she was three. We cannot track what happened to them. We cannot even prove that they are alive or dead. She was found on her own, a note pinned to her, giving her name, date of birth. Someone dropped her off at a police station. I know you've talked with her about how she was never adopted, although her foster family tried their best. There was some sort of documentation with her that she could never be adopted, something to do with her last name.

"There was no issues with her until just before she was 18. I talked to her foster family. The mother indicates something changed a couple of months before she was 18. Her foster sister said the same thing. She thought she had been contacted by someone, someone who terrified her. I have not been able to confirm this. We are looking into going to her apartment in your town, Jeremiah. We're just waiting for the police there to obtain a search warrant for us."

Jeremiah spoke up. "I have her permission from before to go into her place at any time for any reasons. She put it into writing and had a lawyer draw it up. So we can do that tomorrow if you like."

"That will help. Thank you."

"This seems to odd, Samuel." Jacob was trying to puzzle through it all. "Why couldn't she be adopted?"

Samuel shrugged. "That I have no idea why. From what I understand the documentation never said. Her foster parents have a copy and are emailing to me. I'll have it later today and maybe know something more."

Josh had been still, listening to them. "Donald Emms, from this town. How is he connected to the Bronaghs?"

The five men shared a look and then stared at him.

"Why would you ask that?" Blackie had his own issues with Donald, wanting to talk with him about a search he had sent Julia and Blackie on a year ago.

"Because he was standing watching Leah. I saw him when I turned to look for her at one point but I didn't recognize him right away. He disappeared after the building collapsed." Josh's head went back and his eyes closed. "Why would he do this?"

"We don't know that he did, Josh." Simon spoke up. "But we will find out, trust me on that one." He glanced at his watch. "Sorry, Samuel. I'll have to catch up with you later. Let me know if I can do anything to help."

Samuel watched Simon walk away, knowing that Simon would never let this rest, not when it affected a good friend. He prayed for answers, that they could resolve this soon, without either Josh or Leah being hurt again.

"Samuel?" Josh's voice caught his attention. "Can you look into Donald? See where he is in this? I know Blackie wants to talk to him, but so do I. He knows something."

"I plan on doing just that."

The conversation had exhausted Josh, whose eyes slid closed as he slept again. The other men finished their quiet conversation and all left but Jeremiah.

Jeremiah stood for a few minutes at the window, his eyes on the sky, his heart raised in prayer. Sunday was only a few days away and he knew he needed to be working on his sermon, but right now, Josh needed him. He turned, leaning back against the wall, his hands jammed into his pockets, lost in thought before he walked out of Josh's room and down to Leah's. He nodded at the officer at the door and quietly pushed the door open.

Standing beside Leah's bed, he watched as her head turned restlessly before he reached to lay a hand on her shoulder and bow his head to pray for her. He looked up, surprised to see her eyes open and clear. The doctors didn't think she would be awake until the next day.

"Jeremiah? What are you doing here? And just where is here?" She looked around, panic momentarily taking over.

"You're in the hospital in Mistletoe. Don't you remember?"

She stared at him. "Mistletoe? Where's that? And why am I there?"

"You really don't remember?" When she shook her head, he sighed. Thanks, Lord, leaving it to me to break it to her. "You ended up here a few days ago. You couldn't remember anything other than your first name. Apparently you had an accident or something like that. Earlier today, you were in a building that collapsed here in town. They think you hit your head on an old cast-iron stove."

"Why would I be in that building? And why did it collapse?" She paused, a frown in place. "Jeremiah, this does not make sense at all."

"No, I guess it wouldn't." He reached to draw up a chair, knowing he'd be there for a while. "Mistletoe is where Josh lives."

"Joy's brother? But that doesn't explain why you're here."

"We're here because I'm taking over for the pastor for a while. He's off on sick leave. We're staying with Josh. Somehow you and Josh connected. You really don't remember?"

She went to shake her head, then stopped. "Does he have a restaurant or something?"

"He does. Why?"

"Then I do remember. He saved me from someone coming after me with a bat. He was hurt." Her eyes flew to Jeremiah's. "Tell me he didn't get hurt again."

Jeremiah began to laugh, drawing a frown from her. "No. He didn't get hurt again, but they did have to sedate him when he realized you were in the collapsed building. Blackie said he's never seen him fight to get to anyone like he fought his friends."

She sighed, her head going back on the pillow before she reached to the control to raise the head of the bed. "I wish he hadn't."

"Why?"

"Just because."

"Because why, Leah? We know that you were in foster care. A friend's father who is an investigator has found them and talked to them." At her glare, he held up a hand. "We needed to know, Leah. You couldn't remember anything about your previous life. Not one thing. You didn't even remember your last name."

She sighed, the glare disappearing. "That's okay, Jeremiah, in that case. I remember now." A look of fear fluttered across her face.

"What or who are you afraid of, Leah? Let us help you."

"I can't." Her words were barely above a whisper.

"And why not?" Jeremiah and Leah both jumped at Josh's words.

Jeremiah rose, drawing Josh over to the chair. "I'll be outside. You two can hash this out." He walked away, standing out in the hallway for a moment, before he looked around and headed for the chapel. He needed to spend time in prayer for his friends, but also for his new town and church.

Watching the door close after Jeremiah, Josh stood for a moment, lost in thought, before he turned back to Leah, finding her eyes on him. He sank down into the chair Jeremiah had vacated and studied her.

"How are you feeling?" He had to say something, had to break the silence.

She shrugged. "I have a horrible headache and the vision isn't great. Do you know how sick you can feel from double vision?"

He grinned for a moment. "I do. It's not fun. Other than that, how are you?"

She once more shrugged. "I really don't know." She frowned, even as she studied his face. "I'm sorry, but I take it you're Josh?"

"I am. You don't remember me?" When she shook her head slightly, he smiled. "That's okay. We've only known each other for a couple of days, anyway."

"No, it's not okay. I feel like I should remember you, that you've helped me in some way. Tell me how we met. I can remember your restaurant, I think. Jeremiah said it was yours."

"It was. You ran in the back door, tried to run when I approached you, back out the door again. I caught up with you. I ended up taking you to my house where a friend and his wife met us. We had you checked out by a friend, Doc, who said you had had a concussion. Simon, another friend, found your car, battered and beaten, the windows all broken. We think that's how you ended up with a concussion in the first place. We were walking through the downtown area this morning and when I went to talk to a friend, you disappeared. Somehow you ended up in the old schoolhouse, which collapsed around you."

She stared at him. "There is no way all that happened to me. I don't live that kind of life." She was in shock, her eyes huge.

Josh grinned. "It has. All in the space of say three days, four at the most?"

She shook her head. "There is absolutely no way that would happen. And just why would I go into an old building anyway?"

"Apparently to rescue a kitten you heard, that you decided I needed for my two nieces."

"A kitten? There is no way I'd do that. I don't like cats." She stared as he just shook his head and grinned at her. "No way!" When he still grinned at her, she sighed. "I wouldn't do that. I don't rescue animals. I don't go into old buildings on my own."

"Sorry, Leah. This time you did. And Simon, a friend, had to do some talking to get you to give up the kitten, which by the way is now at my house with my sister and her girls. I don't think I'll get to keep it."

She stared at him, knowing he was telling the truth, but seeing the hint of teasing coming through. She knew from Joy that he could tease but that he loved his sister and nieces dearly. "I still can't see me doing that."

"You did. Unfortunately, it ended up with you here in the hospital. The fire chief is still trying to figure out how the building came down, but they think it was set up to get you into it and then bring the building down on top of you."

She stared at him, horror coursing through her. "Then he really did mean it, didn't he?"

Josh was instantly stern and concerned. "Who, Leah? Who are you talking about?"

She shook her head. "I can't tell you." Her voice was barely above a whisper. "He threatened to kill my foster family. He said he had my real parents somewhere. He won't tell me if they are alive or dead." Tears sparkled in her eyes and Josh reached to grasp her hand, finding hers ice cold.

"Leah, you need to tell someone. We can help you. Please, let us. Let me." Josh knew he was begging but he felt he had no choice.

She shook her head, but it was not as forceful as it had been. "I don't want you hurt, Josh."

"And I don't want to see you hurt, not any worse than you have been." He looked up at the ceiling, as if to ask for help, before looking back at her. "All I ask is that you talk to me. Please. You were coming to Mistletoe for a reason. Maybe if you know why, we can figure out who."

She stared at him for a moment, then sighed. "I was coming to find you, I think. Joy has talked so much about you, I thought maybe you could help me or you would know someone who could. I knew it wasn't a very smart idea, but I didn't know who else to turn to."

"I'm glad you did come, Leah. Let's work through what you know and then go from there."

She nodded, pain flickering across her face. "I will, but right now, I just can't think straight."

Josh stood to leave, to let her sleep, just as she reached for his hand.

"Can you stay for a bit, Josh? I don't want to be alone." He nodded as he sank back into the chair, having to pull it closer to the bed as she pulled on his hand. "Thank you. I'll sleep now." Her eyes slid closed and she slept, her hand with Josh's tight in it curled up under her cheek as she turned to her side.

Josh gave a small smile and tried to pull his hand back, finding she would not release his. This is great, he thought. Now what do I do?

He waited for a while and once more tried to free his hand, without success. He sighed and then carefully moved her fingers to release his hand, sitting back in the chair before he rose and quietly placed the chair back to where it usually sat. He stood, his eyes on her, then moved to the door, stopping once more to look back at her before he looked up and seemed to receive confirmation of something.

Simon stood outside the door, waiting for him, and followed Josh back to his room. Josh dropped down on the edge of the bed, feeling restless and in danger, but not knowing why.

"How is she?" Simon studied his friend with concern, seeing something in his face Josh didn't realize he showed.

"She really doesn't remember the last few days. She also says she wouldn't have gone in to find a kitten." He smiled at Simon's snort of laughter.

"Well, she did. I had to take it from her, remember?"

"I do, from what you said. Now, she says someone threatened her foster family and that they know where her real family is."

Simon sat up straighter in the chair he had dropped into. "Say what?"

Josh repeated himself. "Just what I said. She also said she was coming here to find me, hoping I could help or one of my friends could. That I don't get."

"Joy." Josh stared at Simon. "Joy's talked about you. She's talked about your friends. So it would make sense that Leah would head away from home to find someone to help her."

Josh shrugged. "I guess. Or the girls. Maybe even Jeremiah. I still don't get it, though." He paused, his thoughts drifting to something else. "Did you find Donald?"

"No, and that concerns me. We still need to talk to him about what happened with Blackie and Julia last year. We've never been able to."

"No. That was strange, sending them out on that rescue mission, and then disappearing. Did Samuel ever track down his family connection to here?"

"There is none. Donald showed up here about five years ago, became involved in the search and rescue team, and then sort of took it over when the leader retired. He was never formally voted in as leader, and with what he did to Julia, that has rankled a number of the members."

Josh stared at the floor, his arms folded across his chest, as he became lost in thought. Simon watched him, concern in his own eyes for his friend. Just how far is he into this, Lord, Simon asked.

Simon's head turned slightly as he heard soft footsteps walking towards them. Samuel stood for a moment before he reached for a second chair, startling Josh as he did so.

"Samuel! I didn't hear you."

Samuel laughed. "No, I didn't think you did. You were pretty lost in thought. Now, I know you've been to talk to Leah. What can you share?"

Josh sighed, his eyes resting on Simon, who nodded. "I did speak with her. She really doesn't remember the last couple of days. But she is terrified of someone who threatened to kill her foster family, said he knew where her real parents were and that she headed to Mistletoe to find me or one of my friends for help. Does that sound about right?" He looked over at Samuel, catching a slight smile on his face and then frowned. "Samuel?"

"Josh?"

"Oh, and she would never have gone into a building like that, particularly to rescue a cat. She doesn't like them."

Samuel started laughing at that, causing Simon to join him, and then finally Josh.

"Did she really say that?" Samuel's voice held a question he didn't ask.

"She did. I have no idea why she doesn't but that's what she said. Maybe something to ask her family." Josh sighed and then crawled up on the bed, pulling the covers over himself. He was exhausted but not ready to sleep.

"Josh?" Samuel's voice caught his attention and he looked at him, seeing the concern there.

"I'm okay, Samuel. Just tired. Whatever it was they gave me hasn't worn off yet."

Simon began to laugh once more. "Man, you should have seen yourself. You were so determined to get up, we could barely keep you on the ground." He sobered. "That's when you said you knew who was after her. Is that what you meant when you said Donald?"

Josh nodded. "It is. He was there. I can't prove he had anything to do with what happened, though, and I may never."

Samuel shook his head. "Leave it with us and the police, Josh. We have the resources we need. You have enough with your restaurant right now." A spark of mischief lit up his face, making him look a lot like Blackie. "Besides, you have an eight-week-old kitten to name and look after."

Josh groaned as he laid his head back. "Please, do not remind me of that. I can't have a cat in the house."

"And why not?"

Josh shook his head at Simon's question. "I just can't. Besides, I think the girls would be disappointed not to take it with them. After all, she rescued it for me to give to them." He smirked as the two with him broke out into laughter again, hushing as the door squeaked open and the nurse entered.

"Do you need anything, Josh? No? By the way, this was left for you." She dropped an envelope on the table and then walked out.

<hr>

Josh stared at the envelope, not making any effort to touch it. Simon reached into his pocket, felt around and pulled out latex gloves, reaching for the letter at Josh's nod.

Simon studied the envelope, seeing Josh's name written in bold block letters. No much help there, he thought. Unable to trace this more than likely. He flipped the envelope over, finding the flap sealed, and reached into his pocket for his knife.

Slitting open the envelope, he hesitated, his eyes first on Josh, who had sat back up, watching with interesting Simon's movements, and then turning to Samuel, who frowned, seeming to know that whatever the envelope contained, it would change the direction of their investigation and he wasn't ready for that to happen yet.

Josh watched as Simon carefully extracted the paper folded inside, not quite sure what he was facing with it. Simon shot a look at the two men with him before he carefully unfolded it, a frown covering his face.

"Simon?" Josh's voice caught his attention.

"It's blank, Josh. Absolutely nothing on it that I can see. What in the world is going on?"

Samuel stood at Simon's side, his eyes on the paper, watching carefully as Simon flipped it over to inspect the other side. A frown covered his face as a memory niggled at his mind.

"I've seen this before, Josh, Simon. It's been years. Don't tell me he's back."

"Who's back, Samuel?"

"We had an investigation about fifteen years ago. A client would receive letters like this, meant to terrorize them, and it did. There was never anything on the paper. We did every test imaginable to try and bring up words, DNA, anything. Nothing could be found. I suspect that's what your lab will find with that." He pointed to the paper. "And the envelope will be the same. You'll get nothing from the printing."

"So, what happened?" Josh was deeply concerned, knowing that terror would not sit well with him when it came to Leah.

"The letters stopped. It took a good while for my client to get their life back. We had looked into everyone they had contact with and found no one that would have sent something like this."

"But with Leah, you're thinking differently." Simon's keen eyes studied the older man, catching the look in his eyes that said he was.

"I am, Simon. Given what's gone on with her, I would say it is different. I had a chance to speak with your police chief tonight before I came back. It was deliberate, the way the building came down. Someone placed tiny ribbons of explosives in the corners and then laid almost invisible wires from them to the centre of the floor. He thinks that when Leah walked across it, she would step on a sensor and set off a small charge, likely no louder than a pop. He's planning on talking to her to see if she can remember anything."

"That makes sense." Simon studied Josh, who nodded. "It would have to be someone who knows explosives to do something that sophisticated, don't you think?"

Samuel shook his head. "Not necessarily. The internet is a good source of information nowadays, unfortunately. They look for the right wording and they'll find what they want."

Josh nodded, folding his arms back across his chest, and laying his head on the pillow. "I suspect she really won't remember much. Not right now, anyway. She doesn't remember going into the building or rescuing the kitten. She doesn't remember meeting me at all." They could hear the pain in Josh's voice at that sentence and knew that he had found his treasure, his lady, but would he be hers, that was the question unanswered.

Samuel finally stood, staring down at the blank sheet of paper, a frown on his face. "There's something about that paper, Simon, something I'm just not remembering right at the moment. It will come to me." He looked up at Josh. "How serious was she when she said she thought her parents were still alive?"

He shrugged. "I can't tell. I don't know her that well. Ask Joy or Jeremiah. They might have a better read than I do." He sighed. "Just get me out of here, please?"

"Tomorrow, my friend. Then, we'll have to find a place for Leah to stay." Simon held up his hand. "I know Joy and Jeremiah are planning on staying with you for a while. That would work for the first few days. But we really need to find somewhere she'll be safe."

"Yeah, and where's that, Simon? Look what happened with both Jacob and Blackie. They certainly weren't safe. Or Blackie's friends, Cara and Corin."

"No, they weren't." Samuel stood for a moment, eyes on him. "But we'll do our best for your lady, Josh. You can depend on that."

Josh finally nodded. "I know, Samuel. I know you'll do your best. But look at what just happened to her. How do we keep her safe?"

Samuel and Simon exchanged glances, both wondering just how deep Josh's feelings went and just what he would do to keep his lady safe.

They turned as they heard the door open. Then Josh was off the bed and at Leah's side, a smile on his face, but also a questioning look.

"Leah?"

She looked up at him, fear evident on her face. "He was in my room, Josh. I pretended to be asleep, but he was there. I heard him talking to me, telling me I was no good, that I had to be taken care of, just like my parents." Tears sparkled in her eyes, tears that soon overflowed, no matter how much she determined that they not.

Josh gave an inaudible sound and swept her into a hug, turning slightly so he could see the other two men. Simon nodded, already heading out the door to find the officer who should have been at her door.

"Was the officer there when you came out?"

"Officer? What officer? There wasn't anyone in the hall. I just knew you were here somewhere and looked for you." She stared up at him, a frown now on her face. "Why would there be an officer at my door?"

"To protect you, Leah." Samuel gave a gentle smile as she started and then turned to face him, Josh's arms loosening enough so she could.

"I'm sorry?"

"I'm Blackie's father, Samuel. I didn't mean to frighten you. Here. Sit in this chair." Samuel grabbed a blanket and wrapped her in it before she sat, taking care of her just as he would one of his own two daughters.

Josh's hands stayed on her shoulders as he stood behind her, his eyes on her head. Why, Lord, was his question. Can she not have peace of some kind? What is this all about anyway? He felt a peace flow through him, felt the confidence that God really was in control, that no matter what happened, God would walk every step with them.

He felt Leah moving restlessly under his hands and stepped back, his eyes on Samuel, who was studying Leah.

"Leah. What can you tell us about this man?" Samuel glanced up as he heard Simon and then the police chief entering the room. He sighed. This is not the quiet hospital room she should be in. We need to get her out of here, he thought.

She shook her head. "I didn't see him. I just heard him and felt his hand on my arm. He squeezed it as he spoke." She paused, a frown on her face as she thought back over the event. "I am almost sure I know the voice, but I just can't place it. I know I've heard it somewhere."

Samuel shared a glance with Josh and then Simon and Ed. "I suggest we remove Leah from the hospital and take her somewhere we have better control over her visitors. Josh?"

"I agree. My place is fairly secure. It had a good security system already installed when I moved in."

Ed nodded. "The man who had it before you worked for the government and needed extra security. But I am not convinced that will be enough."

Josh was watching him and sighed when he realized what he meant. Was he ready for that step, with someone who didn't know him, didn't remember that he had helped her?

"What happened to the officer, Ed?" Josh instead asked another question.

"He was knocked out. No one saw anything. He's still out, so I can't question him." Ed turned slightly as he heard a tap at the door and cracked it open. "I'll be back. See if you can come up with a plan in the mean while."

Simon turned back from the door, his eyes on Samuel, who nodded towards Josh.

"Josh, can I talk to you for a moment? Let's get Leah back to her room and let her get dressed. We're moving her tonight."

Leah stared up at Simon. "Moving me? The doctor won't let me go. He said so."

"He will. I'll personally talk to him. It's more important that we keep you alive than you stay here. And somehow I don't think you will be alive come morning unless we do move you." Simon hated to scare her but knew he had no choice, seeing her face whiten as his words.

Leah finally stood, Josh's hand on her back as he guided her back to her room, Simon having already searched it.

"I'll be right outside, Leah. Just open the door when you're ready. Do you need me to get the nurse for you?"

She shook her head, regretting doing just that. "No, I think I'll be okay. I'll need help with my shoes, though."

"Come get me." Josh pulled the door closed behind her.

Simon watched as Josh hesitated outside the door, before walking down the hall towards him. Samuel stood guard for Leah, as did the police chief. Josh stopped just inside his room door, searching for what he didn't know, before he reached for his clothes and dressed, leaving the hospital pyjamas and robe on the bed.

"Let's get us out of here, Simon."

Simon's hand came out to stop Josh. "Josh, we need a plan. We can't just wing it, you know."

Josh shook his head. "I have no plan, other than to get Leah to my place. From there, we'll discuss what we need to do."

Simon watched his friend intently. "I know you, Josh. You already have a plan."

Josh shook his head. "No, I don't. Not really. Other than to marry her and take her away from here."

"That won't work, you know."

"What, marrying her?" Josh stared at his friend, seeing the concern there.

"That. And taking her away. He'd just follow you. We need to find out who is it and stop him. Now."

"Before Christmas, please." Josh shrugged into his jacket, his hands shoving into his pocket to reach for his gloves. "What's this?" He pulled out an envelope. "Not another one."

Simon reached for it, knowing there would be no use trying to protect it now. "Let me see it, please." Opening it, he found once more a blank piece of paper. "This is so bizarre. He's got you on his radar now. That makes two of you to keep safe."

"And you're going to say you can't do that with us in two different places." He waved his hand as he walked away, intent on finding Leah.

Leah watched as Josh knelt to tie her shoes, not liking that he had to do that for her, but on the other hand, liking the courtesy he was showing her. Something softened inside her at his actions.

He stood, his eyes on her, seeing the pain in them but also the fear. There was something else he couldn't read, not yet anyway.

"Ready to go?"

She nodded and took the hand he held out for her. "Where to, Josh?"

"Back to my place for now. We need to talk, you and I."

She sighed. "I know we do. Can we in the morning?" She leaned against him for a moment, not even aware that she had. "I'm just so tired, Josh. Tired of running and hiding. I haven't seen my family in years now, not wanting to be near them. I haven't even dared to call."

"We'll get you together. Trust me on that." He released her hand and drew an arm around her. "Lean on me. We're going down the service elevator, Simon tells me."

———

Dumfounded, Leah stood in Josh's home office and stared at him late the next afternoon. She had slept late that morning, needing the rest, and had just finally began to feel somewhat like herself again. Joy had told her that Josh had headed into his restaurant early that morning, wanting to talk with her but needing to be there. She shook her head at what he had asked.

"Josh! That's not what we need to do!" She was in shock, she thought. Lord, how did I get here?

Josh ran his hand through his hair as he watched her begin to pace. This was not how he had planned to talk to her. Joy had left with the two girls, with the understanding they'd be back in an hour or so. She had pointed at Leah, letting him know he needed to address the issue with her, whatever the issue was.

"Leah. I know it's not what you expected. Just listen to me for a moment." He paused, gathering his thoughts. He really needed to talk to his father right about now and that man was still on the road to Mistletoe.

"You're absolutely right, Josh. How can you even begin to ask that question?" She turned, a puzzled look on her face, as she stopped in front of him. "We don't know each other well enough to even consider marrying one another."

Josh nodded. "I know we don't. I'm just trying to come up with a way to keep you safe. I thought that would be one way. I guess not." He turned away, swallowing hard against his disappointment and worry, and moved towards the door. He paused for a moment, then, shaking his head, continued to walk away.

Leah watched him go, her hand on her mouth. She had just received a marriage proposal, she thought, not at all like she had ever dreamed of, though. Lord, what do I do? You know his heart. I don't. I know I have no one else who would even offer his hand to me in such a way. She sighed, her eyes searching the room, seeing Josh's Bible on his desk. She walked over to the desk, her hand resting on the Book and then picking it up, settled herself in an easy chair near the fireplace he had lit earlier. She leafed through the book, finally settling on a favourite chapter, the words filling her with hope and courage. She closed her eyes, her head bowed over the Book, not seeing Josh pause at the doorway on his way back in to apologize to her and say he would come up with another way to ensure her safety. He turned, seeking his own prayer corner. This was not an easy decision for either one of them.

Joy stopped as she saw her brother in the kitchen, standing, coffee pot in hand, staring out the back window, and just shook her head. She knew their parents were due in at any time and she had to prepare him for that. It's what she did as the older sibling. It had been hard when he had been in the armed forces, away for eight years, home for just brief visits. Then when he moved to Mistletoe once he was out, she had felt like he had abandoned her. She knew he hadn't, that he had had a reason for coming here. She just didn't see it or maybe it was that she didn't want to see it.

"Josh?" Her soft question startled him and water sloshed from the coffee pot onto the counter. He filled the reservoir on the maker and set the coffee to perk, reaching for a cloth to wipe up the water.

"Joy? Where are the girls?"

"With Jeremiah. They decided they wanted to do some shopping and he volunteered to help them. I have no idea what they'll come home with." She laughed at the thought, causing him to grin slightly. "What about you? Are you okay?"

He sighed, giving a small shrug. "I don't know, Joy." He looked at her, a bleakness around his eyes she had never seen before. "I just don't know how to keep Leah safe. We have no idea who it is or why, other than it might be related to her last name and this town." He turned, anger emanating from him for a moment. "There are times I wish I had never heard of this town."

Joy's arm went around her brother as she hugged him, her head resting on his arm. "We'll get there, brother. Just let God lead."

"I know that, Joy. I just don't see it right now." He paused as he heard a small sound behind him and glanced over his shoulder, seeing Leah standing in the doorway, hesitation in her manner. He turned, dislodging Joy's arm, and leaned back against the counter. "Leah?"

"Josh? Can we talk?" She was distraught, he could tell as he walked towards her, following her back to the office.

He shut the door behind him, knowing this was one conversation they needed to have in private.

"Leah? What's up?"

Leah walked to stand in front on him, her arms folded around herself, her eyes raised to his. "I've thought about what you asked. I've also spent time in prayer. I know what that answer is, but I'm still so unsure of anything." Tears sparkled in her eyes but she stepped back as he reached for her. "Please. Just let me say my piece."

Josh nodded. "Sure." He tilted his head to watch her face. "That is, if you're going to talk."

She shook her head at his gentle teasing, knowing it came from his tender heart and a desire to ease the situation for her.

"I know why you asked what you did. I'm just not convinced that's the way we should go. I'm not even sure I should be making a decision about a lifelong commitment when I have a head injury." She turned and paced away, stopping with her back to him. "If your question is still on the table, then my answer would be yes."

Josh stood motionless, stunned at her response. It was not what he had expected her to say. "Leah? You're saying yes? You're sure?"

He watched as she hesitated, then nodded her head, her dark red curls shaking with the movement of her head. "I am, Josh. God alone knows why I am, but after praying and waiting, I have a peace that's what we should do." She turned. "I'm just not sure at all, though."

He smiled as he walked towards her, his hands coming down on her shoulders. "One step, one day at a time, sweetheart. That's all we can do." He turned his head slightly as he heard commotion in the hallway. "I think Mom and Dad have just arrived." His hands tightened on her shoulders as she gasped and tried to move back. "You know them, Leah. They will welcome you to their hearts, if they haven't already." His hand slid down her arm and to her hand. "Come. I have something for you."

She sat in his desk chair as he gently pushed her down, her eyes following him as he opened a drawer and pulled out a jeweller's box.

"My grandmother gave me this. Told me it was a treasure for my treasured one." He lifted solemn eyes to Leah as he opened it, to show a beautiful emerald stone in a unique setting. "Gramps bought it for her when they were first married, once he could afford to get her an engagement ring." He paused, his eyes dropping back to the ring. "I know what we're doing is unorthodox. That we don't know each other that well." He raised eyes to hers again. "Will you wear it for me? Wear it as a sign of your trust and faith in me? For now?"

She finally nodded and he reached for her hand. "I promise, Leah, to do everything in my power to protect you, to keep you safe, to learn to love you as I should." He stooped, dropping a kiss on her forehead.

"Thank you, Josh." Her words were barely audible. "I just don't know, though."

"I know, sweetheart. I know. Let's just see how it goes." He turned his head to look at the door. "They'll want to know why and when."

She shook in her anxiety and he drew her up into his arms. She relaxed against him, feeling his strength and courage and determination to keep her safe. "I guess then we need to set a date." She leaned back. "How do we even do that?"

"Let's wait for a day or two and see what happens. If Simon and the chief are able to find the man or men responsible, then there will be no rush. But if things escalate, we'll need to talk again."

She nodded, burrowing against him, hiding her face and the fear she felt. "Okay, then. Let's go face your family." She leaned back again as she felt his body shaking with laughter. "What did I say that's so funny?"

"It sounded like you were walking out to face a judge and jury. You're not. They all love you now. The girls will be over the moon ecstatic."

"That's what I'm afraid of, Josh. I'm afraid I'll disappoint them." She moved to walk towards the door, stopping as his arms surrounded her again.

"Never think like that. You will never disappoint us with this. Even if we both walk away from each other once you're safe, it will not be a disappointment. They understand." He waited until she nodded. "I talked to Simon today. He'll be by later with the chief. They both want to talk to you. But if you're too tired, let me know. You still need a lot of rest, given your head injury. If anything, I'll take you with me to the restaurant tomorrow and they can come talk to you there."

"That might be best, Josh. I'm feeling a trifle overwhelmed right at the moment."

He nodded, his chin brushing against her hair, even as he bowed his head and prayed.

He reached for her hand as they walked towards the kitchen and the laughter and talking they could hear, intermingled with the excited squeals of the girls. He glanced down at her just before he reached the doorway and squeezed her hand.

"Just remember. We're in this together, sweetheart. Together with God."

She nodded, fright flickering across her face for a moment before she seemed to steel herself.

Josh's mother looked up as she heard their footsteps and was across the room to hug her son. Martha held tight for a moment, before she stepped back, her eyes on his face and then nodding. She turned to the woman beside him, surprise on her face.

"Leah? Oh, how nice. Joy mentioned you were in town. I just wasn't expecting to see you here." She looked between Josh and Leah even as Josh's dad, Andrew, greeted his son. "Josh? What's going on?"

Josh stepped back to Leah's side, his arm going around her. "We'll explain later, but Leah has done me the honour of agreeing to marry me."

Gasps could be heard from his parents even as talk broke out. His eyes sought Jeremiah and saw his nod, knowing they would talk later.

Later, as Joy and her mother were with the girls, Andrew and Jeremiah turned to the younger couple.

"Josh, I think you need to explain."

Before Josh could explain, the doorbell rang. He rose, returning with Simon and the police chief. Andrew stayed for a while, then excused himself, heading to the garage apartment. Somehow, he knew his son was in trouble and he needed to spend time in prayer.

Josh finally locked the door. Simon and Ed had little new to add to what they had already talked about. He leant his head against the door for a moment, suddenly exhausted beyond belief. He needed to sleep but didn't know if he could. Leah, he knew, had retired as had the rest of the household.

———

He yawned, stopping mid-yawn as he heard a voice behind him. He spun, seeing Jeremiah standing here.

"I thought you had gone to bed."

"I hadn't. I just wanted to catch you before tomorrow. I know you're planning on taking Leah with you to the restaurant. I'll stop by mid-morning, if you think it will be quiet enough for us to talk. We do need to talk." Jeremiah's heart was troubled for the man he called brother.

"That should be fine. Night." Josh walked by him, feeling Jeremiah's hand on his shoulder for a brief moment. He shuddered with fear suddenly as he closed the door to his bedroom, not knowing exactly why, but knowing that by taking the step they had, they had just opened themselves up to more trouble.

Laughing at Amy's teasing, Josh shook his head the next morning, even as his mind sorted through the lack of information regarding Leah's assailant. He wanted this over for her. She needed that. He sighed to himself. *Lord, I know it's Your timing. Can we just get through this quickly?*

He finally stood in his office doorway, a puzzled look on his face. Leah was seated at his desk and he could see stacks of papers around her. He moved forward, seeing that she had organized his mail and whatever other paperwork he had dropped there three days ago.

She looked up, a smile on her face, then a look of uncertainty. "I thought I was helping you, Josh. Just organizing things for you." She went to rise from his chair but his hand on her arm stopped her.

"That's fine, Leah. I like that you just went ahead." He turned to look at his desk, perching on a corner. "Oh, wonderful. I see you've found the chequebook too and have the cheques ready. That is a huge help. Now I'm not going to be stuck here until early evening catching up." His grin warmed her heart.

"You really don't mind?"

He shook his head. "Not at all. It's nice to have this all taken care of. I'll unlock the filing cabinet for you as well." He reached into the desk drawer and pulled out a set of keys. "Here. These are the building keys. This little one is the filing cabinet. Take them and keep them with you at all times."

"Are you sure?" She really hadn't expected that response from him.

"I am." He grinned at her. "Here, let me grab a pen and I'll sign off on the cheques. Boot up the computer and I'll walk you through my accounting program." He showed her the program, pleased to hear that she knew it from her previous employment. "What about your job, Leah?"

"Oh, that. I quit it just before I left town. I wanted a change." She looked around the office. "How do you manage to do all that you do?"

"It's been hard. The House was losing money when I took it over but I've turned that around. I have great staff, who really care about the people they serve." He looked down at the cheques, then back at her. "I'll employ you here, Leah. I could use someone to do my paperwork and ordering. I think you'd be perfect at it."

She sat back, her eyes on him. "I accept, if you're sure." Her eyes narrowed. "Unless it's just a ploy to keep track of me."

He started to laugh, shaking his head. "That too, but I really would like it if you were working here. It would make my day go faster."

She nodded. "Okay, then. I guess you have a secretary. I'd feel safer tucked away in here too. They'd have to go through a few people to get to me."

He laughed even as he reached for the employee file. "Now, all I have to do are the employees' cheques. They're due out today. Work with me on them, and then next week you're on your own with them."

Josh finally headed back to the kitchen, his mind already on that, leaving Leah to stare after him, then down at the desk he had left cluttered behind him. She sighed and began the task of folding invoice copies around cheques and addressing envelopes.

She finally wandered towards the kitchen, standing back where she couldn't be seen, watching as Josh flipped burgers, plated specials and generally kept flying around the room, stopping every once in a while to wipe his hands on his apron, all the time a smile on his face and teasing words for his staff. She could tell he was respected, that the staff were working their hardest for him.

How will what we're going through change this, Lord? I don't want him hurt, but that's exactly what I fear will happen.

She stepped forward towards the doorway and then froze, a voice reaching to her ears. He was here, she thought. I'm not even safe here. She turned and almost ran for the office, shutting the door behind her and sliding down the wall to sit with her head on her upraised knees, arms tight around her legs. Amy caught sight of her turning and fleeing and turned to find Josh, taking the spatula from his hand with a quiet word and nod towards his office.

Josh hit the office doorway almost on a run, carefully opening the door and searching for Leah. Finding her, he sank down to sit crosslegged on the floor, pulling her onto his lap, his arms wrapped around her, just holding her as she shuddered in shock.

Amy appeared at the door, heading for the closet and the blanket Josh asked her to bring him. She stood, watching as Josh talked with Leah, finally getting a response.

"What happened, Leah? What scared you?"

She looked up at him, Amy seeing the stark fear on her face. "He's in the restaurant, Josh. I heard his voice."

Josh froze for a moment, his eyes on his beloved's face before they raised to Amy.

"Amy, we need the names of everyone who is in the restaurant right now, local or stranger. Come up with something that gets you that information, a free meal, meal on the house next visit, whatever. And call Chief Waters. I need to talk to him."

"On it, boss." Amy was away, not asking why Josh needed the information, just willing to do what she could for him.

———

The chief paced Josh's office, his eyes on the paper Amy had handed him as he approached her. He shook his head. Who would have thought the man would have been so bold? He doubted that the name was there, but he still had to go over the list with Leah, and that didn't look like it was happening in the near future.

Josh covered Leah's sleeping form with the blanket as she lay on the couch in his office before he turned.

"Now what, Ed? He was here. He knows where to find her. How?"

Ed shrugged. "He knows she's with you. It's not hard to figure out where you'd be." He held up the list. "I need to talk to her about this."

"I know you do." Josh sighed. "This is not how I envisioned today."

"What do you mean?" Ed looked between Josh and Leah, not quite understanding.

"I just hired her to work here." Josh didn't say what he really wanted to say, that he had found the love of his life, his treasure, and she had agreed to be his. That wouldn't go over well, he knew.

"That's a good thought, Josh. You can tuck her away here. But obviously someone else has thought of her being here." Ed paced, finally stopping at Josh's desk.

"Where's the list, Josh?"

Josh spun at Leah's words, not realizing she had awakened and sat up while the men were conversing.

"Leah. You're awake. Here, it is." Josh sat beside her as he handed it to her. "Do you recognize any names?"

She started to shake her head, then paused. "This one. Donald. I'm sure it's his voice that I've heard, that he's the one who has been terrorizing me. Who is he?"

"Someone we would really like to talk with. We're finding out he's not who he has said he is." The chief looked grim. "It was really bold of him to come back into town like that, given how the feeling is about him here."

Josh stared at Leah for a moment before he stood, motioning with his head for Ed to follow him out of the room. He stood where he could watch Leah, nodding as Amy approaching and then went to sit with Leah.

"Is he really that bold?" Josh was unsettled.

"It looks as if he is. I have patrols out looking for him now, just from what you said happened when Leah was hurt. No, we haven't found him. He was in town long enough to find some holes to disappear down in." Ed paused. "I wonder if Old Jack has seen him."

"I haven't seen Jack in a couple of days. But then again that's not unusual." Josh didn't continue, not knowing how much Ed knew or had guessed about Old Jack's connection to town.

That night, his three friends, Jeremiah, and his father stood in his kitchen, staring at him, not quite sure to believe what Josh had just said. Joy and his mother had Leah up in the garage apartment, with the little girls, wrapping presents for the youth centre Blackie ran.

"He was in the restaurant?" Simon stared at Josh, who was also watched by Jacob.

"He was that bold. The staff wouldn't have known we wanted to talk to him. I spoke with each one and advised them that if he comes in again, they serve him but call in the police, detaining him until they arrive." Josh turned to pace, worry on his face. "Now, how do I keep Leah safe? We're not sure he knew she was there. She was tucked back in the office all day."

Blackie shook his head. "He's bold, I must say that for him. Did Amy say if she recognized him at all?"

"I didn't get a chance to ask her, but she wasn't out on the floor much, more in the kitchen." Josh sighed as he ran a hand through his hair, lost for a moment as to what to do. "Dad? What do you suggest?"

His father nodded, then pointed to a chair. "Why don't we sit? I, for one, want to get off my feet. Your mother's had me running around all day, Josh, and my feet are very tired." He took the coffee mug he was offered by Jacob with a quiet thanks. He raised his eyes to his son, seeing Josh staring down at his own mug, lost to them for a moment, his hand reaching for the little kitten as she crawled up his leg and settled down on his arm. *Lord, what I am about to say is going to shock him, I know, and it will change his life. I just don't know how to word it. This time, it has to be Your words, not mine.*

"Josh?" Andrew waited until Josh looked up at him. "How serious are you about Leah? I know this is a conversation you and I need to have in private as well, but just let me know it's serious and we'll go on from there."

Josh kept his eyes on his father, not saying a word, his father reading his answer in his eyes before he nodded.

"All right, then. We'll talk later, son. There are some things we do need to decide now though." Andrew had been in law enforcement in his earlier years before he retired to run a book store he had inherited from his mother. "Where do you see this going, Simon?"

Simon sighed. "I have no idea at present, Andrew. We do know that Leah is connected to the town, as one of the descendants from the Bronagh family. We're still working through that relationship, but she is a cousin of sorts to both Julia and Finn, even though it is more distant than that of Julia and Finn to one another. We have been searching for Donald without any luck in finding him."

Josh turned to his friend. "Have you searched the outlying sheds and cabins? I know Donald had a connection to one way back in the bush."

"We've been there and seen evidence someone has been living there, but he wasn't around. We'll be watching it though." Simon turned to Blackie. "What about any of your kids at the centre? Have they said anything?"

Blackie shook his head. "No, and they would come to me if they had. Julia's really popular with the girls and they trust her. They would let her know that Donald was around. They all know what happened to her."

Josh finally rose, not happy that there was nothing they could plan for, nothing concrete they could decide. Simon was right, once again, he thought. There really isn't that much evidence, and I know he's been speaking with Ed. Dad's right, too. Now what, Lord? Where do I go from here?

He rinsed the mugs they had used and stacked them into the dishwasher, reaching under the sink for more detergent to set the machine running. He heard his father's quiet footsteps behind him and then a chair as it gently scraped back across the tiled floor.

He turned, seeing his father's eyes not on him as he expected, but on his Bible. Josh sighed, knowing that the inevitable talk was on the table, and he would have to own up to his feelings about Leah. He slid into a seat across from his father, knowing they likely didn't have a long time to talk. Joy would be back with the girls soon for bed.

Andrew finally looked up at his son, a sigh rising within him. Where do I go with this, Lord? I don't know how to read him now, not in this situation. I know he has a good heart, that he's a man of God.

"Dad? You wanted to talk?" Josh watched as his father finally nodded, his hands folded on his open Bible.

"I do, son, and now I'm not sure how to proceed."

"At the beginning would be a good place as you are wont to say." Josh grinned at his father, receiving an answering grin and a shake of the head in response.

"That's too true. I know how you and Leah met. I know somewhat of the trouble you two are facing. It concerns me that you really don't know her that well, not well enough to take such a big step."

Josh sighed, then nodded. "I know, Dad. It's tough to explain. I am not even sure if I can. It's just that….It seems….." Josh's voice finally died way.

Andrew's soft smile caught Josh's attention and he frowned at his father.

"Dad?"

"You've got it bad, son, don't you? She has you at a loss for words. I was like that when I met your mother. I stumbled over my words all the time. Just couldn't put a sentence together that made sense. Even today, I sometimes look at her and feel the same."

Josh sat back, relief coursing through him that his father understood. "Thanks, Dad. That does help." He nodded towards the Bible. "You've found a verse for me, haven't you?"

Andrew nodded, even as the back door opened and the two little girls flew in, excitement wafting from them as they swarmed their grandfather and uncle, sure of their reception, their chatter about the presents they had just helped to wrap.

"We'll talk later, son."

Josh nodded as he slid his chair back so Heidi could sit on his knee, the kitten now nestled in her arms before it scrambled onto Josh's shoulder, where she thought she'd be safe, drawing a pout from Heidi.

Leah stood for a moment, just inside the door, her hands stilled as she reached to hang up her jacket. Josh was laughing at Heidi as he tried to rescue the kitten from his shoulder. She smiled, realizing that she really did have a knight in shining armour after all, didn't she? She caught a glimpse of a future child, their child, with Josh acting the same way. She just didn't know how bad it would get, not knowing who was after her and not knowing when they would strike again.

She turned as Joy spoke to her, nodding at her word of thanks. She passed the men, heading for her bedroom, not realizing that Josh followed her with his eyes before he turned to answer his mother's question. The four other adults in the room shared a look and a smile, not wanting to speak until the girls had been put to bed.

Josh finally tracked Leah down in his home office. She had seated herself at his desk, a book open in front of her. He dropped into a chair across from her, not speaking, just watching her.

"Josh? What do you know of the history of Mistletoe? I'm told I'm related to the founder but I don't see that at all."

He nodded at the book she had open in front of her. "That tells a lot. Finn's parents know a whole lot more. Why don't we drop in on them tomorrow and talk with them?"

"We can't just drop in on someone like that!" She was horrified at the thought.

Josh reached to grasp her hand, his warm and comforting on hers. "This is a different town than you've lived in, Leah. We can do just that. We can drop in on them without any problems. If you like, I'll call Mary in the morning and make sure she'll be home, but I'm sure she will be. At this time of year, their B&B is booked solid and she's around for their clients."

Leah stared at him, then finally nodded, a shuttered look coming over her face.

"Leah, please don't shut me out. Talk to me." Josh's hand tightened on hers.

She finally sighed, her eyes on his hand. "I really don't know what to think anymore, Josh. You've offered me safety through marriage. You provided work for me. Your family have practically adopted me." She held up a hand as he went to speak, causing a grin to spread across his face. She fought an answering smile. Somehow, he really did make her feel safe and secure, and yes loved and wanted just for being her. "I really don't get it. Why?"

"Why? Which question do you want me to answer?"

"I didn't know I had asked more than one, but I guess I sort of did." She looked down as she felt something brush against her foot. "There's your kitten, Josh. Somehow, I don't think she'll be heading out with the girls when Jeremiah and Joy move into their new home on the weekend."

He reached for the little kitten. "Somehow, I think you're right. You really wanted her for them, you know?" He grinned as she shook her head at him. "We need to name her."

"Terror would likely fit in a few weeks. She's got that look in her eyes, but we can't be outside calling for Terror, now can we?" Her eyes on the kitten, she didn't see the swift startled look Josh sent her, not realizing what she had just said. "I'll come up with a name, seeing as I found her." She smirked at his grin. "That's my privilege, you know." She reached for the kitten who mewed in protest about leaving Josh. "She really is your kitten, isn't she? Now, back to the town. You tell me I'm related to one of the founders, through my last name. Is that why I'm under attack?"

Josh nodded. "It could well be. Julia and Finn went through the same thing." He looked up at her gasp. "I'm sorry. We never told you, did we? Last year about this time, someone tried to kill both Finn and Jacob, then a week or two later, Blackie and Julia. It all goes back to the founding fathers and the town charter. People think they can circumvent a legal document, which has been tried and proven in court to be legal. Because you are a direct descendant (Samuel's proven this), you are entitled to some of the town buildings and there is a bank account with your name on it. I have no idea how much is there, or how many buildings." He sat back, his eyes now on the floor. "We'll need to meet with the town lawyer sometime over the next couple of days. Jeremiah and Simon said they'd clear out your apartment for you."

Chapter 14

Leaving the town lawyer's office the next afternoon, Leah waited for Josh to open her car door and then close it after she had seated herself. She watched as he rounded the front of the vehicle and then slid inside, his hand inserting the key into the ignition, starting the vehicle, and then just sitting.

"Josh?"

Her question caught his attention, and he turned to her with a smile. "Yes, ma'am?"

She shook her head at him. "You're heading for the restaurant, aren't you?"

He turned to look behind him before he pulled away from his parking spot. "Not now. Amy's on the late shift today and will close up. I usually open and she or Stephen close for me. It's working out well." He stared at her for a second before he looked back out the front window. "Would you care to go out for dinner with me tonight, Leah? Somewhere away from here?"

She stared at him, then nodded. "That would be nice, Josh. Somewhere quiet and sane, perhaps? Is there such a place?"

He began to laugh even as he accelerated away from the edge of town and out to the highway. "Let's go to the next town over. It's not that far, really, not out here. I know a nice quiet restaurant where we can catch an early supper."

Josh prayed as they finished their meal, not he thought as he had ever prayed before, even for his friends on the battlefield. He reached for Leah's hand after their plates had been removed and their coffees refilled.

She watched their linked hands, praying that he wasn't going to say he had made a mistake, that he wanted his freedom back. She had had a peace and feeling of safety in the last few hours that she had not felt in years.

"Leah, I know this is really sudden, what we decided. Dad spoke to me this morning when he stopped by. He asked if we had reconsidered our plans at all. When I said no, he then suggested that we set a date and do so quickly. He feels you may have more safety that way."

She tried to retract her hand but Josh's grip tightened. She stared down at him, worry running over her face, before she looked up, finding his eyes on her, concern in them.

"It has to be your decision, Leah. I am fine with whatever you decide. If you need time to pray about it, then we take that time." He had been praying the whole time he was waiting, asking God to bring them to the right decision.

She finally sighed, her hand relaxing under his before she moved it enough to turn it over and grasp his. "I know where your father's heart is. What does

———

277

your mother say?" She paused, biting at her lip. "This is so hard, Josh. I need my own parents to talk to, and I don't have them."

"I know, sweetheart. I know. Talk to Mom or to Finn's Mom, if you need to. They'll answer your questions and concerns."

She finally shook her head. "No, I don't think I need to. I think...." Her voice died away as she raised her eyes to stare out the window, straight at a bridal dress shop. She started to giggle, causing Josh to frown and turn to look out as well.

"What's so funny?"

She had trouble containing her mirth. "Look at the shop right across the street, Josh."

When he focused on it, he too began to laugh. "Is that a sign or what?"

She nodded. "I'm guessing it is. So when?"

"This Saturday? Too soon?"

She shook her head, sadness crossing her face. "I wish I had more time, but I don't think we do. I need to find something to wear."

Josh hooked a thumb over his shoulder. "Right there, sweetheart. They're open late by what the sign says. We'll head over there. You pick out your dress, and I won't look." He grinned at her, not seeing the man sitting at a nearby table, his eyes focused on Leah, anger on his face as he watched her. If she had looked up, she would have recognized him from her past place of employment, and as someone she had feared on the job.

Josh had waited patiently as Leah tried on dresses, finally rising to take the bag from her as she approached him, his arms going out to hug her as he saw the sadness in her eyes.

"I know, sweetheart. I know. You need your parents here and they're not. You need someone to walk you down the aisle, now don't you?"

She nodded her head, then rested her cheek against his chest, not seeing the looks of sympathy the shop owner was sending her.

"Let's go home, Josh. We can talk about this later."

Josh turned towards Mistletoe, an uneasy feeling in his bones as he watched the traffic around him. It was late afternoon, just beginning to get dusk, and he could feel evil approaching him. He watched as a vehicle came towards him at high speed before he turned the wheel and headed into a shop parking lot, bringing an exclamation of surprise from Leah.

"Josh?" She stared at him, then out the window.

"Sorry, Leah. Someone was coming at us at a really high speed. I don't think he'd have stopped before he hit us, not with the oncoming traffic." He reached for his phone, making a quick call. "I've asked for a police escort to

Mistletoe. They're on their way. Simon has talked to them already, so they've been aware of what we may need."

"And just how did he know that?" She was astounded at the friendship between the four men, never having had that, not really, she thought.

"We're friends, Leah. It's how we are. We help one another." He shot her a quick look even as he caught sight of the marked police cruiser pulling in. "I did let Simon know we were heading this way and I had a bad feeling about something happening."

"Looks as if you were right, doesn't it?" She sat back, a blank look on her face, not letting Josh see how scared she really was.

Josh followed her into his house a while later, his eyes on her, distressed that their happy occasion of dinner had been changed so rapidly. He didn't like it, not one bit. He set the bag with her dress down on her bed, watching as she paced before he reached to hug her. It took a bit but she finally hugged him back. He could feel the faint shivers running through her and decided then and there that he would end this, somehow. He would find the man or woman responsible for this.

Jeremiah turned from the counter to study his brother-in-law as he reached for the coffee pot and filled a mug, setting it down with a loud thump.

"Josh?"

"They followed us, Jeremiah. If I hadn't had a chance to pull into a parking lot, who knows what would have happened?" A dark look covered Josh's face at that.

"Josh, don't do anything foolish or rash. Leave it with the police."

"Well, right now, I don't see them doing that great a job, now, are they?" He sighed, shame running through him. "I'm sorry, Jeremiah. That's not true. I know they're doing the best they can. This just scared me."

Jeremiah nodded. "I know it did, and it will continue until the culprit is under arrest." He looked at the kitchen doorway where Joy stood, the two girls on either side of her. He lowered his voice. "My girls are here. I don't want the little ones scared any more than they have been."

"I won't. I promise. It's likely good that you're moving out on the weekend. Things seem to be heating up."

"But where does that leave you?" Jeremiah shared another look with Joy, puzzled as to what Josh and Leah had planned.

"Joy, go find Leah. See what she found today and let her know how beautiful she is. I can't tell her, not yet. I haven't seen it." Josh sent his sister a smile, one that didn't reach his eyes. He watched as Joy and the girls left to find Joy.

"What did you two go and do?" Jeremiah hooked a chair leg with his foot, pulling out the chair and then dropping down. It had been a long day for him, trying to get an understanding of the church.

"Leah found a wedding dress." Josh turned, leaning against the counter, mug in hand as he pointed towards Jeremiah with it. "We want to be married this weekend. If you can do the honours sometime this weekend, that works."

"Wow!" Jeremiah sat back, not really surprised, he found. "Which day? We're moving on Saturday, but the furniture is already there. It's just what personal stuff we have here."

"And you'd be there now if it wasn't for Leah's situation. Saturday afternoon would work. Just a small ceremony is what she wants. She's really missing her parents."

"And she needs someone to walk her to you." Josh looked up as his father pulled out another chair and sat as well. "I'll do it, Josh. I'll be her father after you two wed. Let me do this for her now."

Josh nodded, for a moment unable to speak. "Thanks, Dad." His voice was husky with emotion.

"But what is this I hear about what happened to you two? I just caught part of it as I was coming in. I wasn't meaning to eavesdrop."

"I know you weren't. Someone tried to ram us from behind. At least I think that was their intent. I had a feeling all the time we were at dinner and then shopping that we were being watched and followed."

Andrew nodded. "I can see that." He looked over his shoulder as he heard the excitement in his wife and daughter's voices, as well as the excited chatter of the little girls. "What about a meal afterwards, Josh?"

Josh sighed. "I'm not good at this planning stuff, am I?" He rose, filling a mug of tea for his father, knowing that was his preference in the afternoon. "I wonder if Mary would have time to cater something. I can't ask my staff, not this weekend. It's the tree lighting and they'll be swamped. I've brought in some extra students like other years." He sighed as he sat. "But that isn't the real problem. The real problem is keeping Leah safe."

Saturday afternoon came quicker than anyone had planned. A scurry of activity had happened, with Leah totally overwhelmed with the love and support she was given, not just by Josh's own family, but by his friends and their families. Mary had gladly offered, without being asked, to prepare a meal for them, hugging Leah as she protested, stating that Josh had been there when Finn and Jacob had needed him the year before, and this was the least she could do.

Leah finally stood in the hallway of the rambling house Andrew and Martha had chosen to live in. She paced, knowing that soon her life would change, but just how much, she really hadn't an idea. She didn't know that the man had set up outside and was waiting for her to emerge on her own, ready to take her captive and disappear with her.

Andrew watched as Martha fussed over Leah, knowing his wife's heart was breaking for Leah, not having her own parents there. Martha's mother had been gone by the time Andrew and Martha had married, taken too soon by heart disease, and she knew just how much a mother was missed. Leah had refused to let her foster family come, despite their asking, stating it was too unsafe for that.

Martha finally hugged Leah and walked away to where Simon was waiting to escort her to a seat. The ladies had decorated the living room for Christmas and large pots of fresh flowers sat around as well.

Andrew approached Leah, waiting until she looked up at him, uncertainty in her eyes.

"Leah, welcome to our family. We're noisy and loud at times, as you know, but you're bringing a peace to it that we need. Josh and you make a great couple, a great team. No matter how you two met, it was already designed by God. Never forget that. He's brought you together." He reached to kiss her cheek, a thumb flicking away a tear as he would have done for his own daughter. "I am privileged now to have two daughters, whom I love immensely. Now, let's get you to Josh."

She nodded, still hesitating. "But Andrew, I bring danger with me. I don't want anyone hurt because of me."

"No, the danger is there, not necessarily because of you. We don't know who or why or what, but I suspect it goes back a long time before you were born."

She finally reached to tuck her hand into the crook of his arm. "Okay, then. Thank you, Andrew."

"Call me Dad if you want. I'd like that, but only when you're ready to do so."

She looked up at him, wonder on her face. "I can't remember calling anyone just Dad. I don't remember my own father well enough to know what I called him, and my foster father was always called by his first name with Dad in front of it."

Josh turned as he heard footsteps and stopped at the beauty of his bride. He knew they were rushing it and he felt remorse at that, but knew from what they had discussed that this was the one way they could think of to keep her safe.

Leah wandered Josh's house when they returned, suddenly at a loss. They were alone for the first time there, and she didn't know what to do. She returned to the kitchen, opening the fridge to place the food Mary had sent home with them on the shelves, before she shut the door and then stood, staring out the window. She could hear Josh on the phone with Amy, checking in to hear how the day had been. Amy had dropped in for the ceremony before heading back to the restaurant.

Josh stopped just before the kitchen door, his eyes watchful as Leah moved restlessly around the kitchen. He regretted rushing her into this, not having had the time, he felt, to properly court her as his grandmother would have said. That he really regretted, he decided, and made a vow to make up for it the rest of the married life. He dropped his eyes to the paper he held, found in his mail from yesterday that he hadn't gotten to. He had spoken with Simon and promised to bring it with him tomorrow to church.

Leah turned, spying him in the hallway and walking towards him, stopping as she saw the paper in his hands.

"Another threat, Josh? What this time?"

He looked up, compassion in his glance as he studied her face. "Another one, Leah. It shouldn't be happening. I want this guy and want him yesterday. He was outside Dad and Mom's house yesterday when we were there. This time he sent a picture of you and Joy's girls."

"The girls?" Her hands flew to her mouth as horror struck her. "He won't go after them, will he?"

"Not if we can help it. I've warned Jeremiah and Joy and also Mom and Dad. They'll watch out for them." He signed, his hand reaching out, waiting until she clasped his hand before he led her to the living room and seated her on the couch, sitting beside her, his eyes on the snapping flames in the fireplace. "We need to figure out who this is. Have you thought of anyone at all, Leah? Anyone else who made you uncomfortable or feel frightened?"

She turned from him for a moment, lost in thought, before she turned back. "On my last job, the one I left to come here, there was one man, older than me, I think around your father's age. I never felt comfortable around him. He wanted me to go out with him, but I always refused. He watched me constantly, to the point I had someone walk me out every day. He left just about a week before I did. I never heard why, but I know the manager was talking to him. There had been complaints about him, what complaints I never heard." She looked up at Josh, who was watching her intently. "His is the voice I heard that day, Josh. Is he from this town?"

Josh shook his head. "No. That was Donald you heard. He lived here for about five years, leaving last year after he duped Blackie and Julia into heading out on a rescue and then we think was part of running them off a cliff." He paused, not quite sure how to continue.

"If you're asking, he was only with our company for less than a year. That goes with what you've said, doesn't it?"

"It does. What name did he go by?"

"Not the name on the list. The first name, yes, but not the last name. I don't know if I ever heard it said. This doesn't make sense, does it? The voice I heard was younger."

"I'll pass that on to Simon and to the chief. Let me have the contact information for the company as well." Josh sighed as he sat back, stretching out his legs in front of him, content for the moment. "Are you up for church in the morning, Leah? We can skip if it you need to."

She stared at him, dumbfounded that he would even ask. "No, we need to be there. It's Jeremiah's first Sunday and we need to support him and Joy."

———

282

"They'd understand." He watched as she picked up a cushion and held it against her as she curled up in a corner of the couch. He could see her relaxing as she sat there, her eyes on the fire now. Lord, bless us, please. I know for sure Your hand was in this. Don't let us go wrong, please, dear Lord? Protect my lady.

Sitting beside Josh the next morning for the service, Leah had interested and some questioning looks sent her way and edged closer to Josh without knowing she was. Josh reached an arm around her, resting it along the pew back, just touching her shoulders, not realizing that he had just told the whole church she was his. Not that it mattered anyway. He wanted the world to know.

Leah shivered, her eyes going around. She could feel him somewhere in the church. She knew he was there, waiting for an opportunity to take her away from Josh.

She lifted Holly to her knee as the little girl patted her leg, her arms hugging her back against her as the little one leaned on her, watching her sister carefully as she waited for her Uncle Josh to pick her up, finally giving on that and just climbing up on him, his free arm coming around her to hold her steady. He caught Leah's look and grinned.

Then he sobered as he shot a look around. Yes, he felt those eyes, the eyes that both Jacob and Blackie had said they had felt. Whoever it was, he was here. He shifted slightly, watching around them, not seeing anyone in particular.

He caught Leah's look at him and nodded, seeing her sigh and look of distress before Holly asked her something, drawing her attention back to the little girl and then the service.

Josh stood after the service, his arm around Leah as he held her close to him, not wanting her far away, as he stood and talked with different people from the town, introducing Leah as his wife to their surprised looks, but welcoming words.

He raised his eyes at last, catching sight of Donald as he stood, hatred emanating from him as he watched Leah. Josh turned his body slightly, moving between Donald and Leah, catching Jacob's eye and nodding towards the other man. Jacob whispered quickly to Finn and then moved away, his eyes on Donald.

Leah caught the look between the two friends and peeked around Josh, seeing Donald standing there.

"He's here, Josh."

He could hear the fear in her voice. "He is. Jacob's heading his way and I know Simon and Blackie are as well. We'll let them deal with it. Now, Mary has asked if we'd like to come for lunch with them. She has a buffet going on for her clients and says we're more than welcome."

Leah looked down as her hand was clutched tight, seeing the pleading look on Heidi's face.

"Aunt Leah, please come!"

Leah stopped, her words of refusal choking in her throat. She realized that she was an aunt now, with two little ones she could love without reserve. She crouched down as Heidi's arms hugged her tight. "How can I say no, Heidi? We'll come, at least for a while. Does that suit you?"

Heidi's head bobbed up and down in her glee before she was away, looking for her mother. Leah raised up to a standing position, blinking back tears.

"Leah?" Josh was worried, not quite sure what had just happened.

Leah surprised him by hugging him, his own arms going around her. "She called me Aunt. I just realized I have two little nieces."

"That you do. We need to talk at some point, Leah, about where we want to go. No pressure right now. Our priority is keeping you safe." His voice was low enough that only she heard him as he watched while her eyes slid closed, knowing he had just taken off pressure she had put on herself. "As I said, no pressure, Leah. When or if God wills we have a true marriage, we'll know. Right now, I'm just glad you're mine." He tucked her hand into the crook of his elbow and headed out, determined to make the most of the day, knowing that they'd be back at work early the next day, and the next few weeks would be overwhelming for her as she helped in the restaurant office.

Josh stood watching the women laugh and joke around as they were setting up the buffet, Leah among them, a smile on her face. He was taken aback once more at her beauty. He turned his head to look over his shoulder as he heard footsteps approaching from behind him. Jacob and Blackie walked towards him.

"Josh? We need to talk." Blackie motioned towards Timothy's study. Finn's father had told them to use it whenever they needed to.

Josh perched on the arm of the sofa, as Mary called it, watching Blackie, Jacob and Simon as they settled into seats. He understood that Donald had disappeared before Jacob reached him, and no one could tell them where he was.

"You didn't find him today?" Josh's question was more of a statement.

Jacob shook his head. "We didn't, and we couldn't find anyone who saw where he went. He would have been held on to if some of the men had seen him, I can guarantee you that. They want to talk to him about last year."

Josh nodded. "Then I guess it's time I told you that I had another letter come, this time to the house, and this time with photos from yesterday. He's following us wherever we go."

Simon reached for the envelope Josh pulled from his shirt pocket. "I don't like this, Josh. We can't be everywhere you two are."

"Leah doesn't know about this, not yet. I'll have to tell her. I didn't have time yet this morning since I found it." Josh stared down at the floor. "How do we catch him, Simon?"

"That's a good question, Josh. He seems to know where you two are at all times." He frowned. "I'll be right back."

He returned, a small object in his hand, his face grim.

"Is that what I think it is?" Blackie rose and came to study the object.

"It is. A tracker of some kind. That's how they knew you were out of town, Josh." He frowned, a puzzled look coming over his face. "Just what do they want with Leah? She's not from here, had no knowledge of her ancestry."

Josh frowned as well. "That's what I don't get. She did say she had had to be escorted to her vehicle before she left her last job, Donald causing her that much distress."

The men started as they heard a feminine voice in their midst.

"Simon, what is that thing?" Leah pointed to his hand.

"A tracking device I pulled off Josh's vehicle. This is how they've been following you."

She moved closer, her head bent over Simon's hand. "I've seen something like that before. Someone had it on their desk where I worked." She shook her head at Josh's question. "No, not Donald. Someone else. I can't think of who right at the moment, but it will come to me." She studied it closer. "It's the same one. See that little bit of red paint? It's in the same spot as the one I saw." Her gaze was frightened as she raised it to Simon, and then Josh. "Is Donald not the one after me?"

"We think he is, but this changes it all." Simon nodded at Josh's questioning look. "Josh found an envelope in the mail box this morning, Leah. Pictures of you two from yesterday."

She looked up at Simon before she nodded. "Of course, they would do that, now wouldn't they? I'm sorry. They will not scare me with that. It will take a whole lot more than that now." She turned to stare at Josh, reading his support in his eyes before she spoke again. "No matter what happens, they will not break me. Jacob, Finn mentioned that she needed your help in getting something from the storage shed. Simon, here, distracted me from the purpose of telling you when I entered this room for." With a pretended sniff of disdain, she spun on her heel and walked away, leaving the men staring after her before Josh began to laugh and then rose, heading after his wife.

Blackie stared at him, then at the other men. "Is that our Josh?"

"It is, Blackie. He has it bad, I'd say, and so does she. They just haven't come to that conclusion together yet, but they will." Jacob walked away to find his own wife, knowing exactly what she needed from the shelves in the storage shed, the Christmas box of platters and tableware.

Josh drew Leah aside from the buffet line and sheltered her from the rest of the group for a few minutes.

"Are you okay?" He was concerned, seeing the shadow in her eyes.

"I will be." She looked up at him, wondering how she had managed to find a husband so tall, not what she had ever dreamed about, that was for sure. "It's just disheartening, Josh, to have our day spoiled like that."

He ran a finger down her cheek before his hand rested on her shoulder, the finger on her jaw. "I know, sweetheart. I hate that, too. We'll catch him. It's only a matter of time. But are you okay here with everyone? If you're not, we can make our excuses and leave."

She stared at him, not quite sure that she had heard him right. "You'd leave, just for me?"

"I would. You're the most important one in my life now. Always will be. That's a promise I won't break. I may come close but please remind me if I do. We need to come up with a code word for that." He grinned as she smiled and shook a finger at him. "All right, then. If you're sure, then let's get some food before my friends eat it all. Mary's a fantastic cook."

———

Late the next afternoon, Josh grabbed the bags of garbage that had been set near the back door and headed outside. He knew Leah was tucked away in his office, finishing off the paperwork that had accumulated over the last few weeks. The restaurant was that busy he had to be in the kitchen a lot of the time, which he loved. Paperwork, he thought, now that I hate. He lifted the lid of the dumpster and tossed the bags in, hearing the lid bang back down. The noise of the lid clanging covered the rushed footsteps heading his way and he heard nothing until he felt something slam into his back, throwing him forward into the dumpster, his head crashing into it.

He dropped to his knees, one hand reaching for his head, the other for his back, even as another blow struck him violently in the ribs sending him once more into the corner of the dumpster and then to the ground. He didn't feel the kick lodged into the same ribs or feel the snap as they broke.

His assailant looked around and hearing noise, ducked behind the bin, waiting. He knew Leah would come looking for Josh, it was just a matter of time. He shrugged his coat collar up around his ears, pulling his knitted hat down further and glanced up as the snow started falling. Good, he thought. This makes it even better. It will hide my tracks.

The snow continued to fall, gently covering Josh's body even as he lay, unaware of what was happening around him. Blood trickled from his mouth, freezing finally as it dripped to the ground.

Leah paused in the kitchen doorway, searching for Josh and not seeing him. She had a question about some paperwork she had found, paperwork that disturbed her. It had nothing to do with the restaurant but everything to do with her. She knew it hadn't been there the last time she was in the office as she had cleared off his desk of the most current papers.

"Amy?" As Amy turned, Leah headed her way, weaving among the kitchen staff frantically preparing the meals for their customers. "Have you seen Josh?"

Amy paused, a plate in hand that she handed off to another worker before wiping her hands on a towel and tossing that over her shoulder. "He was here ten minutes ago." She looked around. "He's taken the garbage out. But that doesn't take ten minutes."

Leah stared at her, horror and fear running through her before she ran for the door, slamming it open and then stopping to peer around. The snow had covered Josh's tracks, but she headed for the dumpster, her eyes searching in the dimming light. She stumbled as she caught her foot, catching her balance on the metalbin. She looked down and then dropped to her knees, her hands reaching for Josh as she found him at her feet, her hands frantically feeling his back and then his arm for a heartbeat, brushing at the snow that partially covered him. She breathed a sigh of relief as she felt a faint one.

Her calls and then screams for Amy had Amy out the back door of the restaurant, her eyes searching for Leah, searching for Josh, seeing Leah on her knees and had her starting towards her.

"Amy. An ambulance. Josh is hurt." Leah watched as Amy nodded, her hand opening the back door to call in before she headed across the parking lot, intent on staying with Leah, shrugging into her own jacket, Josh's in her hands to wrap around Leah.

Leah didn't feel the fingers that brushed the back of her sweater as she turned back to Josh, didn't see the dark form slink backwards behind the dumpster as Amy dropped down beside Leah.

"Is he alive?"

"He is, but he's hurt. I can't tell from where though." Leah's worry was palpable. She just knew it was because of her that Josh was hurt, wasn't it? Lord, don't let him die, please, was her cry. Her hands felt through his soaked hair, trying to find a wound on his head, finding nothing. Why was he unconscious? Her worry and fear became palpable. Please, Lord, was her silent cry.

Leah fought against the paramedics and the police officers as they tried to prevent her from riding with Josh. She spun, anger spewing from her, informing them that she was going with him, he was her husband after all. What would they expect her to do?

Chief Waters had approached, listening with a faint smile as the vehement way Leah defended her choice. He finally spoke a quiet word and all resistance dropped. He knew the easier way to keep them both safe was to keep them together.

Leah shot him a look of thanks, then clambered into the rig, finding a seat in a corner, her eyes glued to Josh. She could tell the men were concerned, and so was she.

Leah stood at the head of the stretcher, her eyes on Josh as the medical personnel worked around him, assessing his wounds, running IV lines, preparing him for imaging studies. She refused to move, even when a security officer approached her at a nurse's request. She turned to glare at him, shaking her head, her hand clamped around the stretcher's side rail.

Doc, a friend from church, finally shook his head and told them to let her be, she was fine where she was. He stood back and watched her as the stretcher carrying Josh was wheeled from the examination room, heading for the imagining department. He sighed. Josh, do you know how much this lady loves you? I sure hope you love her that much back.

He headed for the waiting room, knowing Jeremiah and Joy were there and suspecting that Andrew and Martha were as well. He needed someone with Leah and he knew they were the only family she had.

Andrew rose as he saw Doc approaching them, worry on his face.

"Doc?"

"No news yet, Andrew. He's off for some imaging. But I need someone with Leah. She's refusing to move from the examination room, just stands there focused on the door right now. Martha?"

She nodded as she headed back to the room Leah was waiting in. She stood for a moment, her eyes full of compassion on her new daughter. No in law about, she thought. I know she has Josh's heart and he has hers by the looks of it.

"Leah?" Martha's arm came around the younger woman but she found she could not move her. "Leah? Listen, love. Come and sit. He'll be a while."

Leah finally tore her eyes from the door, a tortured look in them. "It's because of me he's hurt, Martha. It's all my fault."

Martha stared at her, dumbfounded for a moment, before she wrapped her arms around Leah. Leah resisted her hug as much as she could before Martha began to pray for her. As the words washed over her, Leah relaxed, Martha heard the suppressed sobs as Leah wept.

Leah still refused to move from her spot. "I need to be here, Martha. I need to be where Josh can find me."

"That's okay, Leah. Just sit in this chair right here. He can see you right there. They'll likely take him to a room soon, anyway." Martha finally convinced Leah to sit, but Leah didn't stay still.

Leah kept shifting in her chair, her eyes on the door, waiting for Josh to come back, waiting for what she just wasn't sure.

Martha stared at the back of Leah's sweater for a moment, perplexed at the mark, before she drew a deep breath and headed for the waiting room. Finding both her husband and Ed, she drew them back to the room, pointing at Leah's sweater.

"Leah?" When she looked up at Ed, she frowned.

"What is it, Chief? Did you find the person?"

"No, but I need to see your sweater. Do you have another top on under it or can we get you one?"

She shrugged before she pulled off the sweater, revealing a V-neck sweater underneath it and handed it to Ed. He threw a quick glance at her even as he studied the sweater back.

"Leah, I need you to think very carefully. When you first got to Josh, did you see anyone around?"

Leah shook her head. "I don't know. I was just focused on him. Why?"

"Because there's some blood on the back of your sweater and it isn't yours. And where it is couldn't have come from Josh."

She paled as she realized what he was saying. "He touched me? He was that close?"

Ed nodded, compassion in his glance. "He was, Leah. You didn't feel or see anything?"

She shook her head, fear on her face. "Nothing. I was just so focused on Josh." She turned to Martha, who stood, arm around Leah's shoulder. "What have I done, Martha?"

"You have done nothing, child. Nothing at all."

Leah spun on her chair as she heard the stretcher coming back and was on her feet at Josh's side before they had even totally placed it back in its spot. Her eyes were glued to his face even as she reached for his hand. She felt Martha beside her, Martha's own hand covering the younger couple's.

"God is here, Leah. He hears your prayers. Trust him."

Leah finally nodded, knowing that was all she had left. She had to trust.

She struggled to release her hand from under Martha's, only to place it on Josh's cheek, her eyes sad as she saw the bruising. I hate this, Lord, she thought. I hate that he was hurt because of me. Why? Tears sparkled in her eyes and on her lashes, tears she refused to let fall.

Martha stood back, her eye on her son, even as she felt Andrew come to a stop near her, his eyes on his son.

"What have they said, Leah?"

She turned, shaking her head. "Nothing as of yet. The nurse said they were waiting for results and that the doctor would be in shortly." She looked back at Josh, her finger lightly tracing the bruising. "Find who did this, Andrew, please. Find him before he kills one of us. That is his intent. I have no idea who it is or if he is even someone I know. Please?"

He nodded, his head turning as he heard footsteps approaching. Doc stood for a moment, chart in hand, studying the notes, before he looked up, watching Leah as she stood. He knew he needed her to leave, to go home and rest, but he also knew that would be a losing battle. The nurses on the floor would just have to accept the fact that she was not leaving and that he would let her stay.

During the early morning hours, Josh began to stir, his eyes finally staying open as he grimaced in his pain, his hand finding the ribs that had been fractured. He gave a low groan, not knowing where he was for a moment. He looked around, squinting as he became accustomed to the low lighting. A hospital room, he thought. Now, why? What happened, Lord, to put me here? I don't remember. All I know is that my back, ribs and head hurt.

He reached carefully to brush at his face, wondering what he could feel tickling it, and caught a lock of hair. He stared at it. Deep red. Leah?

His head turned slightly and he saw his bride curled up on the bed beside him, a light blanket covering her. He gave a small smile. She was here. She hadn't left, like he thought she would. Love for her flooded through his heart and he know he didn't ever want her to leave. Reaching carefully, he withdrew his arm from between them and snuggled her close to him, her head fitting under his chin. He turned so his cheek rested against her head and he slept again.

He roused somewhat later as he felt a hand on his wrist and looked around. One of the nurses stood there, her eyes watching him as she checked his IV.

"How are you feeling, Josh?" Her voice was low.

"Sore, but not as sore as I will be. What happened?"

She shook her head. "I don't know for sure, but someone said you were attacked outside your restaurant. The chief will be by in the morning."

He nodded, his hand going to his ribs. "What did I do to the ribs?"

"You fractured about three. And you have bruised kidneys. Whoever beat you did a good job." She turned and walked away, not seeing him staring after her before he looked down at Leah.

Why, Lord? I need to keep her safe and I can't if I'm laid up like this. Heal me quickly, please?

Leah stirred in the later hours, her hand coming up to rub at her face before she raised her head at a sound. She stilled, seeing a man standing in the room, his eyes on Josh. She could feel the evil coming from him and froze even more, not wanting to let him know she was awake. She tried to see his face but the shadows hid it. He finally walked away, leaving her breathing a sigh of relief but still scared.

Leah turned her head slightly, studying Josh's face, seeing the bruising on his forehead and cheek. Who did this, she wondered once more. Josh was watching her as she turned, a small smile on his face.

"Leah, hi." He had to clear the early morning huskiness from his voice. "You're here."

"Where else would I be? You're hurt. Of course, I'd be here."

He nodded and regretted it as pain pounded through his head, causing his eyes to slide closed. When he cracked them open again, Leah was sitting up, concern on her face, the nurse coming through the door.

"You called the nurse!"

"Of course I did. You need something for pain." Leah pushed herself away from him and off the bed, starting to pace before she walked from the room. She needed some time to think. Being that close to Josh didn't help. She had to come up with a plan to end this, to find the culprit and bring him to justice.

She stopped as she saw the police chief walking towards her.

"Chief? You're here early." She glanced at her watch.

He smiled. "I know I am. I wanted to talk to both you and Josh before the day got going. Is he awake?"

She nodded, as she turned, her hand coming on to stop Ed as he walked by her. "Do you have news who did this?"

He shook his head. "We're still looking at surveillance videos and trying to find the assailant. Did you see anything that you have remembered?"

"I was too focused on finding Josh. I didn't see or hear anything." She frowned at him. "Why?"

"Because we don't see him leaving. We see the assault on Josh and then he disappears behind the dumpster. We see him reach for you and then disappear. He doesn't show up anywhere."

"What does that mean?" She looked at him horrified. "Is he with the emergency services?"

"That would be one explanation. Another is that he managed to hide behind someone and leave." Ed sighed. "Let's go talk to your fellow and see if he remembers anything."

✳ ✳ ✳ ✳

Josh was moved home three days later, worried about his restaurant, even though Amy told him she had it under control, as much as he was missed, that he needed time to heal. He shook his head at her and finally agreed.

He sank gratefully down into his own bed, nodding at his father's help, the nod almost too much of an effort, and then pulling the covers over himself as he laid back on the pillows. His eyes slid shut from relief. The pain medications were kicking in and he knew he'd be out before long. He wanted desperately to be out there hunting for his assailant but knew he just couldn't.

"Do you need anything, son?" Andrew's voice held the concern he knew he could not speak.

"No, I'm fine. Thanks, Dad. Talk to Leah, please. Let her know it's not her fault." His eyes closed and he slept.

Andrew stood for a moment before he headed to look for Leah, finding her standing in the kitchen, her hand on the fridge door, her eyes on the stove.

"That's an interesting position, Leah. Planning on cooking?"

She shook her head as she looked over at him. "Frankly, I have no idea what I'm doing any more, other than being a danger to Josh."

"Now that we don't know for sure, Leah. It could have been anyone who went after him." He pointed to a chair. "Sit. Josh asked me to talk to you. Do you know why?"

She sighed as she pulled out a chair, then turned to reach for the coffee she had poured for them, setting Andrew's down in front of him. "Can I get you anything else?"

Andrew smiled at her, knowing she was putting off the talk they needed to have. "I'm fine, Leah. Sit, please." He waited as she did. "Now, about what happened to Josh. We have no way of knowing who it was and if it was connected to you." He held up a hand as she protested. "It's the truth, Leah. Until the police find whoever it was, we won't know. We can't live our lives as if everyone is out to get us." He watched carefully as she finally relaxed and sat back.

"I know that, Andrew, in my head. It's my heart that I can't convince of that." She shot a look towards the hallway. "Josh was hurt because of me. I just know it."

Andrew shook his head. "Again, Leah. We don't know that for sure. If we did, we'd have you two put somewhere safe." He sipped at his coffee, gathering his thoughts. "Now, about what Josh also wanted me to talk to you about. No, that doesn't make much sense, now does it?"

Leah smiled and reached to pat Andrew's hand. "It made perfect sense. What doesn't make sense is what Josh wanted you to talk to me about."

"Leah, you are a descendent of one of the founding families. You never knew that until the last few days. That may be why someone has targeted you. It may not be." He paused, his eyes seeking the window, before he nodded, having received the words he needed from the Lord. "You do not have to work, ever again. You have buildings you own in this town. Not many but a few. They are rented well and the tenants want to stay. You also have a bank account in your name now." He reached into his pocket and pulled out an envelope. "When you're ready, Josh will take you over to the bank and get it all set up for you. The police chief has spoken to the bank manager and he's just waiting for you to come in."

She stared at him, then at the envelope. "How? Shouldn't someone else get it?"

Andrew shook his head. "No. The town charter is specific. The assets go to the descendants of the families. If there are no descendants, the assets go into a trust and are proportioned out to the remaining families after a certain period of time. Do you understand?" At her nod, he continued. "The assets go to the male heir first and then to the female. It would have gone to your father but because he's not here and you're his heir, it goes to you."

"Wow! That's a lot to take in." Leah stared at him once more, her eyes not blinking. Andrew smiled, thinking she had a "deer in the headlights" look. "This is what Josh wanted you to talk to me about?" She spun to stare at the window behind her, suddenly uncomfortable, feeling as if someone was standing there watching her. She turned back to Andrew. "What about Josh?"

"I have divided what I received between Joy, Josh and myself. He asked for the restaurant. He was a cook in the armed forces and wanted to make a difference in a town with a new style of restaurant. I think he's done that. He's well loved by all."

"Not by all. I'm sorry, Andrew. Someone doesn't like him very much."

"No, they don't." He looked around as he heard a sound and Josh appeared in the doorway, ragged and weary looking.

Leah rose, her arm going around him as he staggered a bit, drawing him to a chair, her hand resting on his shoulder as she watched him closely.

Andrew studied the two as Josh looked up, nodding his thanks. Thank you, Lord. You've provided just who Josh needs in Leah. A strong woman, who knows what she wants and is willing to fight for it. She won't take anything from anyone when it comes to her family and that's what he needs. He's very much a protector and she needs that in her life. Bless them, Lord.

"Dad? Did you talk with Leah?" Josh's head dropped to his folded arms and his voice was muffled.

Leah shared a look of concern with Andrew, who shook his head.

"I did, son. Now, do you want something to eat? If not, let me help you back to bed. You're almost asleep again on your feet."

Leah finally turned off most of the lights in the house late that night, stopping at Josh's bedroom door before she entered. He was asleep but she could see the pain in his face. She hesitated, finally reaching for a blanket and curling up beside him on the bed. She sighed, knowing that tomorrow was another day and there would be no way she'd be able to keep him from the restaurant. She had to go in any way to do paperwork.

Josh roused as Leah settled beside him, his heart raising in prayer for his bride. Lord, she's hurting in ways I can't fix, only You can. This is where I just have to trust you. Please, Lord? End this soon so we can get on with our lives?

❋ ❋ ❋ ❋

Amy looked at the young couple the next morning as Josh sat on a stool near the counter, his eyes on the paperwork Leah had set in front of him, needing his signatures. His arm had come around her waist and she leaned on his shoulder, pointing out what she needed. Amy shook her head. Yep, she thought. Another couple in love. That leaves only Simon, and who could she find for him?

Josh looked up at Leah at that moment, catching her eye and seeing something that gave him hope. She shook her head at him, her eyes going to the staff, before she looked back at him.

"Josh, there's something in the office I think the police need to see. Amy said a parcel was delivered yesterday. I didn't open it. I don't like the looks of it."

He stood, watched as she gathered the paperwork and then swung his arm around her again as she turned to the office. He knew something had spooked her and he wanted to stop that, now. Lord, please! I need to have this stopped. It's slowly killing my bride and I don't like that. Give us strength, please, dear Lord.

He stared at the box, medium sized, wrapped in plain paper with Leah's name and the restaurant address in block print. He reached for his phone even as he sighed. This is not how he planned to spend today, that was a given.

Ed looked at the two and then at the techs as they carefully moved the package. They looked up at him and one spoke quiet enough that the young couple didn't hear what was said. He looked over at them and then spoke, pointing to the box.

The techs took the box as they left, telling Josh and Leah Ed would let them know what was in it. The young couple shared a look before Ed spoke to them.

"I'll follow them to see what they have and then I'll be back. Will you be here or at home?"

Leah spoke. "At home. Josh is at his limit right now."

Josh just stared at her, then began to laugh. "Hen-pecked already, Ed, and that not even after a week." He wrapped Leah in a hug, not letting her see the grimace that came with it, shaking his head slightly at Ed as he went to speak.

Later that night, Leah stepped back from the open door as both Ed and Simon entered, grim looks on their faces. Her eyes shot to where Josh stood in the kitchen doorway.

He pointed to the living room. "Why don't we have a seat in there?" He turned back to kitchen, but Leah was ahead of him, lifting the tray to prevent him from doing so. He stopped her with a hand on her arm, his own eyes studying hers before he dropped a kiss on her cheek and then turned away, not seeing the softening of her face.

Simon took the tray from her and set it down, waiting as she took two mugs and then settled down beside Josh, who reached over and tucked her tight to him, before handing her back her mug. Ed and Simon shared a smile, knowing what they had to say would be difficult for the couple to hear.

Leah finally shared a look with Josh, who took her mug from her, setting it down on the side table, and reaching for her hand. She looked over at Simon and then Ed.

"Ed? Simon?"

The two officers shared a look, before Simon spoke.

"We do have information that really impacts who you are, Leah. I'll let Ed explain what was in the box."

Ed looked down at the folder he had set on the coffee table before he reached for it, his heart sore for what he would have to tell her. *Lord, I need your words. Please speak through me. I'm glad she has Josh right now. He'll get her through this, as sore as he is. He has a strength in him I have seen in few, other than his friends and their families. I know it comes from you.*

"Ed?" Leah's quiet voice broke into his prayer and he looked up, his eyes catching Josh as he looked down at Leah, his heart on his face and in his own eyes.

"Leah. That box was delivered to you and to you only. It has nothing to do with Josh or the restaurant. That doesn't explain how whoever it was knew your married name or where to find you."

"Someone has been watching me very closely, I would say. We already know that."

"That's correct, Leah. Now, as to the contents, I just need to ask a few questions. They're likely questions we've already asked you, but please bear with me. I just need to verify the facts before I go on."

Leah confirmed what Ed asked, a puzzled look on her face, knowing she had already answered those questions before, with both Ed and Simon. She looked at Josh, who was watching her intently, concerned about how it was affecting her.

Ed finally reached for the folder, hesitating before he handed it to her.

"These are photos that the techs took. They are what was contained in the box." He hesitated once more before he handed it to her. "Don't open it yet, please, Leah. This is going to change what you have known about your life. Are you prepared for that?"

She shrugged after pondering his words. "I need to know, Ed. There has always been this question about my life that has never been answered. I know Mom and Dad Whitley wanted to adopt me so badly but were refused every time. That hurt all of us." She reached to open the folder, stopping as Josh's hand covered hers, gripping it tightly. She looked up at him.

"We need to pray first, Leah. If this is as big as Ed says, we need God at the centre. We need His strength." He searched her eyes and face, seeing her agreement, then turned to Simon, who nodded and led them off in a powerful prayer.

Ed finally nodded to the folder. "Open it now, Leah. Look at it very carefully. We have some answers, but not all."

Leah looked at him, apprehension in her eyes before she turned to look at Josh. He nodded to the folder.

"Let's see what we have, Leah."

She slowly opened it, searching through the photos, before she raised her eyes to Ed.

"What does this mean? These are pictures of me over the years."

"They are, Leah. Someone has watched you very carefully. This shows that. What the intent was, we don't know at this point. There is nothing to show us who it has been."

She flipped back through them, pausing at one. "I recognize this one, but who's that in the background? I don't know that person at all. He's so close to us." She passed it back to Simon.

Simon studied it, fear rising in him. If it was who he thought it was, Leah was in more danger than she knew. "I might know who that is, but I need to do some research." He glanced at her.

"Leah, I think Simon needs to talk to you." Josh's quiet words caught her attention.

She looked up at Simon, a frown on her face. "Simon? I thought you were done."

"Sorry, Leah. I'm not. Something has come to our attention, coupled with these photos, that we need to look at." He shared a look with Ed. "Someone has approached our office, asking about a missing child."

She drew in a deep breath. "Me?"

Simon nodded. "It may be. A little three-year-old girl disappeared from the other coast about the same time you appeared in foster care here, about a week to ten days' difference." He reached for his jacket, pulling out a swab kit. "If we can test your DNA, we may be able to link you to that family."

She nodded, then held up a hand. "Is it possible, do you think?"

Simon shared a look with Josh, seeing the worry and hope on Josh's face. "It is, Leah. Let me do the swab and then I have something to show you."

She waited for him to tuck the sample away and then took the folder he handed her, not quite sure what to expect. She just knew it would change her life and she wasn't sure she was ready for that. Her eyes closed as she begged God for strength, for hope, for peace. She felt the folder gently removed from her hands and Josh's arms hugging her tight before a finger traced the tears on her cheeks.

She looked up at him, realizing that she wasn't alone on this journey, that God had provided for her before she even knew what she was facing.

"You open it, Josh. You open it first." She urged him, a pleading look on her face.

"Are you sure?" At her nod, he flipped it open, his hand freezing as he looked at the page with the side-to-side photos. His eyes raised to Simon, who nodded.

"Leah. You need to look at this. But, sweetheart, I need to prepare you." Josh stopped, not sure how to proceed.

"Is it me?" Leah's voice could barely be heard. "It's me, isn't it?"

Josh nodded, sadness on his face. "I think so." He turned the picture to show her and heard her cry of shock and then the sobs. He didn't feel Simon reach for the folder, didn't feel the pain from his ribs and back as he cradled Leah in his arms, his head on hers as she sobbed, her heart broken, her hand fisted in his sweater.

Later, she looked at Simon, meeting his compassionate glance. "Now what, Simon?"

"First, we confirm your DNA. That will take a few weeks, unfortunately. But I will be in touch with the detective who sent this. He's been contacting police services on this side of the country as that had never been done. He's been going back over cold case files and came across yours. He wasn't satisfied with the supposition that you had drowned in a creek in your town. That's what everyone thinks because they found your blanket on the bank and one of your shoes in the water. But the woman who was to have been watching you disappeared the same day you did, and no one has ever been able to find her to question her. There has always been a question in everyone's mind if she took you and left evidence to the contrary." His paused, working to quell his anger. "Your mother has never lost hope that you are still alive and that she'll see you once more. You were their only child. They could have no more."

Leah's tears flowed once more at that. "How cruel!"

Josh held her tight once more, sharing a look with first Simon and then Ed. "How fast can we get confirmation? Do we have to wait for confirmation or can we meet her parents?"

Simon paused, having considered just that. "What I would suggest is that you let either Ed or I contact the detective out there, get his feelings and then go from there. I'm sure the couple would want to come here as soon as possible. But with Leah in danger as she is, we don't want to place anyone else in the line of fire to say the least."

"I think I would want to wait, Simon. Wait for confirmation. I don't want to get their hopes up for nothing. I mean. I know I look like that little girl, our pictures are so similar, but it would be cruel to do this to them. Besides, as you say, we need to solve who it is after me first before I can go on with anything else. And how close are you to that?"

Simon shared another look with Ed and then Josh, finding both men nodding in agreement with Leah. "That's what we'll do then, Leah. I'll get the sample to the lab in the morning. With the possibility of you being the missing child, that will expedite it. I know the couple placed DNA on file a few years ago, so that will help."

Josh turned back from locking the doors after the two men, searching for Leah, finding her in the kitchen cleaning away their coffee mugs and preparing the room for the morning. He paused, leaning against the door jamb.

"Leah?"

She turned, and he saw the fatigue and fear and yet hope on her face. "Do you think it's them, Josh? Will I finally find my family? It's not that the Whitleys weren't family, but they're not blood, and I've always felt that I was missing someone."

He walked towards her, his hands coming to rest on her upper arms. "I think they are but we need to pray hard about this. This will be a shock for them, and I know they'll want to see you right away."

She nodded, then yawned. "You need to be in bed, Josh. Did you get your pain meds?"

"I did, thank you. Head off. I'll make sure everything's locked up and the lights are off." He stopped her as she went to walk past him to drop a kiss on her cheek before he headed for the back door, not seeing the look of surprise she gave him.

Chapter 18

Three months passed without Ed or Simon any closer to finding the person responsible for sending the box to Leah or who had assaulted Josh. They were growing frustrated but there was not a lot they could do about that.

Josh watched as Leah grew white and thin. He hated this for her but knew he could do nothing, except pray. His family joined him in that.

He looked up one day as Simon entered the restaurant office, an official envelope in hand.

"Simon?"

"Is Leah around, Josh?" Simon had some news. He hadn't looked at the results but the tech had handed them to him, a small smile on her face as she did so. Simon had talked to Leah the day before, letting her know he had the results, hadn't seen them, but was given to understand by the tech that they were what they had all suspected.

"She's just down the street at Finn's." Josh looked down at his desk and then rose. "This can wait. Leah wanted some signatures and I'm about done."

Simon dropped into a chair. "Finish this off. I doubt you'll be back today."

Josh's hand froze as he reached for his pen, his eyes on Simon. "Is it good news?"

"I have no idea. Not for sure. Either way, Leah will need you today and that should be away from here. If it's a celebration, take her out somewhere for dinner."

Josh nodded, then quickly scrawled his signature on the cheques. Simon reached for them and folded the copies of the invoices and the cheques into the envelopes Leah had already prepared, stacking them neatly before handing them to Josh.

"Drop these in the mail box on the way by and you can tell Leah you finished the task she assigned you." Simon laughed at the look Josh shot him before Josh rose, grabbing his jacket and the envelopes, calling out to Amy that he was gone for the day.

Finn turned as the door opened and the two men entered, shooting a quick look behind them.

"Afternoon, Finn. How are you this fine day?" Simon grinned as she shook a finger at him.

———

"I'm fine, Simon, but a little confused. Leah left to go back to the restaurant a good thirty minutes, Josh. Did she not make it there?" Concern coloured Finn's face.

Josh shook his head before turning back to the door. He stopped before he spun to face Finn. "Did she say if she planned to stop anywhere between here and there?"

Finn hesitated, then shrugged. "Not that I know of, Josh. She seemed extra happy this morning, as if she had a secret she wanted to share but couldn't."

Josh just grinned at her prying comment. "She was, was she? I'll have to ask her about that when I track her down."

Finn sputtered out words as Josh walked through the door, before she turned to Simon, her words halting as she saw the look on Simon's face and began to fear the worst.

Simon watched Josh as he headed back for the restaurant, disturbed that Leah wasn't at either place.

"Finn? Can you call Blackie for me and have him meet me at the restaurant?" He walked away, not catching her quick glance of concern.

Simon caught up with Josh as he stared around the kitchen of the restaurant, having searched for Leah in the whole building.

"She's not here, Simon. Where is she?"

"Would she have stopped anywhere?"

Josh shrugged, then reached for his phone, walking away from Simon for a moment. He had called their physician's office, knowing that Leah wanted to make an appointment and he prayed that she was there. He turned back to Simon, worry on his face.

"Not where you thought she'd be?" Simon was worried as well, just not wanting to let Josh know that.

"No. She wanted to see the doctor but her appointment isn't until later today." He paced, then headed for the door. "I'm going store to store, Simon. I don't like the feeling I'm getting. Amy, if Leah shows up, have her call me."

Simon took one side of the street as Josh walked the other side, finally meeting up together near the town square. No one had seen Leah since before she had been at Finn's.

"Now what, Simon? Where do we search?" Josh turned in a circle, desperately seeking any sign of Leah.

"I've called Ed. He's sending officers to start searching buildings around the centre of town, working their way out. We'll find her, Josh."

Josh nodded, fear and concern in his heart. He prayed as he didn't think he had prayed before, asking for Leah to come home safely. He walked away from Simon, his eyes seeking his wife, not finding her.

Early evening found Josh in his kitchen, hands jammed into his jeans pockets, not listening to the quiet conversation going on around him, his eyes on Ed and the officers setting up equipment in his living room, just in case a ransom call came in. His mother approached him, but he just shook his head. She stopped, then retreated, Andrew's arm finding its way around her shoulders.

"Let him be, love. He's hurting and he doesn't know how to react right now." Andrew looked over at Jeremiah who nodded his agreement. Joy stood near her brother, wanting to help him but not knowing how, other than to be close. Their two girls were with Finn's parents.

Ed stood quickly from where he was seated, walking away as he pulled out his phone. He spun, his eyes seeking Josh, as relief washed over his face. He pocketed his phone, spoke quietly to the officers, who nodded, and then approached Josh.

Josh had watched Ed take his call and turn to find him. He waited for Ed to speak, but Ed didn't seem to be able to find the words.

"You found her?" At Ed's nod, relief coursed through him, then fear. "She's alive?"

"She is, Josh. She's hurt but they're transporting her to the hospital now. Let's get you there. I'll leave the officers here for now, just in case any calls come through." He looked past Josh at Josh's family, who were scurrying to find their coats. Jeremiah shoved Josh's into his hands, but Josh made no effort to put it on, clutching it tight instead as he headed for the door.

Jeremiah's hand on his arm stopped him. "Let me drive you, Josh."

Josh finally nodded and headed for that vehicle, sliding into the back seat as Joy fastened her seat belt.

Josh almost ran through the doors of the Emergency Department, heading for the desk, desperate to find Leah. The clerk smiled compassionately at him as she asked him to have a seat. She would let the physician know he was here, that Leah was being assessed at the moment. He hesitated before nodding, pleading that they let him go back as soon as they could.

He turned and paced, not seeing his friends come through the door, not seeing the officers Ed had asked to be there for his protection. He didn't see his mother and sister sitting watching him, fear on their faces. His father stood near the door, his eyes flickering between Josh, the door to the examination rooms and the rest of his family and their friends. Jeremiah paced with him, knowing that Josh just needed someone to stand with him, that no conversation was necessary.

It seemed hours later to Josh that the door finally opened and the physician walked towards him. He drew a breath of relief, seeing it was Doc. He approached, stopping suddenly in fear. He couldn't read Doc's face and felt his heart sinking in his chest. How bad was she?

"Doc?" He reached to shake the hand Doc held out.

"Josh. We need to stop meeting like this, you know. Between you and your friends, this is becoming a habit." He gave a small grin as Josh shook his head at him. His eyes saw Josh's family moving to stand behind him.

"Doc?"

"She's okay, Josh. Battered and bruised and very cold but she's fine."

"Did she say what happened?" Josh's brow wrinkled as he puzzled through what Doc had said.

"Not really, other than that she was running down some stairs and tripped and fell." At Josh's quickly indrawn breath, Doc's hand went up. "She slid down about seven stairs. Her back is bruised. She has a hairline fracture in her tibia from the way she landed at the bottom of the stairs. She was there for a few hours before she was found and is very cold and in pain. We're working on warming her up. She's refusing pain medications. She says she won't take them. Maybe you can talk to her and see if you can convince her she needs them." He paused, a slight smile on his face, as he watched Josh take in what he had said.

Josh's eyes slid closed and his heart raised in praise that she wasn't hurt worse. It could have been so much worse. Then, his eyes popped open and he stared at Doc, seeing the slight smile on his face.

"Doc?" When Doc didn't answer, Josh moved closer to him, not realizing how close his family was to him. "The baby?" His voice was low, trying to keep that fact confidential until he saw Leah and he reassured himself both were fine. They had decided not to tell their family or friends yet. It was just too new to them.

Doc's smile widened a bit. "Both are fine. The way Leah made herself fall protected the little one. Come on. Let's get you back to her. We do have a fetal monitor on for now." His voice was equally quiet. Doc was reading Josh's stance and knew he wanted that fact kept quiet but he didn't think it had worked, not by the looks on the faces behind Josh.

Josh walked away, leaving his family staring after him, mouths open.

"Did he just ask about a baby?" Martha turned to Andrew, wonder on her face.

"He did, love. We need to let that go. It's up to them to tell us." He raised his eyes to the rest of them standing there. "Is that understood? He has enough to worry about without any of us asking questions he may not be ready to answer as of yet. If they had known for a while, they would have told us. When they do tell us, we all act as if we knew nothing about it." Andrew nodded towards the exam rooms. "She may still lose it, given what she's been through. We need to let them have this time."

Finn shared a look with Jacob. "That's what I picked up on then today. She was glowing when I saw her earlier." She leaned into her husband's arm. "Please, Lord, don't let them lose it."

Josh stood for a moment just inside the door, watching as the nurse finished her task and then moved away from the bedside, before he approached. He stood by the bedside, his eyes on Leah, watching as she dozed. He searched her face, seeing the pain and fatigue lining it. He reached for her hand, the one she had on the outside of the blankets they were using to warm her body. He rubbed his thumb on the back of it, feeling the chill in her skin, praying that the Lord would warm her quickly.

His eyes raised to the various monitors, stopping as he caught sight of the heartbeat on the fetal monitor, wonder growing within his heart.

He felt his hand squeezed and looked back down at Leah, finding her eyes on him and a faint smile on her face. He laid the back of his fingers against her cheek before he reached to kiss her.

"Hi." Her voice was hoarse.

"Hi, yourself. How are you feeling?"

"Sore. I tried to fall the right way, Josh. I just don't know if I did it right. The doctor said I fractured a leg bone and am bruised." She frowned at him. "I really didn't want to end up bruised like you, you know."

He smiled, reassurance flowing from him that made her relax. "I know you didn't. You'll need to tell me what happened, but not right now. I hear tell you're refusing any pain medication."

She nodded, wincing at the pain. "I am. I just can't, Josh."

"I know, sweetheart." His eyes raised again to the monitor and she followed his line of sight, wonder overcoming her.

"Is that the baby?"

"It is. Doc said the way you fell you protected it." He turned as Doc entered the room, file in hand.

Doc stopped before he reached the bed, a frown on his face, before he looked up, catching their eyes on him. He smiled.

"Everything looks good, Josh. Leah. It doesn't look as if the baby was harmed." He frowned at her. "Now about your pain, young lady."

"I won't take anything. I absolutely refuse." She frowned as Josh began to laugh and Doc grinned, shaking her file at her.

"That's what I thought you said. We plan on keeping you in at least overnight and maybe an extra day, just in case. The obstetrician will be in tomorrow to see you."

He paused, leaning against the end of her bed, crossing his feet. "Do you have any questions at all, either one of you?" When they looked at each other and then shook their heads, he straightened up. "I'll be around for a while if you do. If not, the doctor who's covering for me will be in tomorrow to see you." He shot a look at Josh, not quite sure what to say. "The chief is waiting to speak with you, Leah. Josh, can I have a word?"

Josh looked down at Leah before he nodded, following Doc out of the room.

"Doc? What aren't you saying?"

Doc shook his head. "All is well with Leah. I just thought you should have a head's up that your family may have guessed what's going on. I can't be sure that they do."

Josh sighed. "I figured that out when I looked back at them. I would rather just leave it like it is for now. Leah just told me last night. It's so new we didn't want to say anything yet."

Doc smiled. "From the looks of it, your father was laying down the law." He reached to shake Josh's hand as he saw Ed approaching. "Now, I'm out of here. Call me if you have any concerns."

Ed stood for a moment, his eyes on Josh, seeing the fatigue on the younger man's face and knowing the questions he had to ask would only make it worse.

"Is Leah up to talking with me, Josh?"

Josh looked at the closed door and sighed. "I would rather she wait, but she'll want to do it tonight. Come on, then. The sooner you ask your questions, the sooner I can get her settled."

Leah stood in their kitchen the night before all what happened to her transpired. She stared down at the water in the sink, her hands gripping the edge of the counter, not quite sure how to approach Josh. What she had to tell him was something they really hadn't talked about, and now she was at a loss for words.

Josh watched his wife for a few minutes before he approached her, wrapping her into his arms, his chin on the top of her head. When she didn't move, he turned her to face him.

"Leah? What's going on? You're quiet tonight, and you hardly touched your dinner. Are you sick?" Concern laced his words.

She shrugged, and he saw the faint glimpse of tears in her eyes. Worried, he scooped her into his arms and headed for their favourite chair in the living room, settling down himself and cradling her close on his knee.

"Talk to me, Leah. What is going on?"

Her head on his shoulder, she gripped his hands tightly for a moment, a habit that she was really trying hard to break, that of gripping hard to something when she was scared or uncertain.

She finally spoke. "You had a good day?"

"I did. And you? You left early today. I missed you at the office."

She nodded. "I know. I had to run an errand." She looked up at him, uncertainty in her glance. "We've talked about so many things over the last few months, Josh, but there is one thing we never really touched on."

He tilted his head to study her face, not quite sure where she was going with her words. "And that would be?"

"A family. We never have talked much about that."

"No, we haven't. I guess I figured that you would want to wait, given what you've been through. I know we're still waiting for the test results to come back and I thought we'd talk once they were back."

"Simon talked to me today. I have the tentative test results and need to talk to you about that. That little girl is me. He said he'd talk to the detective on the coast. He'll bring the official results to us tomorrow." There was sadness in her voice and on her face.

"That's good news, isn't it?" Josh was confused at her reaction.

"It is and it isn't. Mom and Dad Whitley will be hurt. We may never know what transpired though to get me here on this coast."

"God knows, sweetheart." Josh studied her face once more, still confused. "But that's not all. What is all this talk about family?"

She stared at him, the answer in her eyes and on her face.

"Leah? Are you telling me something?" Hope surged within him, that they would be starting a family, sooner than he had thought.

She nodded. "I am, Josh. We're having a baby and I don't know that I'm ready for that."

Josh kissed her soundly and then hugged her tight. "We'll get there."

They sat for a while, conversation quiet and light before Leah finally stood, yawning as she did so, Josh standing as well, heading off to finish the work in the kitchen and then to make sure everything was locked up for the night.

The next day, she thought back to Josh's reaction and smiled, her mind really not on the bookwork she was to be doing. She finally rose, having finished everything, and headed for the kitchen, finding Josh deep in the orders flying into the kitchen. She gave a small wave at Amy as she headed for the door. Josh's birthday was coming up and Finn had called, saying she had just the gift Leah was looking for.

Finn looked up as Leah entered, giving a small wave as she handed a customer the box she had just wrapped, before heading for Leah.

"Leah. Thanks for coming in. This way." Finn led the way back to her office, pointing to the chairs. "Sit. Do you want coffee or something?"

"I'm fine, Finn. Did you get it?"

"I did. It took some time, but here is the cookbook you wanted. It's a first edition too, from the late 1800s. I think he'll like it."

Leah took the book carefully into her hands. "Oh, I think he will." She paged through it, excitement growing within her. "Can I leave it here with you until the weekend? I don't know where I would hide it at home. Josh is wanting to change some rooms around."

"Not a problem, Leah. Any word on the DNA results?" Finn knew it had been months and that Leah was getting anxious for the answers, that she needed them in order to move on with her life.

She shook her head. "Simon has them and I've talked to him." She stared at Finn and then started to laugh at the disgruntled look on Finn's face. "Don't worry. Once Josh and I have discussed them, I'll tell you." She glanced at her watch. "I need to run. I have an appointment later this afternoon, and I need to head home for a bit. Thanks again, Finn, for finding this book." She hugged Finn and headed for the door, not looking back, not seeing the puzzled look on Finn's face, who had picked up on something about her friend.

Leah stood for a moment, her face raised to the sky, praise and thanksgiving flowing to her Father in heaven. Josh had taken her news, both parts, well, and that morning was already planning how to turn a room downstairs into a nursery. She had laughed at him, telling him they had months yet to do just that. He had replied that he knew that, he was just dreaming, even as he wrapped her into his arms, his strength comforting in a way she had not felt before.

She didn't hear the heavy footsteps that approached her as she stood in front of the alleyway, lost in thought. She was suddenly wrapped into an iron arm, a hand clasped across her mouth to muffle her cries for help. She was still for a second, then began to fight desperately, wanting to get loose and unable to do just that. She was half-walked, half-carried down the alleyway, her captor searching the area around him. He stopped, turning his body so she was shielded for any eyes that might see them. He then dragged her forward, a warning growled into her ear that if she screamed, Josh would be hurt. He had someone in the restaurant, watching him.

She nodded, fighting back the tears that clouded her vision. She couldn't get a look at the man, not the way he held her, but she knew he wasn't much taller than her and heavyset. She felt his arm loosen from around her and she turned, ready to flee, only to have her upper arm caught into an iron fist and she was dragged along the back streets. She desperately looked for help and saw no one. It was close to lunchtime and everyone was off the streets.

She was shoved into a building and then into a room where she was pushed hard down into a chair. The man paced, his voice rumbling away as he muttered to himself. She finally looked up and froze. No, she thought. Please, God! Not this man! I need Your help to get away. I know I can't do it on my own.

The man turned, his eyes hard on her as she stared back at him before he gave a cruel grin.

She shrank back against the chair, not sure what he had planned, but knowing it was not in her best interest.

"So, Leah. At last I have you where I want you. You'll not get away from me." The man stood in front of her, arms crossed against his ample belly.

"Duane. I should have known it was you. I always knew there was something evil about you."

"Evil?" His voice rose in a scream. "There is nothing evil about me. You should know better." His hand reached out to slap her. Then he stopped. "No, I can't hit you. I can't damage your face."

Leah continued to stare at him, her face blank, her mind racing as she tried to think of a way to get away from him. He was the one person she had prayed never to see again. He had haunted her working days at her last job, trying to get her to go for lunch or dinner, always hanging around when she went to leave, to the point that she always asked someone to walk her to her car. She had spurned the advances, or what she thought were advances, from a man old enough to be her father.

Duane Alberts stormed around the room, his voice echoing from the walls as he talked to himself, his words liberally laced with profanity. He would turn at odd moments, his eyes fastening on Leah as she sat, her eyes on the floor in front of her, her hands folded on her lap, calm and peace flowing from her in contrast to his rage. She listened as he detailed every attempt on their lives, every assault, every package, every envelope that they had received. All from him, and with the express purpose of driving them apart and terrorizing them.

He stormed over to stand in front of her, ready to speak, numerous times before he would step away and begin to pace once more. Leah kept an eye on him, not sure what he had planned or when he would let her go. She was afraid to move, afraid that he was right and someone was watching Josh and would harm him if she disobeyed Duane's commands. Her feet were starting to chill from the cement floor and she knew it was only a matter of time before the chill spread through her whole body, and that she wanted to avoid.

She shuddered as she heard a new voice behind her. Donald. How did he fit into this?

"Dad? What have you done?"

"Donald! What are you doing here? I told you to watch Josh."

"Well, guess what. He's left the restaurant, searching for her." He nodded at Leah. "I can't keep track of him any more, so I came here. What have you done?"

"What have I done?" Duane's voice rose in a screech. "What do you mean, what have I done?"

"Yes, that's what I said. What have you done? Why is Leah here?" He pointed to her. "She shouldn't be."

Duane forged towards Donald, his hand sweeping across Donald's face in a vicious blow, sending his son back against the wall.

"I did this for you. She belongs to you, not him."

"No, she doesn't. She's his wife, not mine." Donald stared at his father, not understanding what Duane was really saying.

"No, she's yours. She always has been. I brought her here just for that."

Donald stared at his father even harder, horror spending through him, not quite sure what he meant. "Dad, what did you go and do?"

Leah's gaze shifted between the two men and she realized she needed to get away and soon. There was no telling what Duane would do to her and she feared for Josh, not knowing if he was safe. Her fear for Josh intensified as she listened to the ranting and raving of the older man and Donald's horrified responses.

As she listened, her heart broke within her, hearing just what the man had done, and how he had affected her life from such an early age. She finally stood, her eyes searching the room.

Duane spun, storming back at her in a rage, threatening her, telling her to sit back down.

———

"I need to use the facilities. Please? Let me use them, and I'll come right back." Leah had no intention of doing that, but she needed him to let her go. She had begun to recognize the building, knowing it was one Josh owned and she had been through it with him just recently. She needed to get away and then she could find a place to hide.

Donald finally convinced his father to let her use the facilities, his eyes unreadable as he motioned her to follow him, not realizing she knew the building.

She thanked him as she shut the door and then locked it, finding a chair to jam under the doorknob, and then searching for somewhere to hide. She opened the window, brushing the snow off, to give the illusion she had snuck out that way. It wasn't that far of a drop to the ground, but she wasn't ready to try that, not yet. If she didn't find somewhere soon to hide, she would.

She searched the room, finding nowhere to hide. She shot a look at the door, knowing she needed to made a move soon before the men broke the door down. She clutched each side of the window and prayed for protection of her unborn child. She pulled herself through the window and dropped, sinking to the ground as she felt pain in her leg, her eyes searching around, desperate to find a hiding place. She rose, running as quickly as she could, or hobbling as she thought, for another building, seeking the travelled portion of the street, where her footsteps would be hidden.

She tried a door of an empty building, finding it open. She slipped inside and searched for a hiding place, knowing she would need one and quickly. She hurried for the stairs to the basement and started down, her wet shoes slipping out from under her in her haste. She muffled her scream as she hit the concrete stairs and slid, ending in a crumpled heap at the bottom of the stairs. Pain blinded her and she sank back, her last conscious thought was a prayer for the little one, that the way she had fallen would have protected it.

Hours later she roused as she heard voices talking to her and hands on her. She tried to fight back until she realized it wasn't either Duane or Donald. She relaxed, letting the paramedics assess her and then lift her to a stretcher, wrapping her in blankets to try and warm her. The older one paused as her words, and then nodded.

Leah's mind came back to the present as she heard the door open and Josh and Ed entered her hospital room. She sighed. She just wanted to sleep but it looked as if that would have to wait. They had promised her that she would be taken upstairs to a room shortly. That's all she wanted, to be in a quiet room, with Josh nearby. She had had a rough two days, given what she had learned yesterday and then today. She reached for Josh's hand, but he was not content with just that. He sat on the side of her bed, wrapping her into his arms, his hands finding hers as he studied first her and then Ed.

Chapter 20

Ed studied the younger couple in front of him. He shook his head as he tried to come up with the words he needed, to find the questions he had to ask. Leah looked exhausted and it was no wonder, given what she had been through in the last couple of days. Simon had shared the news about the DNA results and that the detective on the other coast had talked to her biological parents, who wanted to fly out that night. Simon had in turn spoken with them and had convinced them to wait for a couple of days and then to come.

"Ed?" Leah's quiet voice broke into his thoughts.

"Leah, how are you feeling?"

"Sore. Exhausted. I just want this all over with, Ed. Can you do that?"

"I will do my best. I just need you to tell me what happened today." He watched as her eyes slid closed and her hands gripped Josh's tighter. "If it's okay with you, I'd like to tape it. Then I'll have your statement transcribed, bring it to you and have you go over it and sign it."

"I can, but it's difficult. It affects someone who lived and worked in this town, and I'm still not sure how far he is involved in this." She looked up at Josh, at a loss for words for a moment. She prayed hard, knowing it would be God's strength that got her through what she had to say. She didn't know how either man would take what she had to say.

She sighed, knowing she had to start way back, when she was small and give Ed the information Simon had given her.

"Did Simon talk to you, Ed?" When he nodded, she sighed. "Thank God for that. I don't want to go back to that, but I have to. That's where it all starts." She blinked back tears as Josh's arms tightened around her, not sure where she was going with her words.

"Duane Alberts is the one who abducted me today. He worked at my last workplace. He's the one I was running from. I didn't know why at the time or what he had really done. Donald is his son. Donald has his mother's name, his parents not being married." She looked up, gathering strength to continue.

"Duane apparently abducted me years ago, when I was three, and brought me to this side of the country. He arranged for the sitter that my parents hired, all with this devious plot in mind. He knew who my father's ancestors were. He decided that I would grow up, marry Donald, and Duane would live off the inheritance he knew my father had coming to him."

"Wait! You said Duane Alberts? Donald's his son?" Ed looked up from his notes. "Duane's been on our radar for years. We just haven't been able to prove anything against him. Now, thanks to you, we can." He looked down at his notes. "What else, Leah?"

Leah continued to talk, her voice low at times. Ed finally tucked his notebook away as well as the dictator, knowing his night was not yet over. "Have you any idea where they might be now?"

She shook her head. "I asked the officer who found me but he didn't see them. He said he hadn't planned on searching that building but something made him." She leaned back against Josh, suddenly exhausted beyond what she had ever been. Her eyes closed and she slept.

Ed looked up to ask a question, his words dying on his lips as he watched Josh cradling his wife, his eyes on her face. Ed walked quietly from the room, meeting a nurse heading that say.

"She's sleeping, Nance."

"I thought she would be. We're moving her upstairs. I don't suppose Josh will be heading home any time soon."

Ed started to laugh. "I highly doubt you'll get him to let her out of his sight. At least not for tonight."

Josh stood, watching as the nurses settled Leah into her new room, Leah not arousing at all. He walked back towards her, finding a chair to draw close to the bed, his hand reaching for hers. He settled back, not caring how uncomfortable he was, and slept as well, Leah's hand tight in his.

Before he slept he thought through what all Leah had said, the reasoning behind her kidnapping all those years ago, and his heart broke, first for his wife and then for her parents. He thanked God that she had survived today. If she hadn't managed to get away, he doubted that she would have. He was puzzled, though, on how Donald fit into it and if he knew what his father had really been up to.

Lord, You know. You know the outcome of this and the reasoning why. I hurt for Leah and her parents, for her foster parents and their daughter. But I am thankful she came here, that she's mine. My life would be empty without her. Please, dear Lord, we need Your strength to get through the next few days. Help the authorities to find Duane and Donald quickly before any more harm is done.

His head rested back on the pillow tucked behind his head and he slept, Leah's hand tucked tightly in his. He didn't hear the door swish open and a man enter. Old Jack stood at the foot of the bed for a moment, his eyes assessing his young friends, before he nodded and walked away. He knew where Donald was hiding. He was headed there to find him and convince him to turn himself in.

———

Chapter 21

Leah laughed at the antics of Heidi as she crawled up to cuddle beside her on her hospital bed. Joy had brought Heidi in to see her Aunt Leah at the little girl's insistence. Heidi plopped down tight to Leah, with Leah's arm around her as she placed her picture book on her bent knees and began to tell her aunt a story.

Somewhere in the midst of the story, Heidi's words shocked her mother and made Leah laugh.

"You need to have a baby, Aunt Leah."

Leah's caught back the giggles that wanted to burst from her, sharing an amused glance with Joy. They hadn't told anyone yet, waiting until the timing was right.

"And why should I?"

Heidi shrugged. "Just because. You and Uncle Josh need a baby. Then I'd have someone else to play with at your place."

Joy struggled to hold back her own giggles. "Heidi, I think we need to go. Say goodbye to Aunt Leah. Uncle Josh said he'd stop by later if he could. Remember, you have something to finish for him."

"Oh I do. I do." Heidi scrambled from the bed, her book flying through the air, forgotten, as she headed for her jacket. "Bye, Aunt Leah. I'll be back."

Joy shook her head. "And Aunt Leah is saying that's what she's afraid of. Sorry, Leah. I have no idea where she came up with that."

"It's okay, Joy. It's understandable. Aren't married couples supposed to have families?" Leah laughed at the look on Joy's face. "Go. Josh says he'll stop in before the girls go to bed. Thanks for coming."

Leah laid back on her pillows, her thoughts on the little girl and her questions before she reached for her Bible. She was behind on her readings and missed the strength she drew from each's day Scripture.

She looked up later as the door opened and a head peeked around it. Simon stood there, hesitating before he entered.

"Simon. Hi. You can come in, you know." Laughter filled Leah's words.

"Leah. How are you today?"

She shrugged, her eyes on his face. "I'm fine. Going home tomorrow, thank goodness. But you didn't come here to discuss my health, now did you?"

He grinned at her. "You found me out. Not that I wasn't interested in how you were feeling." He drew up a chair, after handing her a thick envelope. "Here. Your biological parents asked that I give you this. They are in town, but won't come near you until you have read this and have talked to Josh. They are eager to see you, but will understand if you would rather not see them."

Leah's hand rubbed against the envelope. "Thank you, Simon, for what you have done. This will help. I gather it's letters, photos, whatever I need to try and bridge a years-long gap in our history. I do want to see them, but not here. Somewhere neutral and safe."

"That's what I thought you'd say. Jeremiah has suggested that you use a room at the church. The board is in agreement on that."

"Bless him. He's always thinking one step ahead of everyone, isn't he?" She looked up, tears sparkling in her eyes for a moment. "I could be very angry and at times I have had to damp that down. If I had not been kidnapped, I would not have met Josh or any of his friends. My life would be empty without all of you in it. Thank you, Simon, for caring so much, even when you knows it will hurt."

Simon just nodded, fighting back his own emotions. They talked for a while longer before he hugged her and walked away, stopping in the hallway outside her door to lean against the wall, his eyes closing as he prayed for a lady of his own. He saw the happiness his three friends had now and desired that for himself. Help me to be content, Lord, in whatever place You put me.

Josh walked in on Leah an hour later, finding her still sitting with her hands on the envelope, having made no move to open it. She had spent the time in prayer, seeking wisdom and understanding. He kissed her, then looked down at the envelope.

"What's this, sweetheart?"

"Simon was by. This is from my biological parents. They wanted me to have this and look it over before we meet. Jeremiah has offered a room at the church for that."

"That would be good. The prayer room, I think, would be the best one."

She nodded, her face pensive. "Do I really want to do this, Josh? Meet them? I know it wasn't their fault, but it all is so horrible for us. Will wounds be opened up that shouldn't be? It all ties back to Mistletoe and that town charter."

Josh perched himself beside her and wrapped an arm around her, pulling her to him. "It does. But it also goes to Duane's greed. He wanted something that wasn't his to have and he used you to try and get it. He also used Donald."

"Ed was by earlier. Did he talk to you?" Leah tilted her head back to look up at Josh.

"He stopped by but I was too busy to talk. What did he have to say?"

"Apparently, Old Jack found Donald and convinced him to turn himself in. What a mess that is! He wasn't the one who sent Julia and Blackie out that day. He wasn't in town, moving away because of his father. Duane hired a lookalike, figuring in the heat of the moment, no one would notice the slight differences."

"Julia mentioned later that something seemed off about him. Now we know why."

She nodded. "Donald wasn't sure why, but he thinks his father tried to get Julia to marry Donald and she refused."

"That makes sense, in a weird way, I think." Josh looked down at the envelope. "So, do we open this or not?"

"I want to wait until I'm home. There are too many interruptions here. Doc says I'm being released tomorrow."

"I'm glad. The house has been empty without you."

They talked for a while longer before Josh finally stood, his back to the door. "I need to run for a while. I promised Joy's girls I would stop by. I'll be back." He stared at Leah as she started to giggle. "What did I say that was so funny?"

"Not you. Heidi. Joy and Heidi were here earlier. Heidi has decided we need to have a baby because then she'd have someone besides Holly to play with."

Josh broke out into laughter. "Our little logician. What next?"

Leah shrugged. "Who knows? I'm just glad it's almost over, Josh. I'm ready to move on, to meet my parents and get to know them, and to reunite with Mom and Dad Whitley."

Engrossed in their talk, neither heard the door swish quietly open or see the man who entered. A movement had Leah looking up, then screaming at Josh to duck.

Josh partly turned, but not enough to avoid the vicious blow that slammed into his head and shoulders, sending him first into Leah's bed and then to the floor, where he laid in a sprawled heap.

Leah's horrified eyes stared at Duane as he stood, club in hand, watching to ensure that Josh didn't move, before he looked at her, an evil grin on his face.

"Now, my girl, it's time to deal with you. You're coming with me. We'll end this now."

Leah scrambled off the other side of the bed, inching away from Duane, her eyes on him, terror rushing through her. She knew what he was hinting at. She wouldn't survive this time. He meant to kill her. And that she would not allow to happen.

She inched along the wall, seeing a slight movement from Josh that drew Duane's attention. She flew for the door, yanking it open and flying down the hall, seeing hospital security running her way. Her scream when Josh had been hit had alerted them that something was desperately wrong.

One of them caught her into his arms and turned, running with her towards an empty room, where he deposited her on the bed, Doc and a nurse behind him.

Sobs rent through the air as her words tumbled over each other, letting them know that Josh was hurt and that Duane was in there with him, that he wanted to kill her.

Doc tried to reassure her that the police were on their way, that Josh would be okay. She just kept shaking her head, sobs increasing with each breath. Doc turned as Abby Waters, the obstetrician, entered the room, fetal monitor in tow.

"We need to calm her down, Abby. She's refusing any medications, but we need to give her something."

"A mild sedative will be fine, I think. Can we get her laying back, do you think?"

Doc shook his head. "She's absolutely refusing to do just that. She's fighting us." He turned to the nurse, giving an order for a mild sedative. "We need that stat, nurse."

She nodded, running for the door and then the head nurse, who was already on her way to the medication cabinet. The nurse returned, handing the syringe to Doc, who quickly administered it, Leah not even aware of what he had done. Leah finally calmed as the sedative took affect, laying back and closing her eyes. Abby watched her, then moved for the monitor, turning as she heard a commotion in the hallway.

Doc nodded at her and then headed for the door, asking the nurse to stay where she was.

Duane had turned as he heard the door shut, seeing for the first time that Leah had escaped him once again. Rage engulfed him as he stumbled around the room, foam flying from his mouth as he sputtered profanity, before he stood over Josh, seeing that he wasn't moving.

He raged around the room, his words becoming more incoherent the longer he talked, his feet stumbling over one another. Josh watched quietly from where he lay, gathering strength to move. His head and shoulder pounded with pain and he wasn't sure he would be able to even get up.

He watched as Duane finally stood at the window, hands braced on the glass, the club he had been holding dropped on the floor near Josh. Josh reached carefully for it, knowing he would need to defend himself in some way against Duane. He rose as silently as he could and backed towards the door, not realizing that Duane would see him in the glass.

Duane spun and charged for him, anger spewing from him. Josh swung the club, catching Duane on a knee and sending him crashing to the floor, his head thudding in a hollow sound. Josh stood for a few seconds, then ran for the door, pulling it open and running through, right into the arms of the Emergency Task Force officers gathered outside the room. He was quickly moved from the area, towards the room where Leah lay.

Doc looked at him and pointed to a chair.

"Sit, Josh. Let's see how much damage that thick head of yours took." Doc grinned at the look Josh shot him.

"It hurts, Doc, but I've had worse." He tried to peek around the physician, searching for Leah. "Leah?"

"She's sleeping, Josh. We had to give her something to calm her down. She just wouldn't stop. And yes, Abby Waters has been in. The baby's fine." He felt Josh's head and then shoulder. "Nothing broken, but it'll bruise. We'll ice it now and I suggest you ice it every three to four hours as best you can. You won't be using that arm much for a few days." He nodded towards a room door. "Now, go. Find your wife. Given what's happened, I think we'll let her go home today." He turned as an officer approached, a large envelope in hand. "This is addressed to Leah."

Josh reached for it. "It's hers. Simon dropped it off earlier." Josh kept his eyes on it for a moment before he raised them to Doc. "Pray for her, Doc. This is from her biological parents. They want to meet with her."

"I have been, Josh." He patted the younger man on his shoulder. "Now, go find your wife. It will all work out. Trust me. God is in control, even when it looks as if evil will win."

He turned and walked away, knowing he was needed to look at Duane. He stopped as Ed approached him, an unreadable look on his face. A few words and Doc nodded, before continuing on his way towards the room.

Chapter 22

Sunday found Josh and Leah curled up on the couch, the envelope in her hands, his arm around her. Knowing how hard this was for her, Josh prayed for them, waiting as she fingered the flap before opening it and pulling out the sheaf of papers.

"This is hard, Josh. How hard has it been for them all these years, not knowing? I don't even know if they are believers, having God's comfort through all this."

He nodded at the paperwork. "I think that will tell you. Do you want me to start?"

She shook her head. "No, thank you. I have to. I'm just glad you're here, that I have someone with me."

She picked up an envelope, the one on top, and opened it, seeing a birthday card for a four-year-old. Birthday cards, Christmas cards, just-because cards, were next. She read them, then Josh took them from her, watching as she had to pause every once in a while to wipe away the tears.

She fingered through the photos, seeing her early childhood, then photos of her parents through the years. It saddened her that knowing and loving them had been taken from her.

She finally came to a long envelope and hesitated, her hand tracing the name on it. "Leah Rebekah. At least my name is the same. They didn't change that." She looked up, her gaze going towards the front window, seeing the early signs of spring in the buds on the trees. "Josh. I'm afraid. I don't know why."

Josh's lips thinned for a moment as he thought about what Leah had been through for most of her life. "It's understandable, Leah. This is an unknown for you. You've wanted to meet your parents but had no idea who they are or if they even wanted you. That you were stolen never likely crossed your mind." He hugged her tighter, her hands coming up to clasp his arms. "Do you want me to read it for you?"

Tears blocked her vision as she nodded. "Please." Her voice was barely audible.

Josh took another moment to pray aloud for them before he reached for the envelope, setting it aside as he drew a blanket up and over Leah, seeking to bring her warmth and comfort.

He still hesitated as he looked at the envelope before he opened it and unfolded the pages within it, knowing that once it was read, it would change their lives. He prayed they would be ready for that.

"Dearest Leah, our beloved daughter

"It was with fearful hearts we took that call all those months ago that someone fitting your description had been found, on the other side of the country at that. Our hearts raised with hope as we heard that DNA needed to be tested in order to prove that our hopes were real and that you had finally been found.

"You will never know the anguish and pain we felt when we were told you had drowned. That we never ever believed. Our prayer has been that you were alive and well taken care of.

"When we got a call from a detective named Simon, who said he was a friend of yours, and confirmed what detective here had told us, that you were our daughter and that you were alive and well and happily married, our hearts almost burst with happiness and joy. We wanted to come that night but your friend asked that we wait for a couple of days. That allowed us time to prepare what was in this envelope for you, to help you to see and understand us better. It didn't help prepare us to meet you. That can't be done. Not after all these years. The only thing that can prepare us is to actually see you.

"Your friend said you were raised in a loving home with foster parents who so wanted to adopt you but were refused at every turn. You will never know our sorrow at knowing it was because of an inheritance your father never knew about. He lost his father at an early age and never knew his roots, not until now.

"We are in town, and would dearly love to meet you and your husband, Josh I think Simon said his name was. Whenever it feels right for you, let Simon know. He will arrange for us to meet.

"Just know that we have loved you so much all these years and have grieved the loss of the bright and loving daughter you were even at a young age. We have prayed daily for you as has our church family over the years. They were so overjoyed to hear that you are alive and well and happy.

"Love your mother and father."

Leah buried her head against Josh as he finished. "This is just too cruel, for Duane to have done this to them. How could he?"

"Greed, sweetheart. It all comes down to greed. And now he has to answer, not to earthly authorities but to God." Josh had received word that Duane had died the previous night, an undiagnosed brain tumour taking his life. "He wouldn't have lived to stand trial anyway."

"I know, but there are still so many unanswered questions."

"Not really. Ed talked to me at church this morning, just long enough to say that Duane had kept journals over the years, and that what he said about kidnapping you to have you marry Donald was true. He had a sick and twisted mind. He had even decided that if Donald wouldn't marry you, he'd force you to marry himself."

Leah stared at Josh in horror. "That is just so sick. How cruel and how evil!"

Josh nodded. "We'll never know exactly what he was thinking in those last few days. But his journals indicate that he got rid of the woman who helped him. He gave a location and the authorities are searching that area now, likely to find her remains where he said."

Leah shuddered, her head back on Josh's shoulder. "There is just so much evil in the world, Josh. This town has so much hope and good in it. The town founders looked after it all in such a legal manner but there are still those who want it all, to whom it doesn't belong."

"There will always be people like that." Josh hesitated, before he continued. "Do you want to meet with your parents?"

She nodded. "Jeremiah suggested Wednesday afternoon. They have agreed to that, if we agree. I said we'd let him know after we talked."

"We'll plan on that. Now, let's pray, Leah. We'll need God's strength to get us through the next few days." He paused. "What about your foster parents?"

"They're on board. I talked to them earlier today. They want to meet my parents as well, but that will be on another day."

Wednesday found Leah pacing the prayer room at the church, uncertainty in her very movements. Josh leaned against a wall, his eyes on his wife, not knowing how to comfort her in this situation, but knowing she was hurting in more ways than one.

Leah looked up to find Josh watching her and moved quickly to him, welcoming his hug as he wrapped her tight into his arms, his head on hers, a prayer rising between them. Josh looked up as the door opened and Jeremiah entered.

"They're here?" Josh's quiet words had Leah turning in his arms to study him. "What's wrong, Jeremiah?"

Jeremiah just shook his head. "Leah looks so much like her, it's spooky." He paused, at a loss for words. "Are you ready?"

"No. I'm not, but we need to do this." Leah's voice was quite but filled with fear.

Jeremiah nodded as he approached. "Then, as your pastor and also as your family, let me pray with you and for you and for them."

Leah watched as the door opened and a couple entered, her breath coming in a quick gasp as she saw what Jeremiah meant. She really did look like the woman.

Awkwardness was the order of the moment, until Josh stepped in, a hand going out to greet the couple. The woman finally stood, hands on her face as tears flowed.

"Leah! Oh my! How God has protected you all these years! You are so beautiful!"

That broke the silence and they finally sat on the couches in the corner. Jeremiah had made sure to have refreshments available if they needed them.

Silence reigned for a few minutes, until Josh began to ask the questions Leah and he had talked about.

Two hours later, Leah sat between her parents, gripping their hands, tears on their faces, and laughter sounding through the room. Josh sat back, satisfied that Leah was loved by this couple who had missed out on so much with her.

Jeremiah peeked in and then entered, coming to sit near them, not saying anything, but happiness on his face.

"Everything's okay, Jeremiah. Thank you." Leah shared a look with Josh. "We still have a lot of work to do, but Mom and Dad have said they are willing to move here. They're both retired and have nothing to hold them on the other coast now."

"That's correct, Pastor Jeremiah. We have already sold our house, having planned to move somewhere else anyway. Now that Leah is settled here, and I understand I have an inheritance in this town I didn't know about, we're happy to move here." Joseph Bronagh shared a look with his wife. "We both want this, but the final decision rests with Leah."

"I want you here. The Whitleys live about two hours from here, so we can keep in contact. I want you to meet them." She suddenly yawned, exhaustion in her very voice and movements.

Josh stood, reaching to gather her close. "I think I need to take her home. She's had a rough few days. Thank you, Joseph. Anna. I'll call you later today."

They watched as Josh walked away, Leah almost asleep in his arms, knowing she was treasured and loved by so many.

Eight months later, Simon smiled as he watched Josh and Leah move among their family and friends. God has blessed them, he thought, before moving forward to shake Josh's hand and drop a kiss on Leah's cheek, before looking down at the bundle Josh cradled so carefully and close to his heart.

Josh's eyes followed Simon's, to study his sleeping daughter. Rebecca was the image of her mother, to his delight. His finger reached to touch the dark red hair and then his hand reached for Leah's. He was blessed, he thought, thinking of the treasures God had provided for him, Leah and now Rebecca.

They had gone through a lot, Leah thought, watching Josh and their daughter, knowing how much she was loved and just how much he loved their little one. She had had a difficult life, that was a given, but God had blessed her as well. First with a foster family that loved her deeply and had raised her in the Christian faith. Then with Josh, a Godly man who loved her more than she ever dreamed of being loved. And now with their daughter. And being reunited with her parents. Her heart seemed fuller as she felt an arm around her shoulders and her father stood there, her mother beside Josh. She heard a camera click somewhere and smiled. Yes, God had been good to them.

Ed had talked to them earlier that day. It had taken months to finally unravel the web Duane had constructed, but what he had told them was that Duane had been determined to become one of the members of the founding families of Mistletoe, that he decided he needed the money and buildings that came to the heirs.

Donald had helped to unravel that web, but even he had not known the extent of his father's deceit or that he had had a woman murdered. He had cooperated with the authorities and then walked away from Mistletoe, knowing he was not welcome there anymore. He had spoken with Blackie and Julia and then Josh and Leah, apologizing for his father and trying to make amends. The two couples had taken his apologies and then suggested he find God, that that would be the only way he would ever have peace. He had listened to them, talked with Jeremiah, and then walked away.

Leah turned as Heidi and Holly ran towards them, the little girls delighted that Josh and Leah had a baby girl. Though a boy would have been welcome, Heidi acknowledged, not understanding the laughter of the adults as she said that.

Leah's eyes lifted to where her foster parents and foster sister were talking with Josh's parents. She looked up as Josh's arm cradled her close to him, his eyes on her before he kissed her, his other arm still cradling his daughter.

"God has blessed us, sweetheart. He protected us and brought people back into your life that you had lost." He smiled as she blinked back tears.

<hr>

"He has at that, love. Perhaps now we can have a quieter life. God has provided for us and our families." She rested her head on his shoulder, her eyes on Rebecca, not seeing the photographer hired by her parents to take photos of the baby dedication set up and take the perfect family shot for them.

Dear Readers:

Thank you for picking up the story of Josh and Leah, the third in the Mistletoe series. Josh was very determined from the outset on how he was to meet Leah and what would happen to them. Leah was just as determined that Josh needed that little kitten. While working on this story, it has come close to Christmas and a time of year that brings to mind God's gift to us.

Greed plays a huge role in our world today. People are not satisfied with what they have, wanting more and more, not realizing that the best thing in life is God's love and His provision for us, that we can live with Him forever.

Josh's favourite verse is also one of mine - to be strong and of good courage. It is not a coincident that his verse comes from a book that shares his name, the book of Joshua.

As you travel through life, cherish those treasures God has given you: your family, friends, other loved ones. They are never with us long enough.

God bless.

Ronna

Misadventure and Murder In Mistletoe

Mistletoe Treasures Book 4

By

Ronna M. Bacon

Isaiah 41:10. So do not fear, for I am with you; do not be dismayed, for I am your God. I will strengthen you and help you; for I will uphold you with my righteous right hand.

Table of Contents

The woman straightened her jacket and then reached for her small bag and purse. She was leaving and not looking back, she decided. She didn't want what she was leaving here.

She walked from the room, her heels clicking on the tiled floor, avoiding the elevator, instead taking the stairs. She signalled for a taxi, heading for the hotel room she had been staying in, telling the taxi to wait. She gathered her belongings and headed back down, finding another taxi to take her to another hotel, where she found the vehicle she had left there the week before. She tossed the ticket on the windshield and climbed in, driving away, not looking back, not caring about what she had left behind her.

The nurse paused in the hospital room, not seeing the woman, seeing the gown crumpled on the bed, and looked back to check the room number. It was the right room, but the woman had fled. She turned, her steps taking her to find the charge nurse, consternation on her face. She looked down at the little bundle in her arms, sound asleep, a beautiful little girl with auburn hair and green eyes, abandoned by her mother.

Days went by and the mother was not found. Police detectives could not trace her, as she was not from that town. Inquiries went out but returned with no response.

The baby girl grew, placed in a loving foster home at just one week of age, her foster parents adopting her before she was much older. She was loved by all of them, a bright happy child, who still felt a shame that she had been abandoned through no fault of her own.

She grew, her faith in God unshakable. She just knew somewhere, someone did really belong to her and that God would bring her to them at some point.

She didn't see the dark shadows hanging over her head or that of her family. Shadows that spelt doom and death.

Shrugging deeper into his jacket collar, Simon Gardner pulled his toque down further over his ears, his eyes scanning the woods around him, watching for the armed assailant they had been warned was in the area of the local hiking trails. He really didn't want to be out there, he had other things he had planned to do on his Saturday off, but when the Mistletoe police chief had put out a call for help to the county force, Simon had been contacted. He had agreed to help, since Mistletoe was his town even though he worked for the county force. He listened to the crackling voices on his radio and then walked forward, the sun reflecting off the snow and causing him to reach for his sunglasses.

He sighed. It was going to be a long day, he thought. He mentally shook his head. Not the right attitude, now is it, Lord, he asked. I guess I'm just getting tired of this, of hunting for people and worrying about my fellow officers and civilians getting hurt. I'm feeling burnt out and is this Your way of directing me to something else?

He paused as he heard a soft voice and spun trying to find the source before he frowned and then walked forward, stopping in his tracks, surprise colouring his face.

A lady was laying on the ground, her elbows planted on the blanket she had placed underneath her, her hiking boot clad feet crossed at the ankles. Simon leaned to the side, a frown turning to a half-smile as he saw the camera in her hand before he frowned again. Now, just what was she up to?

He raised his eyes, searching the surrounding area, his vision probing into the trees and underbrush. He could sense someone there, but just couldn't see anyone. He glanced back at the woman, having heard her exclamation of triumph and watched as she sat up, fidgeting with her camera before she packed it away into a backpack he hadn't seen. She rose gracefully, folding the blanket and sticking into the pack as well before she picked up the pack and stood, her gaze roaming the area. She walked forward, just as Simon heard a snap from the woods and caught a glimpse of sun reflecting off metal.

He gave a shout and charged forward, throwing himself towards the woman, arms wrapping around her as he threw them both to the ground and then covered her as best he could with his own body, his head raised just enough to glance around. He felt a tug at his jacket sleeve and then saw bursts of snow flying up just beyond them.

A startled cry had been torn from the woman and then she struggled to free herself from him, her voice sharp with fear.

"Get off me, you oaf!"

Simon finally caught her words as he glanced towards the woods, seeing that the assailant had fled, and moved away from her, sitting up and reaching out a hand to her. She turned over, slapping at his hand and pulling herself upright.

"What were you doing?" She was angry, he could tell, even though her cap had not dislodged in the fall.

"Trying to keep you safe." He responded, shocked at the vehemence of her reaction. "Someone was shooting at you."

"Not at me, boyo. More likely at you. I'm a stranger here." She rose and gathered her backpack once more. "Let's hope you didn't damage the cameras." She stood for a moment, her gaze drilling into his, her face shadowed by the sun behind her.

Simon shook his head as he rose. No, this was not Julia, his friend, Blackie's wife, but she looked almost identical to her. Now what, he thought? Lord, please help me to understand because I sure don't right now.

The woman glared at him once more before she stomped off, snow squeaking under her feet.

Simon shook his head, and then his mind turned to what had happened. He reached for his radio, knowing he would have to call it in, and also knowing he had no idea of who the woman was. He spun, seeing she had already disappeared, and sighed. Chief Waters would not like this, he decided, his eyes turning to the holes in the snow where he knew they'd find the bullets.

———

333

Chapter 2

Turning to look back towards the man she had just walked away from, Eavan Walker sighed. She had not been nice, her Gran would tell her. Not one bit. She needed to apologize, she knew. She could feel God's nudge to do just that. She stood hesitating, before she shrugged and walked away. She was sure she had seen him around town at some point, but right now, she had to get back to her studio. She had pictures she needed to take care of. She turned, heading off, her quick strides covering the ground. She didn't see the two men who emerged from the forest, one with a rifle in his hand, and stand watching her, their conversation ugly and angry.

Eavan slipped quietly into her studio, knowing the younger woman she had working for her was up front. She could hear her talking with a customer. She sighed. She wanted so much to be on her own today, didn't want to be around anyone at all, but knew she had to have Maggie out there. She herself refused to work with the customers, preferring to keep herself in the background, a shadowy figure to the studio and website she had created, entitled Reflections by Elf.

She turned as she felt a hand on her back. Her Gran, Megan Walker, stood there, a frown on her face.

"Eavan, what did you go and do this time? Your jacket's wet." Gran looked closer. "And there a hole in it. Did you go and hurt yourself, child?"

Eavan shrugged out of her jacket, seeing for the first time the tear and realizing that whoever that man had been, he had saved her. Her eyes slid closed. Now I really have to a find him, don't I, Lord, and apologize profusely? And you know how hard that will be for me, seeking out someone when I have been hiding for so many years.

"No, I didn't. Something happened today, Gran, and I don't know what to think." She shot a glance at the clock. "I'll tell you but first I have to get these pictures up and see if I caught the one Danny wanted." Her face glowed as she remembered the moment her finger had clicked on the camera and she caught the little mouse peeking out of the snow. "I think I did."

She looked around as Maggie came from the front, a troubled look on her face.

"Eavan, there's a police officer out there, wanting to speak with you." She looked over her shoulder. "He's from the county force."

Gran's hand tightened on her granddaughter's hand. "You need to talk to him."

"Not right at this moment. You know I'm on a deadline and I have exactly three hours to see if it's what Danny wants. I think it is." She brushed past the two women and into her studio, the door clicking behind her.

Simon stood at the counter in the shop, hearing the conversation, a slight smile coming over his face. The smile widened as he heard the door click shut and then the concerned voices of the two women left standing and staring at one another.

He walked away from the counter, studying the photos that hung on the wall, turning as he heard footsteps behind him.

"I'm sorry for Eavan. She will apologize for this. I'm her grandmother, Megan Walker." Her hand went out to shake Simon's even as his head tilted to pick up the lilting accent that traced her words.

"I'm Simon Gardner. I ran into your granddaughter earlier today. I just wanted to apologize to her and see if she is fine."

"By her words and actions, she is." Megan turned, her hand tucking into Simon's arm. "Now, tell me, young man. Are you in a hurry? It's almost lunch time and I have soup on the stove that I would gladly share with you."

Simon's surprise showed on his face for a moment before he shook his head and allowed Megan to lead him to the back of the studio, into the living quarters. He stood for a moment, taking in the simplicity of it, before he walked towards the kitchen, taking the bowls as Megan ladled the soup into them. She paused, her hand on one bowl, her head turning.

"I need to take this to Maggie." She reached for the tray, finding Simon's hands there before hers.

"I can do that for you. Is this ready to go out to her?"

Megan nodded, her eyes following Simon's tall, strong form as he walked back towards the front of the shop, her hand resting on her cheek. Lord, you have brought this man into our lives. He is exactly like the knights I used to weave into stories for my Eavan. Tall, strong, black curls, dark blue eyes. You knew all those years ago that she would find someone just like that.

Simon sat later, his eyes studying the albums Megan had brought to him in the living room, his thoughts on the lady who had taken the photos. He glanced at his watch. He needed to leave soon. His friends had planned a dinner among themselves and wanted him there. He sighed to himself. He felt like a fifth wheel right now, with Jacob, Blackie, and Josh all married to wonderful women, Josh and his Leah the proud parents of a beautiful little girl.

He looked up as he felt a hand on his arm. Megan stood there, her eyes on the far wall, a thoughtful look on her face before she looked down at him. She sat beside him, her hand still on his arm, hesitation in her movements.

"Megan?" She had finally convinced Simon to call her by her first name but it had taken some talking, respect for his elders drilled into his head by his parents.

"Simon, I need to ask you something and I don't want Eavan knowing I have." She looked past him towards the front of the building.

Simon's eyes were on her face as he reached to lay his hand on hers. "What is it, Megan?"

"Eavan won't like me telling you this, but she is hiding from someone. She won't tell me who, but it's been going on since she was young. I ended up raising her where her father died from a heart attack not long after her mother died from cancer. She is all that I have left in the world. I want her to be safe." She looked down. "You have come into our lives at the right time. She needs you but will fight you every step of the way. That's how she is. Just trust me when I say she does really need protection. Just maybe, God willing, you can get her to open up to you."

The sudden opening of a door startled the two and Simon spun to stare towards the front, not quite sure what had happened. He heard rushing footsteps towards the front and excited voices. He rose, a frown on his face as Megan patted his arm and hurried ahead of him.

"Eavan?" Megan's voice cut through the two women's excited chatter.

Eavan almost danced across the room to her grandmother. "I got it, Gran. I got the exact picture Danny needed. I'm just waiting to hear back from him." She shoved a print into her Gran's hands. "Here. What do you think?"

Megan's eyes were on her granddaughter, seeing the excitement in her eyes, then dropped to the photo. "Oh, love. You have indeed got the very essence of his story. How on earth did you manage that?"

"God, I guess, Gran." She lifted her eyes, seeing Simon for the first time. "I got it just before this big oaf tackled me into the snow."

Simon stared at her, finally catching the hint of mischief in her eyes. "What was I supposed to do, may I ask?"

"Walk on by and take whoever it was after you with you." Eavan reached for her phone, excitement still emanating from her. "Danny? Just a moment. Let me put you on speaker. Gran and Maggie are here."

A male voice carried through the room. "Eavan, how did you ever manage to get this photo? It's just so….." His voice died away. "It's too perfect, that's so spooky. How long did you wait for that mouse?"

She began to laugh. "Not really that long. I erased the crumbs from the photo. Bribery worked."

"I don't care how much bribery you used. This is exactly what I need for the book cover. Thank you." His voice died away before he spoke again. "Thank you, Eavan. You don't know how much this means. Suzie would have loved it."

"I know, Danny. I did it for her. Your little girl loved her mice so much." She blinked back tears as Danny abruptly cut off the call.

Megan moved in to hug her granddaughter. "That pleased him, Eavan. His Suzie did love her mice. Now, come. You need to eat. I know you were out early before breakfast and didn't take time to eat, not unless you had some of those bread crumbs you laid out."

Eavan hugged her Gran as she denied doing just that. Her arm around her Gran's shoulders, she turned to the kitchen area, seeing Simon standing there, his eyes watchful.

"Gran, can I have a moment with this gentleman? I fear I owe him an apology."

Megan shook her finger at her granddaughter as she moved back towards Maggie. "Do just that, love. Come and find me when you're done. We need to pray about this attitude of yours."

"Yes, Gran. I know we do. It just keeps rearing its ugly head." She sighed as she said that before moving towards Simon and pointing back towards the kitchen. "Do you have a moment?"

"I do. We need to talk, Eavan. May I call you that?" At her nod, he continued. "My name is Simon Gardner. I'm a detective with the county force."

She nodded as she pointed to a chair at the table. "Forgive me if I eat while we talk? Gran's right. I didn't have breakfast and need something."

Simon moved towards her, pulling out a chair and gently shoving her down, before he moved to fill the soup bowl for her, placing it and the sandwich her grandmother had made for her on the table in front of her. He reached for the teapot, knowing from his conversation with Megan that Eavan loved her tea. He poured their mugs full and then finally sat across from her, finding her eyes on him.

"Eavan?"

"Simon, you didn't have to wait on me. I could have gotten my own meal."

He grinned at the disgruntled look on her face. It's going to fun getting to know her, isn't it, Lord? "I know, but I was raised a gentleman. This is what my Dad would have done and I just followed through. I'm sorry. I shouldn't have."

"No. No. It's all right, I think." Her brow wrinkled as she struggled with her emotions and her thoughts. "It's just that I haven't had a male do this for me since my Dad died."

He smiled, sadness in his eyes as he thought of his own parents, both gone now for years, disease taking them both far too young. "It's okay, Eavan. I guess I'll need to learn to ask before I do something for you."

She glared at him. "And who says there'll be another chance?"

He just shook his head at her. "I'm sure there will be." He looked down at his hands clasped around the mug. "About today. I'm sorry I tackled you so abruptly. Not that I'm sorry I kept you from getting hurt."

"Yes. About today. What was that all about anyway?" She paused, her spoon halfway to her mouth, as she watched his thoughts cross his face. "Simon?"

———

He shook his head. "You look so much like a friend's wife, it's spooky." He reached for his phone, then paused. "First, about today. I really am sorry I tackled you without warning. There was someone in the trees, aiming for you." He pointed to his jacket. "I have the hole in my jacket to prove it."

She paled, her spoon dropping back into her bowl, the liquid splashing outside the bowl. "Simon? Were you hurt?"

He shook his head. "We don't know if it was the man we were after or not. That's why I was out there. I was following up on a report of an armed male out there. Well, myself and other officers." He pointed to her soup. "Eat."

"You're still bossy, you know that." She finally pushed her bowl away, her appetite gone. "What is this about your friend's wife, I think you said?"

He nodded. "I need to prepare you about life in this town." He proceeded to talk, telling her about the founding families and the legacy they had left to their descendants of buildings in town, money in the bank, things that could not be sold or passed out of the families. "Blackie's Julia is one of those families." He smiled. "In fact, my three friends and myself are too. As it turns out, Jacob's Finn and Blackie's Julia are cousins. Josh's Leah is also related to Finn and Julia."

"Just a moment. You said Finn?" Her eyes were watchful.

"I did. Her full name was Finola Bronagh but everyone calls her Finn. Why?"

She paused, then sighed, knowing the Lord had brought Simon into her life, whether or not she liked it. "I was told to find a Finola Bronagh when I came here. I had a letter. Gran doesn't know about it. She also doesn't know why I had to leave where we were living."

"Will you tell me?" He watched as she tilted her mug and then went to rise. He rose, his hand on her shoulder keeping her in her chair as he moved past her, feeling the teapot and then making a fresh pot, giving her a chance to collect her thoughts.

"Simon?"

He paused as she spoke, his eyes searching hers, noting the clear green of them with the flecks of gold and brown scattered through the green, perfectly paired with her dark auburn hair.

"Eavan? What is it?"

"I think he's here. I think he's found me. I have tried so hard to hide. My studio and website don't name me as the photographer. I use an alias for that. But I know he's found me. And I'm scared." Fear shimmered in her eyes, and suddenly nothing else mattered to Simon, except keeping this lady safe and finding the one after her, no matter what it took.

Simon tried to draw out more information from her but she just shook her head, telling him she needed to organize her thoughts and find the paperwork she had somewhere, that she would track him down and give it to him, before reminding him he was to tell her about his friend's wife.

Simon pulled out his phone, flipping through to a picture of Blackie and Julia, studying it before handing his phone to Eavan.

Her hand shaking, she took it, her eyes on him before she dropped them to the picture. Her breath caught in her throat.

"That could be me, Simon. Whatever does this mean?" She looked up at him. "As far as I know, I have never been in this town in my life."

"That's what I would like to look into. If I can have your parents' names and your date of birth, I can have a friend start to research it."

She nodded, giving them to him, turning as Maggie's hand touched her shoulder. "Don't be forgetting to tell Simon you're adopted, love. Adopted as a week-old infant. Your birth certificate was sealed but I think we need to look into who your biological parents are."

Simon's hand froze as he was writing, his thoughts going to Julia and her brother, Jonathan, and the way their mother had been with them. "I have an idea, but I need to run it by someone first. Let me talk to them. In the meanwhile, I'll have my friend start his research." He held up a hand at Eavan's protest. "He will not say a word to anyone but you or I. I can guarantee you that."

Chapter 3

Simon paced the living room of his home later that night, his socked feet whispering quietly on the hardwood floors he had lovingly repaired and refurbished. He ran his hands through his hair, for what time he was sure but he knew it had been many. He was disturbed by Eavan's words and then too there was her likeness to Julia. Where did she fit into this town? He was sure it was no coincidence that she ended up here.

He paused as he heard steps on the wooden porch running across the front of his house and then a tap at the door. He approached cautiously, not expecting anyone that night. He had declined his friends' invitation to dinner, much to their disappointment and among their protests, just shaking his head at them before he walked away, leaving them staring after him.

He opened the door, surprised to see Samuel Blackwell standing here, a folder tucked under his arm. He knew Samuel well, as he was Blackie's father, but he had felt as if Samuel had at times acted in the stead of his own father.

"Samuel? Come in. What brings you out tonight?"

"I have some things to talk over with you, Simon. It's going to take a while. How full is your coffee pot?" He grinned as he followed Simon to the kitchen, knowing full well Simon drank tea but kept a coffee pot on hand for his friends.

"Sit, Samuel. Have you eaten?" Simon finally sat across from him, taking a sip of his tea, watching his friend closely. "What did you need to talk to me about?"

"This." Samuel tapped the folder he had set on the table before he slid it over, not removing his hand as Simon reached for it.

Simon lifted questioning eyes to Samuel, not quite sure why Samuel was preventing him from opening the folder.

"Simon. This is something I have prayed many hours about as has my wife. We want you to come work with us, in a new department. We saw how hard you worked with Leah, to find her parents. We receive contact from people looking for their parents or their missing children. We want to start a new department, dedicated just to that. We want you to work it for us. We've seen the discontent and restlessness in you for the last year. Is that true?"

Simon nodded. "I have felt that way lately. Today, I decided I would resign from the force and find something to do. I just can't continue working like I am. God has been speaking to me, leading me in a different direction than He did when I moved here."

Samuel nodded. "That confirms what I have been getting in my own prayers. Pray over this decision and come to me in a week. I know you would

———

340

give you answer tonight, but you need to seek this guidance from God." He nodded at the folder. "Now, Old Jack has come to me. He says he thinks Julia and Jonathan's mother may have given up a child for adoption, but he can't be sure. He says Julia's father said he finally got her mother to admit that about a week before he died and that he would going to track down this baby."

Simon sighed as he reached for the folder, flipping it open, leafing through the pages, scanning what Samuel had already found. "This is the first one, I take it."

Samuel nodded. "I would like to help Old Jack." His hand went up. "I know. His name is Ben Bronagh. I've known for months. He confided in me." He was puzzled by the look on Simon's face. "Simon?"

"Just a moment." Simon rose and padded away to his office, returning with a folder. "I think I know who the baby is. And she's not going to accept it very well. Not at the present." He slid his own folder over to Samuel.

Samuel gave him a startled look, before he frowned. "How do you know that already?"

"Because I spent today with the lady and her grandmother." He nodded to the folder. "Read what I noted and then we talk. And before you asked, she agreed to a DNA sample, which you know takes time."

Samuel finally took his eyes from his young friend and opened the folder, reading through the neat thorough notes Simon had made. He sat back, stunned at the discovery, hope welling within him as well as caution.

"Do you think it's this girl? How do you pronounce her name anyway?"

"It's pronounced Eve-een. Her parents were Irish. I've met her grandmother as well, and she's convinced that Eavan belongs in this town. Why, she refused to say."

Samuel nodded, his eyes on the photo Simon had snapped of Eavan without her being aware of it, one where she was talking with her grandmother and laughing at something she had said. "She looks so much like Julia. Please, God, let it be her."

Samuel finally stood, filled with mixed emotions, knowing he couldn't talk to his wife or even Blackie, not yet. He and Simon had work to do.

"Who is this person that's looking for Eavan, anyway, Samuel? I'm not getting good vibes about him."

"I don't either. I suggest we stall him as long as we can." He turned, compassion showing briefly in his eyes as he studied Simon. Lord, his heart's already involved, isn't it? Don't let him get hurt. "You'll need to talk to her."

"I know. I don't look forward to that." Simon had admitted to Samuel how he had met Eavan. "She'll likely call me an oaf again."

Samuel started laughing, drawing a wry smile from Simon. "If that's all she calls you, that's good, isn't it? Call me in a week and let me know what you plan. We'll see you at church in the morning."

Simon locked the door behind Samuel, already in prayer about the job offer. It was exactly what he wanted but he had to be sure. He knew without a shadow of a doubt his resignation would be on his lieutenant's desk Monday morning, regardless of whether he took Samuel's offer or not.

Eavan had turned to her grandmother after Simon had walked away late that afternoon, finding her grandmother watching her closely.

"Gran? Why did you ask him to stay for lunch? You never do that."

Megan nodded. "I know. It's as if the good Lord was telling me we needed that man in our lives, in your life. No, I'm not meddling. Just following orders." She turned and walked away, leaving Eavan standing behind her, mouth open until she closed it with a snap.

Eavan whispered a good night to her grandmother, heading for her own bedroom and quiet time with the good Lord, as her Gran called God. She had been out of line today and she knew it. Fear drove her at times. She was ready to face whoever it was and win her freedom. It had gone on long enough.

She fingered the envelope she kept tucked in her Bible, a letter directing her to this very store in Mistletoe, telling her it was rent free. She had no idea who had written the letter but she planned on finding out just that. Maybe Simon could help her, she thought, and then groaned. She had decided she needed to stand on her own two feet and figure this out on her own, and here she was planning on talking to a man she had just met.

Her hand stilled as she pictured him from that morning, sitting back in the snow, his toque in his hands, black hair in tousled curls, and she recognized what her Gran had. He was the knight in all those stories from her childhood. Gran, how did you know? She knew it was a God moment, as her Gran was wont to say.

She stood for a few minutes, the lights out, staring out her bedroom window, her eyes raised to the sky, not seeing the man standing in the shadows of a building across from her, keeping watch. It would have frightened her if she had known.

Old Jack finally turned, his head nodding. He could soon claim his rightful name. His other niece had come home to Mistletoe. He just needed help to prove it. And only one man would do. Simon would be his choice. The other three friends were too close to her, he decided. He would find Simon tomorrow and talk with him.

Simon turned as he heard his name called the next morning, stopping in his walk across the church parking lot. Jacob ran towards him.

"Good morning, Simon. We missed you last night." Jacob wasn't prying, Simon knew, just concerned.

"Good morning. Where's Finn?"

"She's already in the church. Something about helping with the coffee for after church." He walked beside Simon in silence for a moment, before his hand came out and he pulled his friend to a stop. "Simon? What's going on with you?"

"What do you mean?" Simon stared at his friend, wondering where the conversation was headed.

"You're not you. Not the friend we know and love. You're restless and that I haven't seen, not since just before we all left the service. It's back."

Simon sighed, knowing he had to confide in his friend. "I am, Jacob, and could use your prayers. I'm putting in my resignation tomorrow and I really don't know what I'll do. I have had a job offer that I'm praying about."

Jacob nodded. "Finn and I wondered if you would resign. It's burning you out, Simon. You haven't been the same since you worked on Leah's case, helping her to reunite with her parents. That's what you should be doing, you know."

Simon started to laugh as he held the door for his friend. "I should, should I? I guess then I'll have to see what transpires. Now, where are you two sitting today? And don't say up front, because I will not sit with you if you do." He stopped as he felt a hand on his arm and looked down.

"Simon?" Megan stood there, looking up at him. "Would you sit with me this morning? Eavan didn't come. She's off somewhere, somewhere she won't tell me, but I know she's off to spend time in prayer and meditation. That's what she does, goes off on her own."

Simon smiled down at her. "I would be delighted, Megan, and honoured to sit with you. Now, where would you like to sit?"

"About half way to the front is good." She looked around. "What happened to the man you were talking to?"

"Jacob? Oh, he's likely gone to find his wife, Finn. I would really like to introduce you to my friends and their wives. One of the couples have a beautiful little girl who looks so much like her mother."

"Oh, I would like that. Now, this minister. I heard he's good." She settled into a pew, Simon on the end, and began to read over the program or bulletin or whatever it was called, she just could never remember.

Samuel smiled at her words. "He is very good. He also happens to be a good friend. His wife is sister to the couple I told you who have the little baby." He paused as he felt little hands patting his arm and looked down. "Heidi and Holly? What are you doing here?" He looked around for Joy, the minister's wife and saw her heading his way, a smile on her face, which turned to a frown as she saw her daughters climbing up to sit on Simon's knee.

"Heidi and Holly. Is that where you're supposed to be?" She bit back a smile as Heidi shook her head before she looked up with a smile at Simon.

Holly on the other hand nodded. "It is. Sit with Simon today."

Joy reached for her daughters, then stopped as Simon spoke to the girls, who were off his lap and headed for the pew they usually sat in.

"Simon, how did you do that?"

He shrugged and grinned. "Just asked them to do what you said and that I'd be disappointed in them if they didn't." He grinned at Joy, then introduced her to Megan, his mind wandering as he listened to their short conversation.

After church, Megan turned as she heard a voice calling for Simon to wait and searched the crowd, a frown on her face.

"Where's Eavan, Simon? I thought I heard her call you."

Simon froze, realizing what she had said. He realized that Eavan's voice had a quality just like Julia's. "It's not Eavan, Megan. It's my friend, Julia." He watched with compassion as her hand went to her mouth and tears briefly entered her eyes.

"I thought it was Eavan. She sounds like my Eavan."

Simon nodded. "I guess she does. Do you want to meet her today?"

Megan nodded. "Please, but don't tell her about Eavan. They need to meet to have that conversation."

"I won't." He reached to hug Julia as she and Blackie approached.

"We missed you last night, Simon. Blackie said you had another commitment."

"I did, Julia. It's complicated."

She began to laugh even as she shook a finger at him. "It's always complicated with you, Simon, but we understand." She looked with interest at Megan. "And who is this lovely lady, Simon?"

"Blackie. Julia. This is Megan Walker. She's just new to town."

"Oh, how nice. Welcome, Mrs. Walker. This is a great time of year to come to Mistletoe. Where did you come from?"

Megan looked to Simon for help, Blackie catching her look, and then wrapping his wife in his arm.

"Give her time to adjust, Jewel, before you put her through the third degree. We need to get her used to you first." Blackie looked at Megan in apology. "Sorry about that. Julia just has to know people and how they tick. That's so different from when we first met."

Julia dug her elbow into her husband's ribs. "That you deserved this time, Blackie. Would you join us for lunch? We always head to the B&B Finn's people have for brunch on Sundays."

Simon was shaking his head. "I don't think so today, Julia. Megan needs to get home and I volunteered to escort her." He tucked Megan's hand into his elbow and escorted her away, leaving Blackie and Julia staring after them and then at one another.

"Did Simon just walk away from us?" Julia was astounded. He had never done that before.

"He did. Jewel, leave it. God knows what Simon is doing and we need to pray for him. I sense he's involved in something bad and he'll need all the help those prayers can give him."

Julia leaned against her husband, her eyes following Simon. "I fear for him sometimes, Blackie. He has such a difficult, dangerous job. Do you think he's heading for an adventure, just like we did?"

Blackie nodded as he took his wife's hand to lead her away from the church. "I think he will be. Or is already. There's something different about him today."

Simon shut the door carefully behind him before he slipped out of his shoes. He had decided not to head to the B&B after he dropped Megan off. He wanted to talk to Eavan, but she wasn't around and that worried him. Where was she, he wondered? Lord, please keep this lady safe. I fear for her and what she's about to face.

A tap at his door a couple of hours had him frowning and setting aside the book he was attempting to read, without much success. He rose to head for the front door and peeked through the door window, opening the door, surprise on his face.

"Eavan? How did you find me?"

"It wasn't hard, not really. You're well known in town, did you know that?" She gave him a smile that didn't quite reach her eyes. "Can I come in?"

"Oh, sure. Sorry about that. Here, let me have your jacket." He took it, hanging it in the closet, his eyes on the slice that went through the sleeve, knowing it was from the day before. "Can I get you anything? Tea? Water?"

"No, thank you. I'm fine." Eavan wandered through the living room, restless he could tell.

He sighed, heading for the kitchen and the kettle, making a pot of tea, placing it, mugs and cream and sugar on a tray, adding a plate of the cookies that

Heidi had made for him. He smiled as he looked down at the misshaped cookies, laden with icing and sprinkles, knowing he'd eat them and not complain.

He set the tray on the coffee table, his eyes searching for Eavan, finding her standing in front of the fireplace, staring down into the fire he had lit.

"Eavan?" He approached her, not quite sure how to read her mood.

She raised her head and he saw the bleak look around her eyes before she brushed past him to pour herself a cup of tea, eyeing the cookies before she took one.

"Did one of the little girls Gran told me about make these for you?"

He grinned as he poured his own tea. "Heidi did. She is quite the character, that girl." He sat, his eyes searching her face before he nodded.

"Simon, I owe you an apology for yesterday. You scared me when you tackled me. Thank you for saving me, although I am still not sure which one of us the bullet was meant for."

"Bullets." When she stared at him, puzzled, he repeated himself. "Bullets. We found six and there were likely more."

She paled, her hand shaking enough she had to set her cup down. "Six? And there were more?" When he nodded, a grim look on his face, she sat back. "Who? Who did this, Simon?"

"That we're not sure of. But first, tell me about the photo. Yeah, the one of the mouse. How did you ever manage to catch him just as he peeked out through the snow? I swear you can see his nose and whiskers wriggling and his eyes on the crumbs."

She laughed, glad he had changed the subject for now. "I don't know. I just did. God knew I needed that particular frame and gave it to me. I've been trying over the last couple of weeks to get one just like and didn't even raise a mouse no matter how much I tried."

He nodded, knowing she was just waiting for him to ask why she had come to see him, other than to apologize.

"You're not going to ask, are you?" She sound disgruntled and frowned at him as he grinned at her.

"Nope. You'll eventually tell me. And then I'll take you back to your place." He set his mug down as he leaned forward. "Your grandmother talked to you, didn't she? Told you about Julia?"

She nodded. "She did. It really threw her, seeing Julia. She said it was almost like looking at me and she said her voice was a lot like mine. How can that be? We don't even know if we are related."

"No, we don't. We can run DNA testing but that will take months. I did ask my friend to start that investigation we talked about. Stay right there. I'll be right back." He rose and headed for his office, grabbing the file Samuel had given him. He returned to the living room, this time to sit beside her, his hand on the closed file. "He has found preliminary information, Eavan. This contains it."

She looked at the folder, studying his strong hand at the same time, wanting to know what it would be like to have him hold hers when she was scared. "What does it say?" When he didn't answer, she looked up at him. "Simon?"

He shook his head, dispelling a vision of them together for the rest of their lives. That wasn't likely to happen, he thought. "Somehow, Samuel pulled strings and found your original birth certificate. I haven't looked at the folder yet. It was late last night when he came over and with church today and other things, I just let it sit." He looked down at it. "So, this is all new to me too." He handed it to her.

She opened it, seeing photos of herself from her driver's license and other photos. "How did he find these? I didn't think I had had that many taken of me. I hide in the background."

Simon suddenly stared at her. "You were the photographer, weren't you?"

"When?" She was puzzled, not quite sure what he meant.

"At Josh and Leah's baby dedication. That's why you seem familiar."

She sighed. "I was. I didn't realize you knew them. I was in and out and tried to keep my identity as hidden as much as I can. If I remember rightly, her mother hired me through my website, so I never met them in person."

"No, I don't think you did. She mentioned afterwards that she hadn't had a chance to talk with you. You kept a hat on at all times."

"I did when I was doing sessions like that. It helped to hide my face, but it also helped to cut lighting so I could see better." She turned back to the folder, her hand stilling as she reached for a birth certificate, her eyes going to his.

"Do you want me to look at it first?"

She nodded. "Please." Her hands shook as she handed him the paper.

He watched her face for a few minutes before he dropped his eyes. He drew his breath in sharply, and his eyes rose to her, seeing the fear and apprehension and yes hope in hers.

"Simon? What does it say?"

Simon reached to wrap an arm around her, surprising her. "It's what we thought, Eavan. You are Julia and Jonathan's sister. You have a sister and a brother."

"I do? You didn't say anything about a brother."

"Yes, a brother. Oh and an uncle too."

"An uncle? This is getting bizarre. Who would he be?"

"Do you know Old Jack?"

"Old Jack? Sure. Everyone in town knows him." She waited for him to continue, her eyes on the birth certificate. At his silence, she looked up. "He's my uncle?"

Simon nodded. "His name is not Old Jack. That's just a name he chose to use for now. His name is Ben Bronagh. He's your father's brother. There is a long history with your parents that we'll need to discuss. But that's for another night. This is enough of a surprise for you."

She nodded, tears on her cheeks as she swiped at them. "This changes my whole history, you know. I know Gran will still be my Gran, but this will change that. I always knew I was adopted but never really thought about who and why." She looked up at him. "You know why, don't you?"

Simon sighed as he drew her closer to him, his cheek going down on her hair. "I have some idea. Samuel, my friend and actually Julia's father-in-law, runs an investigative firm. He has asked me to come on board and head up a new department. Yours would be the first investigation I undertake."

"Mine? You? But you're a police officer."

He shook his head. "I spoke with my lieutenant today and resigned. With accrued sick time and vacation time, I have enough time so I don't have to report back until I quit. I have to go in for a while tomorrow just to do the paperwork and finish off what I need to do. Then I am full time on this."

"But you can't. Who will pay you?"

"Samuel will. Besides, I don't need to work. With the founding fathers setting it up for their descendants, I have property and a bank account that came down through my father. You see, the Bronaghs and my friends and I are all descendants of the original five founding fathers."

"You are? How does that work?" She shook her head even as she stood, gathering their mugs and picking up the tray, heading for his kitchen. "That I can't understand tonight. My brain has had enough." She paused before she turned back to him. "How do I tell Gran?"

"She already knows, love. She already knows. She met Julia, remember?" He didn't realize an endearment had slipped into his words, but Eavan did and wondered at it.

"I think I need to go now, Simon. I think I'll be awake all night just in prayer."

"You and me both, love. Come on. Let's get you back to your Gran."

———

348

Samuel stood late the next morning in Eavan's studio, looking around at the framed prints. Simon was right, he thought. She has such talent. He thought of the photos Josh and Leah had of baby Rebecca and smiled. Yes, Eavan definitely had talent and it was a shame she had to hide.

He turned as he heard a voice behind him, startled for a moment at the similarity to Julia's. He eyed the young woman in front of him, seeing the similarities that Simon had mentioned. It was spooky, he thought. Lord, help me to help this young woman. I can tell already she has Simon's heart. He has fallen hard and fast, but won't admit it, not yet any way. It was the same with Levi and Julia. He knew right away.

"Can I help you?" Eavan studied the man staring at her, puzzled at his look.

"I'm sorry. I didn't mean to stare." Samuel walked up to the counter, setting down the package that he carried. "I'm Samuel Blackwell. Simon is a good friend of my son, Levi. Or you would have heard of him as Blackie."

"Blackie. That would be Julia's Blackie, if I understand correctly." At his nod, she studied him more openly. "And what can I be doing for you today?"

Samuel smiled at her choice of words, knowing it was likely how her grandmother would have worded the question.

"I understand from Simon that he talked to you yesterday?" He waited until she gave a reluctant nod. "I'm not prying into that conversation, trust me. That was between you and Simon and will remain that way unless either one of you talk to me. That's how I work. I trust the men and women I employ to do their task and come to me if needed. You can't do the kind of work we do if the operatives are micro-managed."

He paused, his heart lifting up in a prayer for the words he needed to say.

She poked at the parcel with one long finger. "And what would be in that?"

He laughed openly at that. She was like Julia, he thought, not wanting to see what was there but still wanting to know. "This is from my wife and I. Julia is a beloved member of our family. Besides Levi, we have two daughters, and we consider Julia a daughter." He nodded at that package. "In that, you'll find photos, letters, what have you from my wife and I, from our girls, from Levi, and more importantly from Julia, from Jonathan." He held up a hand at her protest.

"But they don't know me. Simon promised he wouldn't tell anyone." Tears clouded her vision and she fidgeted with a pen on the counter until a strong hand laid on top of hers stopped her movement.

"We have suspected for a year or so that there was another baby. Ben has confirmed that your father knew and had planned to look for the baby before he was killed." Her eyes shot to his at that. "Yes, your father was killed. I won't go into those facts yet but we will need to talk, either you and I or Simon and you."

She nodded. "Then how did you get all this so soon?" She was genuinely puzzled by that.

"Over the past year, we have all taken photos of ourselves, of places we love, or events we have been involved in. We have all taken time to write letters to the baby sister none of us know. That is, until now. Welcome to the family, Eavan. You will never know the relief I felt when Simon came to me and asked for my help in finding out about you." He held up a hand again as she went to protest. "He didn't go through official police investigative channels to do this. He chose to keep it between himself and me until you give permission for us to share with the family." He nodded towards Megan, who stood in the doorway behind her.

Eavan turned, seeing her Gran there, and reaching out a hand. Megan wrapped her granddaughter in her arms as she wept, heartbreaking sobs wracking her body. Samuel stood, uncertain as to what he should do. He finally nodded to Megan and turned and walked away, standing outside the building, his face raised to the sky, his eyes closed as he prayed for the two women he had just left inside.

Simon stood for a moment, puzzled before he walked towards Samuel, only to have Samuel turn and walk away from him, not having seen him. Simon hesitated, then walked through the door, hearing voices from the back of the building, and heading that way.

Megan turned to him, a helpless look on her face, as she was unable to comfort Eavan. Simon nodded, his jacket tossed to one side, as he sat and gathered Eavan into his arms, turned her face into his shoulder, his clasp as tight as she needed.

Eavan finally relaxed, her sobs easing, her hand clutching Simon's tightly. She didn't see her Gran reach in with a warm damp cloth but felt the softness on her face. She finally tilted her head back to look up at Simon, finding his deep blue eyes on her.

"Simon?"

"Yes, love? You all done with the waterworks?" He gave a small grin at her frown. "What happened?"

"Your friend was here." She pointed towards the front of the building. "He left a package there. Letters from the family, photos, and I don't remember what all. He said they've been preparing them over the last year."

"They have, love. That they have. They have wanted to meet you for so long now. Jonathan, your brother, knew something was wrong when he was a child, when your biological mother disappeared for a few months. He could never get an answer as to where she was. When your father was killed, he dropped it, afraid he would be next if he kept asking questions. Julia, she never said much, but one time she did say she really wanted a sister but was glad she didn't. She wouldn't have wanted her to go through the abuse she suffered at the hands of her stepfather and her mother."

"Her mother? Why? What did she do?" Eavan sat back further, her eyes not leaving his face.

"She was abusive. She was part of the plot to have your biological father killed, thinking she would get his lands and money. The way the charter works in this town is that it does to the children, not the spouses. If there are no children, then it goes into a trust for the remaining families."

"Oh, that's so horrible. How could she?" Eavan's head went back down on Simon's shoulder, not realizing that's what she had done. "And that means she's my mother too. Gran?" Eavan sat up, struggling to free herself from Simon's arms, searching for her Grandmother, who had been her steady rock all of her life.

Megan was there, sitting on beside Eavan, her arms coming around the younger couple as she prayed for them, her words inaudible as her heart broke for her beloved granddaughter.

Simon kept his eyes on Eavan's face, seeing the fear, no, terror, he thought, and knew he needed to get her to open up to him and soon. He could feel something closing in on her and wanted to protect her as much as he could. He hadn't acknowledged it yet, not really, but he wanted to get to know her better. He just knew God had brought her to him for a reason.

Eavan finally stood, heading for her bedroom. Simon stood as well, his eyes following her before he looked down at Megan, whose hand was laid on his arm.

"Let her have a few moments, Simon. She needs that." Megan headed for the front of the shop, returned with Samuel's package, and then going back to the front as the door chimed for a customer.

Simon stirred his mug of tea absentmindedly, his thoughts on the lady he had just been holding to comfort. He sighed. Lord, I have no idea what I'm in for, but You do. Guide each step. Bring comfort to my lady love.

He turned as he heard a small sound behind him. Eavan stood there, almost shamefacedly facing him. He walked towards her, his finger going under her chin to tilt her face to him.

"Look at me, love." When she did, his heart broke at the devastation he saw resting in her eyes. "It's not your fault. None of this is. Your biological mother and her second husband made choices that were wrong and they alone have to answer for them." He pointed to the package. "Now, this. I understand Samuel has been around."

"How did you know? Did you talk to him?" Her voice was barely above a whisper.

He shook his head. "No, I saw him leaving. We need to talk, you and I. I have news other than what we've talked about."

Fear suddenly coursed through her. How did he find out, she wondered? How did he know what she was running from?

He tilted his head to watch the emotions flickering across her face and made a decision.

"Can your Gran run the shop for a couple of hours?"

She nodded. "Why?"

"Because you and I are going for a drive. Leave the package. You're not ready for that yet. I need to talk to you and I would rather your Gran didn't hear, not yet anyway."

She stood for a moment, rebellion rising within her, her eyes on his. He didn't force her, letting her make her choice. She sighed, knowing that she would go with him. She turned, and his hand came to stop her.

"Eavan, love, we don't have to. We can talk here, if you would rather. I won't force you to do anything you don't want to or are not comfortable doing."

She turned as he spoke, searching his face, seeing he spoke from his heart. His heart was in his eyes, without him knowing she could see it. She finally nodded and moved to hug him.

Simon stood for a moment, before he reached for his jacket and shrugged into it, reaching for his keys. He headed to the front, watching as Megan dealt with the customers who had come in, her voice low and pleasant. He waved as she turned, holding up his keys and pointing towards the living quarters. She nodded, then her attention was back on her customer.

Eavan watched as Simon drove away from Mistletoe, not quite sure where he was heading, but feeling safe for the first time in years. Whoever it was that had haunted her seemed so far away today, but she knew that person was still out there, somewhere.

"Eavan?" He glanced at her, not quite sure where her thoughts were.

"Simon? Where are we heading?"

"To Merryville. There's a spot there I think you'll like. I'll bring you back one day and you can bring your camera. Right now, it's the most peaceful spot I can think of. Mistletoe is getting busy, leading up to the tree lighting this Saturday."

"Is that why? I wondered." She watched carefully as he pulled into a parking lot and then came around to open her door, his hand out to help her from the car.

He didn't let go on her hand as he walked them towards a gazebo set in the middle of a park. He searched the area, knowing an officer was patrolling there, having been requested. He sat Eavan down on the bench and then sat beside her, leaning forward with his arms on his thighs, his eyes on the ground.

"Simon?" Eavan's soft voice reached him but he didn't turn to look at her. He felt her hand on his back and finally straightened up, his eyes on her face. Lord, I need words and I don't have them.

"Eavan. I need to talk to you and suddenly I just don't have the words." He searched his mind but couldn't find them. "I really do need to talk to you."

She began to laugh, drawing a frown from him. "That was just so definite, Simon. What is it about? Start there."

He sighed, his arm suddenly going around her and drawing her close to him, surprise on her face at his movement.

"Who's chasing you, love? I know someone is."

"And how would you know that?" She was startled at how easily he went straight to the heart of her troubles.

"I was an MP in the forces, a police officer now. I've learned to read people. You're running. Run to me, please, Eavan. Let me help you."

She finally nodded, her eyes searching his before she turned to stare across the park, a frown now in place.

"I'm still not sure how you knew, Simon, but you're right. For the last ten years, someone has been tracking me. That's why the website and the studio don't mention me by name. I use an alias. But somehow someone has found out the alias and is taunting me. I have no idea why. His taunts are now turning to threats. I haven't shared them with anyone. I can't tell Gran. I haven't felt comfortable in going to the police. I did when it first started and it was brushed aside and I was made to feel that I was making it all up."

"You're not. You never have been. Walk be back through what has happened, starting at the very beginning." He pulled out a notebook and pen.

She missed his arm around her when he moved and wondered at that. "Okay. Let's see. This is hard, Simon." A distressed look covered her face but she refused to cry. She had wept enough over the situation, she refused to weep any more. Lord, is Simon the one? Is he the one who will stop this maniac and his threats? I can handle the threats directed at me, but now that he's going after Gran, I need to stop him.

"I know it is, love, but we need to go back to the very beginning. I know you don't want your grandmother to hear, that's a given."

She nodded, then began to speak, taking him back to the beginning of her troubles, back to when she was just seventeen and starting out with her photography. She paused intermittently to gather her thoughts, to go back over something with him, willing to answer any question he posed, and he didn't ask many, just let her talk.

———

353

Simon read back through his notes, a chill running through him. Whoever this was, he or she was getting more and more vicious and threatening more and more violence. How Eavan had survived this long, he had no idea.

He looked across the park, gathering his thoughts, a frown coming to his face as he saw movement. He rose abruptly, pulling Eavan to her feet and placing himself between what he had seen and her.

"Simon?" Her voice was questioning, but he could see the fright coming into her face.

"Someone is out there, love. An officer is responding. I made sure to have someone here on the perimeter. Let's go somewhere we can get warmed up."

He ushered into a restaurant and to a booth at the back, to the seat facing the front of the building, and sliding in beside her.

She looked at him and then pointed to the seat across from them. "You could sit there, you know. It's empty."

Simon laughed. "I could, but I would rather sit here. They have to get through me to get to you, this way."

She stared at him, disbelief and then fear on her face. He hated that. He wanted this all over for her. He gave their orders and she wondered that he ordered a coffee, when they both drank tea. Her eyes on him, she didn't see the man approaching their booth, who stopped, a hand going to his mouth for a moment as he worked to control his emotions.

Simon looked up and nodded, drawing Eavan's eyes to the man. She watched as he finally slid into the booth across from them, his eyes on her, his mouth working as he tried to speak and was unable to.

"Eavan. I'm sorry to surprise you like this, but I needed help, and this man is the one, the best one, who can." He turned to the man, who nodded, giving his agreement to the unasked question.

"Eavan. This is Old Jack as he is known in town. But he is your Uncle Ben, your biological father's brother. He has information that we need and he has agreed to help."

Shocked beyond what she had ever been, Eavan stared at the older man, not quite sure how to respond. She watched as the man blinked back tears, compassion flowing through her.

"Hi. I'm not quite sure what to say." Eavan looked at Ben and then up at Simon, who sat quietly beside her, a small smile on his face, acceptance on his face. "I never knew. I'm sorry."

"That's okay, girl." Ben's voice was rough with emotion. "I know it's not your fault. It's your biological mother's fault, that's where the fault lies. But you're here now." He paused, reaching for his handkerchief to wipe at his eyes, then reached for the coffee Simon had ordered him.

He finally looked back at Eavan, seeing the tears sparkling on her lashes. "It's like this, girl. Your daddy told me that he had found out he had another daughter, that your mother had given up for adoption as soon as she was born. She had left town before he ever knew that you were on the way. He had finally confronted her, gotten her confirmation, and told me he was heading off to find out about you. He was killed one week later."

She nodded. "Simon mentioned that. But I don't see what that has to do with what I'm going through now."

Ben lifted a hand, silencing her. "I'm coming to that. Hold your horses, girl." He shot a quick look at Simon who was trying to hold back his laughter. "Silence, boy." He shook his head.

"But I'm afraid I still don't understand. How did he not know?"

"That I am afraid we'll never know. I've been and talked to her in prison. She just sits there, stone faced, not saying a word."

"She's in prison?"

Simon spoke up. "She is. She was charged with abuse and murder as well as attempted murder. She tried to kill Julia."

Eavan's breath sucked in so quickly she choked. When she could breathe again, she stared between the two men, seeing confirmation and compassion their faces

Her eyes traced to the front window and she froze. "Simon. He's out there. In that black truck."

Simon followed her line of sight. "You're sure?" When she nodded, he rose, grabbing his jacket. "Ben, stay with her."

Simon was out the door and approaching the truck before she could stop him. She glared at Ben, motioning him to follow Simon.

"Not happening, girl. He left me to watch you. He's a big boy. He can take care of himself."

"Not with the one who is after me. I'm afraid he'll get hurt." She looked up in alarm as she heard squealing tires and shouts from the street, on her feet and running for the door before Ben could stop her. He sighed, grabbed her jacket, even as he dropped money on the table, and ran after her. I'm getting too old for this, Lord. Would you be so kind as to settle all these young ones down?

He searched for Eavan, finding her on her knees beside Simon's still body, her hands assessing him even as she spoke with the officer kneeling across from her.

"Here, girl. On your feet. The paramedics are here. Let them work." Ben drew her to her feet, shoving her arms into her jacket, and then standing with an arm around her. "We'll follow them to the hospital."

He turned as he heard his name called and saw Simon's commanding officer approaching him.

"Old Jack? What happened? Someone said Simon was run down."

Ben nodded grimly. "First, let me correct you. The name's really Ben Bronagh. I've been living undercover for a while now." He nodded towards where they were still assessing Simon, pulling out the neck brace and the backboard. "He was run down. He's helping this young lady and he came out to talk to someone she recognized as being after her."

The man stared at Eavan for a moment. "That's not Blackie's Julia, now is it?"

Ben shook his head. "We've just found out it's her younger sister. That's not for common knowledge yet." He tightened his hold on Eavan as she went to move towards the ambulance. "They won't let you ride with him, girl."

The officer with them shook his head. "Let her go. I'll clear it for her. If what you say is true, then we'll need to provide protection for them while they're here." He was as good as his word. "Now, where is Simon's vehicle? I have his keys and will have it taken to his home. He won't be driving it, not today."

Eavan was scrambling into the back of the ambulance before anyone could say a word, tucking herself back into a corner out of the way, her eyes on Simon. She hated that he had been hurt because of her. Or was it? She really wasn't sure. Not any more.

She followed the stretcher as it was wheeled into the Emergency Department, coming to a stop near the head of it, refusing to move when she was asked to leave the room.

Ben finally found her and arm around her, pulled her from the room and out to a chair, where he gently pushed her down, sitting beside her.

"Let them work on him, girl. They'll come get you." He nodded towards the rooms. "What did you tell them to make them let you stay?"

She shook her head, her eyes not leaving the hallway. "I didn't say anything. I think they thought I was his girlfriend or something."

"That would be about right." He looked around, knowing that Julia and Blackie were on their way. The other two couples had been away for the day together and weren't expected back until later. He hesitated as he saw the man approaching him.

Why now, Lord? I have to have time to prepare him and now I don't.

"Uncle Ben? I heard Simon was brought in. What happened?" Jonathan Bronagh stood there, worry on his face.

"He was, son. That he was. We're waiting on word now."

Jonathan looked around, not recognizing anyone else. "We? Who's we?" He looked up, stepping back as Eavan approached them. "Uncle Ben? Who is this?"

Eavan stared at the younger man, seeing traces of her own features in him. Ben's arm came around her and he pointed them towards a seating area away from the others.

"Jonathan, this is not how I wanted to do this. Simon was to speak with you." Ben looked down at his clasped hands. "You know what your father had discovered and didn't get a chance to investigate." He nodded towards Eavan. "This is the baby that your mother gave away. This is your youngest sister, Eavan Walker. She was adopted when a week old and just in the last few days has found out who her biological parents are."

Jonathan sat back, stunned at the revelation. He turned to Eavan, seeing her sitting there composed. As he went to speak to her, she rose and walked away, towards the nurse heading her way and then following her from the waiting room.

"Uncle Ben? How?"

"I don't know all that happened. Simon knows more. Someone is after her, though. We think that it is why he was run down today."

Jonathan shook his head, reaching for the young woman who sank down beside him. Ben reached over to drop a kiss on Jonathan's wife, Bev's, cheek.

A commotion at the door raised their hands. Jonathan groaned.

"Leave it to Julia to make an entrance." He rose and headed towards her, his steps slowing and finally stopping as he watched Julia head for the desk, her own footsteps stopping as she stared at the woman walking towards her. Julia's eyes followed her as the woman approached Ben.

"Uncle Ben? They've said Simon can go home in about an hour. Will you take us home? I heard the officer say he would have his car driven to his place."

Ben reached to hug Eavan, even as he agreed to drive her and Simon home. "Where's he going to go? They won't let him be on his own."

———

"I know. I called Gran. He'll be welcome to use our spare room for the next few days, if you can grab him some clothes." She stopped, suddenly feeling eyes on her, and turned, coming face to face with a young woman who almost looked like her twin.

They stared at each other, before Julia looked past Eavan to Ben.

"Uncle Ben? Who is this?"

Ben moved towards Julia, even as Blackie wrapped an arm around his wife. Eavan's heart sank, realizing who this and suddenly afraid, wishing with all her heart she had Simon beside her, to buffer this meeting.

"Julia. Keep your voice down, please." Ben stared at his niece until she looked shamefaced and nodded. "There is an explanation due to both you and Jonathan, but now is not the time or place. Suffice it to say, the baby your father wanted to look for is Eaven. This is your baby sister, the sister you always wanted."

Julia's face revealed her shock and puzzlement even as she felt Blackie's arm tighten around her.

"Let it go for now, Jewel. Simon or Ben will explain it all. Right now, Simon's the important one." Blackie's soft words settled Julia's emotions somewhat and she looked back at the young woman, who stood, apprehension on her face, before she turned and walked back towards the exam rooms.

Jonathan reached for his sister, drawing her into a hug, knowing just how this had affected her.

"Are you okay?" He finally asked, leaning back to look down at her.

"I think so. I didn't expect this." She turned with a frown. "But I don't understand how she's back there. Simon didn't say he was dating anyone."

Ben gave a wry grin as he turned her back to face him, moving Jonathan aside to do so. "For now, he is. We need to keep this as low key as we can and right now we're not. I would suggest you and Blackie and Jonathan and Bev head out. I'll call you tomorrow. Take tonight to pray, Julia, about this and your attitude." He gave her a stern look until she nodded.

Blackie waved as he headed off with Julia, her hand tight in his. This was not what either had expected when they showed up here.

"Julia?" Blackie was concerned about her.

"It will take time to sink in, love. I just never expected to have a sister."

"I know. Now, let's do what Ben said. I think we'll need to let him or Simon talk to Jacob and Josh. It's their place, not ours."

Simon settled down carefully onto the bed, nodding as Ben lifted his feet to the bed and then pulled the covers over him. Simon was sore and had a wicked headache, but all things considered, he thought, I came off fortunate.

———

"Eavan's okay?" He was concerned as he watched Ben fold his shirt and jeans and lay them handy for the morning.

"She is, son, but she's scared. She's ready to do something she shouldn't, I think."

Ben stood for a moment, then sank down into a chair. "I know you're hurting, but we need to talk, son. Julia and Jonathan both showed up at the hospital, and met Eavan. Not at all how it should have been."

Simon sighed. "I know. I wanted to prepare them. Now we'll need to warn Blackie to watch Julia. They look enough alike that they may take Julia by mistake."

"That's what I'm thinking." Ben suddenly grinned, causing Simon to frown at him. "Did you know Eavan let on that she was your girlfriend at the hospital? The nurses assumed that she was, she just wouldn't leave you."

"She didn't, did she?" He stared at Ben for a moment, dumbfounded. "And Julia walked in on that, didn't she?"

Ben nodded, knowing what Simon was thinking. "Blackie will talk to her. All she knows is that she suddenly has a sister and nothing more." He looked up as a tap came to the door and then rose and opened it.

Eavan stood there, hesitating, a tray in her hands that she shoved at Ben. "Gran thought Simon might want some soup or tea or something. She thought he'd need something on his tummy, as she put it, when he took his pain medications." She waited until Ben had taken the tray she kept shoving at him before she turned and fled. He watched as the door to her studio closed quietly behind her, shaking his head as he did so.

"Ben?"

Ben turned, coming over to set the tray down. "You'll have to eat something of that, you know, son."

Simon nodded, hardly able to keep his eyes open. "Let me have a moment, please. Watch Eavan. I have no idea what she'll try. I don't know her well enough…" His words died off as he slept.

Ben stood for a moment, watching him sleep, before he picked up the tray and headed for the kitchen. He cleaned up the dishes and then turned, startled to see Eavan standing there, a look on her face he couldn't read.

"Uncle Ben? Talk to me. Tell me what happened. Why I was given up."

Ben sighed to himself. He was exhausted but he knew his day was far from over. This young lady needed answers, some he had, more that he didn't have.

Simon stared at Megan late the next morning, not quite sure he had heard her right

"She did what? She went where?"

"What I said, young man. Now, sit. Here's some soup for you. You're not to have anything solid for another day. That's what the doctor told Eavan."

He sat, mutiny in his heart, before he prayed, asking for forgiveness and a right heart.

"But where would she go?"

Megan shrugged. "I have no idea. She's an adult. She does not answer to me about her comings and her goings." She held up a hand to stop his protest. "She has done this all her life. When she needs to think, she grabs a camera and goes for a walk. Some of her best photos have come from those walks." She sat beside him, her hand just beginning to show the changes arthritis was wreaking in it on his, keeping his on the table. "You need to understand, Simon. She can't be caged. It would kill her. She was like that even as a toddler. Always up for an adventure. I can't begin to tell you the times her parents and I would search for her, to find her walking towards us, a flower or a leaf or a pretty rock in her hand. If you are going to be part of her life, let her have her freedom and solitude. It makes her who she is."

He nodded. "I get that. I'm just worried about her safety, that's all."

"We all are. Ben and I had a good talk this morning before he headed out. I know what she's facing here." She paused, her eyes on their hands as she squeezed his, a prayer in her heart for his understanding. She had seen the looks they were sending one another, each hoping the other wasn't watching them at the time. She could see them falling in love with each other more and more each day. Her prayer had become a prayer for peace for them, for them to realize how much they loved one another.

"But she's facing so much right now." Simon gave a small smile as Megan shook her head at him.

"I know what she's facing here in town, or some of it. I am also well aware of what she's been facing over the years. Whatever she received, I received." She rose, heading for her bedroom, returning with a large manilla envelope that she handed him. "This is for you. Look through it. Eavan has no idea I have these. Please, Simon. Keep her safe. For my sake, and for yours."

"I will do my best, Megan. Trust me on that." He looked down at the envelope, then reached to open it, her hand stopping him as he did so. "Don't open it here. Take it to the room you used, or wait until you go home today. Eavan doesn't need to see this."

He nodded once more, rising to put it with his bag that Ben had brought in for him. He turned as he heard Eavan's happy laughter and headed her way, desperate to see her. He smiled to himself as he thought of her pretending to be his girlfriend the day before. Suddenly, that was a wish he wanted to come true, that she really was his.

Eavan looked up as Simon appeared at the counter in the studio, her face alight with excitement.

"I did it again, Simon. I got another photo I've been trying to get for months." She danced towards him, enveloping him into a hug and holding on just a little bit longer. "How are you feeling today?"

"Sore. The headache better. Ticked off with a young lady." He tried to frown but was unsuccessful. "What photo is that?"

She caught his hand and drew him to the counter. "Here. See this? Someone wanted a close up of a certain type of snowflake. It's so hard to photograph a snowflake, but I did it."

He stared down at the photo, seeing her talent afresh. "You really did, didn't you?"

She nodded. "I did. Now, I just have to finish it off and send it to the client." She turned, her eyes on him. "We need to talk, Simon. I met both Jonathan and Julia last night. Neither one knew about me. I don't like that."

He held up his hands and then pointed at the photo. "Finish with that and then we'll talk. I promise. We didn't have time to talk to either one of them, remember?" His words at the end had a bite to them that drew her back, and then she nodded.

"I realize that, but that doesn't mean I still have to like it. I don't."

She turned and walked away from him, her mind already on her photo and what she needed to do it. Not much, she decided. She sighed as she sank down in front of the large monitor on her desk. Yes, Lord, I get it. I will apologize once again to Simon. I just don't know why I let him get to me like I do.

She finished her work, sent off the proof the client, and then sat back, a sense of foreboding once again coming over her. Lord, are you preparing me for something? I feel that You are, something dangerous and life threatening. I need Your strength and courage from You today.

Simon turned from the front window of her studio where he had stood, watchful for anyone or anything he felt was out of place. So far, he hadn't seen anything, but he knew someone was watching her. He had found evidence of that, as had Chief Waters. He had talked to the Chief earlier and brought him up to date on what was happening.

The Chief had listened to him, given some advice, and then asked what his plans were, since he was quitting the county force. He could use him on the town force, he hinted. Simon had just laughed, told him he was praying over a job offer, and that he wasn't leaving town. Not at all.

———

Eavan hesitated, then reached out a hand for Simon. Maggie had locked up and gone home, her day done, so it was just the two of them right then. She could heard her Gran in the kitchen, singing an old beloved hymn in her sweet alto, preparing their evening meal.

Simon drew Eavan into a hug, knowing both of them needed it. Eavan started and then wrapped her own arms around Simon, feeling safe and secure again. She finally moved back from him, her eyes going everywhere but to him.

"You wanted to talk, Simon?" She finally perched on the stool behind the counter, her hands idly tidying already neat piles of cards and samples of photos.

He reached for her hands, his warm and strong on hers, as he stilled her movements. She finally looked up at him, seeing his heart in his eyes and knowing he didn't realize it was there. She smiled and reached to kiss his cheek.

Simon froze for a moment, then nodded. "We do." He pulled up another stool, his hands going back to hold hers when he was settled. "Ben told me what happened at the hospital. He says you met both Jonathan and Julia."

"I did. I wasn't prepared for that, Simon. I was too worried about you to really take in that anyone else was there." She sighed. "I don't think I made a very good impression, taking over her Uncle Ben like I did, without her knowing. I was with Uncle Ben when he talked to Jonathan and his wife."

"His wife? Jonathan's married? He never said, but then he hasn't been around much for the last year."

"He is. Her name is Bev." Her eyes fell to their hands, as she tried to organize her thoughts. "I don't think Julia was very happy to find out about me."

Simon reached to hug her. "Oh, I think she was. She has wanted a sister so badly for so long. Jonathan left as soon as he could, I can't remember all the circumstances why. But Julia will be happy." He sighed, pulling out his phone. "I hate this. Every time I get into a really good conversation, my phone rings."

"That's why I don't carry one."

"You don't? From now on, you do. Give me yours later and I'll program in some numbers for you."

She nodded, then looked back at the desk, not quite sure how to start. "I don't know where to begin, Simon. I think I've shuttered it away, not wanting to face it."

He waited, letting her gather her thoughts, his experience being that any victim needed this time, a time to reflect and regroup.

"You said it started when you were 17? What triggered that, do you know?"

She shrugged. "I have no idea. I remember whoever it was said something about my photo. Did I pick up something I shouldn't have?"

362

Simon nodded. "You may have and not even known it. Do you have a copy of it?"

She spun on her stool, grabbed his hand and almost ran for her studio. She hunted through a filing cabinet, pulling out a folder, and opening it on the table in the room. "This is it. I have the negatives. I can enlarge it if I have to."

"We can scan it as well to your computer. The quality may not be the best but we can try. I can also take it to our lab or Chief Waters can do that." He studied the photo. "Do you have a magnifying glass?"

She hunted for one, handing it to him. She watched as he scanned the photo once more, stopping at a particular section.

"There, Eaven. There. That's what he's been after all these years. You did pick up on something without knowing it."

She stared at him, horrified at the thought. "What did I do?"

"Here. We'll need to enlarge it, but I think there's someone or something lying on the ground and someone standing in the shadows."

With trembling hand, she reached for the photo and then turned, determination in her stride, to her scanner, sending the photo to her computer. She sat, bringing up her photo program, and hunting for the area Simon had pointed to, enlarging it.

"You're right. I never noticed this before. I was too focused on the overall picture." She printed copies on the enlargement, pulling them off the printer and handing them to Simon. "Now what? Is this what all this has been about?"

Simon shrugged. "I think it's part of it. But I also think someone has watched you since you were a baby, trying to figure out how to get the property that comes to you."

"What property? I have no interest in anything other than what I have." She was shocked, having forgotten what Simon had told her.

"You're part of this town, love, whether you admit it or not. And as such, as a descendant of the founding families, you have property and money coming to you."

"I don't want it."

Simon grinned at her. "I hate to tell you this, but this building? It's actually yours. Ben checked into it today for me."

She stared at him, then went to the door of the office to stare around the studio. "This is mine?" She spun. "So I can do what I want, remodel it how I want to?"

He nodded, grinning at the excitement he could see coming from her, reaching to hug her tightly as she sputtered out plans. He leaned back to look down at her, seeing her heart in her eyes, and knowing he had found his lady, his love, that God had provided for him after all, after all those years.

———

"I hear tell you let on you were my girlfriend yesterday." He grinned as she struggled to get away from him, holding on tighter. "I just want you to know that is what I want too. I want you to be my girlfriend for now. And then we'll see from there. Will you?"

She stared up at him, realizing that as tall as she was for a lady, he was still a lot taller and that she fit just right into his arms. "I guess....I guess." Her words sputtered to a stop as his body shook with his suppressed laughter. "Stop laughing at me, Simon. I can't think with you this close."

"Well, then I guess I'll have to stay this close. I like it when you can't think." He grinned at her as she shook her head.

"What I was trying to say is that yes, I would be delighted to be your girlfriend, unless you don't let me go. Then I'll start calling you an oaf again."

He laughed at her words. "I could get used to that term of endearment. Now, Gran has supper ready, I can tell. Let's go eat. Then I need to head off."

Chapter 8

Simon looked up from his office in Samuel's building as Samuel tapped at his door and then entered, closing the door behind him before he sank into one of the chairs in front of Simon's desk. It had been four days since Simon had been run down and the police were no closer to finding his assailant that they had been that day.

"Simon? I ran that photo you provided. You will not like the name I came up with."

Simon sat back, his pen rolling in his fingers. "Somehow I didn't think I would."

"Your girlfriend has been fortunate so far that she's stayed out of his hands. Not knowing has been to her advantage. Now that she knows he's in that photo, it will be worse for her."

Simon nodded. "Just who are we talking about?"

When Samuel said the name, Simon paled, his pen dropping to his desktop. "I thought he was dead."

"He is, but his son has taken on his holdings and is even more vicious and dangerous than his father. Law enforcement all over are looking for him. They want him for more offences than you can name. They think somehow he's situated himself here in Mistletoe or in the area around here."

"And Eavan moved here. Is that a coincidence? I don't think so. Gran said it was suggested to her that Eavan move here but she can't remember who suggested it. I'll ask her again." He looked down at the paperwork he had been perusing when Samuel interrupted him. "I've been working on Eavan's past. I don't like what I'm finding. Her father somehow was connected to that name."

"I was afraid of that. How deep was he?"

"Not deep. I'm sure he didn't know who he was working for. It was a shell company, so he likely never knew the names. It would seem he was on the legitimate side of the company, which is good news for Eavan."

"That's a blessing then, Simon. Now, how do we keep your lady and her Gran safe?"

Simon shot Samuel a quick look at that, but saw only concern on his face. "I have no idea, Samuel. It's going to be difficult as Eavan will just take off looking for photos. And she refuses to carry a phone. She says she can't when she's out looking for nature photos. Even the vibration may be enough to chase away the perfect shot."

"That's not good. Stay with her as much as you can. You need to get through to her somehow."

———

365

"I know I do, but we're nowhere near that, Samuel. I can't claim all her time."

"I think you can. I was watching her without either of you knowing it. I've seen her around you. I've seen the way she looks at you, watches you when she thinks you're not looking, that no one can see her. She looks at you with her heart in her eyes and on her face." Samuel paused, letting Simon absorb what he had said. "What I'm saying, Simon, is this. She looks at you as if you're the treasure she's been seeking all her life, after God that is. Don't play with her. Take her trust and build from there." He stood, gathering his thoughts.

Simon waited, knowing his friend had something to add. He took what Samuel said to him gracefully, knowing that was how he felt about Eavan and not quite sure how to continue.

"I see how you watch her, Simon. You haven't seen me behind you when you're looking for her, even though she's not in the crowd. The boys have mentioned that something is different about you right now. This is what it is."

Simon nodded. "I know, Samuel. I hear what you're saying. She is my treasure, my heart. I just don't know how to approach her."

Samuel laughed. "This uncertainty, coming from you, Simon?" He took pity on his friend. "You have seen how Levi is with his Julia, Jacob with Finn, Josh with Leah, Jeremiah with Joy. They all want you to find someone to complete your life. Eavan may be that. She may not be. Be prepared in the event that she does walk away. I sense she has issues that she needs to work through. Not the least is that of her heritage."

Samuel stood for a moment, his eyes on his young friend, his heart lifting in prayer, before he walked away, leaving Simon staring after him.

Simon stared at the closed door, then looked back down at his paperwork, immersing himself in it once more. He finally threw down his pen. He needed a break from this, he had found out too much information that he didn't need to know. He sighed, knowing at some point that day he would need to speak with Samuel, and then Chief Ed Waters of town.

He rose, his feet taking him towards Eavan's studio. He entered, not seeing her, and heading for the living quarters, meeting Megan coming towards him.

"Simon. I didn't expect to see you today." She reached to hug him, considering him family all ready.

"I didn't expect to be here. Is Eavan here?"

Megan shook her head. "No, she's not. She took her camera and said she was heading out about town, needing some urban photos. I'm really not sure where you'd find here." She watched as disappointment flickered across Simon's face.

"So I guess there's not much point in waiting, is there?" He started to laugh, sputtering out an apology.

"So I'm not company enough, is that what you're saying?" Megan laughed at the consternation on his face.

"No, that's not what I meant." He reached to hug her once more. "I'm just worried about Eavan."

"I know you are. Go and find her. Come back for dinner when you have."

Simon searched the stores and shops on the main street, then stood, uncertainty in his manner as to where to look next. He headed towards the park where the tree was waiting to be lit on Saturday for the commencement of the Christmas festivities. Somehow he knew he'd find her there.

A sharp cry caught his attention and he spun, then ran towards the gazebo, sliding to a halt just out of sight. Eavan was there, struggling to release her arm from the heavyset man who held her, her foot coming back to kick him in the shin. He gave a sharp yell, his hand releasing her as he reached for the shin. She spun and ran, heading right for Simon, who caught her in his arms and then headed around the gazebo, her hand tight in his as they ran. He heard the yell of outrage behind him.

He pulled Eavan into his arms once more as he stopped behind a large tree, their breaths coming in heavy gasps. He searched her face, seeing the fear on it, and hating that for her.

He listened as he heard the man running by him, his voice calling for Eavan, saying he would find her and she would regret what she had just done.

Simon waited, finally peeking around the tree and searching the area. He looked down at the lady in his arms and hurt for her. She had finally buried her face against him, fear still shaking her.

"Eavan? Come on, love. Let's get you out of here."

She nodded, finally looking up at him. "I can't go back to the studio but I need to." Somehow, in all that she still had her camera. "I need to process these today." She was hesitant as to what she should do, not at all like her usual decisive self.

Simon watched her face, seeing that for once she needed someone else make a decision for her. He reached to kiss her cheek, her hand coming to the spot, her eyes open in wonder as she stared at him.

"Come on, then, love. Let's get you home and to your studio. I need to talk to you at some point anyway."

"But what about your work? Won't Samuel tell you to go back to the office?"

Simon grinned as he led her away from the trees and back to the centre of town. "Nope. He told me to go find you."

Simon watched as Eavan sorted through the photos, selecting the ones she wanted to work on, and then lost her as she became absorbed in her work. He looked around as Megan tapped at the door and then entered, rising to take the tray from her.

"Eavan. You need to eat something. Come on, love. Set your work aside for a few moments."

Eavan finally heard Simon's voice and looked up, surprised that he was still there. "You stayed?"

"I did. Where else would I be?" He watched as her face softened and then she reached to hug him.

"Thank you. Anyone else would have left by now."

"I find it fascinating what you do. Talk to me about it."

She shrugged. "There's not really much I can say. The programs I use are great. Someone has done a lot of work there that makes my work easier." She paused to bite into her sandwich, chewing and then swallowing. "But you wanted to talk to me. What about?"

Simon wiped his mouth with the cloth napkin Megan had provided, his eyes on it as he fingered the softness of it, trying to gather his thoughts. They always seemed to disappear or disintegrate when he was near Eavan.

"Samuel has come up with a name. Someone your father worked for." He held up his hand as she went to speak. "Just let me say my piece. I only want to say it once and then we'll talk. Samuel's willing to meet with us."

Eavan sat back when Simon finished speaking, shock on her face. "He found out all that. He's good. But how much had you found out?"

"I wasn't looking into that. I was looking at your high school classmates, your college classmates, that kind of things. The teachers, professors."

She shivered. "I don't like that there is so much out there about me. I want to stay private and I can't, now can I?" She sighed. "Now what, Simon? How do I stay safe? I know that's what you're planning."

He nodded. "I am. Listen, come with me tonight. My friends and I meet for a Bible study tonight and I would love to have you join us."

She stared at him for a moment, before she nodded. "I guess. I've already been thrown into the deep end without warning. May as well go out further into the lake."

Simon laughed hard at her phrasing. "Out deeper, you say? Then you'll need someone close to rescue you. Let it be me, please?" His laughter had turned to a gentle smile as he traced a finger down her cheek.

She nodded, not looking at him. "How dressed up is this meeting anyway?"

"Not dressy. We'll be meeting at Jeremiah and Joy's tonight. He's our pastor but Joy is twin to Josh. Joy's parents are away so they can't watch the little girls."

"Gran told me about them, how they were adamant they were sitting with you on Sunday. Be careful there, Simon."

"I always am, love. Those two little girls are so precious."

She clasped his hand tight later as they walked up to the front door of a house. She was really apprehensive, not sure what her reception would be. She still saw Julia's face from the other day, the shock on it. Simon stopped her, drawing her into a hug before he spoke.

"They will not bite you. I will leave with you if there is anything negative or you feel uncomfortable at any time."

"You can't do that. They're your friends." Eavan was shocked at his words.

"I can and I will. Tonight, you are the most important thing to me, right after God. Do you understand, Eavan?" He waited for her nod, feeling her hair brush against his chin. "I mean exactly what I said. I will leave and they will understand completely if I do. That's the kind of friends they are."

He turned as he heard the door open and Jeremiah stood there, waiting to welcome them.

"Are we going in or are we leaving? The choice is yours and yours alone. I will not force you to do something you're not ready to do yet."

She finally stepped back, her eyes searching his, seeing the sincerity and determination to please her in them. She turned to the door, seeing Jeremiah standing there, waiting for them.

"I'm sorry. I've kept you waiting."

Jeremiah grinned as he reached to shake her hand, then take her jacket as Simon helped her slip it off. "Not at all. We haven't got started yet. Joy is having trouble getting the girls to bed. They know Simon's coming tonight and for some reason they won't settle until he says good night to them."

Simon started to laugh. "Sure, make me the scapegoat for disobedience, Jeremiah. Is everyone else here?"

Jeremiah shook his head. "Julia and Blackie are running late. She called with some excuse that I can't remember off hand."

Simon laughed again. "That's not you. You know exactly why they're late. Now, where are your girls?" He turned as he heard the patter of bare feet running towards him, and he bent to pick up the two girls.

"Simon, you came. Read story." Holly was adamant that Simon would read the bedtime story that night.

"Not tonight, sweetness. I have a friend I can't leave on her own."

Heidi peeked over her shoulder at Eavan and waved. "She can come listen to it. We'll let her."

Joy choked on the laughter she was trying to keep from bursting forth. "Say good night, girls. Then, it is off to bed with you. Now, please."

Simon watched as the girls clung to their mother's hands, skipping along happily beside her. He shook his head as he turned to find Eavan's eyes on him, laughter brimming in them.

"I think you have a new name."

"And that would be?"

"The Pied Piper, Simon."

Jeremiah howled with laughter at that as they walked into the sunroom where the other two couples were waiting, Josh and Jacob standing as they saw Eavan.

"Up to no good again, are you, Simon?" Josh laughed at the look Simon shot him.

"Me? Never. Now you, that's another story." Simon laughed at the choruses of agreement from the two women, turning as he felt someone behind him, to find Blackie and Julia standing there.

Eavan stood quietly, feeling very much alone and out of place, knowing the people here had been friends for years and she was the outsider.

Julia stopped, her eyes on Eavan's face as she seemed about ready to run from the room, and then approached her, her hands reaching for Eavan's.

"I owe you a huge apology. I was just so taken aback the other night, I didn't act like I normally would. Welcome to Mistletoe. Welcome to the family."

Eavan stared at Julia, seeing how glad Julia seemed to be to have her there. "Thank you, I think." She shot Simon a glare as he laughed quietly before he came to stand beside her, his arm going around her, bringing comfort and peace to her.

"No. I really mean it. I always wanted a sister, always felt there was someone else belonging to Jonathan and I out there. Uncle Ben we discovered just about two years ago now. I had known him for years, never knowing he was my uncle. That's how much he had to keep it quiet." She leaned back against Blackie, emotions getting the better of her for a moment.

"Then, thank you, Julia. I appreciate your words." She looked back at Simon, seeing his nod of approval before looking back at Julia. "Gran said she met you on Sunday. That she heard your voice and thought I was there."

"You two do sound somewhat alike, but you have a different lilt to your voice." Leah walked over and hugged Eavan, taking her by surprise. "Welcome to our family, Eavan. Did I say it right? I've been practicing but wasn't sure. I'm a cousin of sorts, related to both Finn and Julia, and now you. This is great. Another female cousin I can do things with."

Josh had approached as well, reaching out to shake Eavan's hand, seeing how overwhelmed she was. "I'm Josh, Leah's husband. Some day, we'll tell you all about how Leah discovered her roots here in town."

"You mean you're not from here?"

Leah shook her head. "Nope. I'm from the other coast or rather was." She turned to Jacob and Finn. "This is Finn and Jacob. Finn has the antiquities' store in town. I hear you're a photographer. She has a really neat display of old cameras and whatnot. You might be interested in that. And this is her husband, Jacob."

They finally sat, Eavan tight to Simon, his arm around her for reassurance, as they started their Bible study. Eavan was surprised that Jeremiah, as the pastor, didn't lead it, but rather Josh did.

Walking out with the group, Eavan suddenly shivered and looked around. Someone was watching her, she could tell,. Just who, she didn't know, but she felt the oncoming danger and knew she had no way to avoid it, not now. She just prayed that Simon would not be around when it hit, knowing he would take the brunt of whatever happened for her.

Josh was watching her, seeing her glancing around, and then looked around himself, knowing what she was feeling. He would need to talk to Simon, he decided, at some point in the next few days. Little did he know he would not have an opportunity before danger struck, involving not just Eavan.

Eavan looked up from the studio counter, surprised to see the three woman who walked through her door. She watched as they circled the room, studying her photos before Julia approached her.

"Eavan, forgive us for just dropping in. We've been passing this studio for days now, saying we needed to pop in, not realizing it was yours."

Eavan smiled. "No one does, not unless they're told. I've done that on purpose, to keep my personal and professional lives separate."

"Simon told us about the mouse photo. I would love to see it sometime." Leah had approached. "I didn't know it was you Mom had hired to take Rebecca's pictures. We are always asked who the photographer is, they are just exquisite. You captured her so perfectly."

Eavan blushed. "Thank you. She was so precious to photograph. Now, what can I get you ladies? Gran's out, Maggie's not due in today, so it's just me. I have tea, I think coffee, juice, water."

"We're fine, Eavan. It's you we came to see." Finn had walked up to the counter as well. "Any chance you could get away for lunch?"

Eavan shook her head. "Unfortunately, not today. I have to stay here, I think."

"Well, in that case, I'll be right back." Leah headed for the door.

Finn and Julia started to laugh at the look on Eavan's face.

"Don't worry. She's just heading to Josh's restaurant and will be back with lunch for us." Finn took pity on Eavan. "Josh owns The House."

"Oh, he does? We love his food, Gran and I, when we do dine out and that's not often."

Eavan looked up later, her attention briefly distracted from the conversation going on around her. She frowned as she heard the door click in the back of building, then shrugged, thinking it was Gran that had come back earlier than she had planned. Her attention was caught again by Finn's words.

Julia looked up at a sound, fear suddenly showing on her face, as she shoved back her chair and rose. The other three women were startled and then spun as a male voice could be heard.

"So, I finally catch you, Eavan Walker. It's taken years." The man standing near her was younger, but heavy, a weapon held in his right hand trained on her.

Eavan's heart quaked within her, recognizing one of the voices that had tormented her for so many years. Lord, protect these ladies with me. I don't care about me, but don't let any harm come to them.

"Jeff Young. So it's been you all along. Where's your boss? Or are you acting on your own?"

A cruel laugh exploded from him as another man entered the studio and stood just inside the door, his own weapon trained on the women.

Lord, we could use some help right about now, Eavan prayed, but it looks as if it's just us and them. Guide me, Lord, in what I need to do. Grant me the courage and strength to win over this monster. Keep the ladies safe and unharmed.

She listened to the man rant and rave, knowing he was speaking for his employer, a man she had never met but who had made her life miserable for years. At least, that's who she thought it had been.

She finally saw an opportunity, a crack in his demeanour, a chance she just had to take. She shared a look with Leah, who nodded. Of all the women, Leah seemed to understand her the best. Perhaps it was because of what she had been through, but she knew what it was like to be uncertain, to not know who her own family was.

She rose and began to pace her studio, seeming not to watch the man, but keeping her eye on him. He turned to follow her, his weapon now down at his side, his finger off the trigger. She shot a glance at the man near the door and saw his weapon had been holstered, which didn't make a lot of sense. Not unless they were waiting for someone to come, and just who that was, she had no idea and had no intention of letting in the studio.

She turned once more, finding him close to her. His hand came out and struck her across the face, drawing blood from her lip and leaving a red mark on her cheek. She blinked back tears before her eyes shot to the women, watching them closely, seeing Leah's nod. She spun, her booted foot shooting out to connect with the side of his knee, bringing a loud cry from him as they heard cracking of bones and saw him fall, his weapon dropping from his head and sliding a few feet away. Eavan dove for the weapon, grasping it before she rose, training it on the man near the door, who had pulled his own weapon, directing it at her. She waited, not sure for what, seeing Leah standing with her foot ground onto the man's hand, her full weight on his fingers, as he shouted and screamed for her to move. Julia had her phone out, calling for help, even as Finn stood, watching, ready to step in where she needed to.

Finn watched in fascination as a heavy oak walking stick cracked down on the man's wrist, sending his weapon flying, and heard his screams of pain. Megan appeared behind him, brandishing the walking stick.

"That will teach you, you ruffian. Don't ever think you'll get away with threatening my granddaughter or her friends." She peered around him at Eavan. "You're okay, love?"

"I am, Gran, thanks to you. Ladies, meet my Gran. Gran, Leah, Julia and Finn there by the door. Where did you come from anyway?"

"God told me I needed to come home, so I did. I cut my shopping short, and now thanks to these two ruffians, I'll be needing to go out again to finish."

"Not today, Gran. Not today. You'll not be allowed to."

Finn spun as the door was flung open and heavily armed police officers swarmed in. Once they had been assured the women were safe, the men were handcuffed, before the paramedics were allowed in. Ed Waters directed them to the women first, despite the complaints of the two men.

"You'll be looked at. The women come first." Ed studied the five women, his eyes lingering on Eavan, before he nodded. He knew her, he thought, but how he couldn't quite remember. He would, likely the memory waking him up in the middle of the night.

One by one, the woman gave their statements and were then escorted from the building, their eyes searching for their husbands standing behind the police lines, their steps breaking into a run before they were caught in their men's arms and then hurried away by the police.

Simon stood, waiting, fear running through him as the paramedics were in no hurry to come out. He watched as men in handcuffs were led from the building, his attention going back to the door. Finally Tom, an officer he knew well, approached him.

"Simon? The chief asked if you would come with me." He smiled at the apprehension on Simon's face. "It's okay. Your lady's fine. She's just finishing up her statement as is her grandmother." He pointed. "There. Her grandmother is done. The chief said Jeremiah or Samuel would take care of her."

Simon stopped by Megan, before hugging her, smiling briefly at her complaints.

"I have groceries I need to put away, Simon. Will you look after that for me? And they tell me we can't come back tonight. That's not suitable."

"Don't worry, Megan. Samuel here will look after you. His wife will make sure you have what you need."

She grumbled as Samuel tucked her arm into his elbow and led her away, the police tape lifting briefly to let them through.

Simon stood in the door of the studio, seeking the disarray from the afternoon, the photos that had been torn from the wall, the glass and frames smashed. He saw the remnants of the women's lunches dropped on the hardwood floor. He saw the debris from the paramedics as they had treated the wounded men. Who he did not see was Eavan, but he could hear her, her voice calm but taut.

Tom nodded to him as he moved. "Go on back, Simon. She's just finishing up. She needs you, the chief says, and the chief is never wrong."

———

Simon gave a small tight smile even as he headed for the living quarters, sidestepping the techs at work. He would need to find cleaners, he decided, not wanting either Megan or Eavan to clean up the mess.

He stood, his eyes on his lady, seeing the stress and strain she had been under. He couldn't see her face, but her stance as she stood talking with the chief said more than she could.

She finally turned, and he drew in his breath sharply, seeing the bruising on her face, the blood from the cut on her swollen lip.

Eavan stood, shocked to see Simon standing there, but glad, knowing he was just who she needed. She ignored the chief as she swiftly crossed to Simon, to be enveloped in a hard tight hug, one that said he would never let her go and that he was sorry he had not been there.

She didn't hear his quiet words to the chief or the chief's response, just felt him as he shifted to draw off his coat and wrap it around her, his arm around her as well as he led her through the back door and down the streets at the back, her steps stumbling at times. He finally sighed, swept her into his arms and headed for Samuel's place, just a few blocks away.

Blackie's mother, Miriam, waited at the door, her arms going out to hug Eavan. She turned, her arm still around the younger woman.

"Come, love. Let's get you cleaned up. Rachel or Rebecca will have some clothes that will fit you. They're tall like you are. Simon, Samuel's in the kitchen with Megan."

Simon watched as Eavan looked back at him, fear on her face. He nodded towards Miriam.

"She'll take care of you. Trust her. She's been through this with Blackie and Julia."

"You have?" Eavan's attention went to Miriam.

"I have, and I pray that I don't have to with my two girls. My heart just can't take that."

Simon stood for a moment, gathering his thoughts. He grew determined in what he needed to do. Now he just had to convince Eavan of what he wanted. Lord, don't let me rush ahead of You. That I do not want to do. Guide my steps and my words.

Simon was on a hunt a few hours later. Even though it was early, Megan had declared she had had enough excitement for the day and retired. Rachel and Rebecca had moved in together for the next few days, something they were willing and glad to do for their Simon, as they called him, thinking of him as a beloved big brother. Eavan had been avoiding him since they had eaten and he wanted to know why.

"Eavan? What's wrong, love?" Simon stood in front of her where she stood near the French doors of the sun room. "Talk to me."

"I have to leave, Simon. I brought this trouble to your friends. They could have been killed because of me."

"No one blames you, love. No one at all. They know where the blame lies and it isn't with you." He moved closer, his hands on her upper arms. "Please, don't leave. My heart couldn't take it if you did."

She shook her head, sorrow on her face. "I have to, Simon. I can't have someone hurt because of me."

"I can tell you right now someone would be hurt if you do leave. I would be. My heart would never recover." He reached to draw her close, finding her resisting him, and sighed. His hand came up to cup her cheek, his thumb lightly touching the cut on her lip. "I hate that he did this to you. And it wasn't even the one after you. Just one of his henchman."

"His top one, I would imagine. He would send no one else, you know. That's the character of the man who has been chasing me now for years."

Simon nodded, his eyes on her face. "I know, love. I know that. We're gathering information on him. Samuel has pulled men and women off other investigations just for this."

"He shouldn't."

"Well, he has. It was his decision. I've been working on your side of it. He's working on who is behind it." Simon hugged her tighter, his chin on the top of her head. "My heart couldn't take it if you left."

She shoved against him. "And just what do you mean by that?" She stood back from him, her eyes unbelieving as she stared at him. "Tell me. Exactly what do you mean."

Simon sighed to himself once again. This was not how he wanted to tell her she had his heart, that she was the one he had been waiting for all his life. "It's like this, love. You have my heart, have had since you called me an oaf out there in the forest." He watched as her eyes widened in disbelief before they narrowed once again. "I'm in love with you, Eavan. I have been since the first time I saw you. Don't leave me, please."

She shook her head. "You can't. Not so soon. It just doesn't happen that way. Not in real life. Only in books and movies."

Simon smiled at her even as he drew her back to him. "It does, love. It did with me. Just let me know if you'll accept my suit, as my grandmother would say."

He finally felt her nod. Thank You, Lord. Now, don't let me screw this up, please. They stood for a while longer before he bent and kissed the bruise on her cheek, turning her towards the main part of the house.

"You need your rest, love. Sleep well. I'll be bunked down here in Samuel's office. I'm not leaving you alone, not any more."

She stood for a moment, her eyes on his face before she reached and pulled his head down, placing a kiss on his cheek.

"Good night, you big oaf." She had turned her words into an endearment and he loved her for that.

Two days later, Eavan looked up from her monitor, her eyes needing the break. She had been hard at work, trying to meet her deadlines that were closing in on her, having missed a day's work when she was assaulted and the ladies she was coming to know had been put at risk. Her sight landed on Simon, sitting at a desk near her, his attention on his laptop as he researched. What he was working on, he wouldn't or couldn't tell her. He would just laugh at her when she told him he needed to, he was working in her office.

Simon glanced up, catching her watching him, and then sat back from his work. "Almost done, love?"

She nodded, happiness flowing through her. "This is the last one I have pending and I just sent the proofs off. I just need to wait for their decisions and then send the copies they requested." She glanced at his laptop. "How about you?"

"I'm done for the day, too. I have to wait for responses to emails and queries I sent off. That will take a few days." He rose, walking over to perch on the corner of her desk, his eyes assessing her. "Now what?"

"Now what?" She shrugged. "I have no idea. Gran is deep in baking, I think she said, for the afternoon. She is insisting that she has to provide Irish goodies to all your friends. Trust me. They'll love them and want the recipes. That they will never get. I can't even get some of them."

He laughed at the aggrieved tone in her voice. "I'm sure she'll give them to you some day."

A voice spoke from the doorway. "I'll give them to you, Simon, and teach you how to bake them, as long as you promise not to share the recipes." Megan and Simon both began to laugh at the squeal of fake rage that came from Eavan. "What I wanted to ask you, Simon, was if you would let me take you out for a meal, to that restaurant of your friend's? I feel like I need to do something for you, you've done so much for me."

Simon stood, reaching to drop a kiss on Megan's cheek. "I don't need payment for what I've done, you know that. I consider you family and family doesn't need to be paid back."

"I know that, Simon. Just humour me, okay." She patted his cheek before she hurried away, her voice carrying back to them. "Now, hurry up and shut down what you need to. I've made reservations for thirty minutes from now. I spoke to someone named Amy, I think it was."

Simon stared after her before he felt Eavan's finger under his chin, shutting his mouth.

"What's the surprise there, Simon?"

"Josh doesn't do reservations. At least he never has in the past." Simon shook his head, not sure what he was walking into but willing to do anything for his Eavan and her beloved Gran.

Josh watched from the kitchen as Simon escorted Megan and Eavan to a table that Amy had set specifically for them. She had approached him after Megan had called, asking for a reservation for that night. He had stared at her, stating they didn't do reservations.

"I know that, Josh." Amy had begun to laugh, but tears sparkled in her eyes, giving away her tender heart directed towards her employer and his friends. "I just couldn't say no to her. She's so sweet."

Amy stopped beside Josh as he stood. "Well, what did you come up with for dinner for them? And don't say you didn't plan something special. I know you."

He laughed. "I did. It's a good thing there aren't many people in the restaurant. We'd have a revolt on our hands. Here, take out their salads. Their main course will be a few minutes."

Simon watched the two women who had become special in his life enjoy their meal, knowing he didn't want the evening to end but it would at some point. He caught sight of Josh moving around the kitchen and nodded at his wave. Josh and Amy were up to something, he thought, but what he had no idea.

Megan stood and went to find Amy, saying she had to talk to Josh, she wanted to thank him for their meal. Eavan looked after her, then back at Simon.

"That's not Gran. She doesn't do that."

Simon laughed. "Well, tonight she did." He reached for Eavan's hand. "I'm glad she left us on our own for a moment." He hesitated, uncertainty seen his face.

"Simon?" Eavan's quiet voice drew his eyes to her face.

"Eavan, I know we're relative strangers, but you know my heart. You know I love you. Will you trust me and take it one step farther? Will you be mine for life, for however long God gives us? If you don't want to answer now, if you need time, it's fine."

Eavan sat there, tears welling in her eyes. Only Simon, Lord, she thought, would ask me to marry him in the middle of such uncertainty and danger, and in the middle of a restaurant. She was unable to speak, nodding instead, her love for him in her eyes and on her face.

Simon drew a breath of relief, raising her hand to kiss it. "When we're alone, I'll do better than kiss your hand. Thank you, love. God knows our hearts. He knows how long we have with each other. All we can do is trust Him and each other."

He stood as Megan came back, followed by Josh, who eyed the couple, then shook his head. Something had changed but he wasn't sure what. Lord, You alone know.

Simon drew Eavan into her studio, the lights on low as she usually left them. He could hear Megan singing softly to herself. He traced Eavan's face with his hand before he cupped her chin and bent and kissed her. Her hands came up to grasp his, not willing to let him go. He then stood, his forehead on hers, his eyes closed before he spoke.

"Tomorrow, we find your ring and then talk to Jeremiah. I hope you don't want a long engagement."

"Oh, I think a year or two might be best." She giggled as he stared in disbelief at her before he began to laugh and swept her into his arms.

"You had me going there, love. We'll need to tell Gran."

"Tell Gran what?" They jumped as they heard her voice behind them. "That you two are in love? That's been obvious for days. When is the wedding? Soon, I hope."

Megan reached to hug the two of them, her head bowed in prayer as she spoke a blessing on them, asking God's protection and provisions for them.

Simon stood, his arms around both women. "We need to speak with Jeremiah. I have no idea how soon for the wedding. I know Josh and Leah married in less than a week. Julia and Blackie and Finn and Jacob took longer."

"Not a long time, I think, Simon." Eavan looked up at him. "Somehow, I think we're not done with what's his name and that our time is precious."

"That is it. What about a dress and all those doodads?" Simon looked down at Megan as she slapped his arm, laughing as she moved away.

"I have her mother's dress packed away. It will fit her well, I'm thinking. As for the doodads, the baking is done. She'll need flowers, and that's your task, my boy."

Eavan shook her head as she watched her Gran move away. "We've been told, Simon. Now that's settled, where do we live? Here or at your place?"

"My place, I think. There is an in-law suite with its own private entrance that would be perfect for Gran. She'd be close but we'd all have our privacy. Would that work?"

"It will work just fine, my boy." Gran's voice behind him made him jump. She laughed in glee at having surprised him for a second time in just minutes. "Get used to me, boy. You'll have me around for years."

Simon reached to hug her, not having had a grandparent in his life for many years, and loving the idea of Gran being part of their lives.

He paused later as he opened his front door, his hand reaching into the mail box, and pulling out the mail. He dropped it on his office desk before he headed for his bedroom and the jewelry box his mother had left him. He searched through it, finding the rings he knew where there. Would Eavan accept either one, or would she want new?

Simon fingered his mail late that night, then walked away from it. It could wait. He headed for the door to the in-law suite, unlocking it and then flipping on lights as he moved through it. It was furnished, had been for months, he thought. He would bring Eavan and Gran over the next night and let them decide on any changes they wanted to make. And make changes he was determined they would make. He wanted a home for both of them, not just a place to live.

Eavan looked with interest around his home the next night, Gran having headed for the suite that would be hers. She could Gran and Simon talking, Gran determined to leave everything like it was, Simon just as determined she would make the place a home for herself.

She turned from the back door and glanced around the kitchen, liking the light wood on the cupboards and yellow, oranges, rusts and brown Simon had incorporated into the backsplash and countertop. She was glad he had not gone for stainless appliances. She disliked them immensely but had no idea why.

Simon stood watching her, his heart in his eyes, before he moved towards her.

"Eavan?" When she turned, he kissed her, then stood where he was, with Eavan captured in his arms.

"I like your house, Simon. It's comfortable. I don't see what you want me to change."

He sighed, knowing he hadn't worded it right. "I want you to make it into a real home, your home. Just like I want Gran to make the suite her home."

"And we'll do that, Simon." Gran stood watching them. "It just won't be overnight. You have to live in a house to feel its bones, to feel what it wants to tell you, to find out how to decorate." She looked around. "You have done that. Your tastes are so similar to Eavan, it's spooky."

Eavan laughed at her Gran. "They are, aren't they? Now we just have to decide what we want to bring. I think we'll leave the apartment we're in furnished. We'll need supplies there anyway."

Simon hugged her tight to him. "I am so glad." He turned her to the office. "Now, if Gran will excuse us for a moment, I have something I need to ask you, in private, sort of."

"Well, that's definite, isn't it, Simon?" Gran made a shooing motion. "Go on and then come back. I'll find some food for us. I know Simon has tea. I already peeked."

Eavan had drawn her breath at the two rings Simon had presented to her, choosing the emerald in its simple setting, saying it would be an honour to wear his mother's ring. He had kissed her soundly for that before they returned to the kitchen, where Gran waited to see the ring Eavan presented to her.

———

Gran's eyes gleamed with tears as she hugged her granddaughter. She was happy for her but fearful at the same time, knowing danger still surrounded them.

Chapter 11

Simon grabbed up the mail from his home desk the next morning, intent on getting to the office. His lieutenant had called, asking him to call once he was in. He had information for him that he thought Simon could use.

Simon dropped the mail on the desk, intent on making that call, until the mail slid sideways and a plain envelope caught his attention. He scanned it, seeing the name of a lawyer in the corner and then frowned.

Samuel stood for a moment in the hallway, watching Simon. He had been on his way to his own office but stopped as he saw Simon just standing there.

"Simon? Is something wrong?"

Looking up, Simon shrugged. "I'm not sure, Samuel. I found this letter in the mail from home. It's from a lawyer I don't know."

"Then, boot up your computer and see what you can find out. Let me know. I would be interested in what that letter contains. If you don't mind sharing, that is."

Simon nodded, his eyes on his computer monitor as he typed in the name of the lawyer, groaning as he saw who it was.

"Now, why would they be contacting me?"

He slit the envelope open, not seeing the small envelope containing a minute amount of powder. Before he could even draw the letter from the envelope, he began to have difficulty breathing. The sound of his body hitting the floor had his work mates running for his office, Samuel shoving by them to drop on his knees beside the young man, calling for paramedics and the police.

Samuel felt for a pulse, all the while looking around, seeing the open envelope and the spying the small envelope inside it, both slit open with the letter opener.

"Here, give me a hand. Out to the reception area. And close that door. No one comes in here." Samuel gently laid Simon's head down, afraid for him as he saw the struggle to breathe. He prayed for his young friend as he moved back, letting the paramedics in to work on Simon.

The paramedics struggled to work on Simon, desperate to keep him breathing.

"What happened?" One of them looked up even as he reached for the leads to the heart monitor.

"He opened an envelope. I wasn't there but there was a little envelope in the big one. I think he's been drugged." Samuel ran his hands through his hair, knowing exactly what he was saying.

———

"Drugged? As in overdose?" The paramedics worked even harder, one reaching for the kit they carried just for overdoses.

Samuel watched as they finally stabilized Simon enough to move him to a stretcher, preparatory to moving him to the hospital. He watched as they slid the breathing tube in, and started the IV. He turned.

"I'm going to find Eavan. Call me when the police are done." He was out the door, running for his car, his phone in his hand. "Blackie, I need you and Julia at the hospital. Simon's down and I'm heading for Eavan. No. I'm not sure what happened." He listened to Blackie's question even as he heard Blackie calling for Julia. "An overdose somehow. The police will sort out that. Eavan will need someone with her."

Eavan had looked up as Samuel stood in her office doorway, his breath in gasps as he asked her to come with him. She had thrown down her pen, grabbed her jacket, calling to Gran that Simon was hurt and that she'd call. Megan and Maggie had stood, arms around one another, as they watched Samuel drive away.

Eavan paced the waiting room and had been since Samuel ushered her in. It had been three hours since Simon collapsed and they were still working on him. Eavan didn't know that he had been close to death more than once. They had finally found the drug that he had inhaled without knowing and found the antidote that was needed. The paramedics' quick work on the scene had kept him alive long enough for that to happen.

She turned as she felt an arm come around her.   Julia stood there, compassion on her face before she hugged her sister, Blackie's arms coming around the two ladies, his face raised in prayer for his friend. Those two and Josh and Jacob had served in the service together, becoming fast friends, going their own way on discharge, but reuniting again in Mistletoe. Each man had been sent there, why and who was still in a cloud, even though Jacob's lawyer had been behind part of it, before he ended up in prison himself.

Doc stood for a moment, his eyes on the three in the middle of the waiting room, before roaming the room and seeing Simon's friends gathered, Jeremiah standing near the door where he could watch all them. Doc knew he would be in prayer, having gotten to know him well at church.

Doc's eyes came back to the two ladies as they separated, hands wiping at their faces. He paused as he saw the ring on Eavan's finger, knowing that Samuel was right, Simon had made his choice and put his ring on his lady's finger. He thanked God that Simon was still alive, but not conscious. That worried Doc.

Blackie turned at that moment, seeing Doc standing there. Julia saw his movement and turned Eavan towards the physician, introducing her to him.

"Doc? How is he?"

"Very fortunate, Eavan. May I call you that? Simon is a good friend." She nodded and then he continued. "We have him stabilized for now and are moving him up to an ICU bed. He is on a heart monitor, kidney dialysis, and on a ventilator. We need to keep him quiet for now and let the medications we are treating him with do their work. Come. Let me take you back to him. You do want to go, don't you?" He asked the question as she hesitated.

Samuel moved forward, his arm coming around Eavan. "Let me go with you, Eavan. That is, if it's okay with Doc." Doc nodded, grateful that Samuel had stepped in just as he would have with Julia or with one of his own two girls. He knew Samuel thought of Simon as another son and would do just about anything for him.

Eavan stood for a moment, overwhelmed by the sounds of the monitors and the ventilator, her eyes not able to take in all that was in the room before they fell to Simon. With a subdued cry, she was across the room, bending over the stretcher to touch his face, careful of the equipment attached to him. She reached to kiss his forehead, then found his hand, not liking the coldness of it, nor its laxity.

She stood for how long she didn't know before the nurses walked towards her, gently moving her to one side as they moved the stretcher and equipment that was needed. Simon was heading for an ICU unit, still alive but not aware that his love stood near, frozen in her despair. Samuel caught her hand and led her after the stretcher, Miriam appearing beside her, her arm wrapped around the younger woman. Megan, Samuel knew, had arrived and been taken to the waiting room upstairs.

Eavan stood once more at Simon's bedside, not knowing when he would arouse. Doc had been confident that he would, but just when was uncertain. She turned as she felt Gran's hand on her back and then clung to her grandmother, tears falling silently down her cheeks.

Gran let her cry, in her wisdom knowing it was needed before she spoke.

"The police chief is here, child. He wants to talk to you."

"I can't leave him, Gran."

"You can and you will. The nurses have said you need to. They'll come get you when you can come back in."

Ed looked up as Gran came back with Eavan. He was shocked at the devastation he saw on Eavan's face, even though Samuel had warned him the younger couple had become engaged.

"Eavan? Come, sit with me please. I do need to talk with you." Ed waited until she had found a seat, her hand in her grandmother's. "I'm not sure what you have been told, but Simon opened an envelope he had received at home at the office. Thank God he didn't open it at home. We wouldn't be sitting here having this conversation if we had."

Eavan winced and then nodded. "What was in that envelope?"

"We've sent it to the lab. We know it was a drug of some kind and the hospital was able to determine what it was and find the antidote. There was a letter inside as well. I don't have a copy, but it threatened Simon. Just why, that's what we're working on. It doesn't seem to have anything to do with you, before you ask."

She sat back, relief in her motions. "I was afraid it did. But who?"

"That's what we are working on. Samuel has pulled some of his people to do that. Simon's fellow detectives are working on that as well. So are mine. We'll find out who it was." He paused, swallowing hard. "I understand you two are engaged. Is that correct?" At her nod, he continued. "We will need to take precautions with you as well. Given the attempts on your life already and now this, I don't think it's safe for you to go back to your studio. Maggie has agreed to work it and I am putting an officer into the living quarters at the back, rotating every twelve hours. As for you two, we'll put you somewhere safe."

Eavan was shaking her head. "Put Gran somewhere safe. I'm not leaving Simon. Not for one moment." She was on her feet and away from Ed before he could stop her.

Megan gave a short laugh. "That's what you will face, Ed, if you even try to remove her. She'll run and hide somewhere here in the hospital, staying close to her love. That's a given. It's who she is."

Ed grinned at Megan, shaking his head. "That's about what I figured. I have officers here that will be on duty at all times. The county force is sending in some as well. We'll do our best to keep them safe. Now, what about you?"

"I won't go anywhere, Ed. I'll stay right here. She needs me, now more than at any time in her life. She's just found a sister and a brother, found out she's related to the town founding families, and that has thrown her world upside down. Throw into the mix someone wanting her hurt or dead, or whatever it is he wants. Then add a brand new love. Like I said, her world is upside down."

"It is at that. Now about that person who is after her. What do you know about that?"

"Not much. I gave Simon the copies of what I had been sent. The same as was sent to her. He said he had taken it to Samuel, so Samuel may be able to help you out there."

"I'll talk to him. We need to pool our resources. I'm sure he's found out more than I have." Ed sat for a moment, fatigue weighing him down, before he rose and walked away.

Megan sat watching him, before she looked up. Samuel and Miriam stood there, their eyes down the hall, a frown on Samuel's face. Megan rose and walked to the hallway, seeing Eavan slumped to the floor, her head on her knees, arms wrapped around her legs, and rushed to her, dropping to her knees.

"Eavan? What's wrong, child?"

Eavan looked up, a stark look on her face, fear in her eyes. "He took a turn for the worse, Gran. They don't know if he'll survive. What will I do if he doesn't?"

Gran sat, wrapping her arms around her beloved granddaughter. "Pray like you never have before, child. That's what will bring him through. God knows what you're going through. He is there."

"It sure doesn't feel like it." Eavan's face went down on her knees again. "I don't know what I'll do if he doesn't make it."

Samuel finally reached and drew Eavan to her feet, then arm around her, led her back to the waiting room and to a chair. Gran sat on one side of her, Miriam on the other, their arms around the younger woman. Samuel crouched in front of her, reaching for her hands even as he prayed. He finally looked at Eavan.

"Jeremiah's called in the church to pray. Someone will be in the prayer room there, twenty hour hours a day until he's out of danger. Trust me on that, Eavan. It's what we do."

She nodded, her eyes finally going past him to look down the hall. "What if he doesn't make it? What do I do?"

"That's not a question we can answer for you. Only God can. But I have every confidence that God will hear your prayers and answer them. Simon has too much to give to the world yet to be taken home."

She finally nodded, then worked herself free from the two older woman, rising to go and stand in the hallway, leaning against the wall, her eyes trained on Simon's cubicle, watching as the nurses moved in and out, gradually making her way down the hall until she stood at the doorway. Looking around, she finally walked towards him, her eyes first on the monitors, then on his face, seeing the dark stubble that was partially covered and reaching her hand out to lay it on his cheek, bending over to kiss his forehead, resting her cheek against his.

The nurse found her that way and paused, knowing she should make her leave, but not having the heart to do that. She turned instead, asking one of the male orderlies to find her a chair for Eavan. She gently shoved Eavan down in the chair, not breaking Eavan's hold on Simon's hand. Finding Eavan's skin chilly, she headed for the supply closet, returning with a warmed sheet that she wrapped around her. She knew Simon from church and from around town, her prayer rising with those of her fellow Christians.

The man who had sent the letter stood near the waiting room, observing and listening to the quiet conversation. He hadn't meant for Simon to die, not just yet. He still had plans he needed to work out before he wreaked his final plot to destroy Simon. That included Eavan now, he decided. Eavan had no idea that there were now two parties after her, both for their own reasons, but she wouldn't have cared if she had known. She had put her trust in God and her hand in Simon's. She was where she needed to be.

Finally opening his eyes, Simon squinted, not quite sure where he was. He stared around, seeing the medical monitors and then reached for the ventilator tube, not liking the feeling of it down his throat. A hand stopped him. He heard voices around him but darkness claimed him again, and this time it was sleep, not unconsciousness that drove him to darkness.

Eavan stood, her hand on Simon's, relieved that he had awakened, but distressed that he had slipped away on her again. She wanted him awake, to look into his eyes, and see that he was healing.

Doc stood watching for a moment before he moved forward, his words quiet to the nurses. Eavan was escorted from the room and told she would be allowed back in later.

The officer assigned to her walked with her to the waiting room, watching as she sat, not alert at all to who was around her. Megan reached out a hand and Eavan took it.

"He was awake, Gran. He opened his eyes. They said he is in a natural sleep now."

"That's good news, then, love. Let the staff do what they need to. You just sit here and put your head back. You need to sleep more than you have in the last few days."

Eavan nodded, even as she yawned, fatigue claiming her. She curled up, her head going down on her Gran's knee and she slept. Doc found them that way later, and stopped, heading back for a blanket that he used to cover Eavan, before he sat beside Megan.

"Doc? How is our boy?" Megan kept her voice low.

"Better. He's been awake again. We've been able to pull the tube, so he's breathing on his own. It's a miracle, Megan. He should not have survived. I thought for a while we'd lose him."

"So did I. God had other plans, Doc, plans that He hasn't shared with us yet."

Doc gave a low laugh. "No, He has not done that. I took the liberty of calling Jeremiah, to pass on the good news. He still has a long road ahead of him, but he is on the mend." Doc shot a look at the officer standing here. "How long do they have guards on them?"

Megan shrugged. "I have no idea. Ed hasn't said, but he did say they haven't caught either party yet, not quite sure who they are." She looked down at Eavan as she stroked her hair. "Eavan knows who's after her. She hasn't said. Who's after Simon, that I have no idea."

Doc sighed, knowing he needed to move on to another patient, but not willing to walk away. He had gotten to know Megan over the past few days and enjoyed his conversations with her, her wit and wisdom adding to his day.

Eavan finally roused, sitting up and pushing her hair back. She rose, heading for Simon, not seeing the man who was following her, behind the officer. She stopped for a moment, to gather her thoughts. It was night, she saw. She had slept most of the day but was still really tired.

She paused, just inside the door, seeing that some of the monitors had been removed. That she was glad to see. Her feet carried her to the bedside, her hand reaching for Simon's, finding him asleep. At least he's not on the ventilator any more, she thought. Her hand traced his cheek, and he turned his head slightly to trap her hand under his face. She smiled.

Lord, I have no idea where the investigation stands, nor do I really want to know. It is enough that Simon is still here, still alive. She stood for the longest time before she finally gave in to her fatigue and curled up beside him, her head on his pillow, his hand clasped tight in hers.

The night nurse found her like that later, reaching to rouse her, then pulling her hand back. What would it hurt, she asked herself, and instead reached for a blanket, covering Eavan before moving to check Simon's vitals. He was almost out of danger she thought, and who would have thought that even that morning. She was not a believer but decided that she needed to look into this faith this family seemed to have.

She turned from the bed, not seeing the man standing in the darkness in the corner, his eyes on the couple, anger and even rage on his face. He needed to reach them, for his boss, but there just didn't seem to be an opportunity.

Simon stirred in the early morning hours, his eyes opening and staying open this time. He searched the room, a frown in place, seeing the monitors by his bed. His hand raised to his face, feeling the nasal prongs bringing oxygen to his lungs, then dropped to his chest, feeling the leads to the heart monitor. He lifted his hand again, staring at the IV line, following it to the pole and frowning again at the sight of a small bag hanging there as well. He had no memory of the last few days and that scared him. What had happened?

He tried to move and felt a hand tightening on his other hand. He tried to turn his head and realized then that someone's head was beside him. He tilted his head, studying the auburn curls and then following a line of sight to his hand, seeing his hand clasped tightly in her hand, an emerald ring sparkling on her finger.

That's Mom's ring, he thought. Now, how did she get it? Lord, what did I go and do now? He turned as he felt a hand on his shoulders. The night nurse stood there, a smile on her face.

"How are you feeling, Simon?" Her voice was low but comforting.

"Horrible would be how I would describe it. What happened?" He swallowed hard and ran his tongue around his mouth, the dryness preventing him from speaking properly. He drank from the glass the nurse held for him.

"You had a spot of trouble, I would say. Someone tried to kill you. You ended up here." She nodded at Eavan. "She has refused to leave your side. You're a lucky man, Simon, to be loved that much. She was determined you would not die on her, she said, and I would say her prayers worked. Hers and those of your friends."

He nodded, lost for a moment in thought, his face tilting so he could study Eavan, not really recognizing her. His mind was foggy and it hurt to think. He drifted off again.

Eavan finally sat up, her eyes blinking against the early morning light, seeking Simon's face. She slipped from her spot next to him and headed for the door. She knew someone would be waiting for her in the room down the hall and she had to speak with her Gran.

Megan roused as Eavan's hand touched her shoulder.

"Eavan? How is he?"

"Better, I think, Gran. I heard him talking with the nurse earlier but was too tired to rouse properly." Tears sparkled on her lashes. "I don't know that he remembers me though. Doc warned me about that."

"He did at that, love, but he also said it would only be temporary. Simon's system shut down part way to protect him and to let him heal. He'll not have forgotten you." She looked around Eavan as she heard steps coming towards them.

Ed stood for a moment. He had stopped in on his way to the office, having been called in early for another matter. He had news that had come in overnight that he needed to share with Eavan.

"Ed? You're here early." Megan watched Eavan's face pale even more.

"I am, Megan. Eavan, how are you today?" He grinned as she shook her head. "That good, are you? I heard Simon has been awake and talking with the nurse."

Eavan nodded. "He has been, Ed, but he has little memory of what happened."

"We didn't think he would. But that's not why I'm here. I have news." He paused, watching Eavan compose herself. "We identified who sent the envelope to Simon. It has nothing to do with you, and everything to do with his inheritance here in Mistletoe. We're still working on that, to actually determine what all is involved there."

"He is a descendant, isn't he?" Eavan's question caught Ed's attention.

———

"He is, there is no doubt about that. Just as you are. We're working through what you've told us as well. We want these people responsible for hurting both of you. You're family, Eavan, you and Simon, and yes, you, Megan."

Ed finally rose and walked away, heading for the office, and a busy day he knew. Eavan watched him go, then rose, not saying a word to her Gran as she paced back to Simon's room.

She stood at his bedside as she had for so many hours, her hand reaching for his hand, finding it warm this time, not cold as it had been for so long. She sank down into her chair as she thought of it, her head bowed in prayer.

Simon had roused as he felt her take his hand and controlled the jump he almost gave at being touched. His head turned slightly, and he watched as she prayed, a small frown on his face. He knew her but could not remember how close they were. It would seem close, given she was wearing that ring, but he needed to talk to her, and he just wasn't sure how to broach the subject.

His hand moved and Eavan looked up, her hand tightening on his, a smile breaking out on her face and lighting up her eyes.

"Simon, you're awake. Thank God for that."

Simon frowned. "I'm sorry. I just can't remember."

"That's okay. Doc said that would likely be the case. Whatever drug they hit you with has that side effect. Well, one, anyway."

He nodded. "I just need to refresh my memory, I think. It's foggy. How long?"

"Four days since you collapsed in the office. Samuel was there right away, and got you help. If you had opened that letter at home, you wouldn't be here. You needed help that quickly."

He nodded, knowing the truth she was speaking. "And I'm sorry, I just can't remember your name, and I should." He held up her hand. "It looks as if we're a couple, and couple should know their partner's name."

She smiled even as her free hand came to brush the hair from his forehead. "I'm Eavan Walker, and yes, we are a couple. We became engaged the night before you collapsed. That could be why you're having trouble remembering me."

Simon stared down at their hands, memory slowly filtering back. "No, I remember that. Your Gran took us out to Josh's for dinner. You know, he doesn't do reservations."

She laughed. "We know that. So does she. I have no idea what she was up to that night."

"I think I do." Simon paused, swallowing against the dryness in his throat, sipping from the glass she held for him. "I think she wanted to push us to a decision. Apparently we weren't moving fast enough for her."

Eavan smiled, even as she shook her head. "That would be Gran." She sat once more, releasing Simon's hand. "Ed was by earlier. He'll be back to talk to you. He said they've tracked down who sent the envelope but haven't made an arrest yet. Still investigating, I think was what he said."

Simon nodded. "It takes time to put all the pieces together. They need to have a strong case for an arrest and then for court." He sighed. "When am I getting out of here?"

"Not for a few days." She shot a look at the door and then brought her gaze back to him. "We need to make some decisions, Simon, and I'm not sure you're ready for that."

"Decisions?" He watched as she frowned at him. "What? No name calling? No accusing me of being a big oaf?" He smiled as she shook a finger at him.

"There's nothing wrong with your memory," she declared. "Yes, we need to make some decisions. Ed says he needs to keep us together to properly protect us. I just don't see how that can work."

"There is only one way, Eavan, and I'm not sure you're ready for it." Simon watched as she studied his face, comprehension dawning on hers.

"We can't, Simon. We just can't." Panic had begun to set in.

He reached for her hand, tugging her close enough to him that he could wrap an arm around her. "If it means keeping you alive, sweetheart, then yes, we can. I spoke to Jeremiah that night. He was working on getting what we need."

She shook her head, her eyes wide as she stared at him, seeing the confidence he had in her, seeing the love he had for her, and sighed.

"I guess, then. But Simon, what will people say?"

"People will talk. They always do. But our friends and family will understand. They always do. What do we need to do then?"

She finally nodded, her eyes still on his, not turning as she heard the door open behind her.

"Eavan? Samuel's here and needs to speak with both you and Simon." Megan stood at her granddaughter's side, a frown on her face as her eyes shifted between the two in front of her.

"Tell him to come in, Gran. But first, Simon and I have decided not to wait. We'll be married as soon as he's released." Eavan stared at Simon as his head shook. "Yes, when you're released."

"Now that I'm awake, Eavan, they will not let you stay as much as you have. Not as my fiancee. As my wife, yes."

"He's right, love. They've been generous with you up to now, but they do have rules, you know." Megan looked with compassion as the distress colouring Eavan's face before Eavan's stance changed.

———

"Then, we marry here, Simon. Today. Will Jeremiah have what we need?"

"He will. He would have had it the next day."

Eavan blinked back tears. This was not how she had planned her wedding day, but God was in control, she knew. "Gran, what about my dress?"

"I'll have someone get it for us. I'm sure there's a room here we can get you changed in. Simon, I know you'll want something other than the ridiculous nightwear they give you."

Simon gave a shout of laughter, just as Samuel entered the room, hesitating as he did so.

"Simon? I thought you were sick?" Samuel walked over to shake Simon's hand.

"I am, Samuel, but this is my wedding day as well. Just a small one. Please stay."

Samuel nodded. "I can, I guess. Not what I expected when I walked in here, that's for sure."

Eavan and Megan had moved away, Eavan's phone out to call Maggie, asking her to find a box for them that would be picked up.

"Rings, Gran? What about rings?"

"I sure Simon has already taken care of that. Trust him, love."

Hours later, Eavan wandered around Simon's room, her hands busy tidying vases of flowers that had made their way to him, once word got around that he was awake. They had said nothing about their marriage, preferring to keep it quiet for the moment. Other than to Simon's best friends. They had understood his reasoning but not that they couldn't be there.

Simon finally reached for her hand as he stood on shaking legs beside his bed, drawing her to him.

"Eavan? What is it? It's more than just today, isn't it?"

She nodded. "It is. Here. Sit. You'll fall if you keep standing." She sat beside him, his arm keeping her close to him. "I talked to Ed a bit ago. He's worried, Simon. He said he's more worried than he's ever been. They can't find the men after us. They've gone underground and left no trace."

Simon nodded. "I suspected as much, love. That's what these people will do. I've seen it before, but never felt it personally."

She sighed, her eyes holding fear and panic. "So, what do we do? How do we handle this? I know Gran is safe at Samuel's. He's assured me of that, but what about when she's out on her own?"

"Samuel won't let that happen. He'll make sure someone is with her at all times, until we catch these people."

She finally nodded. "I know that, Simon, in my head. I just don't understand how people can be so evil."

A week later, Simon moved through Samuel's office building, back at work, but not in the same office. That had been sealed by the police. He sank gratefully into a chair, his strength still not back fully. Samuel watched him, noting the lack of strength and determined he'd send him home early, if he could.

Eavan, Simon knew, was out and about, one of Samuel's men with her. That was a given, Samuel said. She was not on her own, not at all.

"Simon? Any thoughts on what has happened lately?"

Simon looked up as Samuel sank into a chair across from him. "I have some thoughts, not quite organized. Let me run them by you."

Simon began to speak, Samuel pulling paper and pen across the desk to make notes. He was not surprised that Simon had gone right to the heart of the matter and the men involved. That was the kind of person Simon was.

"You're sure about the names?"

Simon nodded. "I am. They are the only two that make sense." He sat back, his eyes on his own notes. "Now what?"

"Now, we start researching harder. These men have gone underground, but I have contacts that I'll use to try and find them." He looked up at the younger man, finding Simon's eyes on him. "I don't have to warn you how dangerous these men are. You know that already. You've had a taste of what they can and will do."

Simon nodded. "I have. My concern is Eavan and Megan."

"We'll work on keeping them as safe as we can. Unfortunately, we can't promise complete protection and safety. You know that only too well, Simon."

Simon sighed, his thoughts on his young bride. "I know. And I hate that." He stared down at the ring on his finger. "I don't think I could handle losing her, Samuel."

"Then we do everything we can to make sure that doesn't happen." Samuel stood. "I couldn't get your paperwork from your old office. I wasn't allowed, but I know you've put a backup in the company safe. I'll get that for you." He walked to the door, turning as he spoke. "You're only here half a day, remember."

Simon shook his head as he grinned, watching Samuel walk away. He knew Eavan would be here to take him home at that point, and he had work to do before she got there.

Eavan stood later that day, watching Simon work away, his concentration fully on the papers on the desk in front of him. She sighed, knowing she would have to rouse him from his work to get him home. The physicians had been really firm about his getting rest, and she intended to make sure he did just that.

A sound roused Simon from his work, and he looked up, his face lighting up as he stood, walking around his desk to Eavan, catching her into his arms.

"Is it that time already, love?"

"It is. Time to get you out of here. Samuel has a car waiting for us out back, he said. He wants to vary where and when we come and go, not be in too much of a routine." She caught his hand, drawing him from his office, but he stopped her.

"I need to lock up what I've been working on before I go. Just a few minutes." He was as good as his word, his work gathered into a neat bundle and tucked away into the safe before he once more reached for her hand.

Eavan wandered their home later that afternoon. Simon had dozed off on the couch and she had covered him with the blanket she had left there. She knew he's be hungry when he woke up, but she just couldn't concentrate on getting a meal ready for them. Megan had left soup in the fridge, telling her granddaughter to heat that for them, it would be sufficient.

Eavan stopped in front of the fireplace, her hand rubbing against the wooden mantle, until she felt it catch on something. She stooped, feeling along the wood again, her eyes following her fingers, until she reached the spot that had stopped her. She felt around the spot and heard a soft click. Now what, she thought, as she lifted at the mantle. Nothing happened. She turned, surprise on her face as she saw an opening beside the fireplace. She walked towards it, hand to her throat, and peeked in. Just a small room, she thought, looking back over her shoulder at Simon. There was no way she was going in there on her own, she thought, and studied the door, finding the way to close it.

Simon was sitting up, watching as she turned, a frown on his face. "What did you find, love?"

"I have no idea. A secret room, I think." She sank down on the couch beside him, her arm going out to wrap around his as her head leaned against his shoulder. "How are you feeling now?"

"Better, I think. Not quite as drowsy but not ready to run a marathon at this point." He nodded towards the door. "Aren't you going to investigate that?"

She shook her head. "No. Not on my own. I think we should leave it for now. I'm worried about you, Simon. You're not yourself, not yet."

He sighed, knowing she was right. "I know I'm not, but what I am is not an invalid." He paused, a thought crossing his mind. "Tomorrow is Sunday. Are you up for church?"

She shrugged. "I guess. I'm not sure though about facing everyone."

"They will all love you, my sweetness. All of them. They have been after me since I moved here to find someone. Some have tried to play matchmaker."

She laughed at that, the musical sound filling the room and his heart. "And that went over well, didn't it?"

He shrugged. "I was waiting for you. God knew." He reached to kiss her, his hand cupping her cheek.

She leaned back, her own hand on the stubble on his cheek. "I'm liking the beard, Mr. Gardner. It suits you."

"It does? And here I was ready to run for a razor and shave it off. I guess I'll have to keep it if my wife likes it."

She shook his head at his grin. "Gran left soup for us, if you're hungry."

He shrugged, his eyes going back to the panel, and he started to rise, falling back to the couch as she pulled him back.

"Not tonight, Simon. Wait at least until tomorrow. I'm afraid of what we'll find and how it will change something in our lives. I can't explain that."

Simon studied her face, seeing the very emotions she was trying too hard to hide. "Never hide how you're feeling from me, sweetheart. That I don't want you to do. Okay, tomorrow it is then. Now, you said something about food."

The next morning, Eavan sat tight to Simon in a pew near the back of the church, her hands clenched tightly together. She had only been in the church a couple of times before, not sure of her reception in town and wanting to avoid those who called her Julia without realizing she wasn't Julia. Simon reached for her hand, his warm and comforting on hers before he heard two little voices coming towards him.

"Are you ready for them, sweetheart?"

She peeked up, a smile on her face as she saw Heidi and Holly heading their way, big smiles on their faces to see their beloved Simon. Heidi climbed on his knee, hugging him tight, leaving Holly standing near his knee, a pout on her face before she turned to Eavan.

"Julia, up." Eavan gave a gasp and then a smile as the little girl reached for her and then hugged her. "Julia, not fair. I want to hug Simon too."

"You'll get your chance." Eavan shared a look with Simon, knowing she had to correct the little one. "But I'm not Julia. My name is Eavan."

"No, Julia." Holly's bottom lip came out in a pout.

"Sorry, honey. I'm really not Julia. See. Our hair is a different colour as are our eyes. Julia's my sister, though."

Holly studied her, the pout disappearing finally. "You not Julia?" When Eavan shook her head, Holly reached to hug her again. ""Nother Julia, can I now hug Simon?"

Eavan started to laugh. "You may be able to, but I'm not 'Nother Julia. It's Eaven."

"That's a funny name." Holly studied her face, her mind working as she tried to process the grown up terms.

Eavan and Simon heard a gasp from beside him and knew Joy had arrived and was about to correct her daughter. Eavan looked up, giving a small shake of her head.

"Let's see, then, Holly. I'm not Julia, I'm not 'Nother Julia. I'm Eavan. I'm Simon's wife."

"You can't be. I want to marry my Simon." This from Heidi, who had tears welling in her eyes.

Neither woman heard the low words Simon whispered to Heidi, but they saw her reach to hug him and the tears disappear. Eavan turned her attention back to Holly, seeing Joy disappear for a moment, then appear in their pew, to drop into the seat beside her.

"My name's Eavan. Can you say that?"

Holly stared at her, her mouth working as she tried to form the name. "Evie. That's it. Evie."

Her clear voice as she declared her name for Eavan brought laughter and chuckles from those around them, who were delighted to see Eavan with Simon. Simon just knew he'd face questions after church, but right now his attention was on Eavan and Holly, knowing she was handling the little girl just right, not belittling her or talking down to her, but treating her as she should be treated and giving her a choice as to what she did.

Eavan gave a small laugh, seeing Jeremiah on the platform, ready to start the service. "Then, Evie I am. Now, your Daddy's up front, isn't he? Do we have to watch what he's doing?"

"We do. He tells us what to do." Holly squirmed around until she faced the front, her eyes on her Daddy, waiting for him to start talking.

Joy leaned against Eavan's shoulder for a moment. "Thank you. You just handled her like I haven't seen anyone handle her, except for Simon, that is. You'll have to let me know your secret."

Simon stood after the service, watching as Eavan was welcomed by his church family, finally reaching through the crowds to rescue her.

"Thank you, Simon. I couldn't take much more." She walked beside him as he headed for their vehicle.

"I know you couldn't. Listen, I usually head for the B&B for brunch after church. We don't have to, if you'd rather not."

"No, that's fine. I'll have to get used to being around people. I've been hiding for so many years, I'm afraid my conversational skills are rusty." She looked up with a frown as he started laughing. "Now, what did I say?"

"Just thinking about Holly. You handled her just right this morning, Evie."
He teased her with the name Holly had chosen.

"That's just for her to use." She gave a pretended sniff of outrage as he
shut the door behind her. Once he was behind the wheel, she turned to him. "If
you don't mind my asking, what did you say to Heidi?"

He shook his head even as he laughed himself. "I never saw that coming,
not for one moment. I just told her that I was already married, that I was too old
for her, and that God knew her heart, that He would have someone for her when
she was ready."

"Well put, Mr. Gardner. I think I'll keep you and your silver tongue
around." Her attention was drawn to the car following them, vaguely hearing
Simon's shout of laughter.

———

Chapter 14

A week later, Eavan wandered the down town area of Mistletoe, her camera in her hand, being greeted by many of the shop owners. She felt content, loved by a wonderful Christian man, happy to have her Gran loved as well. She stopped as she felt eyes on her and turned, searching for who was watching her and seeing no one. She shuddered, knowing someone was out there, someone who meant her harm.

She stopped in front of Finn's store, finally having made her way to it. She entered, her mouth opening and then closing as she stared around. Here was a treasure trove of photos, she thought, thinking through her client list and knowing just who would want photos from here. She wandered the store, stopping every once in a while to finger a treasure, then move on.

She finally looked up, to find Finn watching her from her from not far away, a grin on her face.

"You made it, finally. I can tell your mind's not on here though."

Eavan shook her head. "I'm not. I have clients who would love to have photos of some of your stock. Can I set up to shoot from here somewhere?"

Finn nodded. "Of course you can. In fact, I'm hiring you to do all new photos for the online store as well. Ann or I have been taking them, but it's time we had a professional do them."

"I would be delighted to do that." Eavan looked around, seeing so much more she wanted to discover. "Unfortunately, I don't have time today to look around as much as I want to. I'm supposed to be heading out to the woods for a shoot, and I'm not at all comfortable about that."

"Who with?"

Eavan pulled out her phone and held it up. "Simon made me get one. Now, let's see." She scrolled through her messages. "Now, that's strange. That message and confirmation for the shoot have disappeared. How can that be?"

Finn froze. "Did you know who it was? I mean, had you met them in person?"

Eavan shook her head. "That's not how my business can work. I often meet up with strangers who book through the website."

Finn shook her head. "Don't do that any more, at least not right now." She saw the fear flit across Eavan's face. "I think it was a set up. The information disappeared because they think they'll have you and that information would lead the police directly to them."

Eavan sank into a chair, her hands to her face. She had set her camera down to look closer at some of the antiquities. "This is what Simon meant, isn't it?"

———

"I'm not sure what he said, but yes, this is likely what he meant. Whoever is after you will stop at nothing to find you." She looked up with a frown as the door opened and two men entered. In a low voice, she spoke to Eavan. "Take your camera and head quietly for that door at the back. It's unlocked. Lock it behind you. It leads to my brother's apartment. No one is up there right now. You'll be safe. I'll come find you once I can."

"I can't let you do that, Finn." Eavan's hand came out to clutch at Finn's arm.

"You're not letting me do anything. I'm just doing it. Now, go. Quickly." She thrust the camera into Eavan's hands and turned her towards the door, giving her a slight shove that way, before she turned and headed for her office, detouring towards the front of the store as she hit that doorway. Eavan could hear her faint conversation with the men before she quietly closed the door behind her and shoved the old-fashioned bolt into place. She just prayed there was another way out of there.

Simon looked up from his work as he heard Jacob's voice and frowned. As far as he could remember, he was not meeting with Jacob that day. Jacob appeared in his doorway and then dropped down into a chair in front of his desk

"And what brings you here today?" Simon frowned as Jacob just grinned at him.

"What? I can't just stop by and see a friend."

Simon shook his head, his eyes on Jacob's face, seeing that his smile didn't reach his eyes. "Jacob? What is going on?"

Jacob sighed, knowing that Simon had read him just like a book. "Finn called. Eavan had stopped in to look around and they were talking. Eavan mentioned that she had a photo shoot in the woods. That bothered Finn and when she questioned her, Eavan discovered that all contact with the party had disappeared from her phone. Then, two men came into the store, Finn thinks looking for your wife. Finn sent her up to the apartment, making her lock herself up there. She called me when the men had left."

"I don't get it. Where was the man who was to be with her today?" Simon rose, intent on finding Samuel, Jacob at his heels, to find Samuel looking for him, a grim look on his face.

"Simon, we have trouble."

"Where's the man who was with Eavan?"

"Ed just called. They found him unconscious behind Finn's store. He's still out so they can't question him. Where's your wife?"

"Finn had her lock herself in the apartment upstairs to the shop." Simon pulled out his phone, his hand shaking as he called Eavan, his coat in his other hand as he headed for the door, Jacob pointing to his truck, Samuel right behind them

"Simon? What are you calling me for? You're supposed to be working." Eavan's voice held a note of fear but more concern that Simon had called. She wasn't used to him calling during working hours, at least not yet. She would become accustomed to that, she supposed, and look forward to that.

"Eavan, sweetheart. I just wanted to talk to you. Where are you? Did you get to your photo shoot you mentioned?" Simon shook his head at Jacob, who was grinning at him.

"No, I did not." Eavan sounded both angry and disgruntled. "And you know that very well. I suppose Finn called Jacob, who tracked you down, and you're both on your way here." There was silence for a moment. "And yes, Samuel is there as well. How did I do at reading you?"

Simon started to laugh, his fear disappearing at her words. "Just about spot on, I would say. We're outside the store. Go on down and open the door, sweetheart. We'll be inside in just a moment."

Simon headed for the back of the store, a hand raised in a wave to Finn, catching Eavan in his arms as she ran to him, her own clinging to him.

"Where's Samuel's man? Did they hurt him?"

"Knocked him out. He'll be fine, sweetheart. What can you tell me?" He heard steps behind him, and looking over his shoulder, saw Ed and another officer standing there.

"I don't know much. Finn sent me upstairs so she could talk to the men. I don't have the information on the client any more. How did they make that disappear?"

"Let Ed have your phone, sweetheart. He'll let the techs take a look at it and see what they can find out."

She gladly thrust the phone at Ed, her hands shaking as she did so. "I don't want it back. I don't like it." She knew she sounded petulant but didn't care.

"We'll get you another one, sweetheart." Simon's arms were still around her as she spoke with Ed.

He finally turned to Samuel and walked away from Eavan to speak with him.

"I found some more information on her father. He was innocent in all his transactions. That much is clear. I have a call in to the police department where they lived, to see what I can find out about her parents' death. Her father had a heart attack. I want the medical examiner's report on that, so you may have to request that. Her mother had stage IV breast cancer and that took her very quickly, I understand."

Samuel nodded, his eyes on Eavan. "I can do just that. Listen. I'll take what you were working on it, look it over and then lock it away for the night. You need to be with her. That's where you're needed most." He held up a hand as Simon protested. "Trust me, Simon. I can work with what you've given me.

She's a priority in the office. Now that Todd's been hurt, it becomes personal for all of us. I have a friend with a security firm. He's sending in people to be with you. You won't see them, but they'll be around you both. And Megan as well, but you know how well that will go over."

Simon chuckled, knowing just how well Gran would take that. "I'll let you be the one to tell her." He turned, his eyes on Eavan. "I'll take her home." Then he stopped. "My car's at the office. Jacob drove us."

"Dan's outside with your car. You left your keys on your desk. He'll drive you home."

Eavan turned as Simon approached, her arms wrapped around herself, before she flung herself at him, burrowing her face against him. This had scared her more than any event in the past, almost as much as what he had gone through. He staggered a bit at her onslaught, then stood, feet apart, as he wrapped her in his arms, his face buried in her hair, not seeing the men and women standing around him, or the customers shooting them curious glances. He finally just scooped her into his arms and headed for the back door, Jacob opening it for him, her camera in his hands before he tucked it into Eavan's.

Simon rose from his chair later that evening, his eyes searching for Eavan and not seeing her. He turned, knowing where he find her. Sure enough, she was wrapped in a blanket, curled up in her favourite wicker rocker in the sun room, her Bible open on the table beside her. He didn't say anything, just stooped and gathered her to his heart and sat in her spot, his arms strong and tight around her.

Eavan finally looked up at him, her head tilted back. He kissed her, then raised himself back to look at her.

"Eavan? Talk to me."

She sighed. "What can I say, Simon? Did I bring danger to Finn today?"

He shook his head. "No, I don't think so. She wasn't sure that the men she spotted were after you. She didn't get that reading from them, and she's excellent at reading people. She did see a car circling the block at a slow speed, that she thinks may have been sent there. She provided the plate number to Ed, but it was a stolen plate, so that doesn't help."

She snuggled down further into his arms. "What do we do now, then, love? We can't continue like we are. Someone will be hurt because of us, and that I couldn't handle."

He nodded. "I know, sweetheart. Samuel has called in a friend with a security team and they're watching us and watching Gran as well. He said we wouldn't see them, but they'd be there. They're on you primarily for now."

She shuddered. "That helps but it doesn't solve the problem. How do we stop these men? They won't stop until they're caught. And just how do we do that? I talked to Ed a while ago, while you were napping. He said he's running down some leads, but right now, nothing makes a lot of sense to him or his team. He said it's the same for the detectives on the county force. And Samuel stopped by. He's found out more than Ed has but had to confirm it before he shared it with us. He said some of it you had found earlier today. When I asked him about the secret room, he suggested that we search it, together, and see what it holds. He wants us to do that tomorrow. I had Maggie bring all my cameras here. I can video us as we do just that."

"That's a good idea. Tomorrow morning, we'll go through that room. Maybe by this time tomorrow, it will be all over." He kissed her forehead, before he leaned his head on hers. "I would like it to be. I want to take you to see the tree at night and I just don't want to take a chance."

"We can't stop living our lives. I've heard you've been asked to help provide security on Friday night."

He nodded. "I have been, but I will only help in setting up schedules. My priority is you."

Eavan drew a deep breath the next morning, her hand tight in Simon's as they stood at the entrance to the secret room, a large-beam flashlight already lighting the room. She entered, staring around, her eyes catching a light switch and reaching for it.

"I didn't expect that." Simon flicked off the flashlight, setting it back outside the room on the floor. He too studied the room, a frown in place.

The room seemed empty, no furniture in it, just shelving with some papers and books on them. Eavan moved around the room, her movement stirring up dust, causing them both to sneeze. She paused as she came to a table, on which rested a large volume.

"What is this, Simon?" She reached for his hand. "What have we found?"

"I don't know, love. Let's see." He brushed at the dust, surprised to see a date for many years ago on the front. "This goes back to the founding of the town. We'll need to open this in front of a lawyer, I think." He picked it up and moved it to the living room, returned to find her packing up the papers and books into boxes she found.

"Eavan, what are you doing?"

"These should likely go to a lawyer as well. I glanced through some. They go back to the founders as well. But there's other stuff as well, more recent. Can we take them to Samuel and have him look after that for us?"

"I'm sure he will. You've taped everything?"

She nodded. "I did. Every speck of dust too." She sneezed again as she looked around. "I don't see that there's anything that we've missed."

"No, I don't think there is." He groaned as his phone chimed and he looked at it. "Samuel. Now how did he know?"

She shrugged as she followed him out, stacking the boxes on the couch as well. "Tell him we need him to come and get these."

Samuel listened as Simon explained what they had found, agreed to come get the material and then arrange for the lawyer handling everything to look it all over. "Did you look at anything at all?"

"No, I didn't. Eavan says she only looked enough to know that we needed a lawyer to go through everything. She has an SD card with the video she took for you as well."

"That's good. She was thinking ahead, wasn't she? I mentioned that but wasn't sure if she had taken that in."

"She did. We'll be here when you get here."

"Good. I have some paperwork for you as well, Simon, from what you were working on yesterday. You both need to see it."

Simon looked up at Eavan after Samuel had come and gone, a thoughtful look on his face. He patted the couch beside him and she finally sat, her hands clasped in her lap.

"What did he bring?" Her voice was barely audible

"I have no idea. I was working on information for your parents yesterday." He raised a hand as she went to protest. "We've already discovered your father was not working for an illegal company, but one of the legitimate ones. We were just looking into his heart attack, to see if there was anything about it that was suspicious." He looked down at the folder in his hand. "Samuel pulled the coroner's report and this is it."

"I can't read it, Simon. You do. Tell me if there is anything about it that we don't already know."

He nodded, his eyes already scanning the report. He finally closed the file with a relieved sigh. "Your father had heart disease all his life, it seems. It ran in his family. Megan never mentioned that?"

"No, but because I'm adopted, it wouldn't have made any different, would it?"

"No, it wouldn't have. Anyway, his heart just gave out. It just stopped beating and they couldn't get it to respond to anything they tried. I'm so sorry, Eavan."

She returned his hug. "It's okay, Simon. I've come to terms with that and with Mom's death. God got me through. God and Gran." She sniffed, blinking back her tears. "What now? Did Samuel have any idea of how long it would take to go through that material?"

Simon shook his head. "The lawyer was waiting at the office, ready to start the preliminary look through. He doesn't seem to think there's a problem. The charter is iron clad and has been proven in court many times. Samuel took a look through the material before he left. He thinks it's just confirmation of what we already know." He paused, a thought coming to his mind. "But how did it end up here? Who put it there?"

"That's the question, isn't it?" Eavan finally rose, heading for the home office. "I have to work on some photos. I have deadlines approaching, Simon. Can I get you anything to eat before I start?"

"No, go ahead, love. I have a conference call in about thirty minutes. I'll take it in the kitchen."

She nodded. "You could use the office. You won't disturb me. I tend to get lost when I'm editing photos."

"No, I think I'll take it out here. Not that it's confidential, but you're too much of a distraction." He waited, a smile lurking in his eyes, for her to respond.

———

406

She was at the office door before she spun, his words finally registering. She stared at him, her mouth slightly open, before he grinned at her. She shook her finger at him and smiled, turning once more to the office.

Simon looked up later from his notes as he felt Eavan touch his shoulder on the way by. She had stood for the longest time, watching him work, seeing his concentration, and not wanting to disturb him. She had had an email from Samuel, letting her know he and Miriam were on their way over and had supper with them.

"Simon, Samuel and Miriam will be here shortly. They're bringing us dinner. We'll need to clear either this table or the dining room."

He stood, looking down at his notes. "I'll move to the office. I have about fifteen minutes left to work, then I'm done for the day." He stooped to kiss her, her hand coming up to rest on his shoulder. "Did you get your editing done?"

"I did, surprisingly. All of it and the proofs are off to the clients. They'll let me know in a few days what they want of the proofs. Right now, I'm at a loss as to what I should be doing. I can't put anyone at risk to do any more outside work."

"Then, head to Finn's and work on the photos she wants for her online store. I think that's a great idea. Another line of work for you."

"Thanks a lot," she grumbled. "Did you think I might want to slow down?"

He grinned before kissing her again. "Now that, I can't see you doing."

Samuel finally sat back, wiping his hands on his napkin, a smile on his face as he listened to Miriam and Eavan teasing Simon. He was glad that Simon had found Eavan, she brought out something in him that had lain dormant. Simon finally looked at Samuel, a grin on his face.

"Now, Samuel, as fun as this has been, I think you have news, don't you?"

"I do, Simon. Hold on a sec while I find my file I dropped somewhere in this house." He was up and then back to the kitchen, a folder in his hand, that he handed to Simon. "Read through this and then pass it on to Eavan."

Eavan was having none of that, her chair in her hands as she moved it to rest beside Simon, his arm around her as she sat and they read through the file together. Samuel and Miriam exchanged glances, both thankful for the younger couple in front of them.

"What are you saying with this, Samuel?" Eavan finally looked up. "Does this mean what I think it means?"

"If you're thinking that this means illegal activities are centred in Mistletoe, then you are correct. Somehow or other, you discovered that fact. The photo that you shot, just on the outskirts of town all those years ago, that's the trigger. You didn't realize it was Mistletoe you were at?"

She shook her heard. "No. We were on a trip and someone asked the bus driver to stop near here so we could take some photos. I never knew it was here."

"And somehow or other, they found out you took that photo and have been after you ever since." Samuel shared a long look with Simon before he asked the next question. "When did your father go to work for that company?"

"Around that time." She stopped her words, her eyes finding Simon's, not quite sure what she had just said. Then, the implication hit her and she sobbed. "It's my fault he went there, isn't it? I know I didn't cause his heart attack, but I knew he wasn't happy there and was looking for something else."

Simon gathered her to his heart, his words soothing and calming her, his love and strength communicating to her through his hold. She finally looked up, turning slightly to face Miriam and Samuel.

"Please, tell me it's not my fault."

"It isn't, Eavan. I know your father had been looking for work and took the employment offered him. I've talked to friends of his, who said he felt something off about his employer and was trying to find somewhere else to work. He had done just that, just before he died. He would have started the next week. He wanted to be there, so much, for you, since your mother died."

She nodded, her head going down on Simon's arm. "He was. We were a team, us and Gran. Does she know?"

Samuel shook his head. "Not that we know of. One thing she never told you, and I am breaking a confidence here because you now need to be aware of the fact, she has been receiving the same material that you have, all these years, in an attempt to keep her and you quiet about what you saw."

"She did? She never ever said anything, just made sure I was okay, all these years." She shared a look with Simon. "Now what, Samuel? Now that we know this, where do we go?"

"For you two, you stay under wraps as much as you can. I know Simon has to be downtown during the day on Friday, and that you plan on being there Friday night, but we need to make sure you two are as safe as we can. The security team I called in will stay with you as close as they can. They won't step in unless there is danger that they see. If they do have to step in, do exactly as they as, without any questions. Your lives, and theirs, may well depend on you doing just that."

She nodded. "I understand. Now, about that material we found in the secret room?"

"That, young lady, we're still going over. The journal clarifies and confirms the charter the town set up. The other material, now, that's interesting. It has nothing to do with the town or the charter. In fact, it's all related to criminal activities. Simon, I'm looking into who had the house before you did, and I'm not liking what I'm finding."

"I didn't think you would. I've been tracing previous owners and see the connection with what's been happening to us. I would say that's why they're after me. They think I already found it."

"I would say just that. Now, Miriam, didn't you bring dessert? Can we change the topic to something more civil and fun?"

Chapter 16

Simon looked around the town square on the Friday morning, working with the town police to set up the security that had been requested by the artist coming in for a concert. While the artist was not well known, they wanted to protect him as much as they could. Eavan reported that her website had been contacted to do photos of the night, but that she had declined, without any explanation. She just didn't feel safe, she said, and Simon had to agree with her.

He finally stood back near a shop, Ed standing beside him, and looked around, satisfied they had done as much as they could.

"I think we're set, Ed, as much as we can possibly be. There are always unexpected events, but I think we've planned for most of them."

"I think we have. Your expertise has been invaluable. I hope we can continue to use you as a security backup when we need to."

"I would like that, Ed. This is what I enjoy. That and digging into investigations without having to worry about safety issues. That's what burnt me out." Simon shrugged his coat collar up higher. He had forgotten his scarf that morning when he left and was wishing for it now.

"Then, we'll plan on that. See me soon about keeping your weapon certificate on and we'll do the paperwork we need to to add you as a consultant to our force. Your lieutenant would like to do the same, he said."

Simon shrugged. "I'm not too sure how much of this I want to do. As long as I can pick and choose, and it doesn't interfere with my time with Eavan, we'll be okay." He turned and shook Ed's hand. "I'll see you later than. I'll do one final check before the concert, which I plan to attend with my wife."

Ed smiled. "You have no idea how glad we all are to hear you say those two words. We've been praying that way for you. You just didn't seem interested in any of the young ladies here in town."

"Yeah, well, there's that. A few were thrown at me by their mothers. That was a delicate situation to extricate myself from."

Ed broke out into laughter, even as he watched Simon walk away. Yes, he thought, Lord, you brought just the right person to him, even if she did call him an oaf at their first meeting. After all, he is tall.

Simon watched as Eavan's eyes widened at the size of the crowd that night. They were standing just outside Josh's restaurant, The House, before entering it. Josh had insisted his friends all join Leah and himself for a meal before the concert

"Is it really this busy, Simon? Does that artist draw that big a crowd?"

He laughed as he held the door open for her. "Not really. But we don't often have concerts in Mistletoe and with the crowds here for the celebrations, it

———

410

has become bigger than we thought. I need you to stay close to me tonight, or close to the security personnel assigned to us.”

Flushed with laughter after the meal, Eavan tucked her hand into Simon’s as they walked through the downtown area, skirting those gathered for the festivities. They could hear the sounds of the concert ringing through the air and she was content, more content than she could remember. Her heart sang praise to God for bringing her to Mistletoe and letting her find Simon, or him find her, whichever it was. Gran was happy too, content with the volunteer work she had found and with the friends she had made.

Simon finally stopped, his eyes searching the area, feeling something off. The concert had finished, and the crowds were dispersing. Still, there was something there, or someone, he wasn’t quite sure what. He turned to the security personnel who had stopped near them, asking them to watch Eavan for him as he moved away, searching for Ed, needing to speak with him.

Eavan watched as he stood near Ed, who had stopped by the lighted tree, their breath showing white in the air, not too far from where she stood. She burrowed deeper into her coat, glad she had worn her long one. She caught a movement to the side, and squinted, a gasp coming from her as she saw the weapon emerging from an alleyway directly across from Simon, pointed at him.

She screamed his name and ran, the security personnel on her heels as they tried to stop her. She shrugged off their hands and ran faster, her cries to Simon bringing his head around and then he started to turn, just as she threw herself at him. Her assault took them down, Simon stunned for a moment, laying still, not moving even as shouts echoed around them and hands moved to help him sit up.

He sat, one leg still curled under him, one leg straight out as he cradled Eavan to him. He froze, knowing she wasn’t moving, her body limp, one arm dangling lifelessly over his, her head on his chest, her hair covering her face.

His hand shook as he desperately pushed at her hair, turning her face to him, her body turning at the same time. He saw the whiteness on her face, that seemed to grow whiter even as he searched it, her lips now with a tinge of blue.

“Eavan? Please, Eavan! Wake up! Eavan? Can you hear me?” His pleas broke the hearts of those near him, seeing that she didn’t respond to the anguish in his voice.

He tried to push away the hands that reached for her, but she was taken from him, a stretcher ready to receive her. Paramedics were still on site and hearing the shouts for medics, they had gathered their gear and ran. Eavan’s screams had drawn the attention of everyone around them, sending people flying for safety, parents gathering their children close to them.

Ed’s hand helped Simon to his feet, his arm across the younger man’s shoulders as he stood, anguish in every breath he took, watching as they worked on his young wife.

———

Murmurs went through the crowd gathered near them as word passed she had been shot, shot trying to protect Simon from his assailant. Officers had scattered but the assailant was gone, disappeared into the crowed with his weapon.

Sudden movement by the paramedics drew Ed's eyes back to them and he watched as they reached to try and stem the flow of blood. Blackie's hands were there, his help needed as they fought for her. He reached for the pressure packings, holding them in place so the other men would work on her. The older paramedic had looked up as Blackie dropped beside them, nodding his thanks, knowing Blackie had been in the service as a medic and had seen far worse than this.

Simon watched as they ran leads from a heart monitor, cut away her coat to run IV lines. He cringed as he saw them intubate her, but knew she had to be. His heart cried out with silent tears to God, asking that He spare her. Simon couldn't live without her. He didn't hear the whispered words around him, the doubt that she'd make it to the hospital, the concern for him, the questions of what had happened.

There were murmurs of air transport to a bigger trauma centre, but the paramedics shook their heads, not saying what they thought. Ed realized what they weren't saying, that she would never make it to the hospital in her condition, not to some place further away than just across town. Hands reached to help them load her stretcher into the ambulance, Blackie jumping in, an officer sliding into the front seat.

Ed motioned for an officer to lead the way and watched as red and blue lights flashing, the two vehicles sped away. His arm around Simon still, he turned him to his vehicle, an officer standing ready to slide behind the wheel as they set out.

Simon sat frozen, not comprehending the words spoken to him, his whole being focused on Eavan. He saw the looks that were exchanged, and knew just how much danger his beloved wife was in. He prayed as he had never prayed before. He felt a hand on his and knew somehow it was Eavan's beloved Gran, offering comfort to him, not taking it for herself. He turned his own hand over, clutching hers in his, their unspoken communication one thought, a prayer flowing from both of them for their beloved Eavan.

Doc finally walked towards them, his hair ruffled, blood staining his white coat, his eyes assessing Simon as the younger man stood and went towards him. He frowned. Something was off about Simon, but he just couldn't put his finger on what it was.

"Simon?" Doc's hand came out to hold Simon's arm as he staggered, his feet stumbling over one another. Doc put it down to stress. "We're taking her to surgery now. She was shot, the bullet going right through. We don't know yet how much damage has been done to her abdomen. Jeremiah has called and is on his way in for you. He's set up the prayer team."

Simon nodded. "Will she live, Doc?" His voice was barely above a whisper.

"That's our prayer, Simon. I won't lie to you. We've almost lost her a few times. We do need to find blood for her, but she has a rare type." He looked up at a sound, seeing Julia, Jonathan and Finn all pulling off their coats and heading away with the nurse, Leah running through the outside door, throwing her coat at Josh, as she heard the murmurs that Eavan needed blood. "Simon?"

"Family, Doc. You haven't heard. She's Julia and Jonathan's youngest sister. Someday, I'll have her tell you the story." He looked with a grateful heart as he watched the four disappear, knowing they were going willing, desperate to help save the sister they had just found, a cousin who no one had known about.

The voices around him began to fade as his vision narrowed to a small circle, where everything in that circle moved in slow motion, while everything outside of it sped by. His legs crumpled and he collapsed, his eyes rolling upwards, Jacob and Josh reaching to catch him before he hit the floor. He didn't hear the call for a stretcher, didn't feel them rush him back to a room, didn't feel them cutting away his jacket.

"Doc?" Blackie stood beside his friend, shock on his face. "He was hit? I thought the blood on him was from Eavan."

"I think we all did. We now know where the bullet ended up, don't we? Let's get him assessed and see what we need to do for him. Surgery, likely, as I don't see an exit wound."

Doc stood in the shambles of the room once they had wheeled Simon away, staring at the blood soaked clothing and the debris from treating him. He walked to the doorway of the room across the hall, staring at the same shambles, only many times worse. His thoughts changed to prayers for his young friends.

Three hours later, the group in the surgical waiting room looked up as they heard footsteps approaching them, his friends who hadn't left, her family who wept at the thought of losing her so soon. The men stood, Gran among them, Blackie with his arm around her, as they waited.

The surgeon's eyes searched, finding Gran and coming towards her. She drew in a deep breath, prepared for the worst, as he stood for a moment.

"Doctor?"

"She's alive, Mrs. Walker. She shouldn't be but she is. She's still unconscious and we have her on life support at present. I'll have a nurse come get you in a while, once we've moved her from Recovery. Thankfully, there was not a lot of damage. I expected there to be more, given her presentation downstairs. No organs were touched and even though a main artery was nicked, the work done as soon as it happened saved her." He looked up, his eyes searching the men until he found Blackie. "Blackie, thank you. I'm told your experience helped our men know how to treat her properly. She owes you her life."

Blackie shook his head. "It was a team effort, Doctor. Your men are good." He paused, his eyes searching his friends' faces. "Simon? How is he?"

"He's in a room now. I can take you back to him. Again, the bullet didn't do a lot of damage. It was slowed passing through Eavan's body." He grimaced at the looks of horror he was given from the women, the tightening of the men's faces. "Sorry, folks. I guess when you work in medicine, you think differently about these things that the ordinary person does. Again, he's resting, not a lot of damage. He was awake, asking about Eavan and about Gran. Mrs. Walker, come with me. I'll take you to him."

She hesitated, searching for someone to go with her, and spying Ben standing near them. "Ben, please? Will you go with me?"

He nodded, surprised that she had chosen him, but willing to go see his young friend. He tucked her arm into his elbow, supporting her as she walked, not as spry as she normally did, but with fatigue and worry evident in every step.

The rest stood around, shock still the main emotion, not willing to leave, but not willing to sit. Jeremiah moved from where he had stood, listening to the update, stopping beside each one, an arm around them as he prayed an individual prayer for each one of Simon and Eavan's friends. It would be a long night, he knew, when he finished, and he turned, seeing Samuel standing beside him, reaching to pray for his pastor.

Fighting against the hands holding him, Simon pleaded with them to let him up, he needed to find Eavan. She wasn't there, and he didn't know where she was. He drifted off, only to wake and try to rise a couple of hours later, fighting with all his strength to get up and go to his beloved Eavan.

"She's calling for me. I need to find her. She's lost. Please, let me go. Let me find my Eavan." His heart-wrenching words tore at his friends and at the nurses. His voice was low, not much above a whisper, but he poured all his love for his bride into them, his eyes opening and closing as he spoke.

Doc stood there, listening, helping to hold him down before he turned and asked for restraints.

"I'm sorry, Megan. We need to restrain him. If we don't, he'll tear open his incision and he'll be back into surgery. Even now, I can't guarantee that he won't be there."

Megan nodded, standing back from the bed, Ben beside her, his arm supporting her. "Do what you need to, Doc. We can't have him doing that, now can we? And you said a sedative won't work?"

Doc shook his head. "We can only give so much medication. He's still recovering from that incident a bit ago."

Megan nodded. "Yes, of course. I didn't realize that." She turned, heading for the door. "I'll just go, then, and see how our Eavan is."

Megan paused outside Simon's room, fighting back tears, knowing how close she still was to losing her beloved granddaughter and now Simon. A hand drew her away from the room and to the waiting area, where she was seated and a bottle of water handed to her. She sipped, and looked up, seeing Joy and Jeremiah there.

"You two need to be with your girls."

Joy smiled. "We're here because of them. Both gave us orders to make sure their Simon and Holly's Evie came home soon. How could we not be here, Megan? You're family, you know."

"What's going on with Simon?" Jeremiah turned, his eyes catching sight of Josh walking towards them.

"He's trying to get up, to get to Eavan. They've had to restrain him."

Joy drew in a deep breath even as Josh's hand came down on her shoulder.

"That's sounds about right, Megan. He's the silent one in our group, but there for us all. He would try to get to her, that I know." Josh shared a look with

Jeremiah before tilting his head away from the women. "I just need to talk to Jeremiah for a moment. Something's come up that I need his advice about."

Joy's eyes narrowed as she watched the two men walk away, turning as Megan patted her hand.

"Let them go, dear. Now, how are your two girls?" Megan succeeded I distracting Joy.

Josh turned to watch his sister, hesitating for a moment to speak.

"Josh? What is this all about? You said you needed to talk to me."

Josh sighed. "I do. Our group is setting up a prayer meeting starting in a few minutes. I know the church has one going around the clock. We just want to spend our time praying for our friends. I know you can't be there, but we just wanted you to know that."

Jeremiah's smile tightened, knowing the bond the four men shared, having been in the armed forces together, and sharing experiences that no one else had with them.

"That's great, Josh. But that's not all."

Josh shook his head. "No, it's not. Ed talked to me. He's increasing security on both Simon and Eavan. They've received word that someone will make an attempt on one of them while they're in here. He said we wouldn't know who his people were, but that the county force would be sending in officers as well." He looked bleak, knowing this was necessary, before he turned, his eyes finding Simon's room. "I want to stop in for a moment, but I'm not sure I should."

"Go, see him, Josh. You need that reassurance yourself that he's still with us."

Simon's eyes finally flickered open and stayed open, his body sore, his mind fogged. He glanced around, not recognizing where he was, trying to move and feeling the restraints. What did I go and do now, Lord, he asked. Where am I? And where is Eavan? I need to get to her.

He felt a hand on his forehead and then his wrist. He looked around, seeing Leah there, her face concerned as she watched him rouse.

"Leah? Why are you here?" He swallowed hard against the dryness in his mouth and throat.

"I'm here because you need us." She watched as the nurse assessed him, then removed the restraints.

"Why the restraints?"

"Because you fought to get up and we couldn't have you breaking open your incision. You'd have been back in surgery if you had done that."

"Incision? I still don't get it. Where's Eavan?" He tried to sit up, but didn't have the strength to do that.

"You were shot, Simon, three days ago. They had to restrain you two days ago. Eavan was hurt as well." She wasn't the one who should be sharing this, she thought, but God seemed to think she was.

"Eavan? How is she?" He watched as tears gathered in Leah's eyes. "Leah? Tell me, please. Tell me she's still alive." The anguish in his voice caught at her heart and she had to blink hard to fight against the tears.

"She's in the room near here, Simon. She was shot as well. She's getting better, but no one can get in to see her. Not yet. They won't let us."

Simon made himself sit up, his breath catching, his heart pounding, as he gripped the side rails of the bed. "Find me someone, Leah, someone who will take me to her. And now." He held up a hand as he gathered his breath. "If you don't, I'll climb out of this bed and go find her. The consequences of that won't be pretty, I can guarantee you that." He didn't tell Leah that he had been shot before while as an MP. He lived through that and would through this. He just didn't know if he'd live if Eavan didn't.

Leah stared at him, then flung herself to the door, pulling it open, startling the officers standing there, who reached for their weapons. She waved them off, seeking someone to help. Doc was heading her way and she almost ran to him, her words spilling over each other as they walked back towards Simon

Doc stood for a moment, assessing Simon, who was once more laying back, his eyes closed. "He's not going anywhere, Leah. He's asleep this time, not unconscious. We'll get him to her in time."

Doc walked away, stopping for a moment, his hand rubbing down his face. He had not had a lot of sleep in the last few days and it was catching up to him. He paused, his hand on the door to Eavan's room, gathering his thoughts and sending up a prayer that she would be better that morning. The nurses had reported she had had a rough night, and he was almost afraid to enter the room. More surgery was a distinct possibility, he decided, depending on the imaging results.

He paused, his eyes on the young woman who lay, kept alive he thought by all the equipment surrounding her. How could he bring Simon in to that?

He stepped quietly to the bed, his hand reaching for her wrist, his eyes on the monitors, a wonder growing within him. The results were better than he had thought, much better than they should have been. Thank you, Lord, he breathed. No more surgery, I take it. You've stepped in as the Great Physician.

He spoke quietly to the nurse, and she moved to follow his instructions. He had decided to remove the ventilator, to see if Eavan could breathe on her own. He waited, his own breath catching as he waited, finally satisfied that she could with just oxygen on her. He inspected her incisions, not finding the redness that had been there the night prior.

The nurse shook her head, a quiet question coming from her.

"It was God, nurse, our Great Physician. She should not have survived before she got here. We almost lost her a number of times down in Emerge and then in surgery. God has a plan for her that He's not sharing. Not just yet. Now, let's see what else we can do for her."

He finally turned, to see Megan standing just inside the door, a hopeful look on her face.

"She's better today, Megan." Doc's voice, though quiet, was jubilant. "She's definitely on the mend. There's a long road ahead of her, but we'll get her better."

Megan nodded, a peaceful look on her face. "I knew she would be, Doc. God told me that in the middle of the night. Now, what do we do about Simon? He needs to see her."

"That he does, and he will. He's asleep right now. Later today, we'll try."

Eavan felt the hand on hers and tried hard to wake up, hearing soft words calling to her. She was too tired, she thought, and slept. Simon watched as she tried to rouse and begged her to wake up, his voice tearing at the hearts of the nurses who stood near him. He bowed his head, his tears falling on their linked hands, before he laid his head down on them, a prayer rising from within that he could not find the words to utter but one he knew had made it to the Father.

Megan turned as Simon was wheeled back to his room, her eyes on him, then rising to the door of her granddaughter's room. This was not right, she thought. They need to be together, but can't be. Lord, please end this and soon.

Ed stood, watching as Simon took in what he had relayed to him. Samuel sat nearby, his eyes on Simon as well.

"So, what you're saying is that you have all the evidence you need to arrest this man, but you can't find him?" At their nods, Simon sighed. "Then, where is he? He could be here in the hospital, just waiting a chance to get to Eavan."

"We know that, Simon. That's why there's extra personnel here. From our force and from the county. We have you under as tight a guard as we can. We have put restrictions in place as to who gets into your rooms."

"I know that, Ed, but they can still get through your defenses. Admit that, will you?" At Ed's nod, Simon stared then at Samuel. "Samuel, what about all that paperwork we found?"

"Now, that was interesting, I must say. As you suspected, the journal does go back to the founding fathers. How it ended up in there, no one can say. It does confirm what all we've been told over the years. It is now locked into a safe, and I'm not telling you where. Suffice it to say, that no one can claim property or monies from the trust funds unless they can prove they are direct descendants.

"Now, about that other paperwork. It was really interesting. The lawyer looked through it and immediately handed it off to Ed. It lists crimes, with dates and victims, from the surrounding area and beyond. We need to find this man, Simon, and soon. What he has been involved in is unspeakable."

"Let me guess. Murder. Kidnapping. Assault. Money laundering. Drugs. Human trafficking. Just to name a few crimes." Simon's face was grim.

"You've nailed just about all of them. Except for extortion and blackmail. That's well documented. He tried to get to Josh over The House, but Josh fought back and for some reason, he walked away."

Simon nodded. "I suspect he's been behind everything the four of us have gone through. Why, that's what we need to determine." He sighed, his fingers plucking at the plastic identification bracelet on his wrist. "Now what, Ed? How do we catch him?"

"That's what we're working on. The federal force has become involved as well, since his crimes seem to be spreading out across the country. He took over the business, shall we say, from his father, and is expanding it, almost too rapidly I would say. We need him, Simon."

Simon sat later lost in thought, after the two men had left, before he turned his wheelchair to the door and set off down the hall to Eavan's room. The staff had gotten used to him making his trek to her room and then staying there for the day, only heading back to his room when he absolutely had to.

———

Simon's hand reached for Eavan's, feeling the thinness of it and not liking it. He had been informed that she was improving each day, that the medications they had used to sedate her were being weaned from her and that today would be the final day for them. He wanted her to wake up, to call him her big oaf, to look at him through her beautiful green eyes. Please, Lord, let today be that day, the day she looks at me again. I need that, please, dear Lord.

Eavan struggled against the darkness, her eyes trying to open. She felt a hand on hers and drew comfort from it. Lord, can I just wake up, please? I need to wake up and find someone, but who that someone is, I just can't remember right now. Please, Lord?

She struggled once more to open her eyes, finally succumbing to the blackness once more, not knowing that Simon sat, watching her struggle, his voice low as he spoke with her.

Simon turned as he heard the door open, seeing Ben entering. Ben had become close to Simon over the last week or so, since the younger couple had been in the hospital.

"Ben, what brings you by today?" Simon was puzzled. Ben had stopped by late the night before and told him he wouldn't be around that day.

Ben just shook his head, his finger on his lips, as he approached. "Things have come to a head faster than we thought, boy. We need to get you and Eavan out of here. The doc's working on that plan right now."

Ben and Simon both turned as the door slid open and a man entered, one they didn't know. Simon was puzzled. He should not have been able to get through the officers outside the door.

"Can we help you? I think you have the wrong room."

The man didn't speak, but his eyes narrowed at Simon's words and then he shook his head, a finger going to his lips. Ben moved away from Simon, and Simon wondered at that.

The man pulled a weapon, pointing at Ben, his finger pointing to Simon. "Stay quiet, and you won't get hurt."

Simon started to rise but sat back down as the weapon swung his way. Lord, I have no idea what's going on, but I'm trusting in You.

Ben made a move, and the weapon was brought back to face him, this time discharging, a silencer muting the sound. Ben flew backwards and lay still. Simon sat for a moment, shock coursing through him, before he turned to face the man, seeing another man had entered the room while he wasn't watching.

"So, Gardner, we finally meet. It's been a long time coming."

Simon frowned. He didn't know this man, so why was he here? "I'm sorry. I don't know you. What did you just go and do?"

The man gave a coarse laugh as he sauntered across the room, to stand at the foot of the bed, his eyes on Eavan. "She's the one I'm after. Not you. You're just collateral."

Simon shook his head. "I'm sorry. I don't know what you mean."

"Sure, you do. I've been watching you for years. I brought you and your friends here to Mistletoe. And there's a reason for that. Think hard and it will come to you."

Simon shook his head, his hand resting on Eavan's as she lay, her breath barely audible. He was afraid this was it for them, that they would be dead before long. His attention was caught by the man who had shot Ben, and his eyes narrowed. There was something different about the man, something he was reading but wasn't sure if he was correct.

The man had his eyes on the younger man, not moving an inch from where he stood. Simon shot a look at Ben, laying on the floor, not moving, and frowned. Did he see his chest rise and fall, or was that wistful thinking?

Simon brought his attention back to the man at the foot of the bed, not quite sure where it was going with him. He frowned again, a memory niggled at the back of his mind.

The man turned to Simon, motioning for him to rise. "You're coming with me. I have plans for you, plans that don't include her." He jerked at thumb at Eavan. "I'll leave her to someone else."

The man turned, grasping Simon's arm and savagely yanking him to his feet. Simon was shoved towards the door, his steps stumbling as he fought to find his balance. The man jerked him to a stop, then waited as the other man followed, his weapon trained on Simon.

Simon hesitated at the door, not willing to pull it open, not sure what he would find on the other side, just knowing he wasn't ready to walk away from Eavan. He spun, his elbow coming up and catching the man in the face. He heard bone crunch and the man's howl of pain before he dropped to the floor, his eyes on the man behind him. He froze, not believing his eyes, as the man reached past him and clicked handcuffs on the first man. He shook his head at Simon and pointed silently to the door.

Simon rose, shaking, as he fumbled for the door handle, finally finding it and pulling it open, to fall into the arms of fully geared police, who swarmed into the room, taking the two men into custody. Simon stumbled to Ben, fear in his heart, his hands shaking as he reached for his friend.

He jumped as Ben's eyes opened and he grimaced with pain, his hand reaching for Simon's arm to pull himself upright.

"Ben? I thought you were dead." Simon couldn't express himself the way he wanted to.

"That's what the plan was, son. We wanted him to think that. Else wise it wouldn't have worked." Ben reached for his chest, and then withdrew his hand, seeing the red on it. He gave a grim smile. "Ed and I concocted this play, even when I stopped by last night to talk to you. We knew that he was in town and was coming after you."

Simon slid to the floor, his hand on his head. "I don't understand."

"I had to draw him out. He knew I had figured out who he was and he wanted to take me out, as they say. Doc was in on this as well. Eavan was never in any danger. Nor were you, not really." Ben pulled a weapon from behind his back. "I had this and was ready to use it." His hand felt his chest once more. "That hurts, you know." He unbuttoned his shirt, removing it and then the vest underneath it. "I knew these worked. Just never expected it to happen to me."

He stood, reaching down to help Simon to his feet. Simon stood for a moment, his eyes on Ben, before he turned back to the bed, finding Eavan rousing. He blanked out anything around him, his focus solely on her.

Eavan's eyes fluttered open, and she squinted, the glare from the lights strong and blinding. She heard her beloved's voice, felt his lips on her cheek, his hand on hers, and she slept, this time not in a nightmare, but in a peaceful sleep, knowing Simon was alive and well and with her.

Eavan rested back on the couch, glad to be finally home. Christmas was a few days away, but she was not thinking of that. As far as she was concerned, she had her Christmas already. Simon sat beside her, his arm around her, almost afraid to let her go, afraid that he would still lose her. Doc had warned them Eavan still had weeks of recovery to make, but all things considered, she would recover and be as good as new.

She looked up as Megan rested her hand on her head, before moving on. This had aged my Gran, Eavan thought, before her eyes turned to Ed and Samuel, who sat across from them. Their friends had gathered around them, knowing that this was the day they would find out what it was all about.

Heidi and Holly had climbed up on them, despite their parents' protest. Eavan had insisted the girls join them, knowing how little time they had spent with their father in the last two weeks. Holly had been very vocal that she needed to see her Evie and had handed her a home-made card, bring tears to Eavan's eyes even as she hugged the little girl.

Ed finally cleared his throat, his eyes on the young couple. He had news to share, news that would affect all four of the couples, five, he corrected himself, seeing Jonathan and his Bev there.

"Ed? What can you tell us?" Simon's voice broke through the silence, the anticipation palpable in the air.

"It's a long story, Simon, and we need to go back to the founders. When they set up the charter and the town, they had no idea how many descendants would eventually show up. Some we haven't been able to track down, but most we have. Samuel here has been invaluable, he and his staff, in that. The monies the original settlers put into trust has multiplied many times over, being invested wisely. If you don't mind my saying this, leave it where it is.

"Now, about the last few years. Jacob, you're first, seeing as it was your lawyer who started the process of bringing all of you to this town. He was employed by our suspect, to bring you all to town. We find now that this is unrelated to the town or the charter, but revenge pure and simple. In his twisted mind, he wanted to bring you down and yes, kill you, in a town such as Mistletoe. Why, we're still working through.

"Your lawyer left a statement before he killed himself earlier this year. I'm sorry to tell you that, Jacob, but we haven't spread that word around too far, knowing who we were after.

"Blackie, he brought you here as well. He was planning on you becoming one of the town's paramedics, and would have used that against you. How, we can only speculate, that perhaps he would have caused someone to die on your watch, and you would have been charged.

"Josh, he's the one who arranged for you to appear when you did, suggesting through the lawyer that you might want to take over The House. He was behind the extortion attempts. What all he planned, we still don't know, but it was not likely pretty. Food poisoning, someone choking on their food and dying, you get my drift?

"Now, Simon. He's the one who suggested your name to the force, dummying up references to start the process. Somehow he planned on having you killed on duty and having a fellow officer charged. You thwarted his plans when you abruptly resigned from the force and he had to change plans in midstream, leading to the confrontation in Eavan's hospital room. Ben knew the man who supposedly killed him. I won't say how or why, as that is a sealed portion of our investigation.

"Now, ladies, it's your turn. Finn, you were never a target. He knew better than to go after you, but through you, he could get to Jacob and tried his best to do so. You overcame every attempt, ones you knew about and the ones you didn't, and there were those. All of you ladies were followed at some point or other and were in danger of being abducted and then likely sent overseas to some country you would never have returned from." He smiled grimly at the shock on their faces, as they turned to stare up at their husbands.

"Julia, he was behind the attempt on your life back in the forest. He was behind it all, Duane was one of his henchman, shall we say? He arranged for everything that happened. He gave approval for your father to be killed, so it wasn't just your mother and stepfather that did that.

"Leah, we have no evidence to show that he was behind Duane's kidnapping of you as a toddler, but he used that to his advantage. He threatened you to keep Duane in line. Donald never knew about his father's working relationship with him. That much we have confirmed.

"Now, Eavan. You're the final one, the one he was really after. He had to do something to get you here, and threatening these ladies and gentlemen were all part and parcel of it. He knew you had a photo of his father you had taken all those years ago, and tried to find it. He threatened you and Megan many times, but you were protected by God, that's all I can say. He was not the one behind your mother leaving when she was expecting you and then putting you up for adoption, but he used that against her. Blackmail was a favourite tool of his. Your biological mother had no choice but to go along with him. Her schemes would have been exposed, and she couldn't have that. He's the one who shot at you and Simon that day, the one behind your incident in the studio, the missing client, the men who showed up at Finn's store."

"But who is he, Ed?" Simon's voice broke through the silence that surrounded them when Ed stopped speaking.

Ed and Samuel shared a look, before Samuel spoke.

"He's someone you know well, the four of you. He was jealous of you and your exemplary service record and wanted to bring you down. He knew he couldn't do it while you were in the service, therefore, he plotted all this for years."

"But that doesn't tell us who it was." Josh spoke up, sharing a look with his three friends.

"When I say his name, I'm sure you'll remember him." Samuel paused at that point, knowing how Blackie would feel about someone he had thought was a friend. "It was Tad Morton."

"Tad?" Shock was in Blackie's voice. "Tad? No wonder he knew how to hurt us."

Josh spoke up. "There was always something about him I never fully trusted. Now I know why. He was always a troublemaker. How many times did you and Simon had to arrest him, Jacob?"

"Too many. He was finally given a dishonourable discharge and we never heard any more about him. When did he take over his father's business, if that's what you can call it?"

"As soon as he returned from the service. There are rumours that he had his father taken down, but we can't prove that. Not yet. Now that he's in jail, we're receiving numerous calls from people that want to speak with us, with information for us about him. We're working through that but it will take time." Ed waited, answering what questions he could before he finally stood, his hand out to shake the hands of the younger men, to give the ladies a hug, before he headed out.

There was silence when he left, as they all looked at one another, before a song was started by Julia and picked up by them all. The words of how God protected and led filled the room, bringing peace and hope to each one.

Late that evening, Simon sat beside Eavan, his arms cradling her to him.

"Do you need anything, love?"

She shook her head. "I have everything I need, right here with you. Gran has taken herself to bed, I think."

"That she has. This was hard on her, you know. We almost lost you. Don't ever do that to me again."

She looked up, a spark of mischief in her eyes. "Do what? Throw myself at my big oaf?"

He laughed. "That and take a bullet for me. I can't handle it if you do that again."

They sat in silence, content, knowing that God had brought them through an adventure they never wanted to repeat.

Simon searched for Eavan just after Christmas, not finding her in the house, or in Gran's apartment. He stood, hands on his hips, trying to think where she would be. He turned as he heard a voice singing from the office and walked that way.

Eavan sat in front of her monitor, her focus on the photos in front of her. How had he missed her, he wondered?

She looked up, delight colouring her face. "You're home, love. Is it that late?"

"No, not late. Samuel sent us all home, told us to take a few days off, that we had worked hard and needed the break. He was planning on doing just that himself." He perched himself on the edge of the desk. "What have you been up to today?"

"Just finishing off some photos for Finn for her online store." She fidgeted with her pen. "There is one thing we need to talk about."

"And that would be?" When she didn't comment, he tilted his head, watching her face.

"Joy approached me. She said because you are so well loved in the community, the church felt slighted that we didn't share our day with them when we married. She has asked if the church can give us a tea or brunch or something like that on Sunday."

He reached to hug her. "I think that's a wonderful idea. I'd like to see you in your dress again. I didn't see much of it before, remember, when I was almost flat on my back."

She grinned. "I know that. I agreed, thinking that it was the least we could do, as a thank you to them." She leaned back. "You do have to arrange for flowers, don't you?"

He shook his head as he hugged her close. "Just a corsage, I think, my love, with a flower matching for me. That will do. If I know Joy and her committee, they've already planned exactly what will be there. We just have to show up." He studied her face. "Are you okay with this?"

She nodded. "I am. I was so lost for so many years, feeling alone, even though I had a Mom and Dad who loved me and Gran who loves me beyond what I ever expected. To have found a brother and sister and cousins has been well beyond my wildest dream. God has been good, Simon. He has given us so many treasures that we will never want for more."

Simon nodded before he kissed her thoroughly. "That I would agree with, sweetheart. He has indeed blessed us in so many ways."

Dear Readers

Thank you for choosing to read this book of Simon and Eavan. It finishes off the Mistletoe Treasures series, with Jacob, Blackie, Josh and Simon finding their treasures, their wives.

God provides treasures for us each and every day. Sometimes we see them. Sometimes we don't. We need to be looking for those, our God moments in our lives. We can be that treasure to someone else. It's just a matter of how much we listen and follow God.

Simon's lady had a mind of her own. I originally planned on calling her Caileigh. She abruptly informed me that was not a suitable name for her, that I was to provide a selection of names for her to choose from. She chose Eavan (Eve-een) which means beautiful in Irish. Ireland has a special place in my heart. My mother's side is from Northern Ireland and my dream trip is to someday visit that land.

God bless each one of you as you travel through life. Just remember to trust Him in everything and when things seem the darkest, He is our light.

Blessings.

Ronna